PENGUIN BOOKS

Assassin's Creed®
Forsaken

Assassin's Creed®

Forsaken

OLIVER BOWDEN

PENGUIN BOOKS

PENGUIN BOOKS

Published by the Penguin Group
Penguin Books Ltd, 80 Strand, London WC2R ORL, England
Penguin Group (USA) Inc., 375 Hudson Street, New York, New York 10014, USA
Penguin Group (Canada), 90 Eglinton Avenue East, Suite 700, Toronto, Ontario,
Canada M4P 2Y3 (a division of Pearson Penguin Canada Inc.)
Penguin Ireland, 25 St Stephen's Green, Dublin 2, Ireland (a division of Penguin Books Ltd)
Penguin Group (Australia), 707 Collins Street, Melbourne, Victoria 3008, Australia
(a division of Pearson Australia Group Pty Ltd)
Penguin Books India Pvt Ltd, 11 Community Centre, Panchsheel Park,
New Delhi – 110 017, India
Penguin Group (NZ), 67 Apollo Drive, Rosedale, Auckland 0632, New Zealand
(a division of Pearson New Zealand Ltd)
Penguin Books (South Africa) (Pty) Ltd, Block D, Rosebank Office Park,
181 Jan Smuts Avenue, Parktown North, Gauteng 2193, South Africa

Penguin Books Ltd, Registered Offices: 80 Strand, London WC2R ORL, England

www.penguin.com

First published 2012
001

Set in 12.75/15.25 pt Garamond MT Std
Typeset by Jouve (UK), Milton Keynes
Printed in England by Clays Ltd, St Ives plc

PAPERBACK ISBN: 978-0-718-19368-3
OM PAPERBACK ISBN: 978-0-718-19454-3

www.greenpenguin.co.uk

Penguin Books is committed to a sustainable
future for our business, our readers and our planet.
This book is made from Forest Stewardship
Council™ certified paper.

MIX
Paper from
responsible sources
FSC
www.fsc.org   FSC™ C018179

ALWAYS LEARNING   **PEARSON**

Prologue

I never knew him. Not really. I thought I had, but it wasn't until I read his journal that I realized I hadn't really known him at all. And it's too late now. Too late to tell him I misjudged him. Too late to tell him I'm sorry.

PART I

Extracts from the Journal of Haytham E. Kenway

6 December 1735

i

Two days ago I should have been celebrating my tenth birthday at my home in Queen Anne's Square. Instead my birthday has gone unremarked; there are no celebrations, only funerals, and our burnt-out house is like a blackened, rotted tooth among the tall, white-brick mansions of Queen Anne's Square.

For the time being we're staying in one of Father's properties in Bloomsbury. It's a nice house, and though the family is devastated and our lives torn apart, there is that to be thankful for at least. Here we'll stay, shocked, in limbo – like troubled ghosts – until our future is decided.

The blaze ate my journals so beginning this feels like starting anew. That being the case, I should probably begin with my name, which is Haytham, an Arabic name, for an English boy whose home is London, and who from birth until two days ago lived an idyllic life sheltered from the worst of the filth that exists elsewhere in the city. From Queen Anne's Square we could see the fog and smoke that hung over the river, and like everybody else we were bothered by the stink, which I can only describe as 'wet horse', but we didn't have to tread through the rivers of stinking waste from tanneries, butchers' shops and the backsides of animals and people. The rancid streams of effluent that hasten the passage of disease: dysentery, cholera, polio . . .

'You must wrap up, Master Haytham. Or the lerg'll get you.'

On walks across the fields to Hampstead my nurses used to steer me away from the poor unfortunates wracked with coughs, and shielded my eyes from children with deformities. More than anything they feared disease. I suppose because you cannot reason with disease; you can't bribe it or take arms against it, and it respects neither wealth nor standing. It is an implacable foe.

And of course it attacks without warning. So every evening they checked me for signs of measles or the pox then reported on my good health to Mother, who came to kiss me good night. I was one of the lucky ones, you see, who had a mother to kiss me good night, and a father who did, too; who loved me and my half-sister, Jenny, who told me about rich and poor, who instilled in me my good fortune and urged me always to think of others; and who employed tutors and nursemaids to look after and educate me, so that I should grow up to be a man of good values, and of worth to the world. One of the lucky ones. Not like the children who have to work in fields and in factories and up chimneys.

I wondered sometimes, though, did they have friends, those other children? If they did, then, while of course I knew better than to envy them their lives when mine was so much more comfortable, I envied them that one thing: their friends. Me, I had none, with no brothers or sisters close to my age either, and, as for making them, well, I was shy. Besides, there was another problem: something that had come to light when I was just five years old.

It happened one afternoon. The mansions of Queen Anne's Square were built close together, so we'd often see our neighbours, either in the square itself or in their grounds at the rear. On one side of us lived a family who had four girls, two around my age. They spent what seemed like hours skipping or playing blind man's buff in their garden, and I used to hear them as I sat in the schoolroom under the watchful eye of my tutor, Old Mr Fayling, who had bushy grey eyebrows and a habit of picking his nose, carefully studying whatever it was that he'd dug from the recesses of his nostrils then surreptitiously eating it.

This particular afternoon Old Mr Fayling left the room and I waited until his footsteps had receded before getting up from my sums, going to the window and gazing out at the grounds of the mansion next door.

Dawson was the family name. Mr Dawson was an MP, so my father said, barely hiding his scowl. They had a high-walled garden, and, despite the trees, bushes and foliage in full bloom, parts of it were visible from my schoolroom window, so I could see the Dawson girls outside. They were playing hopscotch for a change, and had laid out pall-mall mallets for a makeshift course, although it didn't look as if they were taking it very seriously; probably the two older ones were trying to teach the two younger ones the finer points of the game. A blur of pigtails and pink, crinkly dresses, they were calling and laughing, and occasionally I'd hear the sound of an adult voice, a nursemaid probably, hidden from my sight beneath a low canopy of trees.

My sums were left unattended on the table for a moment as I watched them play, until suddenly, almost as if she could *sense* she was being watched, one of the younger ones, a year or so my junior, looked up, saw me at the window, and our eyes locked.

I gulped, then very hesitantly raised a hand to wave. To my surprise she beamed back. And next she was calling her sisters, who gathered round, all four of them, excitedly craning their necks and shielding their eyes from the sun to gaze up at the schoolroom window, where I stood like an exhibit at a museum – except a moving exhibit that waved and went slightly pink with embarrassment, but even so felt the soft, warm glow of something that might have been friendship.

Which evaporated the moment their nursemaid appeared from beneath the cover of the trees, glanced crossly up at my window with a look that left me in no doubt what she thought of me – a peeping Tom or worse – then ushered all four girls out of sight.

That look the nursemaid gave me I'd seen before, and I'd see it again, on the square or in the fields behind us. Remember how my nurses steered me away from the ragged unfortunates? Other nursemaids kept their children away from me like that. I never really wondered why. I didn't question it because . . . I don't know, because there was no reason to question it, I suppose; it was just something that happened and I knew no different.

ii

When I was six, Edith presented me with a bundle of pressed clothes and a pair of silver-buckled shoes.

I emerged from behind the screen wearing my new shiny-buckled shoes, a waistcoat and a jacket, and Edith called one of the maids, who said I looked the spitting image of my father, which of course was the idea.

Later on, my parents came to see me, and I could have sworn Father's eyes misted up a little, while Mother made no pretence at all and simply burst out crying there and then in the nursery, flapping her hand until Edith passed her a handkerchief.

Standing there, I felt grown-up and learned, even as I felt the hotness in my cheeks again. I found myself wondering if the Dawson girls would have considered me rather fine in my new suit, quite the gentleman. I'd thought of them often. I'd catch sight of them from the window sometimes, running along their garden or being shepherded into carriages at the front of the mansions. I fancied I saw one of them steal a glance up at me once, but if she saw me there were no smiles or waves that time, just a shadow of that same look worn by the nursemaid, as though disapproval of me was being handed down, like arcane knowledge.

So we had the Dawsons on one side; those elusive, pigtailed, skipping Dawsons, while on the other side were the Barretts. They were a family of eight children, boys and girls, although again I rarely saw them; as with the Dawsons, my encounters were restricted to the sight of them getting into carriages, or seeing them at a distance in the fields. Then, one day shortly before my eighth birthday, I was in the garden, strolling along the perimeter and dragging a stick along the crumbling red brick of the high garden wall. Occasionally I'd stop to overturn stones with a stick and inspect whatever insects scuttled from beneath – woodlice, millipedes, worms that wriggled as though stretching out their long bodies – when I came upon the door that led on to a passage between our home and the Barretts'.

The heavy gate was padlocked with a huge, rusting chunk of metal that looked as if it hadn't been opened for years, and I stared at it for a while, weighing the lock in my palm, when I heard a whispered, urgent, boyish voice.

'Say, you. Is it true what they say about your father?'

It came from the other side of the gate, although it took me a moment or so to place it – a moment in which I stood shocked and almost rigid with fear. Next, I almost jumped out of my skin when I saw through a hole in the door an unblinking eye that was watching me. Again came the question.

'Come on, they'll be beckoning me in any minute. Is it true what they say about your father?'

Calming, I bent to bring my eye level with the hole in the door. 'Who is this?' I asked.

'It's me, Tom, who lives next door.'

I knew that Tom was the youngest of their brood, about my age. I'd heard his name being called.

'Who are you?' he said. 'I mean, what's your name?'

'Haytham,' I replied, and I wondered if Tom was my new friend. He had a friendly looking eyeball, at least.

'That's a strange sort of name.'

'It's Arabic. It means "young eagle".'

'Well, that makes sense.'

'How do you mean, "makes sense"?'

II

'Oh, I don't know. It just does somehow. And there's only you, is there?'

'And my sister,' I retorted. 'And Mother and Father.'

'Pretty small sort of family.'

I nodded.

'Look,' he pressed. 'Is it true or not? Is your father what they say he is? And don't even think about lying. I can see your eyes, you know. I'll be able to tell if you're lying straight away.'

'I won't lie. I don't even know what "they" say he is, or even who "they" are.'

At the same time I was getting an odd and not altogether pleasant feeling: that somewhere existed an idea of what constituted 'normal', and that we, the Kenway family, were not included in it.

Perhaps the owner of the eyeball heard something in my tone, because he hastened to add, 'I'm sorry – I'm sorry if I said something out of turn. I was just interested, that's all. You see, there is a rumour, and it's awfully exciting if it's true . . .'

'What rumour?'

'You'll think it's silly.'

Feeling brave, I drew close to the hole and looked at him, eyeball to eyeball, saying, 'What do you mean? What do people say about Father?'

He blinked. 'They say he used to be a –'

Suddenly there was a noise from behind him, and I heard an angry male voice call his name: *'Thomas!'*

The shock sent him backwards. 'Oh, bother,' he whispered quickly. 'I've got to go, I'm being called. See you around, I hope?'

And with that he was gone and I was left wondering what he meant. What rumour? What were people saying about us, our *small* family?

At the same time I remembered that I had better get a move on. It was nearly midday – and time for my weapons training.

7 December 1735

i

I feel invisible, like I'm stuck in a limbo between the past and the future. Around me the grown-ups hold tense conversations. Their faces are drawn and the ladies weep. Fires are kept lit, of course, but the house is empty apart from the few of us and what possessions we saved from the burnt-out mansion, and it feels permanently cold. Outside, snow has started to fall, while indoors is a sorrow that chills the very bones.

With little else for me to do but write my journal, I had hoped to get up to date with the story of my life so far, but it seems there's more to say than I'd first thought, and of course there have been other important matters to attend to. Funerals. Edith today.

'Are you sure, Master Haytham?' Betty had asked earlier, with her forehead creased in concern, her eyes tired. For years – as long as I could remember – she had assisted Edith. She was as bereaved as I was.

'Yes,' I said, dressed as ever in my suit and, for today, a black tie. Edith had been alone in the world, so it was the surviving Kenways and staff who gathered for a funeral feast below stairs, for ham and ale and cake. When that was over, the men from the funeral company, who were already quite drunk, loaded her body into the hearse for taking to the chapel. Behind it we took our seats in mourning carriages. We only needed two of them. When it was over I retired to my room, to continue with my story . . .

ii

A couple of days after I'd spoken to Tom Barrett's eyeball, what he'd said was still playing on my mind. So one morning when Jenny and I were both alone in the drawing room together, I decided to ask her about it.

Jenny. I was nearly eight and she was twenty-one, and we had as much in common as I did with the man who delivered the coal. Less, probably, if I thought about it, because at least the man who delivered the coal and I both liked to laugh, whereas I'd rarely seen Jenny smile, let alone laugh.

She has black hair that shines, and her eyes are dark and . . . well, 'sleepy' is what I'd say, although I'd heard them described as 'brooding', and at least one admirer went so far as to say she had a 'smoky stare', whatever that is. Jenny's looks were a popular topic of conversation. She is a great beauty, or so I'm often told.

Although not to me. She was just Jenny, who'd refused to play with me so often I'd long since given up asking her; who whenever I picture her was sitting in a high-backed chair, head bent over her sewing, or embroidery – whatever it was she did with a needle and thread. And scowling. That smoky stare her admirers said she had? I called it scowling.

The thing was, despite the fact that we were little more than guests in each other's lives, like ships sailing around the same small harbour, passing closely but never making contact, we had the same father. And Jenny, being twelve years older than me, knew more about him than I did. So even though I'd had years of her telling me I was too stupid or too young to understand – or too stupid *and* too young to understand; and once even too *short* to understand, whatever that was supposed to mean – I used to try to engage her in conversation. I don't know why, because, as I say, I always came away none the wiser. To annoy her perhaps. But on this particular occasion, a couple of days or so after my conversation with Tom's eyeball, it was because I was genuinely curious to find out what Tom had meant.

So I asked her: 'What do people say about us?'

She sighed theatrically and looked up from her needlework.

'What do you mean, Squirt?' she asked.

'Just that – what do people say about us?'

'Are you talking about gossip?'

'If you like.'

'And what would you care about gossip? Aren't you a bit too –'

'I care,' I interrupted, before we got on to the subject of me being too young, too stupid or too short.

'Do you? Why?'

'Somebody said something, that's all.'

She put down her work, tucking it by the chair cushion at the side of her leg, and pursed her lips. 'Who? Who said it and what did they say?'

'A boy at the gate in the grounds. He said our family was strange and that Father was a . . .'

'What?'

'I never found out.'

She smiled and picked up her needlework. 'And that's what set you thinking, is it?'

'Well, wouldn't it you?'

'I already know everything I need to know,' she said haughtily, 'and I tell you this, I couldn't give two figs what they say about us in the house next door.'

'Well, tell me then,' I said. 'What *did* Father do before I was born?'

Jenny did smile, sometimes. She smiled when she had the upper hand, when she could exert a little power over someone – especially if that someone was me.

'You'll find out,' she said.

'When?'

'All in good time. After all, you are his *male heir*.'

There was a long pause. 'How do you mean, "male heir"?' I asked. 'What's the difference between that and what you are?'

She sighed. 'Well, at the moment, not much, although you have weapons training, and I don't.'

'You don't?' But on reflection I already knew that, and I suppose I had wondered why it was that I did swordcraft and she did needlecraft.

'No, Haytham, I don't have weapons training. No child has weapons training, Haytham, not in Bloomsbury anyway, and maybe not in all of London. Nobody but you. Haven't you been told?'

'Told what?'

'Not to say anything.'

'Yes, but . . .'

'Well, didn't you ever wonder why – *why* you're not supposed to say anything?'

Maybe I had. Maybe I secretly knew all along. I said nothing.

'You'll soon find out what's in store for you,' she said. 'Our lives have been mapped out for us, don't you worry about that.'

'Well, then, what's in store for you?'

She snorted derisively. '*What?* is in store for me is the wrong question. *Who?* is in store would be more accurate.' There was a trace of something in her voice that I wouldn't quite understand until much later, and I looked at her, knowing better than to enquire further, and risk feeling the sting of that needle. But when I eventually put down the book I had been reading and left the drawing room, I did so knowing that although I had learnt almost nothing about my father or family, I'd learnt something about Jenny: why she never smiled; why she was always so antagonistic towards me.

It was because she'd seen the future. She'd seen the future and knew it favoured me, for no better reason than I had been born male.

I might have felt sorry for her. Might have done – if she hadn't been such a sourpuss.

Knowing what I now knew, though, weapons training the following day had an extra frisson. So: nobody else had weapons training but me. Suddenly it felt as though I were tasting forbidden fruit, and the fact that my father was my tutor only made it more succulent. If Jenny was right and there was some calling I was being groomed to answer, like other boys are trained for the priesthood, or as blacksmiths, butchers or carpenters, then good. That suited me fine. There was nobody in the world I looked up to more than Father. The thought that he was passing on his knowledge to me was at once comforting and thrilling.

And, of course, it involved swords. What more could a boy want? Looking back, I know that from that day on I became a more willing and enthusiastic pupil. Every day, either at midday or after evening meal, depending on Father's diary, we convened in what we called the training room but was actually the games room. And it was there that my sword skills began to improve.

I haven't trained since the attack. I haven't had the heart to pick up a blade at all, but I know that when I do I'll picture that room, with its dark, oak-panelled walls, bookshelves and the covered billiard table which had been moved aside to make space. And in it my father, his bright eyes, sharp but kindly, and always smiling, always encouraging me: block, parry, foot-work, balance, awareness, anticipation. Those words he repeated like a mantra, sometimes saying nothing else for an entire lesson at a time, just barking the commands, nodding when I got it right, shaking his head when I did it wrong, occasionally pausing, scoop-ing his hair out of his face and going to the back of me to position my arms and legs.

To me, they are – or were – the sights and sounds of weapons training: the bookshelves, the billiard table, my father's mantras and the sound of ringing . . .

Wood.

Yes, wood.

Wooden training swords we used, much to my chagrin. Steel would come later, he'd say, whenever I complained.

On the morning of my birthday, Edith was extra-specially nice to me and Mother made sure I was given a birthday breakfast of my favourites: sardines with mustard sauce, and fresh bread with cherry jam made from the fruit of the trees in our grounds. I caught Jenny giving me a sneering look as I tucked in but paid it no mind. Since our conversation in the drawing room, whatever power she'd had over me, slim as it had been, had somehow been made less distinct. Before that I might have taken her ridicule to heart, maybe felt a little silly and self-conscious about my birthday breakfast. But not that day. Thinking back, I wonder if my eighth birthday marked the day I began to change from boy to man.

So no, I didn't care about the curl of Jenny's lip, or the pig noises she made surreptitiously. I had eyes only for Mother and Father, who had eyes only for me. I could tell by their body language, tiny little parental codes I'd picked up over the years, that something else was to come; that my birthday pleasures were set to continue. And so it proved. By the end of the meal my father had announced that tonight we would be going to White's Chocolate House on Chesterfield Street, where the hot chocolate is made from *solid blocks of cocoa* imported from Spain.

Later that day I stood with Edith and Betty fussing around me, dressing me in my smartest suit. Then the four of us were stepping into a carriage at the kerb outside, where I sneaked a look up at the windows of our neighbours and wondered if the faces of the Dawson girls were pressed to the glass, or Tom and his brothers. I hoped so. I hoped they could see me now. See us all and think, 'There go the Kenway family, out for the evening, just like a normal family.'

iv

The area around Chesterfield Street was busy. We were able to draw up directly outside White's and, once there, our door was opened and we were helped quickly across the crowded thoroughfare, and inside.

Even so, during that short walk between the carriage and the sanctuary of the chocolate house, I looked to my left and right and saw a little of London red in tooth and claw: the body of a dog lying in the gutter, a derelict retching against some railings, flower sellers, beggars, drunkards, urchins splashing in a river of mud that seemed to seethe on the street.

And then we were inside, greeted by the thick scent of smoke, ale, perfume and of course chocolate, as well as a hubbub of piano and raised voices. People, all of whom were shouting, leaned over gaming tables. Men drank from huge tankards of ale; women, too. I saw some with hot chocolate and cake. Everybody, it seemed, was in a state of high excitement.

I looked at Father, who had stopped short, and sensed his discomfort. For a moment I was concerned he'd simply turn and leave, before a gentleman holding his cane aloft caught my eye. Younger than Father, with an easy smile and a twinkle that was visible even across the room, he was waggling the cane at us. Until with a grateful wave, Father acknowledged him and began to lead us across the room, squeezing between tables, stepping over dogs and even one or two children, who scrabbled at the feet of revellers, presumably hoping for whatever might fall off the gaming tables: pieces of cake, maybe coins.

We reached the gentleman with the cane. Unlike Father, whose hair was straggly and barely tied back with a bow, he wore a white powdered wig, the back of it secured in a black silk bag, and a frock coat in a deep, rich red colour. With a nod, he greeted Father then turned his attention to me and made an exaggerated bow. 'Good evening, Master Haytham, I believe that many happy returns of the day are in order. Remind me please of your age, sir? I can see from your bearing that you are a child of great maturity. Eleven? Twelve, perhaps?'

As he said this he glanced over my shoulder with a twinkly smile and my mother and father chuckled appreciatively.

'I am eight, sir,' I said, and puffed up proudly, as my father completed the introductions. The gentleman was Reginald Birch, one of his senior property managers, and Mr Birch said he was delighted to make my acquaintance then greeted my mother with a long bow, kissing the back of her hand.

His attention went to Jenny next, and he took her hand, bent his head and pressed his lips to it. I knew enough to realize that what he was doing was courtship, and I glanced quickly over to Father, expecting him to step in.

Instead what I saw was he and Mother looking thrilled, though Jenny was stony-faced, and stayed that way as we were led to a private back room of the chocolate house and seated, she and Mr Birch side by side, as the White's staff began to busy themselves around us.

I could have stayed there all night, having my fill of hot chocolate and cake, copious amounts of which were delivered to the table. Both Father and Mr Birch seemed to enjoy the ale. So in the end it was Mother who insisted we leave – before I was sick, or they were – and we stepped out into the night, which if anything had become even busier in the intervening hours.

For a moment or so I found myself disorientated

by the noise and the stench of the street. Jenny wrinkled her nose, and I saw a flicker of concern pass across my mother's face. Instinctively, Father moved closer towards us all, as if to try and ward off the clamour.

A filthy hand was thrust in front of my face and I looked up to see a beggar silently appealing for money with wide, beseeching eyes, bright white in contrast to the dirt of his face and hair; a flower seller tried to bustle past Father to reach Jenny, and gave an outraged 'Oi' when Mr Birch used his cane to block her path. I felt myself being jostled, saw two urchins trying to reach us with their palms out.

Then suddenly my mother gave a cry as a man burst from within the crowd, clothes ragged and dirty, teeth bared and his hand outstretched, about to snatch my mother's necklace.

And in the next second I discovered why Father's cane had that curious rattle, as I saw a blade appear from within as he span to protect Mother. He covered the distance to her in the blink of an eye, but before it cleared its scabbard, he changed his mind, perhaps seeing the thief was unarmed, and replaced it, ramming it home with a thump and making it a cane once again, in the same movement twirling it to knock the ruffian's hand aside.

The thief shrieked in pain and surprise and backed straight into Mr Birch, who hurled him to the street and pounced on him, his knees on the man's chest and a dagger at his throat. I caught my breath.

I saw Mother's eyes widen over Father's shoulder.

'Reginald!' called Father. '*Stop!*'

'He tried to rob you, Edward,' said Mr Birch, without turning. The thief snivelled. The tendons on Mr Birch's hands stood out and his knuckles were white on the handle of the dagger.

'No, Reginald, this is not the way,' said my father calmly. He stood with his arms around Mother, who had buried her face in his chest and was whimpering softly. Jenny stood close by at one side, me at another. Around us a crowd had gathered, the same vagrants and beggars who had been bothering us now keeping a respectful distance. A respectful, *frightened* distance.

'I mean it, Reginald,' said Father. 'Put the dagger away, let him go.'

'Don't make me look foolish like this, Edward,' said Birch. 'Not in front of everybody like this, please. We both know this man deserves to pay, if not with his life then perhaps with a finger or two.'

I caught my breath.

'*No!*' commanded Father. 'There will be no bloodshed, Reginald. Any association between us will end if you do not do as I say this very moment.' A hush seemed to fall on everybody around us. I could hear the thief gibbering, saying over and over again, 'Please sir, please sir, please sir . . .' His arms were pinned to his sides, his legs kicking and scraping uselessly on the filth-covered cobbles as he lay trapped.

Until, at last, Mr Birch seemed to decide, and the dagger withdrew, leaving a small bleeding nick behind. When he stood he aimed a kick at the thief, who needed no further encouragement to scramble to his hands and knees and take off into Chesterfield Street, grateful to escape with his life.

Our carriage driver had recovered his wits, and now stood by the door, urging us to hurry to the safety of our carriage.

And Father and Mr Birch stood facing one another, their eyes locked. As Mother hurried me past, I saw Mr Birch's eyes blazing. I saw my father's gaze meet him equally, and he offered his hand to shake, saying, 'Thank you, Reginald. On behalf of all of us, thank you for your quick thinking.'

I felt my mother's hand in the small of my back as she tried to shove me into the carriage, and craned my head back to see Father, his hand held out to Mr Birch, who glared at him, refusing to accept the offer of accord.

Then, just as I was bundled into the carriage, I saw Mr Birch reach to grasp Father's hand and his glare melt away into a smile – a slightly embarrassed, bashful smile, as though he'd just remembered himself. The two shook hands and my father awarded Mr Birch with the short nod that I knew so well. It meant that everything had been settled. It meant that no more need be said about it.

v

At last we returned home to Queen Anne's Square, where we bolted the door and banished the smell of smoke and manure and horse, and I told Mother and Father how much I had enjoyed my evening, thanked them profusely and assured them that the commotion in the street afterwards had done nothing to spoil my evening, while privately thinking that it had been a highlight.

But it turned out the evening wasn't over yet, because as I went to climb the stairs, my father beckoned me follow him instead, and led the way to the games room, where he lit a paraffin lamp.

'You enjoyed your evening, then, Haytham,' he said.

'I enjoyed it very much, sir,' I said.

'What was your impression of Mr Birch?'

'I liked him very much, sir.'

Father chuckled. 'Reginald is a man who sets great store by appearance, by manners and etiquette and edict. He is not like some, who wear etiquette and protocol as a badge only when it suits them. He is a man of honour.'

'Yes, sir,' I said, but I must have sounded as doubtful as I felt, because he looked at me sharply.

'Ah,' he said, 'you're thinking about what happened afterwards?'

'Yes, sir.'

'Well – what about it?'

He beckoned me over to one of the bookshelves. He seemed to want me closer to the light and his eyes to stare at my face. The lamplight played across his features and his dark hair shone. His eyes were always kindly but they could also be intense, as they were now. I noticed one of his scars, which seemed to shine more brightly in the light.

'Well, it was very exciting, sir,' I replied; adding quickly, 'Though I was most concerned for Mother. Your speed in saving her – I've never seen anybody move so quickly.'

He laughed. 'Love will do that to a man. You'll find that out for yourself one day. But what of Mr Birch? His response? What did you make of it, Haytham?'

'Sir?'

'Mr Birch seemed about to administer severe punishment to the scoundrel, Haytham. Did you think it was deserved?'

I considered it before answering. I could tell from the look on Father's face, sharp and watchful, that my answer was important.

And in the heat of the moment I suppose I had thought the thief deserved a harsh response. There had been an instant, brief as it was, when some primal anger wished him harm for the attack on my mother. Now, though, in the soft glow of the lamp, with Father looking kindly upon me, I felt differently.

'Tell me honestly, Haytham,' prompted Father, as though reading my thoughts. 'Reginald has a keen sense of justice, or what he describes as justice. It's somewhat . . . *Biblical*. But what did you think?'

'At first I felt an urge for . . . revenge, sir. But it soon passed, and I was pleased to see the man granted clemency,' I said.

Father smiled and nodded, and then abruptly turned to the bookshelves, where with a flick of his wrist he operated a switch, causing a portion of books to slide across to reveal a secret compartment. My heart skipped a beat as he took something from it: a box, which he handed to me and, nodding, bade me open.

'A birthday present, Haytham,' he said.

I knelt and placed the box on the floor, opened it to reveal a leather belt that I plucked quickly away, knowing that beneath would be a sword, and not a wooden play sword but a shimmering steel sword with an ornate handle. I took it from the box and held it in my hands. It was a short sword and, though, shamefully, I felt a twinge of disappointment about that, I knew at once that it was a *beautiful* short sword, and it was *my* short sword. I decided at once that it would never leave my side, and was already reaching for the belt when Father stopped me.

'No, Haytham,' he said, 'it stays in here, and is not to be removed or even used without my permission. Is that clear?' He had collected the sword from me and already replaced it in the box, placing the belt on top and closing it.

'Soon you will begin to train with this sword,' he continued. 'There is much for you to learn, Haytham, not only about the steel you hold in your hands, but also the steel in your heart.'

'Yes, Father,' I said, trying not to look as confused and disappointed as I felt. I watched as he turned and replaced the box in the secret compartment, and if he was trying to make sure that I didn't see which book triggered the compartment, well, then, he failed. It was the King James Bible.

8 December 1735

i

There were two more funerals today, of the two soldiers who had been stationed in the grounds. As far as I know, Father's gentleman, Mr Digweed, attended the service for the captain, whose name I never knew, but nobody from our household was at the funeral for the second man. There is so much loss and mourning around us at the moment, it's as if there simply isn't room for any more, callous as it sounds.

ii

After my eighth birthday, Mr Birch became a regular visitor to the house and, when not squiring Jenny on walks around the grounds, or taking her into town in his carriage, or sitting in the drawing room drinking tea and sherry and regaling the women with tales of army life, he held meetings with Father. It was clear to all that he intended to marry Jenny and that the union had Father's blessing, but there was talk that Mr Birch had asked to postpone the nuptials; that he wanted to be as prosperous as possible so that Jenny should have the husband she deserved, and that he had his eye on a mansion in Southwark in order to keep her in the manner to which she'd become accustomed.

Mother and Father were thrilled about that of course. Jenny less so. I'd occasionally see her with red eyes, and she'd developed a habit of flying quickly out of rooms, either in the throes of an angry tantrum or with her hand to her mouth, stifling tears. More than once I heard Father say, 'She'll come round,' and on one occasion he gave me a sideways look and rolled his eyes.

Just as she seemed to wither under the weight of her future, I flourished with the anticipation of my own. The love I felt for Father constantly threatened to engulf me with its sheer magnitude; I didn't just love him, I idolized him. At times it was as if the two of us shared a knowledge that was secret from the rest of the world. For example, he'd often ask me what my tutors had been teaching me, listen intently, and then say, 'Why?' Whenever he asked me something, whether it was about religion, ethics or morality, he would know if I gave the answer by rote, or repeated it parrot fashion, and he'd say, 'Well, you've just told me what Old Mr Fayling thinks,' or, 'We know what a centuries-old writer thinks. But what does it say in here, Haytham?' and he'd place a hand to my chest.

I realize now what he was doing. Old Mr Fayling was teaching me facts and absolutes; Father was asking me to question them. This knowledge I was being given by Old Mr Fayling – where did it originate? Who wielded the quill, and why should I trust that man?

Father used to say, 'To see differently, we must first think differently,' and it sounds stupid, and you might laugh, or I might look back on this in years to come and laugh myself, but at times it felt as though I could feel my brain actually *expand* to look at the world in Father's way. He had a way of looking at the world that nobody else had, so it seemed; a way of looking at the world that challenged the very idea of *truth*.

Of course, I questioned Old Mr Fayling. I *challenged* him one day, during Scriptures, and earned myself a whack across the knuckles with his cane, along with the promise that he would be informing my father, which he did. Later, Father took me into his study and, after closing the door, grinned and tapped the side of his nose. 'It's often best, Haytham, to keep your thoughts to yourself. Hide in plain sight.'

So I did. And I found myself looking at the people around me, trying to look inside them as though I might be able somehow to divine how they looked at the world, the Old Mr Fayling way, or the Father way.

Writing this now, of course, I can see I was getting too big for my boots; I was feeling grown-up beyond my years, which would be as unattractive now, at ten, as it would have been at eight, then nine. Probably I was unbearably supercilious. Probably I felt like the little man of the household. When I turned nine, Father presented me with a bow and arrow for my birthday and, practising with it in the grounds, I hoped that the Dawson girls or the Barrett children might be watching me from the windows.

It had been over a year since I'd spoken to Tom at the gate, but I still sometimes loitered there in the hope of meeting him again. Father was forthcoming on all subjects except his own past. He'd never speak of his life before London, nor of Jenny's mother, so I still held out hope that whatever it was Tom knew might prove illuminating. And, apart from that, of course, I wanted a friend. Not a parent or nursemaid or tutor or mentor – I had plenty of those. Just a friend. And I hoped it would be Tom.

It never will be now, of course.

They bury him tomorrow.

9 December 1735

i

Mr Digweed came to see me this morning. He knocked, waited for my reply then had to duck his head to enter, because Mr Digweed, as well as being balding, with slightly bulging eyes and veiny eyelids, is tall and slim, and the doorways in our emergency residence are much lower than they were at home. The way he had to stoop as he moved around the place, it added to his air of discomfiture, the sense of him being a fish out of water here. He'd been my father's gentleman since before I was born, at least since the Kenways settled in London, and like all of us, maybe even more than the rest of us, he belonged to Queen Anne's Square. What made his pain even more acute was guilt – his guilt that on the night of the attack he was away, attending to family matters in Herefordshire; he and our driver had returned the morning after the attack.

'I hope you can find it in your heart to forgive me, Master Haytham,' he had said to me in the days after, his face pale and drawn.

'Of course, Digweed,' I said, and didn't know what to say next; I'd never been comfortable addressing him by his surname; it had never felt right in my mouth. So all I could add was 'Thank you.'

This morning his cadaverous face wore the same solemn expression, and I could tell that, whatever news he had, it was bad.

'Master Haytham,' he said, standing before me.

'Yes . . . Digweed?'

'I'm terribly sorry, Master Haytham, but there's been a message from Queen Anne's Square, from the Barretts. They wish to make it clear that nobody from the Kenway household is welcome at young Master Thomas's funeral service. They respectfully request that no contact is made at all.'

'Thank you, Digweed,' I said, and watched as he gave a short, sorrowful bow then dipped his head to avoid the low beam of the doorway as he left.

I stood there for some time, gazing emptily at the space where he'd stood , until Betty returned to help me out of my funeral suit and into my everyday one.

ii

One afternoon a few weeks ago, I was below stairs, playing in the short corridor that led off the servants' hall to the heavily barred door of the plate room.

It was in the plate room that the family valuables were stored: silverware which only ever saw the light of day on the rare occasions Mother and Father entertained guests; family heirlooms, Mother's jewellery and some of Father's books that he considered of greatest value – irreplaceable books. He kept the key to the plate room with him at all times, on a loop around his belt, and I had only ever seen him entrust it to Mr Digweed, and then only for short periods.

I liked to play in the corridor nearby because it was so rarely visited, which meant I was never bothered by nursemaids, who would invariably tell me to get off the dirty floor before I wore a hole in my trousers; or by other well-meaning staff, who would engage me in polite conversation and oblige me to answer questions about my education or non-existent friends; or perhaps even by Mother or Father, who would tell me to get off the dirty floor before I wore a hole in my trousers and *then* force me to answer questions about my education or non-existent friends. Or, worse than any of them, by Jenny, who would sneer at whatever game I was playing and, if it was toy soldiers, make a malicious effort to kick over each and every tin man of them.

No, the passageway between the servants' hall and the plate room was one of the few places at Queen Anne's Square where I could realistically hope to avoid any of these things, so the passageway is where I went when I didn't want to be disturbed.

Except on this occasion, when a new face emerged in the form of Mr Birch, who let himself into the passage just as I was about to arrange my troops. I had a lantern with me, placed on the stone floor, and the candle fire flickered and popped in the draught as the passage door opened. From my position on the floor, I saw the hem of his frock coat and the tip of his cane, and as my eyes travelled up to see him looking down upon me, I wondered if he, too, kept a sword hidden in his cane, and if it would rattle, the way my father's did.

'Master Haytham, I rather hoped I might find you here,' he said with a smile. 'I was wondering, are you busy?'

I scrambled to my feet. 'Just playing, sir,' I said quickly. 'Is there something wrong?'

'Oh no,' he laughed. 'In fact, the last thing I want to do is disturb your playtime, though there is something I was hoping to discuss with you.'

'Of course,' I said, nodding, my heart sinking at the thought of yet another round of questions concerning my prowess at arithmetic. Yes, I enjoyed my sums. Yes, I enjoyed writing. Yes, I one day hoped to be as clever as my father. Yes, I one day hoped to follow him into the family business.

But with a wave of his hand Mr Birch bade me back to my game and even set aside his cane and hitched up his trousers in order to crouch beside me.

'And what do we have here?' he asked, indicating the small tin figurines.

'Just a game, sir,' I replied.

'These are your soldiers, are they?' he enquired. 'And which one is the commander?'

'There is no commander, sir,' I said.

He gave a dry laugh. 'Your men need a leader, Haytham. How else will they know the best course of action? How else will they be instilled with a sense of discipline and purpose?'

'I don't know, sir,' I said.

'Here,' said Mr Birch. He reached to remove one of the tiny tin men from the pack, buffed him up on his sleeve and placed him to one side. 'Perhaps we should make this gentleman here the leader – what do you think?'

'If it pleases you, sir.'

'Master Haytham,' smiled Mr Birch, 'this is your game. I am merely an interloper, somebody hoping you can show me how it is played.'

'Yes, sir, then a leader would be fine in the circumstances.'

Suddenly the door to the passageway opened again, and I looked up, this time to see Mr Digweed enter. In the flickering lamplight I saw he and Mr Birch share a look.

'Can your business here wait, Digweed?' said Mr Birch tautly.

'Certainly, sir,' said Mr Digweed, bowing and retreating, the door closing behind him.

'Very good,' continued Mr Birch, his attention returning to the game. 'Then let us move this gentleman here to be the unit's leader, in order to inspire his men to great deeds, to lead them by example and teach them the virtues of order and discipline and loyalty. What do you think, Master Haytham?'

'Yes, sir,' I said obediently.

'Here's something else, Master Haytham,' said Mr Birch, reaching between his feet to move another of the tin soldiers from the pack then placing him next to the nominal commander. 'A leader needs trusted lieutenants, does he not?'

'Yes, sir,' I agreed. There was a long pause, during which I watched Mr Birch take inordinate care placing two more lieutenants next to the leader, a pause that became more and more uncomfortable as the moments passed, until I said, more to break the awkward silence than because I wanted to discuss the inevitable, 'Sir, did you want to speak to me about my sister, sir?'

'Why, you can see right through me, Master Haytham,'

laughed Mr Birch loudly. 'Your father is a fine teacher. I see he has taught you guile and cunning – among other things, no doubt.'

I wasn't sure what he meant so kept quiet.

'How is weapons training going, may I enquire?' asked Mr Birch.

'Very well, sir. I continue to improve each day, so Father says,' I said proudly.

'Excellent, excellent. And has your father ever indicated to you the purpose of your training?' he asked.

'Father says my *real* training is to begin on the day of my tenth birthday,' I replied.

'Well, I wonder what it is that he has to tell you,' he said, with furrowed brow. 'You really have no idea? Not even a tantalizing clue?'

'No, sir, I don't,' I said. 'Only that he will provide me with a path to follow. A creed.'

'I see. How very exciting. And he's never given you any indication as to what this "creed" might be?'

'No, sir.'

'How fascinating. I'll wager you cannot wait. And, in the meantime, has your father given you a man's sword with which to learn your craft, or are you still using the wooden practice batons?'

I bridled. 'I have my own sword, sir.'

'I should very much like to see it.'

'It is kept in the games room, sir, in a safe place that only my father and I have access to.'

'Only your father and *you*?' You mean you have access to it, too?'

I coloured, grateful for the dim light in the passageway so that Mr Birch couldn't see the embarrassment on my face. 'All I mean is that I know where the sword is kept, sir, not that I would know how to access it,' I clarified.

'I see,' grinned Mr Birch. 'A secret place, is it? A hidden cavity within the bookcase?'

My face must have said it all. He laughed.

'Don't worry, Master Haytham, your secret is safe with me.'

I looked at him. 'Thank you, sir.'

'That's quite all right.'

He stood, reached to pick up his cane, brushed some dirt, real or imaginary, from his trousers and turned towards the door.

'My sister, sir?' I said. 'You never asked me about her.'

He stopped, chuckled softly and reached to ruffle my hair. A gesture I quite liked. Perhaps because it was something my father did, too.

'Ah, but I don't need to. You've told me everything I need to know, young Master Haytham,' he said. 'You know as little about the beautiful Jennifer as I do, and perhaps that is how it must be in the proper way of things. Women should be a mystery to us, don't you think, Master Haytham?'

I hadn't the faintest idea what he was talking about

but smiled anyway, and breathed a sigh of relief when
I once again had the plate-room corridor to myself.

iii

Not long after that talk with Mr Birch I was in another
part of the house and making my way towards my
bedroom when as I passed Father's study I heard
raised voices from inside: Father and Mr Birch.

The fear of a good hiding meant I stayed too far
away to hear what was being said, and I was glad I'd
kept my distance, because in the next moment the
door to the study was flung open and out hurried
Mr Birch. He was in a fury – his anger was plain to see
in the colour of his cheeks and blazing eyes – but the
sight of me in the hallway brought him up short, even
though he remained agitated.

'I tried, Master Haytham,' he said, as he gathered
himself and began to button his coat ready to leave. 'I
tried to warn him.'

And with that he placed his tricorne on his head
and stalked off. My father had appeared at the door of
his office and glared after Mr Birch and, though it was
clearly an unpleasant encounter, it was grown-up stuff,
and I didn't concern myself with it.

There was more to think about. Just a day or so later
came the attack.

It happened on the night before my birthday. The attack, I mean. I was awake, perhaps because I was excited about the next day, but also because I was in the habit of getting up after Edith had left the room to sit on my windowsill and gaze out of my bedroom window. From my vantage point I'd see cats and dogs or even foxes passing across the moon-painted grass. Or, if not watching out for wildlife, then just watching the night, looking at the moon, the watery-grey colour it gave the grass and trees. At first I thought what I was seeing in the distance were fireflies. I'd heard all about fireflies but never seen them. All I knew was that they gathered in clouds and emitted a dull glow. However, I soon realized the light wasn't a dull glow at all, but in fact was going on, then off, then on again. I was seeing a signal.

My breath caught in my throat. The flashing light seemed to come from close to the old wooden door in the wall, the one where I'd seen Tom that day, and my first thought was that he was trying to contact me. It seems strange now, but not for a second did I assume the signal was meant for anyone but me. I was too busy dragging on a pair of trousers, tucking my night-shirt into the waistband then hooking my braces over my shoulders. I shrugged on a coat. All I could think of was what an awfully splendid adventure I was about to have.

And of course I realize now, looking back, that in the mansion next door Tom must have been another one who liked to sit on his windowsill and watch the nocturnal life in the grounds of his house. And, like me, he must have seen the signal. And perhaps Tom even had the mirror-image thought to mine: that it was me signalling him. And in response did the same as I did: he scrambled from his perch and pulled on some clothes to investigate . . .

Two new faces had appeared at the house on Queen Anne's Square, a pair of hard-faced former soldiers employed by Father. His explanation was that we needed them because he had received 'information'.

Just that. 'Information' – that's all he'd say. And I wondered then as I wonder now what he meant, and whether it had anything to do with the heated conversation I'd overheard between him and Mr Birch. Whatever it was, I'd seen little of the two soldiers. All I really knew was that one was stationed in the drawing room at the front of the mansion, while the other stayed close to the fire in the servants' hall, supposedly to guard the plate room. Both were easy to avoid as I crept down the steps to below stairs and slid into the silent, moonlit kitchen, which I had never seen so dark and empty and still.

And cold. My breath plumed and straight away I

shivered, uncomfortably aware how chilly it was compared to what I'd thought was the meagre heat of my room.

Close by the door was a candle, which I lit and, with my hand cupped over its flame, held to light the way as I let myself out into the stable yard. And if I'd thought it was cold in the kitchen, then, well . . . outside, it was the kind of cold where it felt as if the world around you was brittle and about to break; cold enough to take my cloudy breath away, to give me second thoughts as I stood there and wondered whether or not I could bear to continue.

One of the horses whinnied and stamped, and for some reason the noise made my mind up, sending me tiptoeing past the kennels to a side wall and through a large arched gate leading into the orchard. I made my way through the bare, spindly apple trees, then was out in the open, painfully aware of the mansion to my right, where I imagined faces at every window: Edith, Betty, Mother and Father all staring out and seeing me out of my room and running amok in the grounds. Not that I really was running amok, of course, but that's what they'd say; that's what Edith would say as she scolded me and what Father would say when he gave me the cane for my troubles.

But if I was expecting a shout from the house, then none came. Instead I made my way to the perimeter wall, began to run quickly along it towards the door.

47

I was still shivering, but as my excitement grew I wondered if Tom would have brought food for a midnight feast: ham, cake and biscuits. Oh, and a hot toddy would be most welcome, too . . .

A dog began barking. Thatch, Father's Irish bloodhound, from his kennel in the stable yard. The noise stopped me in my tracks, and I crouched beneath the bare, low-hanging branches of a willow, until it ceased as suddenly as it had started. Later, of course, I'd understand why it stopped so abruptly. But I didn't think anything of it at the time because I had no reason to suspect that Thatch had had his throat cut by an invader. We now think there were five of them altogether who crept up on us with knives and swords. Five men making their way to the mansion, and me in the grounds, oblivious to it all.

But how was I to know? I was a silly boy whose head buzzed with adventure and derring-do, not to mention the thought of ham and cake, and I continued along the perimeter wall, until I came to the gate.

Which was open.

What had I expected? I suppose, for the gate to be shut and for Tom to be on the other side of it. Perhaps one of us would have climbed the wall. Perhaps we planned to trade gossip with the door between us. All I knew was that the gate was open, and I began to get the feeling that something was wrong, and at last it occurred to me that the signalling I'd seen from my bedroom window might not have been meant for me.

'Tom?' I whispered.

There was no sound. The night was completely still: no birds, no animals, nothing. Nervous now, I was about to turn and leave, return to the house and to the safety of my warm bed, when I saw something. A foot. I edged further out of the gate where the passageway was bathed in dirty-white moonlight which gave everything a soft, grubby glow – including the flesh of the boy sprawled on the ground.

He half lay, half sat, propped up against the opposite wall, dressed almost exactly as I was, with a pair of trousers and a nightshirt, only he hadn't bothered to tuck his in and it was twisted around his legs, which lay at strange, unnatural angles on the hard, rutted mud of the walkway.

It was Tom, of course. Tom, whose dead eyes stared sightlessly at me from beneath the brim of his hat, skew-whiff on his head; Tom, with the moonlight gleaming on blood that had sheeted down his front from the gash at his throat.

My teeth began to chatter. I heard a whimper and realized it was me. A hundred panicked thoughts crowded into my head.

And then things began to happen too quickly for me even to remember the exact order in which they took place, though I think it started with the sound of breaking glass and a scream that came from the house.

Run.

I'm ashamed to admit that the voices, the thoughts jostling in my head, all cried that one word together.

Run.

And I obeyed them. I ran. Only, not in the direction they wanted me to. Was I doing as my father had instructed and listening to my instincts, or ignoring them? I didn't know. All I knew was that though every fibre of my being seemed to want me to flee from what I knew was the most terrible danger, in fact I ran towards it.

Through the stable yard I ran, and burst into the kitchen, hardly pausing to acknowledge the fact that the door hung open on its hinges. From somewhere along the hall I heard more screaming, saw blood on the kitchen floor and stepped through the door towards the stairs, only to see another body. It was one of the soldiers. He lay in the corridor clutching his stomach, eyelids fluttering madly and a line of blood trickling from his mouth as he slid dying to the floor.

As I stepped over him and ran for the stairs, my one thought was to reach my parents. The entrance hall, which was dark, but full of screams and running feet, and the first tendrils of smoke. I tried to get my bearings. From above came yet another scream, and I looked up to see dancing shadows on the balcony, and, briefly, the glitter of steel in the hands of one of our attackers. Meeting him on the landing was one of Father's valets, but the skittering light stopped me from seeing the poor boy's fate. Instead I heard and through my feet *felt* the wet thump of his body as it dropped from the balcony to the wooden floor not far away from me. His assassin gave a howl of triumph, and I could hear running feet as he made his way further along the landing – towards the bedrooms.

'*Mother!*' I screamed, and ran for the stairs at the same time as I saw my parents' door flung open and my father come surging out to meet the intruder. He wore trousers, and his suspenders were pulled over his naked shoulders, his hair untied and hanging free. In one hand he held a lantern, in the other his blade.

'Haytham!' he called as I reached the top of the stairs. The intruder was between us on the landing. He stopped, turned to look at me, and in the light of Father's lantern I could see him properly for the first time. He wore trousers, a black leather-armour waist-coat and a small half-face mask like the kind worn for a masked ball. And he was changing direction. Instead of going up against Father, he was charging back along the landing after me, grinning.

'*Haytham!*' shouted Father again. He pulled away from Mother and began to run down the landing after the intruder. Instantly the gap between them closed, but it wouldn't be enough, and I turned to escape, only to see a second man at the foot of the stairs, sword in hand, blocking my way. He was dressed the same as the first, although I noticed one difference: his ears. They were pointed, and with the mask gave him the look of a hideous, deformed Mr Punch. For a moment I froze, then swung back to see that the grinning man behind me had turned to meet Father, and their swords clashed. Father had left his lantern behind, and it was in the half-dark that they fought. A short, brutal battle punctuated by grunts and the chiming of sword steel. Even in the heat and the danger of the moment I wished it had been light enough to watch him fight properly.

Then it was over and the grinning assassin was grinning no more, dropping his sword, tumbling over the banisters with a scream and hitting the floor beneath. The pointy-eared intruder had been halfway up the stairs but had second thoughts and wheeled around to escape to the entrance hall.

There was a shout from below. Over the banisters I saw a third man, also wearing a mask, who beckoned to the pointy-eared man before both disappeared out of sight beneath the landing. I glanced up and in the low light saw a look pass across my father's face.

'The games room,' he said.

And, in the next instant, before Mother or I could stop him, he'd leapt over the banister to the entrance hall beneath. As he jumped my mother screamed,

'*Edward!*' and the anguish in her voice echoed my own thoughts. No. My one, single thought: he's abandoning us.

Why is he abandoning us?

Mother's nightclothes were in disarray around her as she ran along the landing towards where I stood at the top of the stairs; her face was a mask of terror. Behind her came yet another attacker, who appeared from the stairway at the far end of the landing and reached Mother at the same time as she reached me. He grabbed her from behind with one hand while his sword hand swept forward, about to draw the blade across her exposed throat.

I didn't stop to think. I didn't even think about it at all until much later. But in one movement I stepped up, reached, plucked the dead attacker's sword from the stair, raised it above my head and with two hands plunged it into his face before he could cut her throat.

My aim was true and the point of the sword drove through the eyehole of the mask and into the socket. His scream tore a ragged hole in the night as he span away from Mother with the sword momentarily embedded in his eye. Then it was wrenched out as he fell against the banister, toppled for a moment, sank to his knees and pitched forward, dead before his head hit the floor.

Mother ran into my arms and buried her head in my shoulder, even as I grabbed the sword and took her hand to make our way back down the stairs. How many times had Father said to me, on his way to work for the day, 'You're in charge today, Haytham; you look after Mother for me.' Now, I really was.

We reached the foot of the stairs, where a strange quiet seemed to have descended over the house. The entrance hall was empty now and still dark, though lit by an ominous flickering orange glow. The air was beginning to thicken with smoke, but through the haze I saw bodies: the assassin, the valet who was killed earlier . . . And Edith, who lay with her throat open in a pool of blood.

Mother saw Edith, too, whimpered, and tried to pull me in the direction of the main doors, but the door to the games room was half open, and from inside I could hear the sound of sword fighting. Three men, one of them my father. 'Father needs me,' I said, trying to disentangle myself from Mother, who saw what I was about to do and pulled at me harder, until I snatched my hand away with such force that she collapsed to the floor.

For one strange moment I found myself torn between helping Mother to her feet and apologizing, the sight of her on the floor – on the floor because of me – was so appalling. But then I heard a great cry from inside the games room and it was enough to propel me through the door.

The first thing I saw was that the bookcase compartment was open, and I could see the box holding my sword inside. Otherwise the room was as always, left just as it had been after the last training session, with the covered billiard table moved and space made for me to train; where earlier that day I'd been tutored and scolded by Father.

Where now Father was kneeling, dying.

Standing over him was a man with his sword buried hilt-deep into my father's chest, the blade protruding from his back dripping blood to the wooden floor. Not far away stood the pointy-eared man, who had a large gash down his face. It had taken two of them to defeat Father, and only just at that.

I flew at the killer, who was caught by surprise and without time to retrieve his sword from my father's chest. Instead he span away to avoid my blade, letting go of his sword at the same time as Father dropped to the floor.

Like a fool I continued after the assassin, forgot to protect my flank, and the next thing I saw was a sudden movement out of the corner of my eye as the pointy-eared man danced forward. Whether he meant to do it or mistimed his blow, I'm not sure, but instead of striking me with the blade he clubbed me with the pommel, and my vision went black; my head connected with something it took me a second to realize was the leg of the billiard table, and I was on the floor, dazed, sprawled opposite Father, who lay on his side with the sword handle still protruding from his chest. There was life in his eyes still, just a spark, and his eyelids fluttered momentarily, as if he were focusing, taking me in. For a moment or so we lay opposite one another, two wounded men. His lips were moving. Through a dark cloud of pain and grief I saw his hand reach for me.

'Father –' I said. Then in the next instant the killer had strode over and without pausing bent and pulled his blade from Father's body. Father jerked, his body arched with one last spasm of pain as his lips pulled away from bloodied teeth, and he died.

I felt a boot on my side that pushed me on to my back, and I looked up into the eyes of my father's killer, and now *my* killer, who with a smirk raised his sword two-handed, about to plunge it into me.

If it gave me shame to report that my inner voices had commanded me to run just a few moments before, then it gives me pride to report that now they were calm; that I faced my death with dignity and with the knowledge that I had done my best for my family; with gratitude that I would soon be joining my father.

But of course it was not to be. It's not a ghost who writes these words. Something caught my eye, and it was the tip of a sword that appeared between the killer's legs and in the same instant was driven upwards, opening his torso from the groin up. I've realized since that the direction of the strike had less to do with savagery and more to do with the need to pull my killer away from me, not push him forward. But savage it was, and he screamed, blood splattering as he was split asunder and his guts dropped from the gash to the floor and his lifeless carcass followed suit.

Behind him stood Mr Birch. 'Are you all right, Haytham?' he asked.

'Yes, sir,' I gasped.

'Good show,' he said, then spun with his sword up to intercept the pointy-eared man, who came at him with his blade flashing.

I pulled myself to my knees, grabbed a fallen sword and stood, ready to join Mr Birch, who had driven the pointy-eared man back to the door of the games room when suddenly the attacker saw something – something out of sight behind the door – and danced to one side. In the next instant Mr Birch reared back and held out a hand to prevent me coming forward, while at the doorway the pointy-eared man had reappeared. Only this time he had a hostage. Not my mother, as I at first feared. It was Jenny.

'Get back,' snarled Pointy Ears. Jenny snivelled, and her eyes were wide as the blade pressed into her throat.

Can I admit – can I admit that at that moment I cared far more for avenging my father's death than I did for protecting Jenny?

'Stay there,' repeated Pointy Ears man, pulling Jenny back. The hem of her nightdress was caught around her ankles and her heels dragged on the floor. Suddenly they were joined by another masked man who brandished a flaming torch. The entrance hall was almost full of smoke now. I could see flames coming from another part of the house, licking at the doors to the drawing room. The man with the torch darted to the drapes, put his flame to them, and more of our house began to burn around us, Mr Birch and I powerless to stop it.

I saw my mother out of the corner of my eye and thanked God she was all right. Jenny was another matter, though. As she was dragged towards the door of the mansion, her eyes were fixed on me and Mr Birch as though we were her last hopes. The torch-bearing attacker came to join his colleague, hauled the door open and darted out towards a carriage I could see on the street outside.

For a moment I thought they might let Jenny go, but no. She began to scream as she was dragged towards the carriage and bundled in, and she was still screaming as a third masked man in the driver's seat shook the reins, wielded his crop and the carriage rattled off into the night, leaving us to escape from our burning house and drag our dead from the clutches of the flames.

10 December 1735

i

Even though we buried Father today, the first thing I thought about when I awoke this morning didn't involve him or his funeral, it was about the plate room at Queen Anne's Square.

They hadn't tried to enter it. Father had employed the two soldiers because he was worried about a robbery, but our attackers had made their way upstairs without even bothering to try to raid the plate room.

Because they were after Jenny, that was why. And killing Father? Was that part of the plan?

This was what I thought as I awoke to a room that was freezing – which isn't unusual, that it should be freezing. An everyday occurrence, in fact. Just that today's room was *especially* cold. The kind of cold that sets your teeth on edge; that reaches into your bones. I glanced over to the hearth, wondering why there wasn't more heat from the fire, only to see that it was unlit and the grate grey and dusty with ash.

I clambered out of bed and went to where there

was a thick layer of ice on the inside of the window, preventing me from seeing out. Gasping with cold, I dressed, left my room and was struck by how quiet the house seemed. Creeping all the way downstairs, I found Betty's room, knocked softly, then a little harder. When she didn't answer, I stood debating what to do, a little concern for her gnawing at the insides of my stomach. And when there was still no answer I knelt to look through the keyhole, praying I wouldn't see anything I shouldn't.

She lay asleep in one of the two beds in her room. The other one was empty and neatly made up, although there was a pair of what looked like men's boots at the foot of it, with a strip of silver at the heel. My gaze went back to Betty, and for a moment I watched as the blanket covering her rose and fell, and then decided to let her sleep on, and straightened.

I ambled along to the kitchen, where Mrs Searle started a little as I entered, looked me up and down with a slightly disapproving gaze then returned to her work at the chopping board. It wasn't that Mrs Searle and I had fallen out, just that Mrs Searle regarded everybody with suspicion, and since the attack even more so.

'She's not one of life's most forgiving sorts,' Betty had said to me one afternoon. That was another thing that had changed since the attack: Betty had become a lot more candid, and every now and then would drop hints about how she *really* felt about things. I had never realized that she and Mrs Searle didn't see eye to eye, for example, nor had I any idea that Betty regarded Mr Birch with suspicion. She did though: 'I don't know why he's making decisions on behalf of the Kenways,' she had muttered darkly yesterday. 'He's not a member of the family. Doubt he ever will be.'

Somehow, knowing that Betty didn't think much of Mrs Searle made the housekeeper less forbidding in my eyes, and while before I would have thought twice about wandering into the kitchen unannounced and requesting food, I now had no such qualms.

'Good morning, Mrs Searle,' I said.

She gave a small curtsy. The kitchen was cold, just her in it. At Queen Anne's Square, Mrs Searle had at least three helpers, not to mention sundry other staff who flitted in and out through the great double doors of the kitchen. But that was before the attack, when we had a full complement, and there's nothing like an invasion of sword-wielding masked men for driving the servants away. Most hadn't even returned the following day.

Now there was just Mrs Searle, Betty, Mr Digweed, a chambermaid called Emily, and Miss Davy, who was mother's lady's maid. They were the last of the staff who looked after the Kenways. Or the remaining Kenways, I should say. Just me and Mother left now.

When I left the kitchen it was with a piece of cake

wrapped in cloth handed to me with a sour look by Mrs Searle, who no doubt disapproved of me wandering about the house so early in the morning, scavenging for food ahead of the breakfast she was in the process of preparing. I like Mrs Searle, and since she's one of the few members of staff to have stayed with us after that terrible night I like her even more, but even so. There are other things to worry about now. Father's funeral. And Mother, of course.

And then I found myself in the entrance hall, looking at the inside of the front door, and before I knew it I was opening the door, and without thinking – without thinking too much, anyway – letting myself out on to the steps and out into a world clouded with frost.

ii

'Now, what in the blazes do you plan to do on such a cold morning, Master Haytham?'

A carriage had just drawn up outside the house, and at the window was Mr Birch. He wore a hat that was heavier than usual, and a scarf pulled up over his nose so that, at first glance, he looked like a highwayman.

'Just looking, sir,' I said, from the steps.

He pulled his scarf down, trying to smile. Before when he'd smiled it had set his eyes twinkling, now it was like the dwindling, cooling ashes of the fire, trying but unable to generate any warmth, as strained and tired as his voice when he spoke. 'I think perhaps I know what you're looking for, Master Haytham.'

'What's that, sir?'

'The way home?'

I thought about it and realized he was right. The trouble was, I had lived the first ten years of my life being shepherded around by parents and the nurse-maids. Though I knew that Queen Anne's Square was near, and even within walking distance, I had no idea how to get there.

'And were you planning on a visit?' he asked.

I shrugged, but the truth of it was that, yes, I had pictured myself in the shell of my old home. In the games room there. I'd pictured myself retrieving . . .

'Your sword?'

I nodded.

'It's too dangerous to go in the house, I'm afraid. Would you like to take a trip over there anyway? You can see it, at least. Come inside, it's as cold as a grey-hound's nostril out there.'

And I saw no reason not to, especially when he produced a hat and a cape from within the depths of the carriage.

When we pulled up at the house some moments later it didn't look at all as I had imagined it. No, it was far, far worse. As though a giant God-like fist had pounded into it from above, smashing through the roof and the floors beneath, gouging a huge, ragged hole into the house. It wasn't so much a house now as a cutaway of one.

Through broken windows we could see into the entrance hall and up – through smashed floors to the hallway three flights up, all of them blackened with soot. I could see furniture that I recognized, blackened and charred, burnt portraits hanging lopsided on the walls.

'I'm sorry – it really is too dangerous to go inside, Master Haytham,' said Mr Birch.

After a moment he led me back into the carriage, tapped the ceiling twice with his cane, and we pulled away.

'However,' said Mr Birch, 'I took the liberty of retrieving your sword yesterday,' and reaching beneath his seat he produced the box. It, too, was dusty with soot, but when he pulled it to his lap and opened the lid, the sword lay inside, as gleaming as it had been the day Father gave it to me.

'Thank you, Mr Birch' was all I could say, as he closed the box and placed it on the seat between us.

'It's a handsome sword, Haytham. I've no doubt you'll treasure it.'

'I will, sir.'

'And when, I wonder, will it first taste blood?'

'I don't know, sir.'

There was a pause. Mr Birch clasped his cane between his knees.

'The night of the attack, you killed a man,' he said, turning his head to look out of the window. We passed houses that were only just visible, floating through a haze of smoke and freezing air. It was still early. The streets were quiet. 'How did that feel, Haytham?'

'I was protecting Mother,' I said.

'That was the only possible option, Haytham,' he agreed, nodding, 'and you did the right thing. Don't for a moment think otherwise. But it being the only option doesn't change the fact that it's no small matter to kill a man. For anybody. Not for your father. Not for me. But especially not for a boy of such tender years.'

'I felt no sadness at what I did. I just acted.'

'And have you thought about it since?'

'No, sir. I've thought only of Father, and Mother.'

'And Jenny . . .?' said Mr Birch.

'Oh. Yes, sir.'

There was a pause, and when he next spoke his voice was flat and solemn. 'We need to find her, Haytham,' he said.

I kept quiet.

'I intend to leave for Europe where we believe she is being held.'

'How do you know she is in Europe, sir?'

'Haytham, I am a member of an influential and

important organization. A kind of club, or society. One of the many advantages to membership is that we have eyes and ears everywhere.'

'What is it called, sir?' I asked.

'The Templars, Master Haytham. I am a Templar knight.'

'A knight?' I said, looking at him sharply.

He gave a short laugh. 'Perhaps not exactly the kind of knight you're thinking of, Haytham, a relic of the Middle Ages, but our ideals remain the same. Just as our forebears set out to spread peace across the Holy Land centuries ago, so we are the unseen power that helps to maintain peace and order in our time.' He waved his hand at the window, where the streets were busier now. 'All of this, Haytham, it requires structure and discipline, and structure and discipline require an example to follow. The Knights Templar *are* that example.'

My head span. 'And where do you meet? What do you do? Do you have armour?'

'Later, Haytham. Later, I'll tell you more.'

'Was Father a member, though? Was he a knight?' My heart leapt. 'Was he training *me* to become one?'

'No, Master Haytham, he was not, and I'm afraid that as far as I'm aware he was merely training you in swordsmanship in order that . . . well, the fact that your mother lives proves the worth of your lessons. No, my relationship with your father was not built on my membership of the Order. I'm pleased to say that I was employed by him for my skill at property management rather than any hidden connections. Nevertheless, he knew that I was a knight. After all, the Templars have powerful and wealthy connections, and these could sometimes be of use in our business. Your father may not have been a member, but he was shrewd enough to see the worth of the connections: a friendly word, the passing on of useful information' – he took a deep breath – 'one of which was the tip-off about the attack at Queen Anne's Square. I told him, of course. I asked him why it might be that he had been targeted, but he scoffed at the very idea – disingenuously, perhaps. We clashed over it, Haytham. Voices were raised, but I only wish now I'd been even more insistent.'

'Was that the argument I heard?' I asked.

He looked sideways at me. 'So you did hear, did you? Not eavesdropping, I hope?'

The tone in his voice made me more than thankful I hadn't been. 'No, Mr Birch, sir, I heard raised voices, and that was all.'

He looked hard at me. Satisfied I was telling the truth, he faced forward. 'Your father was as stubborn as he was inscrutable.'

'But he didn't ignore the warning, sir. He employed the soldiers, after all.'

Mr Birch sighed. 'Your father didn't take the threat

seriously, and would have done nothing. When he wouldn't listen to me, I took the step of informing your mother. It was at her insistence that he employed the soldiers. I wish now I had substituted the men for men taken from our ranks. They would not have been so easily overwhelmed. All I can do now is try to find his daughter for him and punish those responsible. To do that I need to know why – what was the purpose of the attack? Tell me, what do you know of him before he settled in London, Master Haytham?'

'Nothing, sir,' I replied.

He gave a dry chuckle. 'Well, that makes two of us. More than two of us, in fact. Your mother knows next to nothing also.'

'And Jenny, sir?'

'Ah, the equally inscrutable Jenny. As frustrating as she was beautiful, as inscrutable as she was adorable.'

'"Was", sir?'

'A turn of phrase, Master Haytham – I hope with all my heart at least. I remain hopeful that Jenny is safe in the hands of her captors, of use to them only if she is alive.'

'You think she has been taken for a ransom?'

'Your father was very rich. Your family might well have been targeted for your wealth, and your father's death unplanned. It's certainly possible. We have men looking into that possibility now. Equally, the mission may have been to assassinate your father, and we have men looking into that possibility also – well, me, because of course I knew him well, and would know if he had any enemies: enemies with the wherewithal to stage such an attack, I mean, rather than disgruntled tenants – and I came up with not a single possibility, which leads me to believe that the object may have been to settle a grudge. If so then it's a long-standing grudge, something that relates to his time before London. Jenny, being the only one who knew him before London, may have had answers, but whatever she knew she has taken into the hands of her captors. Either way, Haytham, we need to locate her.'

There was something about the way he said 'we'.

'As I say, it is thought she will have been taken somewhere in Europe, so Europe is where we will conduct our search for her. And by "we", I mean you and me, Haytham.'

I started. 'Sir?' I said, hardly able to believe my ears.

'That's right,' he said. 'You shall be coming with me.'

'Mother needs me, sir. I can't leave her here.'

Mr Birch looked at me again, in his eyes neither kindliness not malice. 'Haytham,' he said, 'I'm afraid the decision is not yours to make.'

'It is for Mother to make,' I insisted.

'Well, quite.'

'What do you mean, sir?'

He sighed. 'I mean, have you spoken to your mother since the night of the attack?'

'She's been too distressed to see anyone but Miss Davy or Emily. She's stayed in her room, and Miss Davy says I'm to be summoned when she can see me.'

'When you do see her, you will find her changed.'

'Sir?'

'On the night of the attack, Tessa saw her husband die and her little boy kill a man. These things will have had a profound effect on her, Haytham; she may not be the person you remember.'

'All the more reason she needs me.'

'Maybe what she needs is to get well, Haytham – possibly with as few reminders of that terrible night around her as possible.'

'I understand, sir,' I said.

'I'm sorry if that comes as a shock, Haytham.' He frowned. 'And I may well be wrong, of course, but I've been dealing with your father's business affairs since his death, and we've been making arrangements with your mother, I've had the opportunity of seeing her first-hand, and I don't think I'm wrong. Not this time.'

iii

Mother called for me shortly before the funeral.

When Betty, who had been full of red-faced apologies for what she called 'her little lie-in', told me, my first thought was that she had changed her mind about me going to Europe with Mr Birch, but I was wrong. Darting along to her room, I knocked and only just heard her tell me to come in – her voice so weak and reedy now, not at all how it used to be, when it was soft but commanding. Inside, she was sitting by the window, and Miss Davy was fussing at the curtains; even though it was daytime it was hardly bright outside but, nevertheless, Mother was waving her hand in front of her, as if she were being bothered by an angry bird, rather than just some greying rays of winter sunlight. At last Miss Davy finished to Mother's satisfaction and with a weary smile indicated me to a seat.

Mother turned her head towards me, very slowly, looked at me and forced a smile. The attack had exacted a terrible toll on her. It was as though all the life had been leeched out of her; as though she had lost the light she always had, whether she was smiling or cross or, as Father always said, wearing her heart on her sleeve. Now the smile slowly slid from her lips, which settled back into a blank frown, as though she'd tried but no longer had the strength to keep up any pretence.

'You know I'm not going to the funeral, Haytham?' she said blankly.

'Yes, Mother.'

'I'm sorry. I'm sorry, Haytham, I really am, but I'm not strong enough.'

She never usually called me Haytham. She called me 'darling'.

'Yes, Mother,' I said, knowing that she was – she was strong enough. *'Your Mother has more pluck than any man I've ever met, Haytham,'* Father used to say.

They had met shortly after they moved to London, and she had pursued him – 'like a lioness in pursuit of her prey', Father had joked, 'a sight as blood-curdling as it was awe-inspiring', and earned himself a clout for that particular joke, the kind of joke you thought might have had an element of truth to it.

She didn't like to talk about her family. 'Well to do' was all I knew. And Jenny had hinted once that they had disowned her because of her association with Father. Why, of course, I never found out. On the odd occasion I'd pestered Mother about Father's life before London, she'd smiled mysteriously. He'd tell me when he was ready. Sitting in her room, I realized that at least part of the grief I felt was the pain of knowing that I'd never hear whatever it was Father was planning to tell me on my birthday. Although it's just a tiny part of the grief, I should make clear – insignificant compared to the grief of losing Father and the pain of seeing Mother like this. So . . . *reduced*. So lacking in that pluck Father spoke of.

Perhaps it had turned out that the source of her strength was him. Perhaps the carnage of that terrible evening had simply been too much for her to take.

They say it happens to soldiers. They get 'soldier's heart' and become shadows of their former selves. The bloodshed changes them somehow. Was that the case with Mother? I wondered.

'I'm sorry, Haytham,' she added.

'It's all right, Mother.'

'No – I mean, you are to go to Europe with Mr Birch.'

'But I'm needed here, with you. To look after you.'

She gave an airy laugh: 'Mama's little soldier, uh?', and fixed me with a strange, searching look. I knew exactly where her mind was going. Back to what had happened on the stairs. She was seeing me thrust a blade into the eye socket of the masked attacker.

And then she tore her eyes away, leaving me feeling almost breathless with the raw emotion of her gaze.

'I have Miss Davy and Emily to look after me, Haytham. When the repairs are made to Queen Anne's Square we'll be able to move back and I can employ more staff. No, it is me who should be looking after you, and I have appointed Mr Birch the family comptroller and your guardian, so that you can be looked after properly. It's what your father would have wanted.'

She looked at the curtain quizzically, as if she was trying to recall why it was drawn. 'I understand Mr Birch was going to speak to you about leaving for Europe straight away.'

'He did, yes, but –'

'Good.' She regarded me. Again, there was something

discomfiting about the look; she was no longer the mother I knew, I realized. Or was I no longer the son she knew?

'It's for the best, Haytham.'

'But, Mother . . .'

She looked at me, then away again quickly.

'You're going, and that's the end of it,' she said firmly, her stare returning to the curtains. My eyes went to Miss Davy as though looking for assistance, but I found none; in return she gave me a sympathetic smile, a raise of the eyebrows, an expression that said, 'I'm sorry, Haytham, there's nothing I can do, her mind is made up,' and there was silence in the room, no sound apart from the clip-clopping of hooves from outside, from a world that carried on oblivious to the fact that mine was being taken apart.

'You are dismissed, Haytham,' Mother said, with a wave of her hand.

Before – before the attack, I mean – she had never used to 'summon' me. Or 'dismiss' me. Before, she had never let me leave her side without at least a kiss on the cheek, and she'd told me she loved me, at least once a day.

As I stood, it occurred to me that she hadn't said anything about what had happened on the stairs that night. She had never thanked me for saving her life. At the door I paused and turned to look at her, and wondered whether she wished the outcome had been different.

Mr Birch accompanied me to the funeral, a small, informal service at the same chapel we had used for Edith, with almost the same number in attendance: the household, Old Mr Fayling, and a few members of staff from Father's work, whom Mr Birch spoke to afterwards. He introduced me to one of them, Mr Simpkin, a man I judged to be in his mid-thirties, who I was told would be handling the family's affairs. He bowed a little and gave me a look I'm coming to recognize as a mix of awkwardness and sympathy, each struggling to find adequate expression.

'I will be dealing with your mother while you are in Europe, Master Haytham,' he assured me.

It hit me that I really was going; that I had no choice, no say whatsoever in the matter. Well, I do have a choice, I suppose – I could run away. Not that running away seems like any kind of choice.

We took carriages home. Trooping into the house, I caught sight of Betty, who looked at me and gave me a weak smile. The news about me was spreading, so it seemed. When I asked her what she planned to do, she told me that Mr Digweed had found her alternative employment. When she looked at me her eyes shone with tears, and when she left the room I sat at my desk to write my journal with a heavy heart.

11 December 1735

i

We depart for Europe tomorrow morning. It strikes me how few preparations are needed. It is as though the fire had already severed all my ties with my old life. What few things I had left were only enough to fill two trunks, which were taken away this morning. Today I am to write letters, and also to see Mr Birch in order to tell him about something that occurred last night, after I'd gone to bed.

I was almost asleep when I heard a soft knocking at the door, sat up and said, 'Come in,' fully expecting it to be Betty.

It wasn't. I saw the figure of a girl, who stepped quickly into the room and shut the door behind her. She raised a candle so I could see her face and the finger she held to her lips. It was Emily, blonde-haired Emily, the chambermaid.

'Master Haytham,' she said, 'I have something I need to tell you, which has been preying on my mind, sir.'

'Of course,' I said, hoping my voice wouldn't betray the fact that I felt suddenly very young and vulnerable.

'I know the maid of the Barretts,' she said quickly. 'Violet, who was one of those who came out of their houses that night. She was close to the carriage they put your sister in, sir. As they bundled Miss Jenny past her and the carriage, Miss Jenny caught Violet's eye and told her something quickly, which Violet has told me.'

'What was it?' I said.

'It was very quick, sir, and there was plenty of noise, and before she could say any more they bundled her into the carriage, but what Violet thinks she heard was "Traitor". Next day, a man paid Violet a visit, a man with a West Country accent, or so she said, who wanted to know what she'd heard, but Violet said she'd heard nothing, even when the gentleman threatened her. He showed her an evil-looking knife, sir, out of his belt, but even then she said nothing.'

'But she told you?'

'Violet's my sister, sir. She worries for me.'

'Have you told anyone else?'

'No, sir.'

'I shall tell Mr Birch in the morning,' I said.

'But, sir . . .'

'What?'

'What if the traitor *is* Mr Birch?'

I gave a short laugh and shook my head. 'It isn't possible. He saved my life. He was there fighting the . . .' Something struck me. 'There is someone who *wasn't* there, though.'

Of course I sent word to Mr Birch at the first opportunity this morning, and he reached the same conclusion I had.

An hour later another man arrived, who was shown into the study. He was about the same age my father had been and had a craggy face, scars and the cold, staring eyes of some species of sea-life. He was taller than Mr Birch, and broader, and seemed to fill the room with his presence. A *dark* presence. And he looked at me. Down his nose at me. Down his wrinkled-with-disdain nose at me.

'This is Mr Braddock,' said Mr Birch, as I stood fixed into place by the newcomer's glare. 'He is also a Templar. He has my total and utmost trust, Haytham.' He cleared his throat, and said loudly, 'And a manner sometimes at odds with what I know to be in his heart.'

Mr Braddock snorted, and shot him a withering look.

'Now, Edward,' chided Birch. 'Haytham, Mr Braddock will be in charge of finding the traitor.'

'Thank you, sir,' I said.

Mr Braddock looked me over then spoke to Mr Birch. 'This Digweed,' he said, 'perhaps you can show me his quarters.'

When I moved to follow them, Mr Braddock glared

at Mr Birch, who nodded almost imperceptibly then turned to me, smiling, with a look in his eyes that begged my forbearance.

'Haytham,' he said, 'perhaps you should attend to other matters. Your preparations for leaving, perhaps,' and I was compelled to return to my room, where I surveyed my already packed cases then retrieved my journal, in which to write the events of the day. Moments ago, Mr Birch came to me with the news: Digweed has escaped, he told me, his face grave. However, they will find him, he assured me. The Templars always catch their man and, in the meantime, nothing changes. We still depart for Europe.

It strikes me this will be my last entry at home here in London. These are the last words of my old life, before my new one begins.

PART II

1747, Twelve Years Later

10 June 1747

I watched the traitor today as he moved around the bazaar. Wearing a plumed hat, colourful buckles and garters, he strutted from stall to stall and twinkled in the bright, white Spanish sun. With some of the stallholders he joked and laughed; with others he exchanged cross words. He was neither friend nor despot, it seemed, and indeed, the impression I formed of him, albeit one I formed at a distance, was of a fair man, benevolent even. But then again it's not those people he was betraying. It is his Order. It is us.

His guards stayed with him during his rounds, and they were diligent men, I could tell. Their eyes never stopped moving around the market, and when one of the stallholders gave him a hearty clap on the back and pressed on him a gift of bread from his stall, he waved to the taller of the two guards, who took it with his left hand, keeping his sword hand free. Good. Good man. Templar-trained.

Moments later a small boy darted out from the

crowds, and straight away my eyes went to the guards, saw them tense, assess the danger and then . . .

Relax?

Laugh at themselves for being jumpy?

No. They stayed tense. Stayed watchful, because they're not fools and they knew the boy might have been a decoy.

They were good men. I wondered if they had been corrupted by the teachings of their employer, a man who pledged allegiance to one cause while promoting the ideals of another. I hoped not, because I'd already decided to let them live. And if it appears to be somewhat convenient that I've decided to let them live, and that maybe the truth has more to do with my apprehension of going into combat with two such competent men, then that appearance is false. They may be vigilant; undoubtedly they would be expert swordsmen; they would be skilled in the business of death.

But then, I am vigilant. I am an expert swordsman. And I am skilled in the business of death. I have a natural aptitude for it. Although, unlike theology, philosophy, classics and my languages, particularly Spanish, which is so good that I'm able to pass as a Spaniard here in Altea, albeit a somewhat reticent one, I take no pleasure in my skill at death. Simply, I am good at it.

Perhaps if my target was Digweed – perhaps then I might take some small measure of gratification from his death at my hands. But it is not.

For the five years after we left London, Reginald and I scoured Europe, moving from country to country in a travelling caravan of staff and fellow Knights who shifted around us, drifting in and out of our lives, we two the only constants as we moved from one country to the next, sometimes picking up the trail of a group of Turkish slavers who were believed to be holding Jenny, and occasionally acting on information concerning Digweed, which Braddock would attend to, riding off for months on end but always returning empty-handed.

Reginald was my tutor, and in that respect he had similarities to Father; first in that he tended to sneer at almost anything from books, constantly asserting that there existed a higher, more advanced learning than could be found in dusty old schoolbooks, which I later came to know as Templar learning; and second, in that he insisted I think for myself.

Where they differed was that my Father would ask me to make up my own mind. Reginald, I came to learn, viewed the world in more absolute terms. With Father I sometimes felt as if the thinking was enough – that the thinking was a means unto itself and the conclusion I reached somehow less important than the journey. With Father, facts, and, looking back over past journals I realize even the entire concept of *truth*, could feel like shifting, mutable properties.

There was no such ambiguity with Reginald, though, and in the early years when I might say otherwise, he'd smile at me and tell me he could hear my father in me. He'd tell me how my father had been a great man and wise in many ways, and quite the best swordsman he had ever known, but his attitude to learning was not as scholarly as it might have been.

Does it shame me to admit that over time I came to prefer Reginald's way, the stricter Templar way? Though he was always good-tempered, quick with a joke and smile, he lacked the natural joy, even mischief, of Father. He was always buttoned and neat, for one thing, and he was fanatical about punctuality; he insisted that things be orderly at all times. And yet, almost despite myself there was something fixed about Reginald, some certainty, both inner and outer, that came to appeal to me more and more as the years passed.

One day I realized why. It was the absence of doubt – and with it confusion, indecision, uncertainty. This feeling – this feeling of 'knowing' that Reginald imbued in me – was my guide from boyhood to adulthood. I never forgot my father's teachings; on the contrary, he would have been proud of me because I *questioned* his ideals. In doing so I adopted new ones.

We never found Jenny. Over the years, I'd mellowed towards her memory. Reading back over my journals, the young me could not have cared less about her, something I'm somewhat ashamed of, because I'm a grown man now, and I see things in different terms. Not that my youthful antipathy towards her did anything to hinder the hunt for her, of course. In that mission, Mr Birch had more than enough zeal for the two of us. But it wasn't enough. The funds we received from Mr Simpkin in London were handsome, but they weren't without end. We found a chateau in France, hidden near Troyes, in the Landes of Champagne, in which to make our base, where Mr Birch continued my apprenticeship, sponsoring my admittance as an Adept and then, three years ago, as a fully fledged member of the Order.

Weeks would go by with no mention of either Jenny or Digweed; then months. We were involved in other Templar activities. The War of the Austrian Succession had seemed to gobble the whole of Europe into its greedy maw, and we were needed to help protect Templar interests. My 'aptitude', my skill at death, became apparent, and Reginald was quick to see its benefits. The first to die – not my first 'kill', of course; my first assassination, I should say – was a greedy merchant in Liverpool. My second was an Austrian prince.

After the killing of the merchant, two years ago, I returned to London, only to find that building work was continuing at Queen Anne's Square, and

Mother . . . Mother was too tired to see me that day, and would be the following day as well. 'Is she too tired to answer my letters, too?' I asked Mrs Davy, who apologized and averted her gaze. Afterwards I rode to Herefordshire, hoping to locate Digweed's family, to no avail. The traitor in our household was never to be found, it seemed – or *is* never to be found, I should say.

But then, the fire of vengeance in my gut burns less fiercely these days, perhaps simply because I've grown; perhaps because of what Reginald has taught me about control of oneself, mastery of one's own emotions.

Even so, dim it may be, but it continues to burn within me.

iii

The *hostale* owner's wife has just been to visit, throwing a quick look down the steps before she closed the door behind her. A messenger arrived while I was out, she said, and handed his missive to me with a lascivious look that I might have been tempted to act upon if I hadn't had other things on my mind. The events of last night, for example.

So instead I ushered her out of my room and sat down to decode the message. It told me that as soon as I was finished in Altea, I was to travel not home, to France, but to Prague, where I would meet Reginald in the cellar rooms of the house in Celetna Lane, the Templar headquarters. He has an urgent matter to discuss with me.

In the meantime, I have my cheese. Tonight, the traitor meets his end.

i

It is done. The kill, I mean. And though it was not without its complications, the execution was clean insofar as he is dead and I remain undetected, and for that I can allow myself to take a measure of satisfaction in having completed my task.

His name was Juan Vedomir, and supposedly his job was to protect our interests in Altea. That he had used the opportunity to build an empire of his own was tolerated; the information we had was that he controlled the port and market with a benign hand, and certainly on the evidence of earlier that day he seemed to enjoy some support, even if the constant presence of his guards proved that wasn't always the case.

Was he *too* benign, though? Reginald thought so, had investigated, and eventually found that Vedomir's abandonment of Templar ideologies was so complete as to amount to treachery. We are intolerant of traitors in the Order. I was despatched to Altea. I watched him. And, last night, I took my cheese and left my *hostale* for the last time, making my way along cobbled streets to his villa.

'Yes?' said the guard who opened his door.

'I have cheese,' I said.

'I can smell it from here,' he replied.

'I hope to convince Señor Vedomir to allow me to trade at the bazaar.'

His nose wrinkled some more. 'Señor Vedomir is in the business of attracting patrons to the market, not driving them away.'

'Perhaps those with a more refined palate might disagree, señor?'

The guard squinted. 'Your accent. Where are you from?'

He was the first to question my Spanish citizenship. 'Originally from the Republic of Genoa,' I said, smiling, 'where cheese is one of our finest exports.'

'Your cheese will have to go a long way to beat Varela's cheese.'

I continued to smile. 'I am confident that it does. I am confident that Señor Vedomir will think so.'

He looked doubtful but stood aside and let me into a wide entrance hall, which though the night was warm, was cool, almost cold, as well as being sparse, with just two chairs and a table, on which were some cards. I glanced at them. A game of piquet, I was pleased to see, because piquet's a two-player game, which meant there were no more guards hiding in the woodwork.

The first guard indicated for me to place the wrapped cheese on the card table, and I did as I was told. The second man stood back, one hand on the hilt of his sword as his partner checked me for weapons, patting my clothes thoroughly and next searching the bag I wore around my shoulder, in which were a few coins and my journal, but nothing more. I had no blade.

'He's not armed,' said the first guard, and the second man nodded. 'The first guard indicated my cheese. 'You want Señor Vedomir to taste this, I take it?'

I nodded enthusiastically.

'Perhaps I should taste it first?' said the first guard, watching me closely.

'I had hoped to save it all for Señor Vedomir,' I replied with an obsequious smile.

The guard gave a snort. 'You have more than enough. Perhaps *you* should taste it.'

I began to protest. 'But I had hoped to save it for –'

He put his hand to the hilt of his sword. '*Taste it,*' he insisted.

I nodded. 'Of course, señor,' I said, and unwrapped a piece, picked off a chunk and ate it. Next he indicated I should try another piece, which I did, making a face to show how heavenly it tasted. 'And now that it's been opened,' I said, proffering the wrapping, 'you might as well have a taste.'

The two guards exchanged a look, then at last the first smiled, went to a thick wooden door at the end of the passageway, knocked and entered. Then they appeared again and beckoned me forward, into Vedomir's chamber.

Inside, it was dark and heavily perfumed. Silk billowed gently on the low ceiling as we entered. Vedomir sat with his back to us, his long black hair loose, wearing a nightshirt and writing by the light of a candle at his desk.

'Would you have me stay, Señor Vedomir?' asked the guard.

Vedomir didn't turn around. 'I take it our guest isn't armed?'

'No, señor,' said the guard, 'although the smell of his cheese is enough to fell an army.'

'To me the scent is a perfume, Cristian,' laughed Vedomir. 'Please show our guest to a seat, and I shall be over in a moment.'

I sat on a low stool by an empty hearth as he blotted the book then came over, stopping to pick up a small knife from a side table as he came.

'Cheese, then?' His smile split a thin moustache as he lifted his nightshirt to sit on another low stool, opposite.

'Yes, señor,' I said.

He looked at me. 'Oh? I was told you were from the Republic of Genoa, but I can hear from your voice that you are English.'

I started with shock, but the big grin he wore told

me I had nothing to worry about. Not yet at least. 'And there I was, thinking me so clever to hide my nationality all this time,' I said, impressed, 'but you have found me out, señor.'

'And the first to do so, evidently, which is why your head is still on your shoulders. Our two countries are at war, are they not?'

'The whole of Europe is at war, señor. I sometimes wonder if anybody knows who is fighting whom.'

Vedomir chuckled and his eyes danced. 'You're being disingenuous, my friend. I think we all know your King George's allegiances, as well as his ambitions. Your British navy is said to think itself the best in the world. The French, the Spanish – not to mention the Swedes – disagree. An Englishman in Spain takes his life in his hands.'

'Should I be concerned for my safety now, señor?'

'With me?' He spread his hands and gave a crooked, ironic smile. 'I like to think I rise above the petty concerns of kings, my friend.'

'Then who do you serve, señor?'

'Why, the people of the town, of course.'

'And to whom do you pledge allegiance if not to King Ferdinand?'

'To a higher power, señor,' smiled Vedomir, closing the subject firmly and turning his attention to the wrappings of cheese I'd placed by the hearth. 'Now,' he went on, you'll have to forgive my confusion. This cheese. Is it from the Republic of Genoa or is it English cheese?'

'It is *my* cheese, señor. My cheeses are the best wherever one plants one's flag.'

'Good enough to usurp Varela?'

'Perhaps to trade alongside him?'

'And what then? Then I have an unhappy Varela.'

'Yes, señor.'

'Such a state of affairs might be of no concern to you, señor, but these are the matters that vex me daily. Now, let me taste this cheese before it melts, eh?'

Pretending to feel the heat, I loosened my neck scarf then took it off. Surreptitiously, I reached into my shoulder bag and palmed a doubloon. When he turned his attention to the cheese I dropped the doubloon into the scarf.

The knife glittered in the candlelight as Vedomir cut off a chunk of the first cheese, holding the piece with his thumb and sniffing at it – hardly necessary; I could smell it from where I sat – then popped it into his mouth. He ate thoughtfully, looked at me, then cut off a second chunk.

'Hm,' he said, after some moments. 'You are wrong, señor, this is not superior to Varela's cheese. It is in fact *exactly the same* as Varela's cheese.' His smile had faded and his face had darkened. I realized I had been found out. 'In fact, this *is* Varela's cheese.'

His mouth was opening to shout for help as I

dropped the doubloon into the scarf, twirled the silk into a garrotte with a flick of my wrists and leapt forward with crossed arms, dropping it over his head and around his neck.

His knife hand arced up, but he was too slow and caught unawares, and the knife thrashed wildly at the silk above our heads as I secured my *rumal*, the coin pressing in on his windpipe, cutting off any noise. Holding the garrotte with one hand, I disarmed him, tossed the knife to a cushion then used both hands to tighten the *rumal*.

'My name is Haytham Kenway,' I said dispassionately, leaning forward to look into his wide-open, bulging eyes. 'You have betrayed the Templar Order. For this you have been sentenced to execution.'

His arm rose in a futile attempt to claw at my eyes, but I moved my head and watched the silk flutter gently as the life left him.

When it was over I carried his body to the bed then went to his desk to take his journal, as I had been instructed. It was open, and my eye fell upon some writing: '*Para ver de manera diferente, primero debemos pensar diferente.*'

I read it again, translating it carefully, as though I were learning a new language: 'To see differently, we must first think differently.'

I stared at it for some moments, deep in thought, then snapped the book shut and stowed it in my bag, returning my mind to the job at hand. Vedomir's death would not be discovered until morning, by which time I would be long gone, on my way to Prague, where I now had something to ask Reginald.

18 June 1747

i

'It's about your mother, Haytham.'

He stood before me in the basement of the head-quarters on Celetna Lane. He had made no effort to dress for Prague. He wore his Englishness like a badge of honour: neat and tidy white stockings, black breeches and, of course, his wig, which was white and had shed most of its powder on the shoulders of his frock coat. He was lit by the flames from tall iron cressets on poles on either side of him, while mounted on stone walls so dark they were almost black were torches that shone with halos of pale light. Normally he stood relaxed, with his hands behind his back and leaning on his cane, but today there was a formal air about him.

'Mother?'

'Yes, Haytham.'

She's ill, was my first thought, and I instantly felt a hot wave of guilt so intense I was almost giddy with it. I hadn't written to her in weeks; I'd hardly even thought about her.

'She's dead, Haytham,' said Reginald, casting his

eyes downward. 'A week ago she had a fall. Her back was badly hurt, and I'm afraid that she succumbed to her injuries.'

I looked at him. That intense rush of guilt was gone as quickly as it had arrived and in its place an empty feeling, a hollow place where emotions should be.

'I'm sorry, Haytham.' His weathered face creased into sympathy and his eyes were kind. 'Your mother was a fine woman.'

'That's quite all right,' I said.

'We're to leave for England straight away. There's a memorial service.'

'I see.'

'If you need . . . anything, then please don't hesitate to ask.'

'Thank you.'

'Your family is the Order now, Haytham. You can come to us for anything.'

'Thank you.'

He cleared his throat uncomfortably. 'And if you need . . . you know, to talk, then I'm here.'

I tried not to smile at the idea. 'Thank you, Reginald, but I won't need to talk.'

'Very well.'

There was a long pause.

He looked away. 'Is it done?'

'Juan Vedomir is dead, if that's what you mean.'

'And you have his journal?'

'I'm afraid not.'

For a moment his face fell, then it grew hard. Very hard. I'd seen his face do that before, in an unguarded moment.

'What?' he said simply.

'I killed him for his betrayal of our cause, did I not?' I said.

'Indeed . . .' said Reginald carefully.

'Then what need did I have of his journal?'

'It contains his writings. They are of interest to us.'

'Why?' I asked.

'Haytham, I had reason to believe that Juan Vedomir's treachery went beyond the matter of his adherence to the doctrine. I think he may have advanced to *working* with the Assassins. Now tell me the truth, please, do you have his journal?'

I pulled it from my bag, gave it to him, and he moved over to one of the candelabras, opened it, quickly flicked through then snapped it shut.

'And have you read it?' he asked.

'It's in code,' I replied.

'But not all of it,' he said equably.

I nodded. 'Yes – yes, you're right, there were some passages I was able to read. His . . . *thoughts* on life. They made interesting reading. In fact, I was particularly intrigued, Reginald, by how much Juan Vedomir's philosophy was consistent with what my father once taught me.'

'Quite possibly.'

'And yet you had me kill him?'

'I had you kill a traitor to the Order. Which is something else entirely. Of course, I knew your father felt differently to me concerning many – perhaps even most – of the tenets of the Order, but that's because he didn't subscribe to them. The fact that he wasn't a Templar didn't make me respect him less.'

I looked at him. I wondered if I had been wrong to doubt him. 'Why, then, is the book of interest?'

'Not for Vedomir's musings on life, that much is certain,' smiled Reginald, and gave me a sideways smile. 'As you say, they were similar to your father's, and we both know our feelings about that. No, it's the coded passages I'm interested in, which, if I'm right, will contain details of the keeper of a key.'

'A key to what?'

'All in good time.'

I made a sound of frustration.

'Once I have decoded the journal, Haytham,' he pressed. 'When, if I'm right, we'll be able to begin the next phase of the operation.'

'And what might that be?'

He opened his mouth to speak, but I said the words for him. '"All in good time, Haytham," is that it? More secrets, Reginald?'

He bristled. '"Secrets"? Really? Is that what you think? What exactly have I done to deserve your suspicion, Haytham, other than to take you under my wing, sponsor you in the Order, give you a life? You know, I might be forgiven for thinking you rather ungrateful at times, sir.'

'We were never able to find Digweed, though, were we?' I said, refusing to be cowed. 'There never was a ransom demand for Jenny, so the main purpose of the raid had to be Father's death.'

'We *hoped* to find Digweed, Haytham. That's all we could ever do. We *hoped* to make him pay. That hope was not satisfied, but that doesn't mean we were derelict in our attempt. Moreover, I had a duty of care to *you*, Haytham, which was fulfilled. You stand before me a man, a respected Knight of the Order. You overlook that, I think. And don't forget that I hoped to marry Jenny. Perhaps in the heat of your desire to avenge your father, you see losing Digweed as our only significant failure, but it's not, is it, because we've never found Jenny, have we? Of course, you spare no thought for your sister's hardship.'

'You accuse me of callousness? Heartlessness?'

He shook his head. 'I merely request that you turn your stare on your own failings before you start shining light on mine.'

I looked carefully at him. 'You never took me into your confidence regarding the search.'

'Braddock was sent to find him. He updated me regularly.'

'But you didn't pass those updates to me.'

'You were a young boy.'

'Who grew up.'

He bent his head. 'Then I apologize for not taking that fact into account, Haytham. In future I will treat you as an equal.'

'Then start now – start by telling me about the journal,' I said.

He laughed, as though caught in check at chess. 'You win, Haytham. All right, it represents the first step towards the location of a temple – a first-civilization temple, thought to have been built by Those Who Came Before.'

There was a moment's pause in which I thought, *Is that it?* Then laughed.

At first he looked shocked, perhaps remembering the first time he'd ever told me about Those Who Came Before, when I'd found it difficult to contain myself. 'Those who came before what . . . ?' I'd scoffed.

'Before *us*,' he'd replied tightly, 'Before man. A previous civilization.'

He frowned at me now. 'You're still finding it amusing, Haytham?'

I shook my head. 'Not amusing so much, no. More . . .' I struggled to find the words '. . . hard to fathom, Reginald. A race of beings who existed before man. Gods . . .'

'Not gods, Haytham, first-civilization humans who controlled humanity. They left us artefacts, Haytham, of immense power, such that we can only dream of. I believe that whoever can possess those artefacts can ultimately control all of human destiny.'

My laugh dwindled when I saw how serious he had become. 'It's a very grand claim, Reginald.'

'Indeed. If it was a modest claim then we would not be so interested, no? The Assassins would not be interested.' His eyes gleamed. The flames from the cressets shone and danced in them. I'd seen that look in his eyes before, but only on rare occasions. Not when he'd been tutoring me in languages, philosophy, or even in the classics or the principles of combat. Not even when he taught me the tenets of the Order.

No, only when he talked about Those Who Came Before.

Sometimes Reginald liked to deride what he saw as a surfeit of passion. He thought of it as a shortcoming. When he talked about the beings of the first civilization, however, he talked like a zealot.

ii

We are staying the night in the Templar headquarters here in Prague. As I sit here now in a meagre room with grey stone walls, I can feel the weight of thousands of years of Templar history upon me.

My thoughts go to Queen Anne's Square, to which

the household returned when the work was done. Mr Simpkin had kept us abreast of developments; Reginald had overseen the building operation, even as we moved from country to country in search of Digweed and Jenny. (And yes, Reginald was right. Failing to find Digweed: that fact eats at me; but I almost never think of Jenny.)

One day Simpkin sent us the word that the household had returned from Bloomsbury to Queen Anne's Square, that the household was once again in residence, back where it belonged. That day my mind went to the wood-panelled walls of the home I grew up in, and I found I could vividly picture the people within it – especially my mother. But, of course, I was picturing the mother I had known growing up, who shone, bright like the sun and twice as warm, on whose knee I knew perfect happiness. My love for Father was fierce, perhaps stronger, but for Mother it was purer. With Father I had a feeling of awe, of admiration so grand I sometimes felt dwarfed by him, and with that came an underlying feeling I can only describe as anxiety, that somehow I had to live up to him, to grow into the huge shadow cast by him.

With Mother, though, there was no such insecurity, just the almost overwhelming sense of comfort and love and protection. And she was a beauty. I used to enjoy it when people compared me to Father because he was so striking, but if they said I looked like Mother

I knew they meant *handsome*. Of Jenny, people would say, 'She'll *break* a few hearts'; 'She'll have men *fighting* over her.' They applied the language of struggle and conflict. But not with Mother. Her beauty was a gentle, maternal, nurturing thing, to be spoken of not with the wariness Jenny's looks inspired, but with warmth and admiration.

Of course, I had never known Jenny's mother, Caroline Scott, but I had formed an opinion of her: that she was 'a Jenny', and that my father had been captivated by her looks just as Jenny's suitors were captivated by hers.

Mother, though, I imagined to be an entirely different sort of person altogether. She was plain old Tessa Stephenson-Oakley when she met my father. That's what she had always said, anyway: 'plain old Tessa Stephenson-Oakley,' which didn't sound at all plain to me, but never mind. Father had moved to London, arriving alone with no household, but a purse large enough to buy one. When he had rented a London home from a wealthy landowner, the daughter had offered to help my father find permanent accommodation, as well as employing the household to run it. The daughter, of course, was 'plain old Tessa Stephenson-Oakley' . . .

She had all but hinted that her family wasn't happy about the liaison; indeed, we never saw her side of the family. She devoted her energies to us and, until that dreadful night, the person who had her undivided attention, her unending affection, her unconditional love, was me.

But the last time I had seen her there was no sign of that person. When I think back to our final meeting now, what I remember is the suspicion in her eyes, which I realize was contempt. When I killed the man about to kill her, I changed in her eyes. I was no longer the boy who had sat on her knee.

I was a killer.

20 June 1747

En route to London, I re-read an old journal. Why? Some instinct, perhaps. Some sub-conscious nagging . . . doubt, I suppose.

Whatever it was, when I re-read the entry of 10 December 1735, I all of a sudden knew exactly what I had to do when I reached England.

2-3 July 1747

Today was the service, and also . . . well, I shall explain.

After the service, I left Reginald talking to Mr Simpkin on the steps of the chapel. To me, Mr Simpkin said that he had some papers for me to sign. In the light of Mother's death, the finances were mine. With an obsequious smile he said he hoped that I had considered him more than satisfactory in managing the affairs so far. I nodded, smiled, said nothing committal, told them I wanted a little time to myself, and slipped away, seemingly to be alone with my thoughts.

I hoped that the direction of my wanderings looked random as I made my way along the thoroughfare, staying clear of carriage wheels that splashed through mud and manure on the highway, weaving through people thronging the streets: tradesmen in bloodied leather aprons, whores and washerwomen. But it wasn't. It wasn't random at all.

One woman in particular was up ahead, like me, making her way through the crowds, alone and, probably, lost in thought. I had seen her at the service, of course. She'd sat with the other staff – Emily, and two or three others I didn't recognize – on the other side of the chapel, with a handkerchief at her nose. She had looked up and seen me – she must have done – but she made no sign. I wondered, did Betty, my old nursemaid, even recognize me?

And now I was following her, keeping a discreet distance behind so she wouldn't see me if she happened to glance backwards. It was getting dark by the time she reached home, or not home but the household for which she now worked, a grand mansion that loomed in the charcoal sky, not too dissimilar to the one at Queen Anne's Square. Was she still a nursemaid, I wondered, or had she moved up in the world? Did she wear the uniform of a governess beneath her coat? The street was less crowded than before, and I lingered out of sight, watching as she took a short flight of stone steps down towards the below-stairs quarters and let herself in.

When she was out of sight I crossed the highway and sauntered towards the house, aware of the need to look inconspicuous in case eyes were seeing me from the windows. Once upon a time I was a young boy who had looked from the windows of the house in Queen Anne's Square, watched passers-by come and go and wondered about their business. Was there a little boy in this household watching me now, wondering who is this man? Where has he come from? Where is he going?

So I wandered along the railings at the front of the mansion and glanced down to see the lit windows of what I assumed were the servants' quarters, only to be rewarded with the unmistakable silhouette of Betty appearing at the glass and drawing a curtain. I had the information I'd come for.

I returned after midnight, when the drapes at the windows of the mansion were shut, the street was dark and the only lights were those fixed to the occasional passing carriage.

Once again I made my way to the front of the house, and with a quick look left and right scaled the railings and dropped silently down into the gully on the other side. I scuttled along it until I found Betty's window, where I stopped and very carefully placed my ear to the glass, listening for some moments until I was satisfied that there was no movement from within.

And then, with infinite patience, I applied my fingertips to the bottom of the sash window and lifted, praying it wouldn't squeak and, when my prayers were answered, letting myself in and closing the window behind me.

In the bed she stirred slightly – at the breath of air from the open window perhaps; some unconscious sensing of my presence? Like a statue I stood and waited for her deep breathing to resume, and felt the air around me settle, my incursion absorbed into the room so that after a few moments it was as though I were a part of it – as though I had always been a part of it, like a ghost.

And then I took out my sword.

It was fitting – ironic, perhaps – that it should have been the sword given to me by my father. These days, I rarely go anywhere without it. Years ago, Reginald asked me when I expected it to taste blood, and it has, of course, many times. And if I was right about Betty, then it would once again.

I sat on the bed and put the blade of the sword close to her throat, then clamped my hand over her mouth.

She woke. Immediately her eyes were wide with terror. Her mouth moved and my palm tickled and vibrated as she tried to scream.

I held her thrashing body still and said nothing, just allowed her eyes to adjust until she could see me, and she must have recognized me. How could she not, when she nursed me for ten years, was like a mother to me? How can she not have recognized Master Haytham?

When she had finished struggling, I whispered, 'Hello, Betty,' with my hand still over her mouth. 'I have something I need to ask you. To answer you will need to speak. For you to speak I'll need to take my hand from your mouth and you may be tempted to scream, but if you scream . . .' I applied the tip of the sword to her throat to make my point. And, then, very gently, I lifted my hand from her mouth.

Her eyes were hard, like granite. For a moment I felt myself retreat to childhood and was almost intimidated by the fire and fury there, as though the sight of them triggered a memory of being scolded that I couldn't help but respond to.

'I should put you over my knee for this, Master Haytham,' she hissed. 'How dare you creep into a lady's room when she sleeps? Did I teach you nothing? Did Edith teach you nothing? Your mother?' Her voice was rising. *'Did your father teach you nothing?'*

That childhood feeling stayed with me, and I had to reach into myself to find resolve, fighting an urge simply to put away my sword and say, 'Sorry, Nurse Betty,' promise never to do it again, that I would be a good boy from now on.

The thought of my father gave me that resolve.

'It's true you were like a mother to me once, Betty,' I said to her. 'It's true that what I'm doing is a terrible, unforgivable thing to do. Believe me, I'm not here lightly. But what you've done is terrible, and unforgivable, too.'

Her eyes narrowed. 'What do you mean?'

With my other hand I reached inside my frock coat and retrieved a folded piece of paper, which I held for her to see in the near-dark of the room. 'You remember Laura, the kitchen maid?'

Cautious, she nodded.

'She sent me a letter,' I went on. 'A letter that told me all about your relationship with Digweed. For how long was Father's gentleman your fancy man, Betty?'

There was no such letter; the piece of paper I held contained nothing more revelatory than the address of my lodgings for the night, and I was relying on the low light to fool her. The truth was that when I'd re-read my old journals I'd been taken back to that moment many, many years ago when I had gone to look for Betty. She had been having her 'little lie-in' that cold morning, and when I peered through her keyhole I'd seen a pair of men's boots in her room. I hadn't realized at the time because I was too young. I'd seen them with the eyes of a nine-year-old and thought nothing of them. Not then. Not ever since.

Not until reading it afresh, when, like a joke that suddenly makes sense, I had understood: the boots had belonged to her lover. Of course they had. What I was less certain of was that her lover was Digweed. I remember that she used to speak of him with great affection, but then so did everyone; he had fooled us all. But when I left for Europe in the care of Reginald, Digweed had found alternative employment for Betty.

Even so, it was a guess that they were lovers – a considered, educated guess, but risky, with terrible consequences, if I was wrong.

'Do you remember the day you had a little lie-in, Betty?' I asked. 'A "little lie-in", do you remember?'

She nodded her head warily.

'I came to see where you were,' I continued. 'I was cold, you see. And in the passage outside your room –

well, I don't like to admit it, but I knelt down and I looked through your keyhole.'

I felt myself colour slightly, despite everything. She'd been staring balefully up at me, but now her eyes went flinty and her lips pursed crossly, almost as though this ancient intrusion were as bad as the current one.

'I didn't see anything,' I clarified quickly. 'Not unless you count you, slumbering in bed, and also a pair of men's boots that I recognized as belonging to Digweed. Were you having an affair with him, is that it?'

'Oh, Master Haytham,' she whispered, shaking her head and with sad eyes, 'what has become of you? What sort of man has that Birch turned you into? That you should be holding a knife to the throat of a lady of my advancing years is bad enough – oh, that's bad enough. But look at you now, you're ladling hurt on hurt, accusing me of having an *affair*, being a home-wrecker. It was no affair. Mr Digweed had children, that's true, who were looked after by his sister in Herefordshire, but his wife died many years before he even joined the household. Ours was not an affair the way you're thinking with your dirty mind. We were in love, and shame on you thinking otherwise. Shame on you.' She shook her head again.

Feeling my hand tighten on the handle of the sword, I squeezed my eyes shut. 'No, no, it's not me who should be made to feel at fault here. You can try and come high and mighty with me all you like, but the fact is that you had a . . . relationship of some kind, of whatever kind – it doesn't *matter* what kind – with Digweed, and Digweed betrayed us. Without that betrayal my father would be alive. Mother would be alive, and I would not be sitting here with a knife to your throat, so don't blame me for your current predicament, Betty. Blame him.'

She took a deep breath and composed herself. 'He had no choice,' she said at last, 'Jack didn't. Oh, that was his name, by the way: Jack. Did you know that?'

'I'll read it on his gravestone,' I hissed, 'and knowing it makes not a blind bit of difference, because he did have a choice, Betty. Whether it was a choice between the devil and the deep blue sea, I don't care. He had a choice.'

'No – the man threatened Jack's children.'

'"Man"? What man?'

'I don't know. A man who first spoke to Jack in town.'

'Did you ever see him?'

'No.'

'What did Digweed say about him? Was he from the West Country?'

'Jack said he had the accent sir, yes. Why?'

'When the men kidnapped Jenny, she was screaming about a traitor. Violet from next door heard her, but the following day a man with a West Country accent came to speak to her – to warn her not to tell anyone what she'd heard.'

West Country. Betty had blanched, I saw. 'What?' I snapped. 'What have I said?'

'It's Violet, sir,' she gasped. 'Not long after you left for Europe – it could even have been the day after – she met her end in a street robbery.'

'They came good on their word,' I said. I looked at her. 'Tell me about the man giving Digweed his orders,' I said.

'Nothing. Jack never said anything about him. That he meant business; that if Jack didn't do as they told him then they would find his children and kill them. They said that if he told the master then they'd find his boys, cut them and kill them slowly, all of that. They told him what they were planning to do to the house, but on my life, Master Haytham, they told him that nobody would be hurt; that it would all happen at the dead of night.'

Something occurred to me. 'Why did they even need him?'

She looked perplexed.

'He wasn't even there on the night of the attack,' I continued. 'It wasn't as if they required help getting in. They took Jenny, killed Father. Why was Digweed needed for that?'

'I don't know, Master Haytham,' she said. 'I really don't.'

When I looked down at her, it was with a kind of numbness. Before, when I'd been waiting for darkness to fall, anger had been simmering, bubbling within me, the idea of Digweed's treachery lighting a fire beneath my fury, the idea that Betty had colluded, or even known, adding fuel to it.

I'd wanted her to be innocent. Most of all I'd wanted her dalliance to be with another member of the household. But if it was with Digweed then I wanted her to know nothing about his betrayal. I wanted her to be innocent, for if she was guilty then I had to kill her, because if she could have done something to stop the slaughter of that night and failed to act, then she had to die. That was . . . that was *justice*. It was cause and effect. Checks and balances. An eye for an eye. And that's what I believe in. That's my ideology. A way of negotiating a passage through life that makes sense even when life itself so rarely does. A way of imposing order upon chaos.

But the last thing I wanted to do was kill her.

'Where is he now?' I asked softly.

'I don't know, Master Haytham.' Her voice quavered with fear. 'The last time I heard from him was the morning he disappeared.'

'Who else knew you and he were lovers?'

'Nobody,' she replied. 'We were always so careful.'

'Apart from leaving his boots in view.'

'They were moved sharpish.' Her eyes hardened.

'And most folk weren't in the habit of peering through the keyhole.'

There was a pause. 'What happens now, Master Haytham?' she said, a catch in her voice.

'I should kill you, Betty,' I said simply, and looking into her eyes I saw the realization dawn on her that I could if I wanted to; that I was capable of doing it.

She whimpered.

I stood. 'But I won't. There's already been too much death as a result of that night. We will not meet again. For your years of service and nurture I award you your life and leave you with your shame. Goodbye.'

14 July 1747

i

After neglecting my journal for almost two weeks I have much to tell and should recap, going right back to the night I visited Betty.

After leaving I'd returned to my lodgings, slept for a few fitful hours, then rose, dressed and took a carriage back to her house. There I bid the driver wait some distance away, close enough to see, but not close enough to draw suspicion, and as he snoozed, grateful for the rest, I sat and gazed out of the window, and waited.

For what? I didn't know for sure. Yet again I was listening to my instinct.

And yet again it proved correct, for not long after daybreak, Betty appeared.

I dismissed the driver, followed her on foot and, sure enough, she made her way to the General Post Office on Lombard Street, went in, reappeared some minutes later, and then made her way back along the street until she was swallowed up by the crowds.

I watched her go, feeling nothing, not the urge to

follow her and slit her throat for her treachery, not even the vestiges of the affection we once had. Just . . . nothing.

Instead I took up position in a doorway and watched the world go by, flicking beggars and street sellers away with my cane as I waited for perhaps an hour until . . .

Yes, there he was – the letter carrier, carrying his bell and case full of mail. I pushed myself out of the doorway and, twirling my cane, followed him, closer and closer until he moved on to a side road where there were fewer pedestrians, and I spotted my chance . . .

Moments later I was kneeling by his bleeding and unconscious body in an alleyway, sorting through the contents of his letter case until I found it – an envelope addressed to 'Jack Digweed'. I read it – it said that she loved him, and that I had found out about their relationship; nothing in there I didn't already know – but it wasn't the contents of the letter I was interested in so much as the destination, and there it was on the front of the envelope, which was bound for the Black Forest, for a small town called St Peter, not far from Freiburg.

Almost two weeks of journeying later, Reginald and I came within sight of St Peter in the distance, a cluster of buildings nestled at the bottom of a valley otherwise rich with verdant fields and patches of forest. That was this morning.

We reached it at around noon, dirty and tired from our travels. Trotting slowly through narrow, labyrinthine streets, I saw the upturned faces of the residents, glimpsed either from pathways or turning quickly away from windows, closing doors and drawing curtains. We had death on our minds, and at the time I thought they somehow knew this, or perhaps were easily spooked. What I didn't know was that we weren't the first strangers to ride into town that morning. The townspeople were *already* spooked.

The letter had been addressed care of the St Peter General Store. We came to a small plaza, with a fountain shaded by chestnut trees, and asked for directions from a nervous townswoman. Others gave us a wide berth as she pointed the way then sidled off, staring at her shoes. Moments later we were tethering our horses outside the store and walking in, only for the sole customer to take a look at us and decide to stock up on provisions another time. Reginald and I exchanged a confused look, then I cast an eye over the store. Tall, wooden shelves lined three sides, stocked with jars and packets tied up with twine, while at the back was a high counter behind which stood the storekeeper, wearing an apron, a wide moustache and a smile that had faded like an exhausted candle on getting a good look at us.

To my left was a set of steps used to reach the high shelves. On them sat a boy, about ten years old, the storekeeper's son, by the look of him. He almost lost his footing in his haste to scuttle off the steps and stand in the middle of the floor with his hands by his side, awaiting his orders.

'Good afternoon, gentlemen,' said the shopkeeper in German. 'You look like you have been riding a long time. You need some supplies to continue your journey?' He indicated an urn on the counter before him. 'You need some refreshments perhaps? A drink?'

Next he was waving a hand at the boy. 'Christophe, have you forgotten your manners? Take the gentlemen's coats . . .'

There were three stools in front of the counter and the shopkeeper waved a hand at them, saying, 'Please, please, take a seat.'

I glanced again at Reginald, saw he was about to move forward to accept the storekeeper's offer of hospitality, and stopped him.

'No, thank you,' I said to the shopkeeper. 'My friend and I don't intend to stay.' From the corner of my eye I saw Reginald's shoulders sag, but he said nothing. 'All we need from you is information,' I added.

A cautious look fell across the shopkeeper's face like a dark curtain. 'Yes?' he said warily.

'We need to find a man. His name is Digweed. Jack Digweed. Are you acquainted with him?'

He shook his head.

'You don't know him at all?' I pressed.

Again the shake of the head.

'Haytham . . .' said Reginald, as though he could read my mind from the tone of my voice.

I ignored him. 'Are you quite sure about that?' I insisted.

'Yes, sir,' said the shopkeeper. His moustache quivered nervously. He swallowed.

I felt my jaw tighten; then, before anybody had a chance to react, I'd drawn my sword and with my outstretched arm tucked the blade beneath Christophe's chin. The boy gasped, raised himself on his tiptoes, and his eyes darted as the blade pressed into his throat. I hadn't taken my eyes off the shopkeeper.

'Haytham . . .' said Reginald again.

'Let me handle this, please, Reginald,' I said, and addressed the storekeeper: 'Digweed's letters are sent care of this address,' I said. 'Let me ask you again. Where is he?'

'Sir,' pleaded the shopkeeper. His eyes darted from me to Christophe, who was making a series of low noises, as though he were finding it difficult to swallow. 'Please don't hurt my son.'

His pleas fell on deaf ears.

'Where is he?' I repeated.

'Sir,' pleaded the owner. His hands implored. 'I cannot say.'

With a tiny flick of the wrist I increased the pressure of my blade on Christophe's throat and was rewarded with a whimper. From the corner of my eye I saw the boy rise even higher on his tiptoes and felt, but did not see, Reginald's discomfort to the other side of me. All the time, my eyes never left those of the shopkeeper.

'Please sir, please sir,' he said quickly, those imploring hands waving in the air as though he were trying to juggle an invisible glass, 'I can't say. I was warned not to.'

'Ah-ha,' I said. 'Who? Who warned you? Was it him? Was it Digweed?'

'No, sir,' insisted the shopkeeper. 'I haven't seen Master Digweed for some weeks. This was . . . someone else, but I can't tell you – I can't tell you who. These men, they were serious.'

'But I think we know that I, too, am serious,' I said with a smile, 'and the difference between them and me is that I am here and they are not. Now tell me. How many men, who were they and what did they want to know?'

His eyes flicked from me to Christophe, who though brave and stoic and displaying the kind of fortitude under duress that I'd hope for my own son, whimpered again nonetheless, which must have made up the storekeeper's mind, because his moustache trembled a little more, then he spoke, quickly, the words tumbling from him.

'They were here, sir,' he said. 'Just an hour or so ago. Two men with long black coats over the red tunics of the British Army, who came into the store just as you did and asked the whereabouts of Master Digweed. When I told them, thinking little of it, they became very grave, sir, and told me that some more men might arrive looking for Master Digweed, and, if they did, then I was to deny all knowledge of him, on pain of death, and not to say that they had been here.'

'Where is he?'

'A cabin, fifteen miles north of here in the woods.'

Neither Reginald nor I said a word. We both knew we didn't have a minute to spare, and without pausing to make more threats, or to say goodbye, or perhaps even apologize to Christophe for frightening him half to death, we both dashed out of the door, untethered and mounted our steeds, and spurred them on with yells.

We rode as hard as we dared for over half an hour, until we had covered maybe eight miles of pasture, all of it uphill, our horses now becoming tired. We came to a tree line, only to discover that it was a narrow band of pine, and we arrived on the other side to see a ribbon of trees stretching around the summit of a hill on either side. Meanwhile, in front of us the ground sloped down into more woodland, then away, undulating like a huge blanket of green, patched with forestry, grass and fields.

We pulled up and I called for the spyglass. Our horses snorted and I scanned the area in front of us, swinging the spyglass from left to right, crazily at first, with the emergency getting the better of me, panic making me indiscriminate. In the end I had to force myself to calm down, taking deep breaths and screwing up my eyes tight then starting again, this time moving the spyglass slowly and methodically across the landscape. In my head I divided the territory into a grid and moved from one square to another, back to being systematic and efficient, back to having logic in charge, not emotion.

A silence of gentle wind and birdsong was broken by Reginald. 'Would you have done it?'

'Done what, Reginald?'

He meant kill the child.

'Kill the boy. Would you have done it?'

'There is little point in making a threat if you can't carry it out. The storekeeper would have known if I was shamming. He would have seen it in my eyes. He would have known.'

Reginald shifted uneasily in his saddle. 'So, *yes*, then? Yes, you would have killed him?'

'That's right, Reginald, I would have killed him.'

There was a pause. I completed the next square of land, then the next.

'When was the killing of innocents ever part of your teaching, Haytham?' said Reginald.

I gave a snort. 'Just because you taught me to kill, Reginald, it doesn't give you the final say on whom I kill and to what end.'

'I taught you honour. I taught you a code.'

'I remember you, Reginald, about to dispense your own form of justice outside White's all those years ago. Was that honourable?'

Did he redden slightly? Certainly he shifted uncomfortably on his horse. 'The man was a thief,' he said.

'The men I seek are murderers, Reginald.'

'Even so,' he said, with a touch of irritation, 'perhaps your zeal is clouding your judgement.'

Again I gave a contemptuous snort. 'This from you. Is your fascination with Those Who Came Before strictly speaking in line with Templar policy?'

'Of course.'

'Really? Are you sure you haven't been neglecting your other duties in favour of it? What letter-writing, what journalling, what reading have you been doing lately, Reginald?'

'Plenty,' he said indignantly.

'That *hasn't* been connected with Those Who Came Before,' I added.

For a moment he blustered, sounding like a red-faced fat man given the wrong meat at dinner. 'I'm here now, aren't I?'

'Indeed, Reginald,' I said, just as I saw a tiny plume of smoke coming from the woodland. 'I see smoke in the trees, possibly from a cabin. We should head for there.'

At the same time there was a movement not far away in a crop of fir trees and I saw a rider heading up the furthest hill, away from us.

'Look, Reginald, there. Do you see him?'

I adjusted the focus. The rider had his back to us of course and was a distance away, but one thing I thought I could see was his ears. I was sure he had pointed ears.

'I see one man, Haytham, but where is the other?' said Reginald.

Already pulling on the reins of my steed, I said, 'Still in the cabin, Reginald. Let's go.'

iii

It was perhaps another twenty minutes before we arrived. Twenty minutes during which I pushed my steed to her limit, risking her through trees and over wind-fallen branches, leaving Reginald behind as I raced towards where I'd seen the smoke – to the cabin where I was sure I'd find Digweed.

Alive? Dead? I didn't know. But the storekeeper had said there were two men asking for him, and we'd only accounted for one of them, so I was eager to know about the other one. Had he gone on ahead?

Or was he still in the cabin?

There it was, sitting in the middle of a clearing. A squat wooden building, one horse tethered outside, with a single window at the front and tendrils of smoke puffing from the chimney. The front door was open. Wide open. At the same time as I came bolting into the clearing I heard a scream from inside, and I spurred my steed to the door, drawing my sword. With a great clatter we came on to the boards at the front of the house and I craned forward in my saddle to see the scene inside.

Digweed was tied to a chair, shoulders sagging, head tilted. His face was a mask of blood, but I could see that his lips were moving. He was alive, and standing over him was the second man, holding a bloodstained knife – a knife with a curved, serrated blade – and about to finish the job. About to slit Digweed's throat.

I'd never used my sword as a spear before and, take it from me, it's a far from ideal use for it, but at that exact moment my priority was keeping Digweed alive. I needed to speak to him, and, besides, nobody was going to kill Digweed but me. So I threw it. It was all I had time to do. And though my throw had as little power as it did aim, it hit the knifeman's arm just as the blade arced down, and it was enough – enough to send him staggering back with a howl of pain at the same time as I threw myself off the horse, landed on the boards inside of the cabin, rolled forward and snatched out my short sword at the same time.

And it had been enough to save Digweed.

I landed right by him. Bloodstained rope kept his arms and legs tied to the chair. His clothes were torn and black with blood, his face swollen and bleeding. His lips still moved. His eyes slid lazily over to see me and I wondered what he thought in the brief moment that he took me in. Did he recognize me? Did he feel a bolt of guilt, or a flash of hope?

Then my eyes went to a back window, only to see the knifeman's legs disappearing through it as he squeezed himself out and fell with a thump to the ground outside. To follow through the window meant putting myself in a vulnerable position – I didn't fancy being stuck in the frame while the knifeman had all the time in the world to plunge his blade into me. So instead I ran to the front door and back into the clearing to give chase. Reginald was just arriving. He'd seen the knifeman, had a better view of him than I did, and was already taking aim with his bow.

'Don't kill him,' I roared, just as he fired, and he howled in displeasure as the arrow went wide.

'Damn you, man, I had him,' he shouted. 'He's in the trees now.'

I'd rounded the front of the cabin in time, feet kicking up a carpet of dead and dry pine needles just in time to see the knifeman disappear into the tree line. 'I need him alive, Reginald,' I shouted back at him. 'Digweed's in the cabin. Keep him safe until I return.'

And with that I burst into the trees, leaves and branches whipping my face as I thundered on, short sword in hand. Ahead of me I saw a dark shape in the foliage, crashing through it with as little grace as I was.

Or perhaps *less* grace, because I was gaining on him.

'Were you there?' I shouted at him. 'Were you there the night they killed my father?'

'I didn't have that pleasure, boy,' he called back over his shoulder. 'How I wish I had been. I did my bit, though. I was the fixer.'

Of course. He had a West Country accent. Now, who had been described as having a West Country accent? The man who had blackmailed Digweed. The man who had threatened Violet and shown her an evil-looking knife.

'Stand and face me!' I shouted. 'You're so keen for Kenway blood, let's see if you can't spill mine!'

I was nimbler than he was. Faster, and closer now. I'd heard the wheeze in his voice when he spoke to me, and it was only a matter of time before I caught him. He knew it, and rather than tire himself further he decided to turn and fight, hurdling one final wind-fallen branch, which brought him into a small clearing, spinning about, the curved blade in his hand. The curved, serrated, 'evil-looking' blade. His face was grizzled and terribly pockmarked, as though scarred from some childhood disease. He breathed heavily as he wiped the back of his hand across his mouth. He'd lost his hat in the chase, revealing close-cropped, grey-ing hair, and his coat – dark, just as the storekeeper had described it – was torn, fluttering open to reveal his red army tunic.

'You're a British soldier,' I said.

'That's the uniform I wear,' he sneered, 'but my allegiances lie elsewhere.'

'Indeed, do they? To whom do you swear loyalty, then?' I asked. 'Are you an Assassin?'

He shook his head. 'I'm my own man, boy. Something you can only dream of being.'

'It's a long time since anybody's called me boy,' I said.

'You think you've made a name for yourself, Haytham Kenway. The killer. The Templar blademan. Because you've killed a couple of fat merchants? But to me you're a boy. You're a boy because a man faces his targets, man to man, he doesn't steal up behind them in the dead of night, like a snake.' He paused. 'Like an *Assassin*.'

He began to swap his knife from one hand to the other. The effect was almost hypnotic – or at least that's what I let him believe.

'You think I can't fight?' I said.

'You're yet to prove it.'

'Here's as good a place as any.'

He spat and beckoned me forward with one hand, rolling the blade in the other. 'Come on,' he goaded me. 'Come be a warrior for the first time. Come see what it feels like. Come on, boy. Be a man.'

It was supposed to anger me, but instead it made me focus. I needed him alive. I needed him to talk.

I leapt over the branch and into the clearing, swinging a little wildly to push him back but recovering my stance quickly, before he could press forward with a counter-attack of his own. For some moments we circled one another, each waiting for the other to launch his next attack. I broke the stalemate by lunging forward, slashing, then instantly retreating to my guard.

For a second he thought I'd missed. Then he felt the blood begin to trickle down his cheek and touched a hand to his face, his eyes widening in surprise. First blood to me.

'You've underestimated me,' I said.

His smile was a little more strained this time. 'There won't be a second time.'

'There will be,' I replied, and came forward again, feinting towards the left then going right when his body was already committed to the wrong line of defence.

A gash opened up in his free arm. Blood stained his tattered sleeve and began dripping to the forest floor, bright red on brown and green needles.

'I'm better than you know,' I said. 'All you have to look forward to is death – unless you talk. Unless you tell me everything you know. Who are you working for?'

I danced forward and slashed as his knife flailed wildly. His other cheek opened. There were now two scarlet ribbons on the brown leather of his face.

'Why was my father killed?'

I came forward again and this time sliced the back of his knife hand. If I'd been hoping he'd drop the knife, then I was disappointed. If I'd been hoping to give him a demonstration of my skills, then that's exactly what I'd done, and it showed on his face. His now bloody face. He wasn't grinning any more.

But he still had fight in him, and when he came forward it was fast and smooth and he swapped his knife from one hand to the other to try to misdirect me, and almost made contact. Almost. He might even have done it – if he hadn't already showed me that particular trick; if he hadn't been slowed down by the injuries I'd inflicted on him.

As it was, I ducked easily beneath his blade and struck upwards, burying my own in his flank. Immediately I was cursing, though. I'd hit him too hard and in the kidney. He was dead. The internal bleeding would kill him in around thirty minutes; but he could pass out straight away. Whether he knew it himself or not I don't know, for he was coming at me again, his teeth bared. They were coated with blood now, I noticed, and I swung easily away, took hold of his arm, twisted into his body and broke it at the elbow.

The sound he made wasn't a scream so much as an anguished inhalation, and as I crunched the bones in his arm, more for effect than for any useful purpose, his knife dropped to the forest floor with a soft thump and he followed it, sinking to his knees.

I let go of his arm, which dropped limply, a bag of broken bones and skin. Looking down, I could see the blood had already drained from his face, and around his midriff was a spreading, black stain. His coat pooled around him on the ground. Feebly, he felt for his loose and limp arm with his good hand, and when he looked up at me there was something almost plaintive in his eyes, something pathetic.

'Why did you kill him?' I asked evenly.

Like water escaping from a leaking flask he crumpled, until he was lying on his side. All that concerned him now was dying.

'Tell me,' I pressed, and bent close to where he now lay, with pine needles clinging to the blood on his face. He was breathing his last breaths into the mulch of the forest floor.

'Your father . . .' he started, then coughed a small gobbet of blood before starting again. 'Your father was not a Templar.'

'I know,' I snapped. 'Was he killed for that?' I felt

my brow furrow. 'Was he killed because he refused to join the Order?'

'He was an . . . an Assassin.'

'And the Templars killed him? They killed him for that?'

'No. He was killed for what he had.'

'What?' I leaned forward, desperate to catch his words. 'What did he have?'

There was no reply.

'Who?' I said, almost shouting. 'Who killed him?'

But he was out. Mouth open, his eyes fluttered then closed, and however much I slapped him he refused to regain consciousness.

An Assassin. Father was an Assassin. I rolled the knifeman over, closed his staring eyes and began to empty his pockets on to the ground. Out came the usual collection of tins, as well as a few tattered bits of paper, one of which I unfurled to find a set of enlistment papers. They were for a regiment, the Coldstream Guards to be precise, one and a half guineas for joining, then a shilling a day. The paymaster's name was on the enlistment papers. It was Lieutenant-Colonel Edward Braddock.

And Braddock was with his army in the Dutch Republic, taking arms against the French. I thought of the pointy-eared man I'd seen riding out earlier. All of a sudden I knew where he was heading.

I turned and crashed back through the forest to the cabin, making it back in moments. Outside were the three horses, grazing patiently in bright sunshine; inside, it was dark and cooler, and Reginald stood over Digweed, whose head lolled as he sat, still tied to the chair, and, I knew, from the second I clapped eyes on him . . .

'He's dead,' I said simply, and looked at Reginald.

'I tried to save him, Haytham, but the poor soul was too far gone.'

'How?' I said sharply.

'Of his wounds,' snapped Reginald. 'Look at him, man.'

Digweed's face was a mask of drying blood. His clothes were caked with it. The knifeman had made him suffer, that much was certain.

'He was alive when I left.'

'And he was alive when I arrived, damn it,' seethed Reginald.

'At least tell me you got something from him.'

His eyes dropped. 'He said he was sorry before he died.'

With a frustrated swish of my sword I slammed a beaker into the fireplace.

'That was all? Nothing about the night of the attack? No reason? No names?'

'Damn your eyes, Haytham. Damn your eyes, do you think I killed him? Do you think I came all this way, neglected my other duties, just to see Digweed dead? I wanted to find him as much as you did. I wanted him *alive* as much as you did.'

It was as though I could feel my entire skull harden. 'I doubt that very much,' I spat.

'Well, what happened to the other one?' asked Reginald back.

'He died.'

Reginald wore an ironic look. 'Oh, I see. And whose fault was that, exactly?'

I ignored him. 'The killer, he is known to Braddock.'

Reginald reared back. 'Really?'

Back at the clearing I'd stuffed the papers into my coat, and I brought them out now in a handful, like the head of a cauliflower. 'Here – his enlistment papers. He's in the Coldstream Guards, under Braddock's command.'

'Hardly the same thing, Haytham. Edward has a force fifteen hundred-strong, many of them enlisted in the country. I'm sure every single man has an unsavoury past and I'm sure Edward knows very little about it.'

'Even so, a coincidence, don't you think? The storekeeper said they both wore the uniform of the British Army, and my guess is the rider we saw is on his way to them now. He has – what? – an hour's head start?

I'll not be far behind. Braddock's in the Dutch Republic, is he not? That's where he'll be heading, back to his general.'

'Now, careful, Haytham,' said Reginald. Steel crept into his eyes and into his voice. 'Edward is a friend of mine.'

'I have never liked him,' I said, with a touch of childish impudence.

'Oh, pish!' exploded Reginald. 'An opinion formed by you as a boy because Edward didn't show you the deference you were accustomed to – because, I might add, he was doing his utmost to bring your father's killers to justice. Let me tell you, Haytham, Edward serves the Order, is a good and faithful servant and always has been.'

I turned to him, and it was on the tip of my tongue to say, 'But wasn't Father an Assassin?' when I stopped myself. Some . . . feeling, or instinct – difficult to say what it was – made me decide to keep that information to myself.

Reginald saw me do it – saw the words pile up behind my teeth and maybe even saw the lie in my eyes.

'The killer,' he pressed, 'did he say anything else at all? Were you able to drag any more information out of him before he died?'

'Only as much as you could get from Digweed,' I replied. There was a small stove at one end of the cabin and by it a chopping block, where I found part of a loaf, which I stuffed into my pocket.

'What are you doing?' said Reginald.

'Getting what provisions I can for my ride, Reginald.'

There was a bowl of apples, too. I'd need those for my horse.

'A stale loaf. Some apples? It isn't enough, Haytham. At least go back to the town for supplies.'

'No time, Reginald,' I said. 'And, anyway, the chase will be short. He only has a short head start and he doesn't know he's being pursued. With any luck I can catch him before I have need of supplies.'

'We can collect food on the way. I can help you.'

But I stopped him. I was going alone, I said, and before he could argue I'd mounted my steed and taken her in the direction I'd seen the pointy-eared man go in, my hopes high I could catch him shortly.

They were dashed. I rode hard, but in the end the dark drew in; it had become too dangerous to continue and I risked injuring my horse. In any case, she was exhausted, so reluctantly I decided to stop and let her rest for a few hours.

And as I sit here writing, I wonder why, after all the years of Reginald being like a father to me, a mentor, a tutor and guide – why did I decide to ride out alone? And why did I keep from him what I'd discovered about Father?

Have I changed? Has he changed? Or is it that the bond we once shared has changed?

The temperature has dropped. My steed – and it seems only right that I should give her a name and so, in honour of the way she's already starting to nuzzle me when in need of an apple, I've called her Scratch – lies nearby, her eyes closed, and seems content, and I write in my journal.

I think about what Reginald and I talked of. I wonder if he's right to question the man I have become.

15 July 1747

I rose early in the morning, as soon as it was light, raked over the dying coals of my fire and mounted Scratch.

The chase continued. As I rode I mulled over the possibilities. Why had Pointy Ears and the knifeman gone their separate ways? Were they both intending to journey to the Dutch Republic and join Braddock? Would Pointy Ears be expecting his confederate to catch him up?

I had no way of knowing. I could only hope that, whatever their plans, the man ahead of me had no idea I was in pursuit.

But if he didn't – and how could he? – then why wasn't I catching him?

And I rode fast but steadily, aware that coming upon him too quickly would be just as disastrous as not catching him at all.

After about three quarters of an hour I came upon a spot where he had rested. If I'd pushed Scratch for longer, would I have disturbed him, taken him by surprise? I knelt to feel the dying warmth of his fire. To my left, Scratch muzzled something on the ground, a bit of discarded sausage, and my stomach rumbled. Reginald had been right. My prey was much better equipped for the journey than I was, with my half a loaf of bread and apples. I cursed myself for not going through the saddlebags of his companion.

'Come on Scratch,' I said. 'Come on, girl.'

For the rest of the day I rode, and the only time I even slowed down was when I retrieved the spyglass from my pocket and scanned the horizon, looking for signs of my quarry. He remained ahead of me. Frustratingly ahead of me. All day. Until, as light began to fade I started becoming concerned I had lost him altogether. I could only hope I was right about his destination.

In the end I had no choice but to rest again for the day, make camp, build a fire, allow Scratch to rest, and pray that I hadn't lost the trail.

And as I sit here I wonder, Why haven't I managed to catch him?

16 July 1747

i

When I woke up this morning it was with a flash of inspiration. Of course. Pointy Ears was a member of Braddock's army and Braddock's army had joined with forces commanded by the Prince of Orange in the Dutch Republic, which was where Pointy Ears should have been. The reason he was hurrying was because . . .

Because he had absconded and was rushing to get back, presumably before his absence was discovered.

Which meant that his presence in the Black Forest wasn't officially sanctioned. Which meant that Braddock, as his lieutenant-colonel, didn't know about it. Or *probably* didn't know about it.

Sorry, Scratch. I rode her hard again – it would be her third successive day – and noticed the tiredness in her, the fatigue that slowed her down. Even so, it was only around half an hour before we came upon the remains of Pointy Ears' camp and, this time, instead of stopping to test the embers, I urged Scratch on and only let her rest at the next hilltop, where we stopped as we pulled out the spyglass and scanned the area ahead of us, square by square, inch by inch – until I saw him. There he was, a tiny speck riding up the hill opposite, swallowed up by a clump of trees as I watched.

Where were we? I didn't know whether or not we had passed over the border into the Dutch Republic. I hadn't seen another soul for two days, had heard nothing but the sound of Scratch and my own breathing.

That was soon to change. I spurred Scratch and some twenty minutes later was entering the same band of trees I'd seen my quarry disappear into. The first thing I saw was an abandoned cart. Nearby, with flies crawling over sightless eyes, was the body of a horse, the sight of which made Scratch rear slightly, startled. Like me, she had been used to the solitude: just us, the trees, the birds. Here suddenly was the ugly reminder that in Europe one is never far from conflict, never far from war.

We rode on more slowly now, being careful among the trees and whatever other obstacles we might find. Moving onwards, more and more of the foliage was blackened, broken or trampled down. There'd been some action here, that much was certain: I began to see bodies of men, splayed limbs and staring, dead eyes, dark blood and mud rendering the corpses anonymous apart from flashes of uniform: the white of the French army, the blue of the Dutch. I saw broken muskets, snapped bayonets and swords, anything of use having already been salvaged. When I emerged from the tree line we were in a field, the field of battle, where there were even more bodies. Evidently it had been only a small skirmish by the standards of war but, even so, it felt as though death was everywhere.

How long ago it had been I couldn't say with certainty: enough time for scavengers to strip the field of battle but not enough for the bodies to be removed; within the last day, I would have thought, judging by the state of the corpses and the blanket of smoke that still hung over the pasture – a shroud of it, like morning fog but with the heavy yet sharp scent of gunpowder smoke.

Here the mud was thicker, churned up by hooves and feet, and as Scratch began to struggle, I reined her to the side, trying to take us around the perimeter of the field. Then just as she stumbled in the mud and almost pitched me forward over her neck I caught sight of Pointy Ears ahead of us. He was the length of the field away, perhaps half a mile or so, a hazy, almost indistinct figure also struggling in the claggy terrain. His horse must have been as exhausted as mine, because he'd dismounted and was trying to pull it by the reins, his curses carrying faintly across the field.

I pulled out my spyglass to get a better look at him. The last time I'd seen him close up was twelve years ago and he'd been wearing a mask, and I found myself wondering – hoping, even – that my first proper look at him might contain some kind of revelation. Would I recognize him?

No. He was just a man, weathered and grizzled, like his partner had been, filthy and exhausted from his ride. Looking at him now there was no sense of suddenly knowing. Nothing fell into place. He was just a man, a British soldier, same as the one I had killed in the Black Forest.

I saw him crane his neck as he stared through the haze at me. From his coat he produced his own spyglass, and for a moment the two of us studied one another through our telescopes, then I watched as he ran to the muzzle of his horse and with renewed vigour began yanking at the reins, at the same time throwing glances back across the field at me.

He recognized me. Good. Scratch had regained her feet and I pulled her to where the ground was a little harder. At last we were able to make some headway. In front of me, Pointy Ears was becoming more distinct and I could make out the effort on his face as he pulled out his own horse, then saw the realization dawn on him that he was stuck, and I was gaining on him and would be upon him in a matter of a few short moments.

And then he did the only thing he could do. He dropped the reins and started to run. At the same time the verge around us gave way sharply, and once again Scratch was finding it difficult to keep her feet. With a quick and whispered 'thank you' I jumped from her to give chase on foot.

The efforts of the last few days caught up with me in a rush that threatened to engulf me. The mud sucked at my boots, making every step not like running but like wading, and the breath was jagged in my lungs, as though I were inhaling grit. Every muscle screamed in protest and pain at me, begging me not to go on. I could only hope that my friend ahead was having it just as hard, even harder perhaps, because the one thing that spurred me on, the one thing that kept my legs pumping and my chest pulling ragged breaths from the air was the knowledge that I was closing the gap.

He glanced behind and I was close enough to see his eyes widen in fear. He had no mask now. Nothing to hide behind. Despite the pain and exhaustion I grinned at him, feeling dry, parched lips pulling back over my teeth.

He pressed on, grunting with the effort. It had begun to rain, a drizzle that gave the day an extra layer of haze, as though we were stuck inside a landscape coloured in charcoal.

Again he risked another look behind and saw that I was even closer now; this time he stopped and drew his sword, held it in two hands with his shoulders slumped, breathing heavily. He looked exhausted. He looked like a man who'd spent day after day riding hard with little sleep. He looked like a man waiting to be beaten.

But I was wrong; he was luring me forward and, like a fool, I fell for it, and in the next instant was stumbling forward, literally falling as the ground gave way and I waded straight into a vast pool of thick, oozing mud that stopped me in my tracks.

'Oh, God,' I said.

My feet disappeared, then my ankles, and before I knew it I was in up to my knees, desperately yanking at my legs, trying to pull them free, while at the same time bracing myself with one hand on the firmer ground around me, trying to keep my sword raised with the other.

My eyes went to Pointy Ears, and it was his turn to grin now as he came forward and brought his sword down in a chopping, two-handed blow that had plenty of force but was clumsy. With a grunt of effort and a ring of steel I met it and parried, sending him back a couple of steps. Then, as he was off balance, I pulled one of my feet clear of the mud, and my boot, saw my white stocking, filthy as it was, bright compared to the dirt around it.

Seeing his advantage being squandered, Pointy Ears pressed forward again, this time stabbing forward with his sword, and I defended once and then twice. For a second there was only the sound of clashing steel, of grunts and the rain, harder now, slapping into the mud, me silently thanking God his reserves of cunning were exhausted.

Or were they? At last he realized I would be beaten more easily if he moved to the rear of me, but I saw what was on his mind and lashed out with my sword, catching him at the knee just above his boot and sending him crashing back, howling in agony. With a cry of pain and indignity he got to his feet, driven on perhaps by outrage that his victory wasn't being given to him more easily, and kicked out with his good foot.

I caught it with my other hand and twisted it as hard as I could, hard enough to send him spinning and sprawling face first to the mud.

He tried to roll away, but was too slow, or too dazed, and I stabbed downwards with my sword, driving it through the back of his thigh, straight into the ground and spearing him there. At the same time I used the handle as a grip and with a wrench pulled myself from the mud, leaving my second boot behind.

He screamed and twisted, but was held in place by my sword through his leg. My weight on him as I used the sword as leverage to drag myself from the ooze must have been unbearable, and he shrieked in pain and his eyes rolled back in their sockets. Even so, he slashed wildly with his sword and I was unarmed so that, as I flopped on to him, like a badly landed fish, the blade caught me on the side of the neck, opening a cut and letting out blood that felt warm on my skin.

My hands went to his, and suddenly we were grappling for possession of the sword. Grunting and cursing we fought, when from behind I heard something – something that was surely the sound of approaching feet. Then voices. Somebody speaking in Dutch. I cursed.

'No,' said a voice, and I realized it was me.

He must have heard it, too.

'You're too late, Kenway,' he snarled.

The tramping of the feet from behind me. The rain. My own cries of, 'No, no, *no*,' as a voice said, in English, 'You there. Stop at once.'

And I twisted away from Pointy Ears, smacking the wet mud in frustration as I pulled myself upright, ignoring the sound of his harsh and jagged laugh as I rose to meet the troops who appeared from within the fog and rain, trying to bring myself to full height as I said, 'My name is Haytham Kenway, and I am an associate of Lieutenant-Colonel Edward Braddock. I demand this man be given into my custody.'

The next laugh I heard, I wasn't sure if it came from Pointy Ears, who lay still pinned to the ground, or perhaps from one of the small band of troops who had materialized before me, like wraiths delivered from the field. Of the commander I saw a moustache, a dirty, wet, double-breasted jacket trimmed with sodden braid that had once been the colour gold. I saw him raising something – something that seemed to flash across my eye line – and realized he was striking me with the hilt of the sword an instant before he made contact, and I lost consciousness.

ii

They don't put unconscious men to death. That would not be noble. Not even in an army commanded by Lieutenant-Colonel Edward Braddock.

And so the next thing I felt was cold water slapping into my face – or was it an open palm on my face? Either way, I was being rudely awakened, and as my senses returned I spent a moment wondering who I was, where I was . . .

And why I had a noose around my neck.

And why my arms were tied behind my back.

I was at one end of a platform. To my left were four men, also, like me, with their necks in nooses. As I watched, the man on the far left jerked and juddered, his feet kicking at empty air.

A gasp went up in front of me and I realized that we had an audience. We were no longer in the battlefield but in some smaller pasture where men had assembled. They wore the colours of the British Army and the bearskin hats of the Coldstream Guards, and their faces were ashen. They were here under sufferance, it was clear, forced to watch as the poor unfortunate at the end of the line kicked his last, his mouth open, and the tip of his tongue, bleeding from having been bitten, protruding, his jaw working in to try and gulp air.

He continued to twitch and kick, his body shaking the scaffold, which ran the length of the platform above our heads. I looked up and saw my own noose tied to it, cast my eyes downwards to the wooden stool on which I stood, and saw my feet, my stockinged feet.

There was a hush. Just the sound of the hanged man dying, the creak of the rope and the complaint of the scaffold.

'That's what happens when you're a thief,' screeched the executioner, pointing at him then striding down the platform towards the second man, calling out to the stock-still crowd, 'You meet your maker at the end of a rope, orders of Lieutenant-Colonel Braddock.'

'I know Braddock,' I shouted suddenly 'Where is he? Bring him here.'

'Shut your mouth, you!' bawled the executioner, his finger pointed, while at the same time his assistant, the man who'd thrown water in my face, came from my right and slapped me again, only this time not to bring me to my senses but to silence me.

I snarled and struggled with the rope tying my hands, but not too vigorously, not enough so that I would overbalance and fall from the stool on which I was so perilously perched.

'My name is Haytham Kenway,' I called, the rope digging into my neck.

'I said, "Shut your mouth!"' the executioner roared a second time, and again his assistant struck me, hard enough so that he almost toppled me from the stool. For the first time I caught sight of the soldier strung up to my immediate left and realized who it was. It was Pointy Ears. He had a bandage that was black with blood around his thigh. He regarded me with cloudy, hooded eyes, a slow, sloppy smile on his face.

By now the executioner had reached the second man in the line.

'This man is a deserter,' he screeched. 'He left his comrades to die. Men like you. He left *you* to die. Tell me, what should his punishment be?'

Without much enthusiasm, the men called back, 'Hang him.'

'If you say so,' smirked the executioner, and he stepped back, planted his foot in the small of the condemned man's back and pushed, savouring the revolted reaction of the watching men.

I shook the pain of the assistant's blow from my head and continued to struggle just as the executioner reached the next man, asking the crowd the same question, receiving the same muted, dutiful reply then pushing the poor wretch to his death. The platform quaked and shook as the three men jerked on the end of the ropes. Above my head the scaffold creaked and groaned, and glancing up I saw joints briefly part before coming back together.

Next the executioner reached Pointy Ears.

'This man – this man enjoyed a small *sojourn* in the Black Forest and thought he could sneak back undetected, but he is wrong. Tell me, how should he be punished?'

'Hang him,' mumbled the crowd unenthusiastically.

'Do you think he should die?' cried the executioner.

'Yes,' replied the crowd. But I saw some of them surreptitiously shaking their heads no, and there were others, drinking from leather flasks, who looked happier about the whole affair, the way you might if you were being bribed with ale. Indeed, did that account for Pointy Ears' apparent stupor? He was still smiling, even when the executioner moved behind him and planted his foot in the small of his back.

'It's time to hang a deserter!' he shouted, and shoved at the same time as I cried, '*No!*' and thrashed at my bonds, desperately trying to break free. 'No, he must be kept alive! Where is Braddock? Where is Lieutenant-Colonel Edward Braddock?'

The executioner's assistant appeared before my eyes, grinning through a scratchy beard, with hardly a tooth in his mouth, 'Didn't you hear the man? He said

"Shut your mouth."' And he pulled back his fist to punch me.

He didn't get the chance. My legs shot out, knocked the stool away and in the next instant were locked around the assistant's neck, crossed at the ankle – and tightening.

He yelled. I squeezed harder. His yell became a strangulated choke and his face began to flush as his hands went to my calves, trying to prise them apart. I wrenched from side to side, shaking him like a dog with prey in its jaws, almost taking him off his feet, straining my thigh muscles at the same time as I tried to keep the weight off the noose at my neck. Still, at my side, Pointy Ears thrashed on the end of his rope. His tongue poked from between his lips and his milky eyes bulged, as if about to burst from his skull.

The executioner had moved to the other end of the platform, where he was pulling on the legs of the hanged men to make sure they were dead, but the commotion at the other end caught his attention and he looked up to see his assistant trapped in the vice grip of my legs then came dashing up the platform towards us, cursing at the same time as he reached to draw his sword.

With a shout of effort, I twisted my body and wrenched my legs, pulling the assistant with me and by some miracle timing it just right so that his body slammed into the executioner as he arrived. With a shout the executioner tumbled messily from the platform.

In front of us the men were standing, open-mouthed with shock, none moving to get involved.

I squeezed my legs even more tightly together and was rewarded with a cracking, crunching sound that came from the assistant's neck. Blood began pouring from his nose. His grip on my arms began to slacken. Again I twisted. Again I shouted as my muscles protested and I wrenched him, this time to the other side, where I slammed him into the scaffold.

The shaking, creaking, coming-apart scaffold.

It creaked and complained some more. With a final effort – I had no more strength left, and if this didn't work then here was where I died – I rammed the man into the scaffold again and, this time, at last, it gave. At the same time as I began to feel myself black out, as though a dark veil were being brought across my mind, I felt the pressure at my neck suddenly relax as the support crashed to the ground in front of the platform, the crossbar toppled, then the platform itself gave way with the sudden weight of men and wood, falling in on itself with a splintering and crashing of disintegrating wood.

My last thought before I lost consciousness was, *Please let him be alive*, and my first words on regaining consciousness inside the tent where I now lie were, 'Is he alive?'

'Is who alive?' asked the doctor, who had a distinguished-looking moustache and an accent that suggested he was higher born than most.

'The pointy-eared man,' I said, and tried to raise myself upright, only to find his hand on my chest guiding me back down to a lying position.

'I'm afraid I haven't the foggiest idea what you're talking about,' he said, not unkindly. 'I hear that you are acquainted with the lieutenant-colonel. Perhaps he will be able to explain everything to you when he arrives in the morning.'

Thus, I now sit here, writing up the events of the day, and awaiting my audience with Braddock . . .

17 July 1747

He looked like a larger, smarter version of his men, with all of the bearing that his rank implied. His shining black boots were up to the knee. He wore a frock coat with white trim over a dark, buttoned-up tunic, a white scarf at his neck, and on a thick brown leather belt at his waist hung his sword.

His hair was pulled back and tied with a black ribbon. He tossed his hat to a small table at the side of the bed where I lay, put his hands to his hips and regarded me with that deep, colourless gaze I knew well.

'Kenway,' he said simply, 'Reginald did not send word that you were due to be joining me here.'

'It was a spur-of-the-moment decision, Edward,' I said, suddenly feeling young in his presence, intimidated almost.

'I see,' he said. 'You thought you'd just drop in, did you?'

'How long have I been here?' I asked. 'How many days have passed?'

'Three,' replied Braddock. 'Dr Tennant was concerned you might develop a fever. According to him, a feebler man may not have been able to fight it off.

You're lucky to be alive, Kenway. Not every man gets to escape both the gallows *and* a fever. Fortunate for you, too, that I was informed about one of the men to be hanged calling for me personally; otherwise my men might well have finished the job. You see how we punish wrongdoers.'

I put my hand to my neck, which was bandaged from the fight with Pointy Ears and still painful from the rope burn. 'Yes, Edward, I have had first-hand experience of how you treat your men.'

He sighed, waved away Dr Tennant, who retired, closing the flaps of the tent behind him, then sat heavily, putting one boot to the bed as though to stake his claim on it. 'Not my men, Kenway. *Criminals*. You were delivered to us by the Dutch in the company of a deserter, a man who had gone absent with a companion. Naturally, you were assumed to be the companion.'

'And what of him, Edward? What of the man I was with?'

'This is the man you've been asking about, is it? The one Dr Tennant tells me you're especially interested in, a – what did he say now? –"a pointy-eared man"?' He couldn't keep the sneer out of his voice as he said it.

'That man, Edward – he was there the night of the attack on my home. He's one of the men we have been seeking these last twelve years.' I looked at him hard. 'And I find him enlisted in *your* army.'

'Indeed – in my army. And what of it?'

'A coincidence, don't you think?'

Braddock always wore a scowl, but now it deepened. 'Why don't you forget the insinuations, boy, and tell me what's really on your mind. Where *is* Reginald, by the way?'

'I left him in the Black Forest. No doubt he's halfway home by now.'

'To continue his research into myths and folk tales?' said Braddock with a contemptuous flick of his eyes. Him doing that made me feel strangely loyal to Reginald and his investigations, despite my own misgivings.

'Reginald believes that if we were able to unlock the secrets of the storehouse, the Order would be the most powerful it has been since the Holy Wars, perhaps ever. We would be poised to rule completely.'

He gave a slightly tired, disgusted look. 'If you really believe that then you're as foolish and idealistic as he is. We don't need magic and tricks to persuade people to our cause, we need steel.'

'Why not use both?' I reasoned.

He leaned forward. 'Because one of them is a rank waste of time, that's why.'

I met his gaze. 'That's as maybe. However I don't think the best way to win men's hearts and minds is to execute them, do you?'

'Again. Scum.'

'And has he been put to death?'

'Your friend with – sorry, what was it? – "pointy ears"?'

'Your ridicule means nothing to me, Edward. Your ridicule means as much to me as your respect, which is nothing. You may think you tolerate me only because of Reginald – well, I can assure you the feeling is entirely mutual. Now, tell me, the pointy-eared man, is he dead?'

'He died on the scaffold, Kenway. He died the death he deserved.'

I closed my eyes and for a second lay there aware of nothing but my own ... what? Some evil, boiling broth of grief, anger and frustration; of mistrust and doubt. Aware, also, of Braddock's foot on my bed and wishing I could lash out with a sword and purge him from my life for ever.

That was his way, though, wasn't it? It wasn't my way.

'So he was there that night, was he?' asked Braddock, and did he have a slightly mocking tone in his voice? 'He was one of those responsible for killing your father, and all of this time he's been among us, and we never knew. A bitter irony, wouldn't you say, Haytham?'

'Indeed. An irony or a coincidence.'

'Be careful, boy, there's no Reginald here to talk you out of trouble now, you know.'

'What was his name?'

'Like hundreds of men in my army his name was Tom Smith – Tom Smith of the country; much more about them we don't know. On the run, probably from the magistrates, or perhaps having killed his landlord's son in a duel, or deflowered a landowner's daughter, or perhaps romped with his wife. Who's to say? We don't ask questions. If you were to ask does it surprise me that one of the men we hunted was here among my army all of the time, then my answer would be no.'

'Did he have associates in the army? Somebody that I could talk to?'

Slowly, Braddock took his foot from my cot. 'As a fellow Knight you are free to enjoy my hospitality here and you may of course conduct your own enquiries. I hope that in return I can also call upon your assistance in our endeavours.'

'And what may they be?' I asked.

'The French have laid siege to the fortress of Bergen op Zoom. Inside are our allies: the Dutch, Austrians, Hanoverian and Hessians, and of course the British. The French have already opened the trenches and are digging a second set of parallel trenches. They will soon begin their bombardment of the fortress. They will be trying to take it before the rains. They think it will give them a gateway to the Netherlands, and the Allies feel that the fortress must be held at all costs. We need every man we can get. You see now why we do not tolerate deserters. Do you have a heart for the battle, Kenway, or are you so focused on revenge that you cannot help us any more?'

PART III

1753, Six Years Later

7 June 1753

i

'I have a job for you,' said Reginald.

I nodded, expecting as much. It had been a long time since I'd last seen him and I'd had the feeling that his request to meet wasn't just an excuse to catch up on tittle-tattle, even if the venue was White's, where we sat supping an ale each, an attentive and – it hadn't escaped my notice – buxom waitress keen to bring us more.

To the left of us a table of gentlemen – the infamous 'gamesters of White's' – were playing a rowdy game of dice, but otherwise the house was empty.

I hadn't seen him since that day in the Black Forest, six years ago, and a lot had happened since. Joining Braddock in the Dutch Republic, I'd served with the Coldstreams at the Siege of Bergen op Zoom, then until the Treaty of Aix-la-Chapelle the following year, which marked the end of that war. After that I'd remained with them on several peace-keeping campaigns, which had kept me away from Reginald, whose correspondence arrived either from London or from the chateau in the Landes Forest. Aware that my own letters could be read before they were sent, I'd kept my correspondence vague while privately looking forward to the moment I could at last sit down with Reginald and talk over my fears.

But, returning to London, and once again taking up residence at Queen Anne's Square, I found he was not available. That was what I was told: he had been sequestered with his books – he and John Harrison, another Knight of the Order, and one who seemingly was as obsessed with temples, ancient storehouses and ghostly beings from the past as he was.

'Do you remember we came here for my eighth birthday?' I said, wanting, somehow, to put off the moment when I learnt the identity of the person I would have to kill. 'Do you remember what happened outside, the hot-headed suitor prepared to dispense summary justice on the street?'

He nodded. 'People change, Haytham.'

'Indeed – you have. You've been mainly preoccupied with your investigations into the first civilization,' I said.

'I'm so close now, Haytham,' he said, as if the thought of it shrugged off a weary shroud he'd been wearing.

'Were you ever able to decode Vedomir's journal?'

He frowned. 'No, worse luck, and not for want of

trying, I can tell you. Or should I say "not yet", because there is a code-breaker, an Italian Assassin affiliate – a woman, would you believe? We have her at the French chateau, deep within the forest, but she says she needs her son to help her decode the book, and her son has been missing these past few years. Personally, I doubt what she says and think she could very well decode the journal herself if she chose. I think she's using us to help reunite her with her son. But she has agreed to work on the journal if we locate him and, finally, we have.'

'Where?'

'Where you will soon be going to recover him: Corsica.'

So I'd been wrong. Not an assassination, a babysitting job.

'What?' he said, at the look on my face. 'You think it below you? Quite the opposite, Haytham. This is the most important task I have ever given you.'

'No, Reginald,' I sighed, 'it's not; it simply appears that way in your thinking.'

'Oh? What are you saying?'

'That perhaps your interest in this has meant you have neglected affairs elsewhere. Perhaps you have let certain other matters become out of control . . .'

Perplexed, he said, 'What "matters"?'

'Edward Braddock.'

He looked surprised. 'I see. Well, is there something you want to tell me about him? Something you've been keeping from me?'

I indicated for more ales and our waitress brought them over, set them down with a smile then walked away with her hips swaying.

'What has Braddock told you of his movements in recent years?' I asked Reginald.

'I have heard very little from him, seen him even less,' he replied. 'In the last six years we've met just once, as far as I can recall and his correspondences have become increasingly sporadic. He disapproves of my interest in Those Who Came Before and, unlike you, has not kept his objections to himself. It appears we differ greatly on how best to spread the Templar message. As a result, no, I know very little of him; in fact, if I wanted to know about Edward, I dare say I'd ask someone who has been with him during his campaigns –' He gave a sardonic look. 'Where might I find such a person, do you think?'

'You'd be a fool to ask me,' I chortled. 'You know full well that, where Braddock is concerned, I'm not an especially impartial observer. I began by disliking the man and now like him even less, but in the absence of any more objective observations, here's mine: he has become a tyrant.'

'How so?'

'Cruelty, mainly. To the men suffering under him,

but also to innocents. I've seen it with my own eyes, for the first time, in the Dutch Republic.'

'How Edward treats his men is his business,' said Reginald with a shrug. 'Men respond to discipline, Haytham, you know that.'

I shook my head. 'There was one particular incident, Reginald, on the last day of the siege.'

Reginald settled back to listen: 'Go on . . .'; as I continued.

'We were retreating. Dutch soldiers were shaking their fists at us, cursing King George for not sending more of his men to help relieve the fortress. Why more men had not arrived I don't know. Would they have even made any difference? Again, I don't know. I'm not sure any of us who were stationed within those pentagonal walls knew how to contend with a French onslaught that was as committed as it was brutal, and as ruthless as it was sustained.

'Braddock had been right: the French had dug their parallel trench lines and begun their bombardment of the city, pressing close to the fortress walls, and they were on them by September, when they dug mines beneath the fortifications and destroyed them.

'We made attacks outside the walls to try to break the siege, all to no avail until, on 18 September, the French broke through – at four in the morning, if memory serves. They caught the Allied forces quite literally napping, and we were overrun before we knew it. The French were slaughtering the entire garrison. We know, of course, that eventually they broke free of their command and inflicted even worse damage on the poor inhabitants of that town, but the carnage had already begun. Edward had secured a skiff at the port, and had long since decided that, were a day to come when the French broke through, he would use it to evacuate his men. That day had arrived.

'A band of us made our way to the port, where we began to oversee the loading of men and supplies on to the skiff. We kept a small force at the port walls to keep any marauding French troops back, while Edward, I and others stood by the gangplank, over-seeing the loading of men and supplies on to the skiff. We took some fourteen hundred men to the fortress at Bergen op Zoom, but the months of fighting had depleted numbers by about half. There was room on the skiff. Not lots of it – it wasn't as though we could have taken a great many passengers; certainly not the numbers who needed to evacuate from the fortress – but there was space.' I looked hard at Reginald. 'We could have taken them, is what I'm saying.'

'Could have taken whom, Haytham?'

I took a long pull on my ale. 'There was a family who approached us on the port. Included in their number was an old man who could barely walk, as well as children. From among them came a young man, who approached us and asked me if we had room on the boat. I nodded yes – I saw no reason why not – and indicated to Braddock, but instead of waving them aboard as I expected, he held up a hand and ordered them off the port, beckoning his men to board the boat more quickly. The young man was as surprised as I was, and I opened my mouth to protest, but he got there before me; his face darkened and he said something to Braddock that I didn't catch, but was obviously an insult of some kind.

'Braddock told me later that the insult was "craven". Hardly the most insulting affront, certainly not worth what happened next, which was that Braddock drew his sword and plunged it into the young man where he stood.

'Braddock kept a small party of the men nearby at most times. His two regular companions were the executioner, Slater, and his assistant – his new assistant, I should say. I killed the old one. These men, you might almost have called them bodyguards. Certainly they were much closer to him than I was. Whether or not they had his ear I couldn't say, but they were fiercely loyal and protective and were rushing forward even as the young man's body fell. They set about the family, Reginald, Braddock and these two of his men, and cut them down, every single one of them: the two men, an older woman, a younger woman, and of course the children, one of them an infant, one of them a babe in arms . . .' I felt my jaw clench. 'It was a bloodbath,

Reginald, the worst atrocity of war I have seen – and I'm afraid I've seen a great many.'

He nodded gravely. 'I see. Naturally, this hardened your heart against Edward.'

I scoffed. 'Of course – of course it has. We are all men of war, Reginald, but we are not barbarians.'

'I see, I see.'

'Do you? Do you see at last? That Braddock is out of control?'

'Steady on, Haytham. "Out of control"? The red mist descending is one thing. "Out of control" is quite another.'

'He treats his men like slaves, Reginald.'

He shrugged. 'So? They're British soldiers – they expect to be treated like slaves.'

'I think he is moving away from us. These men he has serving him, they're not Templars, they're free agents.'

Reginald nodded. 'The two men in the Black Forest. Were these men part of Braddock's inner circle?'

I looked at him. I watched him very carefully as I lied: 'I don't know.'

There was a long pause and, to avoid meeting his eye, I took a long drink on my ale and pretended to admire the waitress, pleased to have the subject changed when Reginald at last leaned forward to give me more details of my forthcoming journey to Corsica.

Reginald and I parted outside White's and went to our carriages. When my carriage was some distance away I tapped on the ceiling to stop, and my driver climbed down, looked left and right to check that nobody was watching, then opened the door and joined me inside. He sat opposite me and removed his hat, placing it to the seat beside him and regarding me with bright, curious eyes.

'Well, Master Haytham?' he said.

I looked at him, took a deep breath and stared out of the window. 'I'm due to leave by sea tonight. We will return to Queen Anne's Square, where I will pack, then straight to the docks, if you would.'

He doffed an imaginary cap. 'At your service, Mr Kenway, sir, I'm getting quite used to this driving lark. Lots of waiting around, mind, could do without all that, but otherwise, well, at least you ain't got Frenchmen shooting at you, or your own officers shooting at you. In fact, I'd say the lack of blokes shooting at you is a real perk of the job.'

He could be quite tiresome sometimes. 'Quite so, Holden,' I said, with a frown that was intended to shut him up, although chance would be a fine thing.

'Well, anyway, sir, did you learn anything?'

'I'm afraid nothing concrete.'

I looked out of the window, wrestling with feelings of doubt, guilt and disloyalty, wondering if there was anyone I truly trusted – anyone to whom I remained truly loyal now.

Ironically, the person I trusted most was Holden.

I had met him while in the Dutch Republic. Braddock had been as good as his word and allowed me to move among his men, asking them if they knew anything of the 'Tom Smith' who had met his end on the scaffold, but I wasn't surprised when my investigations proved fruitless. No man I asked would even admit to knowing this Smith, if indeed Smith was his name – until, one night, I heard a movement at the door of my tent and sat up in my cot in time to see a figure appear.

He was young, in his late twenties, with close-cropped, gingery hair and an easy, impish smile. This, it would turn out, was Private Jim Holden, a London man, a good man who wanted to see justice done. His brother had been one of those who had been hanged the same day I almost met my own end. He had been executed for the crime of stealing stew – that was all he had done, steal a bowlful of stew because he was starving; a flogging offence, at worst, but they hanged him. His biggest mistake, it seemed, had been to steal the stew from one of Braddock's own men, one of his private mercenary force.

This was what Holden told me: that the fifteen-hundred-strong force of Coldstream Guards was made up mainly of British Army soldiers like himself, but that there was within that a smaller cadre of men personally selected by Braddock: mercenaries. These mercenaries included Slater and his assistant – and, more worryingly, the two men who had ridden to the Black Forest.

None of these men wore the ring of the Order. They were thugs, strong-arms. I wondered why – why Braddock chose men of this stripe for his inner circle, and not Templar knights? The more time I'd spent with him, the more I thought I had my answer: he was moving away from the Order.

I looked back at Holden now. I had protested that night, but he was a man who had glimpsed the corruption at the heart of Braddock's organization. He was a man who wanted to see justice for his brother and, as a result, no amount of my protesting made the slightest bit of difference. He was going to help me whether I liked it or not.

I had agreed, but on the understanding that his assistance was kept secret at all times. In the hope of hoodwinking those who always seemed one step ahead of me, I needed it to appear as though I'd dropped the matter of finding my father's killers – so that they might no longer be one step ahead of me.

Thus, when we left the Dutch Republic Holden

took on the title of my gentleman's gentleman, my driver, and, to all intents and purposes, as far as the outside world was concerned, that's exactly what he was. Nobody knew that in fact he was carrying out investigations on my behalf. Not even Reginald knew that.

Perhaps *especially* not Reginald.

Holden saw the guilt written across my face.

'Sir, it ain't lies you're telling Mr Birch. All you're doing is what he's been doing, which is withholding certain bits of information, just until you've satisfied yourself that his name is clear – and I'm sure it will be, sir. I'm sure it will be, him being your oldest friend, sir.'

'I wish I could share your optimism on the matter, Holden, I really do. Come, we should move on. My errand awaits.'

'Certainly, sir, and where is that errand taking you, may I ask?'

'Corsica,' I said. 'I'm going to Corsica.'

'Ah, in the midst of a revolution, so I hear . . .'

'Quite right, Holden. A place of conflict is a perfect place to hide.'

'And what will you be doing there, sir?'

'I'm afraid I can't tell you. Suffice to say, it has nothing to do with finding my father's killers and is therefore of only peripheral interest to me. It's a job, a duty, nothing more. I hope that, while I'm away, you will continue your own investigations?'

'Oh, certainly sir.'

'Excellent. And see to it that they remain covert.'

'Don't you be worrying about that, sir. As far as anybody is concerned, Master Kenway has long since abandoned his quest for justice. Whoever it is, sir, their guard will drop eventually.'

25 June 1753

i

It was hot on Corsica during the day, but at night the temperature dropped. Not too much – not freezing – but enough to make lying on a rock-strewn hillside with no blanket an uncomfortable experience.

Cold as it was, though, there were even more pressing matters to attend to, such as the squad of Genoese soldiers moving up the hill, who I'd like to have said were moving stealthily.

I'd like to have said that, but couldn't.

At the top of the hill, on a plateau, was the farmhouse. I'd been keeping watch on it for the past two days, my spyglass trained on the doors and windows of what was a large building and a series of smaller barns and outbuildings, taking note of comings and goings: rebels arriving with supplies and leaving with them, too; while on the first day a small squad of them – I counted eight – had left the complex on what, when they returned, I realized had been some kind of attack: the Corsican rebels, striking out against their Genoese masters. There were only six of them when they came back, and those six looked exhausted and bloodied, but, nevertheless, without words or gestures, wore an aura of triumph.

Women arrived with supplies not long afterwards, and there was celebration far into the night. This morning, more rebels had arrived, with muskets wrapped in blankets. They were well equipped and had support, it seemed; it was no wonder the Genoese wanted to wipe this stronghold off the map.

I had spent the two days moving around the hill so as to avoid being seen. The terrain was rocky and I kept a safe distance away from the buildings. On the morning of the second day, however, I realized I had company. There was another man on the hill, another watcher. Unlike me, he had remained in the same position, dug into an outcrop of rocks, hidden by the brush and the skeletal trees that somehow survived on the otherwise parched hillside.

ii

Lucio was the name of my target, and the rebels were hiding him. Whether they, too, were affiliates of the Assassins, I had no idea, and it didn't matter anyway; he was the one I was after: a 21-year-old boy who was the key to solving a puzzle that has tormented poor Reginald for six years. An unprepossessing-looking boy, with shoulder-length hair, who, as far as I could tell from watching the farmhouse, helped out by carrying pails of water, feeding the livestock and, yesterday, wringing the neck of a chicken.

So he was there: that much I'd established. That was good. But there were problems. Firstly, he had a bodyguard. Never far away from him was a man who wore the gowns and cowl of an Assassin; his gaze would often sweep the hillside while Lucio fetched water or scattered chicken feed. At his waist was a sword, and the fingers of his right hand would flex. Did he wear the famous hidden blade of the Assassins? I wondered. No doubt he would. I'd have to beware of him, that much was for certain; not to mention the rebels who were based at the farmhouse. The compound seemed to be crawling with them.

One other thing to take into account: they were clearly planning to leave soon. Perhaps they'd been using the farmhouse as a temporary base for the attack; perhaps they knew that the Genoese would soon be seeking revenge and come looking for them. Either way, they had been moving supplies into the barns, no doubt piling carts high with them. My guess was that they would leave the next day.

A night-time incursion then, would seem to be the answer. And it had to be tonight. This morning I managed to locate Lucio's sleeping quarters: he shared a medium-sized outhouse with the Assassin and at least six other rebels. They had a code phrase they used when entering the quarters, and I read their lips through my spyglass: *'We work in the dark to serve the light.'*

So – an operation that required some forethought, but, no sooner was I preparing to retire from the hillside in order to concoct my plans, than I saw the second man.

And my plans changed. Edging closer to him, I had managed to identify him as a Genoese soldier. If I was right, that meant he was the forward party of men who would be attempting to take the stronghold; the rest would be along – when?

Sooner, I thought, rather than later. They would want to exact swift revenge for the previous day's raid. Not only that, but they would want to be *seen* to be reacting quickly to the rebels. Tonight, then.

So I left him. I let him continue his surveillance and, instead of withdrawing, stayed on the hillside concocting a different plan. My new plan involved Genoese troops.

The observation man had been good. He'd stayed out of sight and then, when dark fell, retreated stealthily, noiselessly, back down the hill. Where, I wondered, was the rest of the force?

Not far away; and an hour or so later I began to notice movement at the bottom of the hill and even, at one point, heard a muffled curse in Italian. By this stage I was about halfway up and, realizing that they would soon begin to advance, I moved even closer to the plateau and the fence of an animal enclosure. Maybe fifty yards away I could see one of the sentries. Last night, they'd had five altogether, around the entire perimeter of the farmyard. Tonight, they would no doubt increase the guard.

I took out my spyglass and trained it on the nearest guard, who stood, silhouetted by the moon at his back, diligently scanning the hillside below him. Of me, he would see nothing, just another irregular shape in a landscape of irregular shapes. No wonder they were deciding to move so quickly after their ambush. It wasn't the most secure hideout I'd ever seen. In fact, they'd have been sitting ducks were it not for the fact that the approaching Genoese soldiers were so damned clumsy. The conduct of their observation man flattered the operation as a whole. These were men to whom stealth was clearly a foreign and unfamiliar idea, and I was beginning to hear more and more noise from the bottom of the hill. The rebels were almost certain to hear them next. And if the rebels heard them, they would have more than enough opportunity to make their escape. And if the rebels made their escape, they would take Lucio with them.

So I decided to lend a hand. Each guard had responsibility for a pie-slice of the farmyard. Thus, the one nearest to me would move slowly back and forth across a distance of about twenty-five yards. He was good; he made sure that even while he was scanning one section of his area the rest of it was never fully out of sight. But he was also on the move and, when he was, I had a precious few seconds in which to move closer.

So I did. Bit by bit. Until I was close enough to see the guard: his bushy, grey beard, his hat with the brim covering eyes like dark shadows, and his musket slung over his shoulder. And while I couldn't see or hear the marauding Genoese soldiers *yet*, I was aware of them, and soon he would be, too.

I could only assume that the same scene was being played out on the other side of the hill, which meant I had to work fast. I drew my short sword and readied myself. I felt sorry for the guard and offered up a silent apology. He had done nothing to me but be a good and diligent guard and he did not deserve to die.

And then, there on the rocky hillside, I paused. For the first time in my life, I doubted my ability to go through with it. I thought of the family on the port, cut down by Braddock and his men. Seven senseless deaths. And all of a sudden I was struck by the conviction that I was no longer prepared to add to the death toll. I couldn't put this guard, who was no enemy of mine, to the sword. I couldn't do it.

The hesitation almost cost me dear, because at that same moment the clumsiness of the Genoese soldiers finally made its presence felt, and there were the sounds of clattering rock and a curse from further down the hill that was carried on the night air, first to my ears, then to the sentry.

His head jerked, and straight away he was reaching for his musket, craning his neck as he strained his eyes, staring down the hill. He saw me. For a second our eyes locked. My moment of hesitation was over and I sprang, covering the distance between us in one leap.

I led with my empty right hand outstretched in a claw, and my sword held in my left. As I landed I grabbed the back of his head with my right hand and plunged the sword into his throat. He had been about to alert his comrades, but the shout died to a gurgle as blood gushed over my hand and down his front. Holding his head secure with my right hand, I embraced him then lowered him gently and noiselessly to the dry dirt of the farmyard.

I crouched. About sixty yards away was the second guard. He was a dim figure in the dark, but I could see that he was about to turn and, when he did, he was likely to spot me. I ran – so fast that, for a moment, I could hear the rush of the night, and caught him just as he turned. Again, I took the back of the man's neck with my right hand and slammed the sword into him. Again, the man was dead before he hit the dirt.

From further down the hill I heard more noise from the Genoese assault troop, which was blissfully unaware that I had prevented their advance being heard. Sure enough, though, their comrades on the other side had been just as inept, and without a Kenway guardian angel *had* been heard by the sentries on their side. Straight away the cry went up and, in moments, lights were being lit in the farmhouse and rebels were pouring out carrying lit torches, pulling boots on over their britches, dragging jackets across their backs and passing each other swords and muskets. As I crouched, watching, I saw the doors to a barn thrown open and two men begin pulling out a cart by hand, already piled high with supplies, while another hurried across with a horse.

The time for stealth was over and the Genoese soldiers on all sides knew it, abandoning their attempts to storm the farm quietly and rushing up the hill towards the farmyard with a shout.

I had an advantage – I was already in the farmyard, plus I was not in the uniform of a Genoese soldier, and in the confusion I was able to move among the running rebels without attracting suspicion.

I moved towards the outhouse where Lucio was quartered and almost ran into him as he came darting out. His hair was untied but otherwise he was dressed, and he was calling to another man, exhorting him to make his way to the barn. Not far away was the Assassin, who ran, pulling his robes across his chest and pulling his sword at the same time. Two Genoese raiders appeared around the side of the outhouse and straight away he engaged them, calling back over his shoulder, 'Lucio, run for the barn.'

Excellent. Just what I wanted: the Assassin's attention diverted.

Just then I saw another trooper come running on to the plateau, crouch, raise his musket and take aim. Lucio, holding the torch, was his target, but the soldier didn't get a chance to fire before I had darted over and was upon him before he even saw me. He gave a single, muted cry as I buried my sword hilt-deep in the back of his neck.

'Lucio!' I yelled, and at the same time jogged the dead man's trigger finger so that the musket discharged – but harmlessly, into the air. Lucio stopped, shielding his eyes to look across the yard, where I made a show of tossing away the limp corpse of the soldier. Lucio's companion ran on, which was just what I wanted. Some distance away, the Assassin was still fighting, and for a second I admired his skills as he fended off the two men at the same time.

'Thank you,' called Lucio.

'Wait,' I responded. 'We've got to get out of here before the farmyard's overrun.'

He shook his head. 'I need to make my way to the cart,' he called; 'Thank you again, friend.' Then he turned and darted off.

Damn. I cursed and took off in the direction of the barn, running parallel to him but out of sight in the shadows. To my right I saw a Genoese raider about to come off the hillside and into the yard and was close enough to see his eyes widen as our gaze met. Before he could react, I'd grabbed his arm, span and thrust my sword into his armpit, just above his chest plate, and let him fall, screaming, backwards to the rock, snatching his torch at the same time. I kept going, staying parallel with Lucio, making sure he was out of danger. I reached the barn just ahead of him. As I passed by, still in the shadows, I could see inside the still-open front doors, where two rebels were tethering a horse to the cart while two stood guard, one firing his musket while the other reloaded then knelt to fire. I continued running then darted close to the wall of the barn, where I found a Genoese soldier about to let himself in through a side door. I thrust the sword blade upwards at the base of his spine. For a second he writhed in agony, impaled on the blade, and I shoved his body through the door ahead of me, tossed the lit torch into the back of the cart and stayed back in the shadows.

'Get them!' I called, in what I hoped was an approximation of the voice and accent of a Genoese soldier. 'Get the rebel scum.'

Then: 'The cart's ablaze!' I shouted, this time in what I hoped was an approximation of the voice and accent of a Corsican rebel, and at the same time I moved forward out of the shadows, clasping my

Genoese corpse, and let him drop as though he were a fresh kill.

'The cart's ablaze!' I repeated, and now turned my attention to Lucio, who had just arrived at the barn. 'We've got to get out of here. Lucio, come with me.'

I saw two of the rebels exchange a confused look, each wondering who I was and what I wanted with Lucio. There was the report of musket fire, and wood splintered around us. One of the rebels fell, a musket ball embedded in his eye, and I dived on the other one, pretending to shield him from the musket fire but punching the knife blade into his heart at the same time. It was Lucio's companion, I realised, as he died.

'He's gone,' I said to Lucio, rising.

'No!' he shouted, tearful already. No wonder they'd considered him fit only for feeding livestock, I thought, if he was going to dissolve into tears the first time a comrade was killed in action.

By now the barn was ablaze around us. The other two rebels, seeing that there was nothing they could salvage, made their escape and ran pell-mell across the yard towards the hillside, melting into the dark. Other rebels were making their escape, and across the yard I saw that Genoese soldiers had put torches to farm buildings as well.

'I must wait for Miko,' called Lucio.

I gambled that Miko was his Assassin bodyguard.

'He's otherwise engaged. He asked me, a fellow member of the Brotherhood, to take care of you.'

'Are you sure?'

'A good Assassin questions everything,' I said. 'Miko has taught you well. But now is not the time for lessons in the tenets of our creed. We must go.'

He shook his head. 'Tell me the code phrase,' he said firmly.

'Freedom to choose.'

And at last I seemed to have established enough trust to persuade Lucio to come with me, and we began to make our way down the hillside; me, gleeful, thanking God that at last I had him; him, not so sure. Suddenly, he stopped.

'No,' he said, shaking his head. 'I can't do it – I can't leave Miko.'

Great, I thought.

'He said to go,' I replied, 'and to meet him at the boom of the ravine, where our horses are tethered.'

Behind us at the farmyard, the fires raged on and I could hear the remnants of the battle. The Genoese soldiers were clearing up the last of the rebels. Not far away was the sound of a clattering stone, and I saw other figures in the darkness: a pair of rebels escaping. Lucio saw them, too, and went to call to them, but I clamped a hand over his mouth.

'No, Lucio,' I whispered. 'The soldiers will be after them.'

His eyes were wide. 'These are my comrades. They are my friends. I need to be with them. We need to ensure that Miko is safe.'

From high above us drifted the sound of pleading and screaming, and Lucio's eyes darted as though trying to deal with the conflict in his head: did he help his friends above or join those escaping? Either way, I could see he had decided that he didn't want to be with me.

'Stranger . . .' he began, and I thought, 'Stranger', now, eh?

'I thank you for all that you have done to help me and I hope that we can meet again in happier circumstances – perhaps when I can express my gratitude even more thoroughly – but at the moment I'm needed with my people.'

He stood up to go. With a hand on his shoulder I brought him down to my level again. He pulled away with his jaw set. 'Now, Lucio,' I said, 'listen. I've been sent by your mother to take you to her.'

At this he reared back. 'Oh no,' he said. 'No, no, no.'

Which wasn't the reaction I'd been expecting.

I had to scramble across rock to catch him up. But he began to fight me off. 'No, no,' he said. 'I don't know who you are, just leave me alone.'

'Oh, for the love of God,' I said, and silently admitted defeat as I grabbed him in a sleeper hold, ignoring his struggles and applying pressure, restricting the flow of his carotid artery; not enough to cause him permanent damage but enough to render him unconscious.

And as I threw him over my shoulder – a tiny slip of a thing, he was – and carried him down the hill, careful to avoid the last pockets of rebels fleeing the Genoese attack, I wondered why I hadn't simply knocked him out in the first place.

iii

I stopped at the ravine edge and lowered Lucio to the floor, then found my rope, secured it and lowered it into the darkness below. Next I used Lucio's belt to tie his hands, looped the other end under his thighs and tied it so that his limp body was slung across my back. Then I began the slow climb down.

About halfway down, the weight became unbearable, but it was an eventuality I'd prepared for, and I managed to hang on until I reached an opening in the cliff face that led into a dark cave. I scrambled in and pulled Lucio off my back, feeling my muscles relax gratefully.

From ahead of me, in the cave, came a noise. A movement at first, like a shifting sound, and then a click.

The sound an Assassin's hidden blade makes when it is engaged.

'I knew you'd come here,' said a voice – a voice that belonged to Miko, the Assassin. 'I knew you'd come here, because that's what I would have done.'

And then he struck, came shooting forward from within the cave, using my shock and surprise against me. I was already drawing my short sword and had it out as we clashed, his blade slicing at me like a claw and meeting my sword with such force that it was knocked out of my hand, sent skittering to the lip of the cave, and into the blackness below.

My sword. My father's sword.

But there was no time to mourn it, for the Assassin was coming at me a second time and he was good, very good. In a confined space, with no weapon, I had no chance. All I had, in fact, was . . .

Luck.

And luck is all it was, that, as I pressed myself against the cave wall, he had miscalculated slightly, enough to overbalance a fraction. In any other circumstances, against any other opponent, he would have recovered immediately and finished his kill – but this wasn't any other circumstances and I wasn't any other opponent, and I made him pay for his tiny error. I leaned into him, grabbed his arm, twisted and helped him on his way, so that he, too, sailed out into the blackness. But he held on, pulled me with him, dragged me to the edge of the cave so that I was screaming in pain as I tried to stop myself being dragged out into open space. Lying flat on my belly, I looked out and saw him, one arm grabbing mine, the other trying to reach for the rope. I could feel the brace of his hidden blade, brought my other hand forward and began fumbling with the fastenings. Too late he realized what I was doing and abandoned trying to catch hold of the rope, instead focusing his efforts on trying to stop me unfastening the brace. For some moments our hands flapped at each other for possession of the blade, which, as I opened the first catch, suddenly slipped further up his wrist and sent him lurching to one side, his position even more precarious than before, his other arm pinwheeling. It was all I needed, and with a final shout of effort I unclipped the last fastening, wrenched the brace free and at the same time bit into the hand that gripped my wrist. A combination of pain and lack of traction was enough to dislodge him at last.

I saw him swallowed up by the dark and prayed he wouldn't hit my horse when he landed. But nothing came. No sound of a landing, nothing. The next thing I saw was the rope, taut and quivering, and I craned my neck, strained my eyes to search the darkness and was rewarded by the sight of Miko, some distance below, very much alive, and beginning to climb up towards me.

I pulled his blade to me and held it to the rope.

'If you climb much higher the fall will kill you when I cut the rope,' I called. He was already close enough so that I could look into his eyes when he stared up at me, and I could see the indecision in them. 'You shouldn't suffer such a death, friend,' I added. 'Start your descent and live to fight another day.'

I began to saw slowly at the rope, and he stopped, looked down into the dark, where the bottom of the ravine was not in sight.

'You have my blade,' he said.

'To the victor the spoils.' I shrugged.

'Perhaps we will meet again,' he said, 'and I can reclaim it.'

'I sense that only one of us will survive a second meeting,' I said.

He nodded. 'Perhaps,' he said, and soon had shimmied down into the night.

The fact that I now had to climb back up, and had been forced to surrender my horse, was awkward. But rather that than face the Assassin again.

And for now we are resting. Well, I am resting; poor Lucio remains unconscious. Later, I will hand him over to associates of Reginald, who will take him in a covered wagon, make the passage across the Mediterranean to the South of France and then to the chateau, where Lucio will be reunited with his mother, the code-breaker.

Then I'll charter a ship to Italy, being sure to be seen doing it, referring to my 'young companion' once or twice. If and when the Assassins come looking for Lucio, that's where they'll concentrate their efforts.

Reginald says I'm no longer needed after that. I am to melt away in Italy, leave no trace, no trail to follow.

12 August 1753

i

I began the day in France, having doubled back from Italy. No small undertaking; it's all very well writing it down, but one doesn't simply 'double back' from Italy to France. My reason for being in Italy was to misdirect the Assassins when they came looking for Lucio. So, by returning to France, to the very place where we were holding Lucio and his mother, I was endangering not just my recently accomplished mission but everything Reginald had been working for these past years. It was risky. It was so risky, in fact, that if I thought about it, the risk took my breath away. It made me wonder, was I stupid? What kind of fool would take such a risk?

And the answer was, a fool with doubt in his heart.

ii

One hundred yards or so from the gate, I came upon a lone patrol, a guard dressed as a peasant, with a musket slung across his back, who looked sleepy, but was alert and watchful. As we drew up to him our eyes met for a moment. His flickered briefly as he recognized me, and he jerked his head slightly to let me know I was free to pass. There would be another patrol, I knew, on the other side of the chateau. We came out of the forest and followed the tall perimeter wall until we came to a large, arched wooden gate inset with a smaller wicket gate, where a guard stood, a man I recognized from my years spent at the chateau.

'Well, well,' he said, 'if it isn't Master Haytham, all grown up.' He grinned and took the reins of my horses as I dismounted, before opening the wicket gate, which I stepped through, blinking in the sudden sunlight after the comparative gloom of the forest.

Ahead of me stretched the chateau lawn, and walking across it I felt a strange crawling sensation in my belly that I knew to be nostalgia for the time I had spent at this chateau in my youth, when Reginald had . . .

. . . continued my father's teachings? He'd said so. But of course I now know he'd been misleading me about that. In the ways of combat and stealth, perhaps, he had done so, but Reginald had raised me in the ways of the Templar order, and taught me that the way of the Templar was the *only* way; and that those who believed in another way were at best misguided, at worst evil.

But I'd since learnt that Father was one of those

misguided, evil people, and who's to say what he would have taught me as I grew up. Who's to say?

The grass was straggly and overgrown, despite the presence of two gardeners, both of whom wore short swords at their waists, hands going to the hilts as I made my way towards the front door of the chateau. I came close to one of them, who, when he saw who I was, nodded his head. 'An honour finally to meet you, Master Kenway,' he said. 'I trust your mission was successful?'

'It was, thank you, yes,' I replied to the guard – or gardener, whatever he was. To him I was a knight, one of the most celebrated in the Order. Could I really hate Reginald when his stewardship had brought me such acclaim? And, after all, had I ever doubted his teachings? The answer was no. Had I been *forced* to follow them? Again, no. I'd always had the option to choose my own path but had stayed with the Order because I believed in the code.

Even so, he has lied to me.

No, not lied to me. How had Holden put it? 'Withheld the truth'.

Why?

And, more immediately, why had Lucio reacted that way when I told him he was to see his mother?

At the mention of my name, the second gardener looked at me more sharply, then he too was genuflecting as I made my way past, acknowledging him with a nod, feeling taller all of a sudden and all but puffing out my chest as I approached the front door that I knew so well. I turned before I knocked, to look back across the lawn, where the two guards stood watching me. I had trained on that lawn, spent countless hours honing my sword skills.

I knocked, and the door was opened by yet another similarly attired man who also wore a short sword at his waist. The chateau had never been this fully staffed when I had lived here, but then again, when I lived here, we never had a guest as important as the code-breaker.

The first familiar face I saw belonged to John Harrison, who looked at me then did a double take. 'Haytham,' he blustered, 'what the hell are you doing here?'

'Hello, John,' I said equably, 'is Reginald here?'

'Well, yes, Haytham, but Reginald is *supposed* to be here. What are *you* doing here?'

'I came to check on Lucio.'

'You what?' Harrison was becoming somewhat red-faced. 'You "came to check on Lucio"?' He was having trouble finding his words now. 'What? Why? What on earth do you think you're doing?'

'John,' I said gently, 'please calm yourself. I was not followed from Italy. Nobody knows I'm here.'

'Well, I should bloody well hope not.'

'Where's Reginald?'

'Below stairs, with the prisoners.'

'Oh? Prisoners?'

'Monica and Lucio.'

'I see. I had no idea they were considered prisoners.'

But a door had opened beneath the stairs, and Reginald appeared. I knew that door; it led down to the cellar, which, when I lived there, was a dank, low-ceilinged room, with mouldering, mainly empty wine racks along one side and a dark, damp wall along the other.

'Hello, Haytham,' said Reginald, tight-lipped. 'You were not expected.'

Not far away lingered one of the guards, and now he was joined by another. I looked from them back to Reginald and John, who stood like a pair of concerned clergyman. Neither was armed, but even if they had been, I thought I could probably take all four. If it came to it.

'Indeed,' I said, 'John was just telling me how surprised he was by my visit.'

'Well, quite. You've been very reckless, Haytham . . .'

'Perhaps, but I wanted to see that Lucio was being looked after. Now I'm told he is a prisoner here, so perhaps I have my answer.'

Reginald chortled. 'Well, what did you expect?'

'What I was told. That the mission was to reunite mother and son; that the code-breaker had agreed to work on Vedomir's journal if we were able to rescue her son from the rebels.'

'I told you no lies, Haytham. Indeed, Monica has

been working on decoding the journal since being reunited with Lucio.'

'Just not on the basis I imagined.'

'The carrot doesn't work, we use the stick,' said Reginald, his eyes cold. 'I'm sorry if you had formed the impression that there was more carrot than stick involved.'

'Let's see her,' I said, and with a short nod, Reginald agreed. He turned and led us through the door, which opened on to a flight of stone steps leading down. Light danced on the walls.

'Regarding the journal, we're close now, Haytham,' he said as we descended. 'So far, we've been able to establish that there exists an amulet. Somehow it fits with the storehouse. If we can get hold of the amulet . . .'

At the bottom of the steps, iron cressets on poles had been set out to light the way to a door, where a guard stood. He moved to one side and opened the door for us to pass through. Inside, the cellar was as I remembered it, lit by the flickering light of torches. At one end was a desk. It was bolted to the floor and Lucio was manacled to it, and beside him was his mother, who was an incongruous sight. She sat on a chair that looked as though it had been brought into the cellar from upstairs especially for the purpose. She was wearing long skirts and a buttoned-up blouse and would have looked like a churchgoer were it not for the rusting iron restraints around her wrists and the arms of the chair, and especially the scold's bridle around her head.

Lucio swivelled in his seat, saw me and his eyes burned with hatred, then he turned back to his work.

I had stopped in the middle of the floor, halfway between the door and the code-breakers. 'Reginald, what is the meaning of this?' I said, pointing at Lucio's mother, who regarded me balefully from within the scold's bridle.

'The branks is temporary, Haytham. Monica has been somewhat vocal in her condemnation of our tactics this morning. Hence we have moved them here for the day.' He raised his voice to address the code-breakers, 'I'm sure they can return to their usual residence tomorrow, when they have recovered their manners.'

'This is not right, Reginald.'

'Their usual quarters are much more pleasant, Haytham,' he assured me testily.

'Even so, they should not be treated this way.'

'Neither should the poor child in the Black Forest have been scared half to death with your blade at his throat,' snapped Reginald.

I started, my mouth working but lost for words. 'That was . . . That was . . .'

'Different? Because it involved your quest to find your father's killers? Haytham . . .' He took my elbow and led me out of the cellar and back out into the corridor, and we began to climb the steps again. 'This is even more important than that. You may not think so, but it is. It involves the entire future of the Order.'

I wasn't sure any more. I wasn't sure what was more important, but said nothing.

'And what happens when the decoding is over?' I asked as we reached the entrance hall once again.

He looked at me.

'Oh no,' I said, understanding. 'Neither is to be harmed.'

'Haytham, I don't much care for you giving me orders . . .'

'Then don't think of it as an order,' I hissed. 'Think of it as a threat. Keep them here when their work is over if you must, but if they are harmed then you will have me to answer to.'

He looked at me long and hard. I realized that my heart was hammering and hoped to God it wasn't somehow visible. Had I ever gone against him like this? With such force? I didn't think so.

'Very well,' he said, after a moment, 'they will not be harmed.'

We spent dinner in near-silence, and the offer of a bed for the night was made reluctantly. I leave in the morning; Reginald promises to be in touch with news concerning the journal. The warmth between us, though, is gone. In me, he sees insubordination; in him, I see lies.

18 April 1754

i

Earlier this evening I found myself at the Royal Opera House, taking a seat next to Reginald, who was settling in for a performance of *The Beggar's Opera* with evident glee. Of course, the last time we'd met, I'd threatened him, which wasn't something I had forgotten, but evidently he had. Forgotten or forgiven, one of the two. Either way, it was as though the confrontation had never taken place, the slate wiped clean, either by his anticipation of the night's forthcoming entertainment or by the fact that he believed the amulet to be near.

It was inside the opera house, in fact, around the neck of an Assassin who had been named in Vedomir's journal then tracked down by Templar agents.

An Assassin. He was my next target. My first job since rescuing Lucio in Corsica, and the first to feel the bite of my new weapon: my hidden blade. As I took the opera glasses and looked at the man across the hall – my target – the irony of it suddenly struck me.

My target was Miko.

I left Reginald in his seat and made my way along

the corridors of the opera house, along the back of the seats, past the opera's patrons, until I found myself at the stalls. At the box where Miko sat I let myself in silently then tapped him gently on the shoulder.

I was ready for him, if he tried anything, but though his body tensed and I heard him give a sharp intake of breath, he made no move to defend himself. It was almost as though he expected it when I reached and took the amulet from his neck – and did I sense a feeling of . . . relief? As though he were grateful to relinquish the responsibility, pleased no longer to be its custodian?

'You should have come to me,' he sighed, 'We would have found another way . . .'

'Yes. But then you would have known,' I replied.

There was a click as I engaged the blade, and I saw him smile, knowing it was the one I had taken from him in Corsica.

'For what it's worth, I'm sorry,' I told him.

'As am I,' he said, and I killed him.

ii

Some hours later, I attended the meeting at the house on Fleet and Bride, standing around a table with others, our attention focused on Reginald, as well as the book on the table before us. It was open, and I could see the symbol of the Assassins on the page.

'Gentlemen,' said Reginald. His eyes were shining, as though he were close to tears. 'I hold in my hand a key. And if this book is to be believed, it will open the doors of a storehouse built by Those Who Came Before.'

I contained myself. 'Ah, our dear friends who ruled, ruined and then vanished from the world,' I said. 'Do you know what it is we'll find within?'

If Reginald picked up on my sarcasm, then he made no sign. Instead, he reached for the amulet, held it up and basked in the hush from those assembled as it began to glow in his hand. It was impressive, even I had to admit, and Reginald looked over at me.

'It could contain knowledge,' he replied. 'Perhaps a weapon, or something as of yet unknown, unfathomable in its construction and purpose. It could be any of these things. Or none of them. They are still an enigma, these precursors. But of one thing I am certain – whatever waits behind those doors shall prove a great boon to us.'

'Or our enemies,' I said, 'should they find it first.'

He smiled. Was I beginning to believe, at last?

'They won't. You've seen to that.'

Miko had died wanting to find another way. What had he meant? An accord of Assassin and Templar? My thoughts went to my father.

'I assume you know where this storehouse is?' I said, after a pause.

'Mr Harrison?' said Reginald, and John stepped forward with a map, unfurling it.

'How fare your calculations?' said Reginald, as John circled an area of the map which, leaning closer, I saw contained New York and Massachusetts.

'I believe the site lays somewhere within this region,' he said.

'That's a lot of ground to cover.' I frowned.

'My apologies. Would that I could be more accurate . . .'

'That's all right,' said Reginald. 'It suffices for a start. And this is why we've called you here, Master Kenway. We'd like for you to travel to America, locate the storehouse, and take possession of its contents.'

'I am yours to command,' I said. To myself, I cursed him and his folly, and wished I could be left alone to continue my own investigations, then added, 'Although a job of this magnitude will require more than just myself.'

'Of course,' said Reginald, and handed me a piece of paper. 'Here are the names of five men sympathetic to our cause. Each is also uniquely suited to aid you in your endeavour. With them at your side, you'll want for nothing.'

'Well, then I'd best be on my way,' I said.

'I knew our faith in you was not misplaced. We've booked you a passage to Boston. Your ship leaves at dawn. Go forth, Haytham – and bring honour to us all.'

8 July 1754

i

Boston twinkled in the sun as squawking gulls circled overhead, water slapped noisily at the harbour wall and the gangplank banged like a drum as we disembarked from the *Providence*, weary and disorientated by over a month at sea but weak with happiness at finally reaching land. I stopped in my tracks as sailors from a neighbouring frigate rolled barrels across my path with a sound like distant thunder, and my gaze went from the glittering emerald ocean, where the masts of Royal Navy warships, yachts and frigates rocked gently from side to side, to the dock, the wide stone steps that led from the piers and jetties to the harbour thronging with redcoats, traders and sailors, then up past the harbour to the city of Boston itself, the church spires and distinctive red-brick buildings seemingly resisting any attempts at arrangement, as though flung by some godly hand on to the side of the hill. And, everywhere, Union flags that fluttered gently in the breeze, just to remind visitors – in case they had any doubts – that the British were here.

The passage from England to America had been eventful, to say the least. I had made friends and discovered enemies, surviving an attempt on my life – by Assassins, no doubt – who wanted to take revenge for the killing at the opera house and to recover the amulet.

To the other passengers and crew of the ship I was a mystery. Some thought I was a scholar. I told my new acquaintance, James Fairweather, that I 'solved problems', and that I was travelling to America to see what life was like there; what had been retained from the empire and what had been discarded; what changes British rule had wrought.

Which were fibs, of course. But not outright lies. For though I came on specific Templar business, I was curious, too, to see this land I had heard so much about, which was apparently so vast, its people infused with a pioneering, indomitable spirit.

There were those who said that spirit might one day be used against us, and that our subjects, if they harnessed that determination, would be a formidable foe. And there were others who said America was simply too big to be governed by us; that it was a powder keg, ready to go off; that its people would grow tired of the taxes imposed upon them so that a country thousands of miles away could fight wars with other countries thousands of miles away; and that when it did go off we might not have the resources to protect our interests. All of this I hoped to be able to judge for myself.

But only as an adjunct to my main mission, though, which . . . well, I think it's fair to say that, for me, the mission has changed en route. I'd stepped on the *Providence* holding a particular set of beliefs and stepped off having had them first challenged, then shaken and, finally, changed, and all because of the book.

The book that Reginald had given me: I'd spent much of my time aboard the ship poring over it; I must have read it no fewer than two dozen times, and still I'm not sure I have made sense of it.

One thing I do know, though. Whereas before, I'd thought of Those Who Came Before with doubt, as would a sceptic, an unbeliever, and considered Reginald's obsession with them to be at best an irritation, at worst a preoccupation that threatened to derail the very workings of our Order, I no longer did. I *believed*.

The book seemed to have been written – or should I say written, illustrated, decorated, *scrawled* – by a man, or maybe several of them: several lunatics who had filled page after page with what, at first, I took to be wild and outlandish claims, fit only for scoffing at then ignoring.

Yet, somehow, the more I read, the more I came to see the truth. Over the years, Reginald had told me (I used to say 'bored me with') his theories concerning a race of beings that predated our own. He'd

212

always asserted that we were born of their struggles and thus obliged to serve them; that our ancestors had fought to secure their own freedom in a long and bloody war.

What I discovered during my passage was that all of this originated from the book, which as I read it, was having what I can only describe as a profound effect upon me. Suddenly I knew why Reginald had become so obsessed with this race. I'd sneered at him, remember? But, reading the book, I felt no desire to sneer at all, just a sense of wonderment, a feeling of lightness inside me that at times made me feel almost giddy with an excitement and a sense of what I can describe as 'insignificance', of realizing my own place in the world. It was as though I had peered through a keyhole expecting to see another room on the other side but had seen a whole new world instead.

And what had become of Those Who Came Before? What had they left behind, and how could it benefit us? That I didn't know. It was a mystery that had confounded my Order for centuries, a mystery I'd been asked to solve, a mystery that had brought me here, to Boston.

'Master Kenway! Master Kenway!'

I was being hailed by a young gentleman who appeared from within the throng. Going over to him, I said, carefully, 'Yes? May I help you?'

He held out his hand to be shaken. 'Charles Lee, sir.

A pleasure to make your acquaintance. I've been asked to introduce you to the city. Help you settle in.'

I had been told about Charles Lee. He was not with the Order but was keen to join us and, according to Reginald, would want to ingratiate himself with me in the hope of securing my sponsorship. Seeing him reminded me: I was Grand Master of the Colonial Rite now.

Charles had long dark hair, thick sideburns and a prominent, hawk-like nose and, even though I liked him straight away, I noticed that, while he smiled when he spoke to me, he reserved a look of disdain for everybody else on the harbour.

He indicated for me to leave my bags, and we began to thread our way through the crowds of the long pier, past dazed-looking passengers and crew still getting their bearings on dry land; through dock workers, traders and redcoats, excited children and dogs scuttling underfoot.

I tipped my hat to a pair of giggling women then said to him, 'Do you like it here, Charles?'

'There's a certain charm to Boston, I suppose,' he called back over his shoulder. 'To all of the colonies, really. Granted, their cities have none of London's sophistication or splendour, but the people are earnest and hard-working. They've a certain pioneer spirit that I find compelling.'

I looked around. 'It's quite something, really – watching a place that's finally found its feet.'

'Feet awash in the blood of others, I'm afraid.'

'Ah, that's a story old as time itself, and one that's not likely to change. We're cruel and desperate creatures, set in our conquering ways. The Saxons and the Franks. The Ottomans and Safavids. I could go on for hours. The whole of human history is but a series of subjugations.'

'I pray one day we rise above it,' replied Charles earnestly.

'While you pray, I'll act. We'll see who finds success first, hmm?'

'It was an expression,' he said, with a wounded edge to his voice.

'Aye. And a dangerous one. Words have power. Wield them wisely.'

We lapsed into silence.

'Your commission is with Edward Braddock, is it not?' I said, as we passed a cart laden with fruit.

'Aye, but he's yet to reach America, and I figured I might . . . well . . . at least until he arrives . . . I thought . . .'

I stepped nimbly to the side to avoid a small girl in pigtails. 'Out with it,' I said.

'Forgive me, sir. I had . . . I had hoped that I might study under you. If I am to serve the Order, I can imagine no better mentor than yourself.'

I felt a small surge of satisfaction. 'Kind of you to say, but I think you overestimate me.'

'Impossible, sir.'

Not far away, a red-faced paperboy wearing a cap yelled out news of the battle at Fort Necessity: 'French forces declare victory following Washington's retreat,' he bawled. 'In response, the Duke of Newcastle pledges more troops to counter the foreign menace!'

The foreign menace, I thought. The French, in other words. This conflict they were calling the French and Indian War was set to escalate, if the rumours were to be believed.

There was not an Englishman alive who didn't detest the French, but I knew one Englishman in particular who hated them with a vein-bulging passion, and that was Edward Braddock. When he did arrive in America, that's where he'd be heading, leaving me to go about my own business – or so I hoped.

I waved away the paperboy when he tried to extort sixpence from me for the broadsheet. I had no desire to read about more French victories.

Meanwhile, as we reached our horses and Charles told me that we were to ride for the Green Dragon Tavern, I wondered what the other men would be like.

'Have you been told why it is I've come to Boston?' I asked.

'No. Master Birch said I should know only as much

as you saw fit to share. He sent me a list of names and bade me ensure you could find them.'

'And have you had any luck with that?'

'Aye. William Johnson waits for us at the Green Dragon.'

'How well do you know him?'

'Not well. But he saw the Order's mark and did not hesitate to come.'

'Prove yourself loyal to our cause and you may yet know our plans as well,' I said.

He beamed. 'I should like nothing more, sir.'

ii

The Green Dragon was a large brick building with a sloping pitch roof and a sign over the front door that bore the eponymous dragon. According to Charles, it was the most celebrated coffee house in the city, where everybody from patriots to redcoats and governors would meet to chat, to plot, to gossip and trade. Anything that happened in Boston, the chances were it originated here, on Union Street.

Not that Union Street itself was at all prepossessing. Little more than a river of mud, it slowed our pace as we approached the tavern, being sure not to splash any of the groups of gentlemen who stood outside, leaning on canes and chattering intently. Avoiding carts and giving curt nods to soldiers on horseback, we reached a low, wooden stables building where we left our horses, then made our way carefully across the streams of muck to the tavern. Inside, we immediately became acquainted with the owners: Catherine Kerr, who was (without wishing to be ungentlemanly), a little on the large side; and Cornelius Douglass, whose first words I heard upon entering were, 'Kiss my arse, ya wench!'

Fortunately, he wasn't talking either to me or to Charles, but to Catherine. When the two of them saw us, their demeanours instantly changed from warlike to servile and they saw to it that my bags were taken up to my room.

Charles was right: William Johnson was already there, and in a room upstairs we were introduced. An older man, similarly attired to Charles but with a certain weariness to him, an experience that was etched into the lines on his face, he stood from studying maps to shake my hand. 'A pleasure,' he said, and then, as Charles left to stand guard, leaned forward and said to me, 'A good lad, if a bit earnest.'

I kept any feelings I had on Charles to myself, indicating with my eyes that he should continue.

'I'm told you're putting together an expedition,' he said.

'We believe there is a precursor site in the region,'

I said, choosing my words carefully, then adding, 'I require your knowledge of the land and its people to find it.'

He pulled a face. 'Sadly, a chest containing my research has been stolen. Without it, I'm of no use to you.'

I knew from experience that nothing was ever easy. 'Then we'll find it,' I sighed. 'Have you any leads?'

'My associate, Thomas Hickey, has been making the rounds. He's quite good at loosening tongues.'

'Tell me where I can find him and I'll see about speeding things along.'

'We've heard rumours of bandits operating from a compound south-west of here,' said William. 'You'll likely find him there.'

iii

Outside the city, corn in a field waved in a light night-time breeze. Not far away was the high fencing of a compound that belonged to the bandits, and from inside came the sound of raucous festivities. Why not? I thought. Every day you've avoided death by the hang-man's noose or on the end of a redcoat's bayonet is a cause for celebration when you lived life as a bandit.

At the gates there were various guards and hangers-on milling around, some of them drinking, some attempting to stand guard, and all of them in a constant state of argument. To the left of the compound, the cornfield rose to a small hill peak and on it sat a lookout tending to a small fire. Sitting tending a fire isn't quite the desired position for a lookout, but, otherwise, he was one of the few on this side of the compound who seemed to be taking his job seriously. Certainly, they'd failed to post any scouting parties. Or if they had, then the scouting parties were lounging under a tree somewhere, blind drunk, because there was nobody to see Charles and I as we crept closer, approaching a man, who was crouching by a crumbling stone wall, keeping watch on the compound.

It was him: Thomas Hickey. A round-faced man, a little shabby, and probably too fond of the grog himself, if my guess was correct. This was the man who, according to William, was good at loosening tongues? He looked like he'd have problems loosening his own drawers.

Perhaps, arrogantly, my distaste for him was fed by the fact that he was the first contact I'd met since arriving in Boston to whom my name meant nothing. But, if that annoyed me, it was nothing compared to the effect it had on Charles, who drew his sword.

'Show some respect, boy,' he snarled.

I laid a restraining hand on him. 'Peace, Charles,' I said, then addressed Thomas: 'William Johnson sent us in the hopes we might . . . expedite your search.'

'Don't need no expediting,' drawled Thomas. 'Don't need none of your fancy London-speak, neither. I've found the men done the theft.'

Beside me, Charles bristled. 'Then why are you just lazing around?'

'Figurin out how to deal with those varlets,' said Thomas, indicated the compound then turned to us with expectant eyes and an impudent grin.

I sighed. Time to go to work. 'Right, I'll kill the lookout and take a position behind the guards. You two approach from the front. When I open fire on a group, you charge in. We'll have the element of surprise on our side. Half will fall before they've even realized what's happening.'

I took my musket, left my two comrades and crept to the edge of the cornfield, where I crouched and took aim at the lookout. He was warming his hands with his rifle between his legs, and probably wouldn't have seen or heard me if I'd approached riding a camel. It felt almost cowardly to squeeze the trigger, but squeeze it I did.

I cursed as he pitched forward, sending up a shower of sparks. He'd start to burn soon, and if nothing else the smell was going to alert his compatriots. Hurrying now, I returned to Charles and Thomas, who drew closer to the bandit compound while I took up position not far away, pushed my rifle butt into my shoulder and squinted along the sights at one of the bandits, who stood – though 'swayed' might have been more accurate – just outside the gates. As I watched he began to move towards the cornfield, perhaps to relieve the sentry I'd already shot, who even now was roasting on his own fire. I waited until he was at the edge of the cornfield, pausing as there was a sudden lull in the merriment from inside the compound, and then, as a roar went up, squeezing the trigger.

He dropped to his knees then keeled over to one side, part of his skull missing, and my gaze went straight to the compound entrance to see if the shot had been heard.

No, was the answer. Instead the rabble at the gate had turned their attention on Charles and Thomas, drawn their swords and pistols and began to shout at them: 'Clear off!'

Charles and Thomas loitered, just as I'd told them. I could see their hands itching to draw their own weapons, but they bided their time. Good men. Waiting for me to take the first shot.

The time was now. I drew a bead on one of the men, whom I took to be the ringleader. I pulled the trigger and saw blood spray from the back of his head, and he lurched back.

This time my shot was heard, but it didn't matter, because at the same time Charles and Thomas drew their blades and struck and two more of the guards keeled over with blood fountaining from neck wounds.

The gate was in disarray and the battle began in earnest.

I managed to pick off two more of the bandits before abandoning my musket, drawing my sword and running forward, leaping into the fray and standing side by side with Charles and Thomas. I enjoyed fighting with companions for once, and felled three of the thugs, who died screaming even as their companions made for the gates and barricaded themselves inside.

In no time at all, the only men left standing were me, Charles and Thomas, all three of us breathing hard and flicking the blood from our steel. I regarded Thomas with a new respect: he'd acquitted himself well, with a speed and skill that belied his looks. Charles, too, was looking at him, though with rather more distaste, as though Thomas's proficiency in battle had annoyed him.

Now we had a new problem, though: we'd taken the outside of the compound, but the door had been blocked by those retreating. It was Thomas who suggested we shoot the powder keg – another good idea from the man I'd previously dismissed as a drunk – so I did, blowing a hole in the wall, through which we poured, stepping over the torn and ragged corpses littering the hallway on the other side.

We ran on. Thick, deep carpets and rugs were on the floor, while exquisite tapestries had been hung at the windows. The whole place was in semi-darkness.

There was screaming, male and female, and running feet as we made our way through quickly, me with a sword in one hand and a pistol in the other, using both, slaying any man in my way.

Thomas had looted a candlestick, and he used it to cave in the head of a bandit, wiping brains and blood from his face just as Charles reminded us why we were there: to find William's chest. He described it as we raced along more gloomy corridors, finding less resistance now. Either the bandits were staying clear of us or were marshalling themselves into a more cohesive force. Not that it mattered what they were doing: we needed to find the chest.

Which we did, nestled at the back of a boudoir which stank of ale and sex and was seemingly full of people: scantily clad women who grabbed clothes and ran screaming, and several thieves loading guns. A bullet smacked into the wood of the doorway by my side and we took cover as another man, this one naked, raised his pistol to fire.

Charles returned fire around the door frame, and the naked man crashed to the carpet with an untidy red hole at his chest, grabbing a fistful of bedclothes as he went. Another bullet gouged the frame, and we ducked back. Thomas drew his sword as two more bandits came hurtling down the corridor towards us, Charles joining in.

'Lay down your weapons,' called one of the remaining bandits from inside the boudoir, 'and I'll consider letting you live.'

'I make you the same offer,' I said from behind the door. 'We have no quarrel. I only wish to return this chest to its rightful owner.'

There was a sneer in his voice. 'Nothing *rightful* about Mr Johnson.'

'I won't ask again.'

'Agreed.'

I heard a movement nearby and flitted across the doorway. The other man had been trying to creep up on us, but I put a bullet between his eyes and he flopped to the floor, his pistol skittering away from him. The remaining bandit fired again and made a dive for his companion's gun, but I'd already reloaded and anticipated his move, and I put a shot in his flank as he stretched for it. Like a wounded animal he jackknifed back to the bed, landing in a wet mess of blood and bedclothes and staring up at me as I entered cautiously, gun held in front of me.

He gave me a baleful look. This can't have been how he planned for his night to end.

'Your kind has no need for books and maps,' I said, indicating William's chest. 'Who put you up to this?'

'Never seen a person,' he wheezed, shaking his head. 'It's always dead drops and letters. But they always pay, so we do the jobs.'

Everywhere I went I met men like the bandit, who would do anything, it seemed – anything for a bit of coin. It was men like him who had invaded my childhood home and killed my father. Men like him who set me on the path I walk today.

They always pay. We do the jobs.

Somehow, through a veil of disgust, I managed to resist the urge to kill him.

'Well, those days are done. Tell your masters I said as much.'

He raised himself slightly, perhaps realizing I planned to let him live. 'Who do I say you are?'

'You don't. They'll know,' I said. And let him go.

Thomas began grabbing more loot while Charles and I took the chest, and we made our way out of the compound. Retreating was easier, most of the bandits having decided that discretion was the better part of valour and staying out of our way, and we made it outside to our horses and galloped away.

iv

At the Green Dragon, William Johnson was once again poring over his maps. Straight away he was digging through the chest when we returned it to him, checking his maps and scrolls were there.

'My thanks, Master Kenway,' he said, sitting back at

his table, satisfied that everything was in order. 'Now tell me what it is you need.'

Around my neck was the amulet. I'd found myself taking it off and admiring it. Was it my imagination, or did it seem to glow? It hadn't – not on the night I took it from Miko at the opera house. The first time I had seen it glow was when Reginald held it up at Fleet and Bride. Now, though, it seemed to do in my hand what it had done in his, as though it were powered – how ridiculous it seemed – by belief.

I looked at him, then reached my hands to my neck, removed the amulet from over my head and handed it across the table. He held my gaze as he took it, sensing its importance, then squinted at it, studying it carefully as I said, 'The images on this amulet – are they familiar to you? Perhaps one of the tribes has shown you something similar?'

'It appears Kanien'kehá:ka in origin,' said William.

The Mohawk. My pulse quickened.

'Can you trace it to a specific location?' I said, 'I need to know where it came from.'

'With my research returned, perhaps. Let me see what I can do.'

I nodded my thanks. 'First, though, I'd like to know a little more about you, William. Tell me about yourself.'

'What's to tell? I was born in Ireland, to Catholic parents – which, I learnt early in life, severely limited my opportunities. So I converted to Protestantism and journeyed here at the behest of my uncle. But I fear my Uncle Peter was not the sharpest of tools. He sought to open trade with the Mohawk – but chose to build his settlement away from the trade routes instead of *on* them. I tried to reason with the man . . . But . . .' He sighed '. . . as I said, not the sharpest. So I took what little money I'd earned and bought my own plot of land. I built a home, a farm, a store and a mill. Humble beginnings – but well situated, which made all the difference.'

'So this is how you came to know the Mohawk?'

'Indeed. And it has proved a valuable relationship.'

'But you've heard nothing of the precursors' site? No hidden temple or ancient constructs?'

'Yes and no. Which is to say, they have their fair share of sacred sites but none matching what you describe. Earthen mounds, forest clearings, hidden caves . . . All are natural, though. No strange metal. No . . . odd glows.'

'Hmmm. It is well hidden,' I said.

'Even to them, it seems.' He smiled. 'But cheer up, my friend. You'll have your precursor treasure. I swear it.'

I raised my glass. 'To our success, then.'

'And soon!'

I smiled. We were four now. We were a team.

10 July 1754

i

We now have our room at the Green Dragon Pub —
a base, if you like — and it was this I entered, to
find Thomas, Charles and William: Thomas drinking,
Charles looking perturbed and William studying his
charts and maps. I greeted them, only to be rewarded
with a belch from Thomas.

'Charming,' spat Charles.

I grinned. 'Cheer up, Charles. He'll grow on you,' I
said, and sat next to Thomas, who gave me a grateful
look.

'Any news?' I said.

He shook his head. 'Whispers of things. Nothin
solid at the moment. I know you're lookin for word of
anything out the ordinary . . . Dealin with temples and
spirits and ancient times and whatnot. But . . . so far,
can't say my boys have heard much.'

'No trinkets or artefacts being moved through
your . . . shadow market?'

'Nothin new. Couple ill-gotten weapons — some jewellery likely lifted from a living thing. But you said to

listen for talk of glows and hums and look out for strange sights, right? An I ain't heard nothin 'bout that.'

'Keep at it,' I asked.

'Oh, I will. You done me a great service, mister – and I fully intend to repay my debt – thricefold, if it pleases.'

'Thank you, Thomas.'

'Place to sleep and meal to eat is thanks enough. Don't you worry. I'll get you sorted soon.'

He raised his tankard, only to find it was empty, and I laughed, clapped him on the back and watched as he stood and lurched off in search of ale from elsewhere. Then I turned my attention to William, moving over to his lectern and pulling up a chair to sit down beside him. 'How fares your search?'

He frowned up at me. 'Maps and maths aren't cutting it.'

Nothing is ever simple, I rued.

'What of your local contacts?' I asked him, taking a seat opposite.

Thomas had bustled back in, with a tankard of foaming ale in his fist and a red mark on his face from where he'd been very recently slapped, just in time to hear William say, 'We'll need to earn their trust before they'll share what they know.'

'I have an idea on how we might be effectin that,' slurred Thomas, and we turned to look at him with varying degrees of interest, Charles in the way he usually regarded Thomas, with a look as though he'd just trodden in dog mess, William with bemusement, and me with a genuine interest. Thomas, drunk or sober, was a sharper customer than either Charles or William gave him credit for. He went on now: 'There's a man who was taken to enslavin natives. Rescue 'em and they'll owe us.'

Natives, I thought. The Mohawk. Now there was an idea. 'Do you know where they're being held?'

He shook his head. But Charles was leaning forward. 'Benjamin Church will. He's a finder and a fixer – he's also on your list.'

I smiled at him. Good work, I thought. 'And there I was, wondering who we might solicit next.'

ii

Benjamin Church was a doctor, and we found his house easily enough. When there was no answer at his door, Charles wasted no time kicking it down, and we hurried in, only to find that the place had been ransacked. Not only had furniture been upturned and documents spread all over the floor, disrupted during a messy search, but there were also traces of blood on the floor.

We looked at one another. 'It seems we're not the

only ones looking for Mr Church,' I said, with my sword drawn.

'Dammit!' exploded Charles. 'He could be anywhere. What do we do?'

I pointed to a portrait of the good doctor hanging over the mantelpiece. It showed a man in his early twenties, who nonetheless had a distinguished look. 'We find him. Come, I'll show you how.'

And I began telling Charles about the art of surveillance, of blending into your surroundings, disappearing, noticing routines and habits, studying movement around and adapting to it, becoming at one with the environment, becoming part of the scenery.

I realized how much I was enjoying my new role as tutor. As a boy I'd been taught by my father, and then Reginald, and I had always looked forward to my sessions with them – always relished the passing on and imparting of new knowledge – *forbidden* knowledge, the sort you couldn't find in books.

Teaching it to Charles, I wondered if my father and Reginald had felt the way I did now: serene, wise and worldly. I showed him how to ask questions, how to eavesdrop, how to move around the city like a ghost, gathering and processing information. And after that we parted, carried out our investigations individually, then an hour or so later came back together, faces grim.

What we had learnt was that Benjamin Church had

been seen in the company of other men – three or four of them – who had been bearing him away from his house. Some of the witnesses had assumed Benjamin was drunk; others had noticed how bruised and bloodied he had been. One man who went to his aid had received a knife in his guts as thanks. Wherever they were going, it was clear that Benjamin was in trouble, but where were they going? The answer came from a herald, who stood shouting out the day's news.

'Have you seen this man?' I asked him.

'It difficult to say . . .' He shook his head. 'So many people pass through the square, it's hard to . . .'

I pressed some coins into his hand and his demeanour changed at once. He leaned forward with a conspiratorial air: 'He was being taken to the waterfront warehouses just east of here.'

'Thank you kindly for your help,' I told him.

'But hurry,' he said. 'He was with Silas's men. Such meetings tended to end poorly.'

Silas, I thought, as we weaved our way through the streets on our way to the warehouse district. Now, who was Silas?

The crowds had thinned considerably by the time we reached our destination, well away from the main thoroughfare, where a faint smell of fish seemed to hang over the day. The warehouse sat in a row of similar buildings, all of them huge and exuding a sense of erosion and disrepair, and I might have walked straight past if it hadn't been for the guard who lounged out-side the main doors. He sat on one barrel, his feet up on another, chewing, not as alert as he should have been, so that it was easy enough to stop Charles and pull him to the side of the building before we were spotted.

There was an entrance on the wall closest to us, and I checked it was unguarded before trying the door. Locked. From inside we heard the sounds of a strug-gle then an agonized scream. I'm not a gambling man, but I would have bet on the owner of that agonized scream: Benjamin Church. Charles and I looked at each other. We had to get in there, and fast. Craning around the side of the warehouse, I took another look at the guard, saw the telltale flash of a key ring at his waist, and knew what I had to do.

I waited until a man pushing a barrow had passed then, with a finger to my lips, told Charles to wait and emerged from cover, weaving a little as I came around to the front of the building, looking to all intents and purposes as though I'd had too much to drink.

Sitting on his barrel, the sentry looked sideways at me, his lip curled. He began to withdraw his sword from its sheath, showing a little of its gleaming blade. Staggering, I straightened, held up a hand to acknow-ledge the warning and made as though to move away, before stumbling a little and brushing into him.

'Oi!' he protested, and shoved me away, so hard that

I lost my footing and fell into the street. I picked myself up and, with another wave of apology, was on my way.

What he didn't know was that I left in possession of the key ring, which I had lifted from his waist. Back at the side of the warehouse we tried a couple of the keys before, to our great relief, finding one that opened the door. Wincing at every phantom creak and squeak, we eased it open then crept through, into the dark and damp-smelling warehouse.

Inside, we crouched by the door, slowly adjusting to our new surroundings: a vast space, most of it in darkness. Black, echoing hollows seemed to stretch back into infinity, the only light coming from three braziers which had been set out in the middle of the room. We saw, at last, the man we had been looking for, the man from the portrait: Dr Benjamin Church. He sat tied to a chair, a guard on either side of him, one of his eyes purple and bruised, his head lolling and blood dripping steadily from a gashed lip to the dirty white scarf he wore.

Standing in front of him was a sharp-dressed man – Silas, no doubt – and a companion, who was sharpening a knife. The soft swooshing sound it made was almost gentle, hypnotic, and for a moment was the only noise in the room.

'Why must you always make things so difficult, Benjamin?' asked Silas, with an air of theatrical sadness.

He had an English accent, I realized, and sounded high-born. He continued: 'Merely provide me with recompense and all shall be forgiven.'

Benjamin regarded him with an injured but defiant gaze. 'I'll not pay for protection I don't need,' he snapped back, undaunted.

Silas smiled and airily waved a hand around at the dank, wet and dirty warehouse. 'Clearly, you do require protection, else we wouldn't be here.'

Benjamin turned his head and spat a gobbet of blood, which slapped to the stone floor, then turned his eyes back to Silas, who wore a look as though Benjamin had passed wind at dinner. 'How very gauche,' he said. 'Now, what shall we do about our guest?'

The man sharpening the knives looked up. This was his cue. 'Maybe I take his hands,' he rasped. 'Put an end to 'is surgerin? Maybe I take 'is tongue. Put an end to 'is wagglin? Or maybe I take 'is cock. Put an end to 'is fuckin us.'

A tremor seemed to go through the men, of disgust, fear and amusement. Silas reacted: 'So many options, I can't possibly decide.' He looked at the knifeman and pretended to be lost in indecision, then added, 'Take all three.'

'Now hold on a moment,' said Benjamin quickly. 'Perhaps I was hasty in refusing you earlier.'

'I'm so very sorry, Benjamin, but that door has closed,' said Silas sadly.

'Be reasonable . . .' started Benjamin, a pleading note in his voice.

Silas tilted his head to one side, and his eyebrows knitted together in false concern. 'I rather think I was. But you took advantage of my generosity. I won't be made a fool of a second time.'

The torturer moved forward, holding the knife-point up to his own eyeball, bugging his eyes and grinning maniacally.

'I fear I lack the constitution to bear witness to such barbarism,' said Silas, with the air of an easily offended old woman. 'Come and find me when you've finished, Cutter.'

Silas went to leave as Benjamin Church screamed, 'You'll regret this, Silas! You hear me? I'll have your head!'

At the door Silas stopped, turned and looked at him. 'No,' he said with the beginnings of a giggle. 'No, I rather think you won't.'

Then Benjamin's screams began as Cutter began his work, snickering slightly as he began to wield the knife like an artist making his first painterly strokes, as though at the outset of a much larger project. Poor old Dr Church was the canvas and Cutter was painting his masterpiece.

I whispered to Charles what needed to be done, and he moved away, scuttling through the dark to the rear of the warehouse, where I saw him put a hand to his mouth to call, 'Over here, y' bastards,' then immediately move away, quick and silent.

Cutter's head jerked up, and he waved the two guards over, glancing warily around the warehouse at the same time as his men drew their swords and moved carefully towards the back, where the noise had come from – even as there was another call, this time from a different pocket of blackness, an almost whispered, 'Over here.'

The two guards swallowed, exchanged a nervous glance, while Cutter's gaze roamed the shadows of the building, his jaw set, half in fear, half in frustration. I could see his mind working: was it his own men playing a prank? Kids messing about?

No. It was enemy action.

'What's going on?' snarled one of the heavies. Both craned their necks to stare into the dark spaces of the warehouse. 'Get a torch,' the first snapped at his companion, and the second man darted back into the middle of the room, gingerly lifted one of the braziers, and then was bent over with the weight of it as he tried to move it over.

Suddenly there was a yelp from within the shadows and Cutter was shouting: 'What? What the hell is going on?'

The man with the brazier set it down then peered into the gloom. 'It's Greg,' he called back over his shoulder. 'He ain't there no more, boss.'

Cutter bridled. 'What do you mean, "he ain't there"? He was there before.'

'Greg!' called the second man. 'Greg?'

There was no reply. 'I'm telling you, boss, he ain't there no more.' And just at that moment, as though to emphasize the point, a sword came flying from the dark recesses, skittered across the stone floor and stopped to rest by Cutter's feet.

The blade was stained with blood.

'That's Greg's sword,' said the first man nervily. 'They got Greg.'

'Who got Greg?' snapped Cutter.

'I don't know, but they got him.'

'Whoever you are, you better show your face,' shouted Cutter. His eyes darted to Benjamin, and I could see his brain working, the conclusion he came to: that they were being attacked by friends of the doctor; that it was a rescue operation. The first thug remained where he was by the safety of the brazier, the tip of his sword glinting in the firelight as he trembled. Charles stayed in the shadows, a silent menace. I knew it was only Charles, but to Cutter and his pal he was an avenging demon, as silent and implacable as death itself.

'You better get out here, before I finish your buddy,' rasped Cutter. He moved closer to Benjamin, about to hold the blade to his throat, and, his back to me, I saw my chance and crept out of my hiding place, stealthily moving towards him. At the same time, his pal turned, saw me, yelped, 'Boss, behind you!' and Cutter wheeled.

I leapt and at the same time engaged the hidden blade. Cutter panicked, and I saw his knife hand tauten, about to finish Benjamin. At full stretch I managed to knock his hand away and send him flying back, but I too was off balance and he had the chance to draw his sword and meet me one on one, sword in one hand, torture knife in the other.

Over his shoulder I saw that Charles hadn't wasted his opportunity, had come flying out at the guard, and there was the chime of steel as their blades met. In seconds Cutter and I were fighting, too, but it swiftly became clear he was out of his depth. Good with a knife he may have been, but he wasn't used to opponents who fought back; he was a torture master not a warrior. And while his hands moved quickly and his blades flicked across my vision, all he showed me were tricks, sleight of hand, moves that might terrify a man tied to a chair, but not me. What I saw was a sadist – a frightened sadist. And if there's one thing more loathsome and pathetic than a sadist, it's a frightened one.

He had no anticipation. No footwork or defensive skills. Behind him, the fight was over: the second thug dropped to his knees with a groan, and Charles planted a foot to his chest and withdrew his sword, letting him fall to the stone.

Cutter saw it, too, and I let him watch, stood back

and allowed him to see his companion, the last of his protection, die. There was a thumping on the door – the guard from outside had at last discovered the theft of his keys and was trying and failing to get in. Cutter's eyes swivelled in that direction, looking for salvation. Finding none. Those frightened eyes came back to me and I grinned then moved forward and began some cutting of my own. I took no pleasure in it. I merely gave him the treatment he deserved, and when he at last folded to the floor with a bright-red gash open in his throat and blood sheeting down his front, I felt nothing besides a detached sense of gratification, of justice having been served. No one else would suffer by his blade.

I'd forgotten about the banging at the door until it stopped, and in the sudden silence I glanced at Charles, who came to the same conclusion I did: the guard had gone for help. Benjamin groaned and I went to him, sliced through his bindings with two slashes of my blade then caught him as he fell forward from the chair.

Straight away my hands were slick with his blood, but he seemed to be breathing steadily and, though his eyes occasionally squeezed shut as he flinched with pain, they were open. He'd live. His wounds were painful but they weren't deep.

He looked at me. 'Who ... who are you?' he managed.

I tipped my hat. 'Haytham Kenway at your service.'

There were the beginnings of a smile on his face as he said, 'Thank you. Thank you. But . . . I don't understand . . . why are you here?'

'You are a Templar knight, are you not?' I said to him.

He nodded.

'As am I, and we don't make a habit of leaving fellow knights at the mercy of knife-wielding madmen. That, and the fact I need your help.'

'You have it,' he said. 'Just tell me what you need . . .'

I helped him to his feet and waved Charles over. Together we helped him to the side door of the warehouse and let ourselves out, savouring the cool, fresh air after the dank smell of blood and death inside.

And as we began to make our way back to Union Street and the sanctuary of the Green Dragon, I told Dr Benjamin Church about the list.

13 July 1754

i

We were gathered in the Green Dragon, beneath the low, dark beams of the back room that we now called our own, and which we were rapidly expanding to fill, stuffing ourselves into the dusty eaves: Thomas, who liked to lounge in a horizontal position whenever he wasn't hoisting tankards of ale or bothering our hosts for more; William, whose frown lines deepened as he laboured over charts and maps spread out over a table, moving from that to his lectern and occasionally letting out a frustrated gasp, waving Thomas and his ale-slopping tankard away whenever he lurched too close; Charles, my right-hand man, who took a seat beside me whenever I was in the room, and whose devotion I felt sometimes as a burden, at other times as a great source of strength; and now, of course, Dr Church, who had spent the last couple of days recuperating from his injuries in a bed that had been begrudgingly provided for him by Cornelius. We had left Benjamin to it; he had dressed his own wounds, and when he at last rose, he assured us that none of the injuries to his face were likely to be permanent.

I had spoken to him two days before, when I interrupted him in the process of dressing the worst of his wounds, certainly the most painful-looking: a flap of skin that Cutter had removed.

'So, a question for you,' I said, still feeling I hadn't quite got the measure of the man: 'Why medicine?'

He smiled grimly. 'I'm supposed to tell you I care for my fellow man, right? That I chose this path because it allows me to accomplish a greater good?'

'Are these things not true?'

'Perhaps. But that's not what guided me. No . . . for me it was a less abstract thing: I like money.'

'There are other paths to fortune,' I said.

'Aye. But what better ware to peddle than *life*? Nothing else is as precious – nor so desperately craved. And no price is too great for the man or woman who fears an abrupt and permanent end.'

I winced. 'Your words are cruel, Benjamin.'

'But true as well.'

Confused, I asked, 'You took an oath to help people, did you not?'

'I abide by the oath, which makes no mention of price. I merely require compensation – fair compensation – for my services.'

'And if they lack the required funds?'

'Then there are others who will serve them. Does a

baker grant free bread to a beggar? Does the tailor offer a dress to the woman who cannot afford to pay? No. Why should I?'

'You said it yourself,' I said: 'Nothing is more precious than life.'

'Indeed. All the more reason one should ensure one has the means to preserve it.'

I looked at him askance. He was a young man – younger than me. I wondered, had I been like him once?

ii

Later, my thoughts returned to matters most pressing. Silas would want revenge for what had happened at the warehouse, we all knew that; and it was just a matter of time before he struck at us. We were in the Green Dragon, perhaps the most visible spot in the city, so he knew where we were when he wanted to launch his strike. In the meantime, I had enough experienced swordsmen to give him pause for thought and I wasn't minded to run or go into hiding.

William had told Benjamin what we were planning – to curry favour with the Mohawk by going up against the slaver – and Benjamin leaned forward now. 'Johnson has told me what you intend,' he said. 'As it happens, the man who held me is the same one you seek. His name is Silas Thatcher.'

Inwardly, I cursed myself for not having made the connection. Of course. Beside me, the penny had dropped with Charles, too.

'That fancy lad is a slaver?' he said disbelievingly.

'Don't let his velvet tongue deceive you,' said Benjamin, nodding. 'A crueller and more vicious creature I've never known.'

'What can you tell me of his operation?' I asked.

'He hosts at least a hundred men, more than half of whom are redcoats.'

'All of this for some slaves?'

At this Benjamin laughed. 'Hardly. The man is a commander in the King's Troop, in charge of the Southgate Fort.'

Perplexed, I said, 'But if Britain stands any chance of pushing back the French, she must *ally* with the natives – not enslave them.'

'Silas is loyal only to his purse,' said William from his lectern perch. 'That his actions harm the Crown is irrelevant. So long as there are buyers for his product, he'll continue to procure it.'

'All the more reason to stop him, then,' I said grimly.

'My days are spent in congress with the locals – attempting to convince them that we're the ones they should trust,' added William; 'that the French are merely using them as tools, to be abandoned once they've won.'

'Your words must lose their strength when held against the reality of Silas's actions.' I sighed.

'I've tried to explain that he does not represent us,' he said with a rueful look. 'But he wears the red coat. He commands a fort. I must appear to them either a liar or a fool . . . Likely both.'

'Take heart, brother,' I assured him. 'When we deliver them his head, they will know your words were true. Firstly, we need to find a way inside the fort. Let me think on it. In the meantime, I'll attend to our final recruit.'

At this, Charles perked up. 'John Pitcairn's our man. I'll take you to him.'

iii

We found ourselves at a military encampment outside the city, where redcoats diligently checked those entering and leaving. These were Braddock's men, and I wondered if I'd recognize any from my campaigns all those years ago.

I doubted it; his regime was too brutal, his men mercenaries, ex-convicts, men on the run who never stayed in one place for long. One stepped forward now, looking unshaven and shabby despite his redcoat uniform.

'State your business,' he said, as his eyes ranged over us, not much liking what he saw.

I was about to answer when Charles stepped forward, indicated me and said to the guard, 'New recruit.'

The sentry stood to one side. 'More kindling for the pyre, eh?' he smirked. 'Go on then.'

We moved through the gates into the camp.

'How did you manage that?' I said to Charles.

'Did you forget, sir? My commission is with General Braddock – when I'm not attending to you, of course.'

A cart on its way out of the camp trundled past, led by a man in a wide-brimmed hat, and we stepped aside for a group of washerwomen who crossed our path. Tents were dotted around the site, over which hung a low blanket of smoke from fires around the campsite, tended to by men and children, camp followers whose job it was to brew coffee and make food for their imperial masters. Washing hung on lines stretched from canopies at the front of the tents; civilians loaded crates of supplies on to wooden carts, watched over by officers on horseback. We saw a knot of troops struggling with a cannon stuck in the mud and more men stacking crates, while in the main square was a troop of twenty or thirty redcoats being put through its paces by an officer screaming barely intelligibly.

Looking around, it struck me that the camp was unmistakably the work of the Braddock I knew: busy and ordered, a hive of industry, a crucible of discipline. Any visitor would have thought it a credit to the British Army and to its commander, but if you looked harder, or if you knew Braddock of old, as I did, you could sense the resentment that pervaded the place: the men gave off a begrudging air about their activities. They worked not out of a sense of pride in their uniform but under the yoke of brutality.

Talking of which ... We were approaching a tent and, as we grew closer to it, I heard, with a crawling and deeply unpleasant sensation in the pit of my stomach, that the voice I could hear shouting belonged to Braddock.

When was the last time I'd seen him? Several years ago, when I'd left the Coldstreams, and never had I been so pleased to turn my back on a man as I had been with Braddock that day. I'd departed the company swearing I would do my utmost to see to it that he answered for the crimes I'd witnessed during my time with him – crimes of cruelty and brutality. But I'd reckoned without the ties that bind the Order; I'd reckoned without Reginald's unswerving loyalty to him; and, in the end, I'd had to accept that Braddock was going to continue as he always had. I didn't like it. But I had to accept it. The answer was simply to steer clear of him.

Right now, though, I couldn't avoid him.

He was inside his tent as we entered, in the middle of lecturing a man who was about my age, dressed in civilian clothes but obviously a military man. This was John Pitcairn. He was standing there, taking the full blast of Braddock's rage – a rage I knew so well – as the general screamed: '... were you planning to announce yourself? Or did you hope my men wouldn't notice your arrival?'

I liked him immediately. I liked the unblinking way he responded, his Scots accent measured and calm, unintimidated by Braddock as he replied, 'Sir, if you'd allow me to explain ...'

Time had not been kind to Braddock, though. His face was ruddier than ever, his hair receding. He became even more red-faced now, as he replied, 'Oh, by all means. I should like very much to hear this.'

'I have not deserted, sir,' protested Pitcairn, 'I am here under Commander Amherst's orders.'

But Braddock was in no mood to be impressed by the name of Commander Jeffrey Amherst; and, if anything, his mood darkened.

'Show me a letter bearing his seal and you might be spared the gallows,' he snarled.

'I have no such thing,' replied Pitcairn, swallowing – the only sign of nerves he'd shown; perhaps thinking of the noose tightening around his neck – 'the nature of my work, sir ... it's ...'

Braddock reared back as though bored of the whole facade – and might well have been about to order Pitcairn's summary execution – when I took the opportunity to step forward.

'It's not the sort of thing best put to paper,' I said.

Braddock turned to look at me with a jerky movement, seeing Charles and I there for the first time and taking us in with varying degrees of irritation. Charles, he didn't mind so much. Me? Put it this way: the antipathy was mutual.

'Haytham,' he said simply, my name like a swear word on his lips.

'*General* Braddock,' I returned, without bothering to hide my distaste for his new rank.

He looked from me to Pitcairn and, perhaps, at last, made the connection. 'I suppose I shouldn't be surprised. Wolves often travel in packs.'

'Master Pitcairn won't be here for a few weeks,' I told him, 'and I shall return him to his proper post once our work is finished.'

Braddock shook his head. I did my best to hide my smile and succeeded, mainly, in keeping my glee internal. He was furious, not only that his authority had been undermined but, worse, that it had been undermined by me.

'The devil's work, no doubt,' he said. 'It's bad enough my superiors have insisted I grant you use of Charles. But they said nothing about this traitor. You will not have him.'

I sighed. 'Edward . . .' I began.

But Braddock was signalling to his men. 'We are done here. See these gentlemen out,' he said.

'Well, that didn't go as I expected,' sighed Charles.

We were once again outside the walls, with the camp behind us and Boston ahead of us, stretching away to glittering sea on the horizon, the masts and sails of boats in the harbour. At a pump in the shade of a cherry tree, we stopped and leaned on the wall, from where we could watch the comings and goings at the camp without attracting attention.

'And, to think, I used to call Edward a brother . . .' I said ruefully.

It had been a long time ago now, and difficult to recall, but it was true. There was a time when I'd looked up to Braddock, thought of him and Reginald as my friends and confederates. Now, I actively despised Braddock. And Reginald?

I still wasn't sure about him.

'What now?' asked Charles. 'They'll chase us off if we try and return.'

Gazing into the camp, I could see Braddock striding out of his tent, shouting as usual, gesticulating at an officer – one of his hand-picked mercenaries, no doubt – who came scuttling over. In his wake came John. He was still alive, at least; Braddock's temper had been either abated or directed somewhere else. Towards me, probably.

As we watched, the officer gathered the troops we'd seen drilling on the barracks square and organized them into a patrol, then, with Braddock at their head, began leading them out of the camp. Other troops and followers scurried out of their way, and the gate, which had previously been thronged with people, promptly cleared to allow the marchers through. They passed us by, a hundred yards or so away, and we watched them between the low-hanging branches of the cherry tree, as they made their way down the hill and towards the outskirts of the city, proudly bearing the Union flag.

A strange kind of peace descended in their wake, and I pushed myself off the wall and said to Charles, 'Come along.'

We stayed more than two hundred yards behind, and even then we could hear the sound of Braddock's voice, which, if anything, began to increase in volume as we made our way into the city. Even on the move he had the air of someone who was holding court, but what quickly became clear was that this was a recruitment mission. Braddock began by approaching a blacksmith, ordering the squad to watch and learn. All signs of his former fury were gone and he wore a warm smile to address the man, more in the manner of a concerned uncle than of the heartless tyrant he really was.

'You seem in low spirits, my friend,' he said, heartily. 'What's wrong?'

Charles and I stayed some distance away. Charles in particular kept his head low and remained out of sight, from fear of being recognized. I strained my ears to hear the blacksmith's reply.

'Business has been poor as of late,' he said. 'I have lost my stall and wares both.'

Braddock threw up his hands as though this were an easily solved problem, because . . .

'What if I told you I could wipe your troubles away?' he said.

'I'd be wary, for one –'

'Fair enough! But hear me out. The French and their savage companions lay waste to the countryside. The king has commissioned men such as me to raise an army that we might force them back. Join my expedition, and you will be richly compensated. Just a few weeks of your time, and you'll return loaded with coin and able to open a new store – bigger and better!'

As they were talking, I noticed officers ordering members of the patrol to approach other citizens and start the same patter. Meanwhile, the blacksmith was saying, 'Truly?'

Braddock was already handing him commission papers, which he'd fished from his jacket.

'See for yourself,' he said proudly, as though he were handing the man gold, rather than papers to enlist in the most brutal and dehumanizing army I had ever known.

'I'll do it,' said the poor, gullible blacksmith. 'Only tell me where to sign!'

Braddock walked on, leading us to a public square, where he stood to deliver a short speech, and more of his men began wandering off.

'Hear me out, good people of Boston,' he announced, in the tone of an avuncular gent about to impart great news. 'The king's army has need of strong and loyal men. Dark forces gather to the north, desirous of our land and its great bounty. I come before you today with a request: if you value your possessions, your families, your very lives – then join us. Take up arms in service to God and country both, that we might defend all we have created here.'

Some of the townspeople shrugged their shoulders and moved on; others conferred with their friends. Still others approached the redcoats, presumably keen to lend their services – and earn some money. I couldn't help but notice a definite correlation between how poor they looked and how likely they were to be moved by Braddock's speech.

Sure enough, I overheard him talking to his officer. 'Where shall we head next?'

'Perhaps down to Marlborough?' replied the trusty lieutenant, who, though he was too far away for me to see properly, had a familiar-sounding voice.

'No,' replied Braddock, 'its residents are too content. Their homes are nice; their days untroubled.'

'What of Lyn or Ship Street?'

'Yes. Those fresh arrived are often soon in dire straits. They're more likely to seize upon an opportunity to fatten their purses and feed their young.'

Not far away stood John Pitcairn. I wanted to get closer to him. Looking at the surrounding redcoats, I realized that what I needed was a uniform.

Pity the poor soul who peeled off from the group to relieve himself. It was Braddock's lieutenant. He sauntered away from the group, shouldered his way past two well-dressed women in bonnets and snarled when they tutted his way – doing a great job of winning local hearts and minds in the name of His Majesty.

At a distance, I followed, until he came to the end of the street, where there was a squat wooden building, a storehouse of some kind, and, with a glance to make sure he wasn't being watched, he leaned his musket against the timber then undid the buttons of his britches to have a piss.

Of course, he *was* being watched. By me. Checking to see there were no other redcoats nearby, I drew close, wrinkling my nose at the acrid stench; many a redcoat had relieved himself in this particular spot, it seemed. Then I engaged my blade with a soft *chk*, which he heard, tensing slightly as he pissed, but not turning.

'Whoever that is, he better have a good reason for standing behind me when I'm having a piss,' he said, shaking then putting his cock back in his britches. And

I recognized his voice. It was the executioner. It was . . .

'Slater,' I said.

'That's my name: don't wear it out. And who might you be?'

He was pretending to have trouble with his buttons, but I could see his right hand straying towards the hilt of his sword.

'You might remember me. My name is Haytham Kenway.'

Again he tensed, and his head straightened. 'Haytham Kenway,' he rasped. 'Indeed – now there's a name to conjure with, so it is. I had hoped I'd seen the last of you.'

'And me of you. Turn around, please.'

A horse and cart passed in the mud as, slowly, Slater turned to face me, his eyes going to the blade at my wrist. 'You an Assassin now, are ya?' he sneered.

'A Templar, Slater, like your boss.'

He sneered. 'Your lot have no attraction for General Braddock any more.'

Just as I'd suspected. That was why he'd been trying to sabotage my efforts to recruit a team for Reginald's mission. Braddock had turned against us.

'Go for your sword,' I told Slater.

His eyes flickered. 'You'll run me through if I do.'

I nodded. 'I can't kill you in cold blood. I'm not your general.'

'No,' he said, 'you're a fraction of the man he is.'

And he went for his sword . . .

A second later the man who had once tried to hang me, whom I had watched help slaughter a whole family at the Siege of Bergen op Zoom, lay dead at my feet, and I looked down at his still-twitching corpse, thinking only that I needed to take his uniform before he bled all over it.

I took it and rejoined Charles, who looked at me with raised eyebrows. 'Well, you certainly look the part,' he said.

I gave him an ironic smile. 'Now to make Pitcairn aware of our plans. When I give you the signal, you're to cause a fracas. We'll use the distraction to slip away.'

Meanwhile, Braddock was issuing orders. 'All right men, we move,' he said, and I used the opportunity to slip into the ranks of the patrol, keeping my head down. Braddock, I knew, would be concentrating on the recruitment and not on his men; equally, I trusted that the men of the patrol would be so terrified of incurring his wrath that they would also be too concerned with enlisting new men to notice a new face in their ranks. I fell in beside Pitcairn and, my voice low, said, 'Hello again, Jonathan.'

By my side, he started slightly, looked at me and exclaimed, 'Master Kenway?'

I shushed him with a hand and glanced up to ensure we hadn't attracted any unwanted attention before continuing: 'It wasn't easy slipping in . . . but here I am, come to rescue you.'

This time he kept his voice down. 'You don't honestly think we can get away with this?'

I smiled. 'Have you no faith in me?'

'I hardly know you –'

'You know enough.'

'Look,' he whispered, 'I'd very much like to help. But you heard Braddock. If he catches wind of this, you and I are both finished.'

'I'll take care of Braddock,' I reassured him.

He looked at me. 'How?' he asked.

I gave him a look to say I knew exactly what I was doing, put my fingers in my mouth and whistled loudly.

It was the signal Charles had been waiting for, and he came rushing from between two buildings into the street. He'd taken his shirt off and was using it to obscure his face; the rest of his clothes were in disarray, too: he'd used mud on himself so that he looked nothing like the army officer he truly was. He looked, in fact, like a madman, and promptly behaved like one, standing in front of the patrol, which came to a disorganized halt, too surprised or bemused even to raise weapons, as Charles began to shout, 'Oi! You're thieves and scoundrels one and all! You swear the empire will . . . will reward and honour us! But in the end you deliver only death! And for what? Rocks and ice, trees and streams? A few dead Frenchmen? Well, we don't want it! Don't need it! So take your false promises, your dangled purses, your uniforms and guns – take all those things that you hold so dear, and shove them up your arse!'

The redcoats looked at one another, open-mouthed with disbelief, so taken aback that, for a moment, I worried they weren't going to react at all. Even Braddock, who was some distance away, simply stood, his jaw hanging open, not sure whether to be angry or amused by this unexpected outburst of pure lunacy.

Were they simply going to turn around and carry on their way? Perhaps Charles had the same worry, because all of a sudden he added, 'Fie on you and your false war,' then added his crowning touch. He reached, scooped up a piece of horseshit and flung it in the general direction of the group, most of whom turned smartly away. The lucky ones, that was – General Edward Braddock not included.

He stood, with horseshit on his uniform, no longer undecided about whether to be amused or angry. Now he was just angry, and his roar seemed to shake the leaves in the trees: '*After him!*'

Some of the men peeled away from the group and went to grab Charles, who had already turned and was now running, past a general store then left from the street between the store and a tavern.

This was our chance. But instead of seizing it, John merely said, 'Dammit.'

'What's wrong?' I said. 'Now's our chance to escape.'

'I'm afraid not. Your man just led them into a dead end. We need to rescue him.'

Inwardly, I groaned. So it *was* a rescue mission – just not of the man I had intended to rescue. And I, too, went running towards the passageway: only I had no intention of satisfying our noble general's honour; I simply had to keep Charles from harm.

I was too late. By the time I got there he was already under arrest, and I stood back, cursing silently as he was dragged back into the main thoroughfare and brought to stand before a seething General Braddock, who was already reaching for his sword when I decided things had gone too far.

'Unhand him, Edward.'

He turned to me. If it was possible for his face to darken more than it already had, then it did. Around us, breathless redcoats gave each other confused looks, while Charles, held by a redcoat on either side and still shirtless, shot me a grateful look.

'You again!' spat Braddock, furious.

'Did you think I wouldn't return?' I replied equably.

'I'm more surprised about how easily you were unmasked,' he gloated. 'Going soft, it seems.'

I had no wish to trade insults with him. 'Let us go – and John Pitcairn with us,' I said.

'I will not have my authority challenged,' said Braddock

'Nor I.'

His eyes blazed. Had we really lost him? For a moment I pictured myself sitting down with him, showing him the book and watching the transformation come over him, just as it had with me. Could he feel that same sense of suddenly knowing that I had? Could he return to us?

'Put them all in chains,' he snapped.

No, I decided he couldn't.

And, again, I wished for Reginald's presence, because he would have nipped this argument in the bud: he would have prevented what happened next.

Which is that I decided I could take them; and I made my move. In a trice my blade was out and the nearest redcoat died with a look of surprise on his face as I ran him through. Out of the corner of my eye I saw Braddock dart to the side, draw his own sword and yell at another man, who reached for his pistol, already primed. John reached him before I did, his sword flashing down and chopping at the man's wrist, not quite severing the hand but slicing through the bone, so that for a moment his hand flapped at the end of his arm and the pistol fell harmlessly to the ground.

Another trooper came at me from my left and we exchanged blows – one, two, three. I pushed forward until his back was against the wall, and my final thrust was between the straps across his tunic, into his heart.

I wheeled and met a third man, deflected his blow and swept my blade across his midriff, sending him to the dirt. With the back of my hand I wiped blood from my face in time to see John run another man through and Charles, who had snatched a sword from one of his captors, finish the other with a few confident strokes.

Then the fight was over and I faced the last man standing – and the last man standing was General Edward Braddock.

It would have been so easy. So easy to have ended this here. His eyes told me that he knew – he knew that I had it in my heart to kill him. Perhaps, for the first time, he realized that any ties that had once bound us, those of the Templar, or mutual respect for Reginald, no longer existed.

I let the moment hang then dropped my sword. 'I stay my hand today because you were once my brother,' I told him, 'and a better man than this. But should we cross paths again, all debts will be forgotten.'

I turned to John. 'You're free now, John.'

The three of us – me, John and Charles – began to walk away.

'*Traitor!*' called Braddock. 'Go on then. Join them on their fool's errand. And when you find yourself lying broken and dying at the bottom of some dark pit, I pray my words today are the last that you remember.'

And, with that, he strode off, stepping over the

corpses of his men and shouldering his way past bystanders. You were never too far from a redcoat patrol on Boston's streets and, with Braddock able to call on reinforcements, we decided to make ourselves scarce. As he left, I cast my eye over the bodies of the felled redcoats lying in the mud and reflected that, as recruitment drives go, it had not been the most successful afternoon.

No wonder townsfolk gave us a wide berth as we hurried back along the streets towards the Green Dragon. We were mud-splattered and bloodstained, and Charles was struggling back into his clothes. John, meanwhile, was curious to know about my animosity towards Braddock, and I told him about the slaughter at the skiff, finishing by saying, 'Things were never the same after that. We campaigned together a few more times, but each outing was more disturbing than the last. He killed and killed: enemy or ally, civilian or soldier, guilty or innocent – it mattered not. If he perceived someone to be an obstacle, they died. He maintained that violence was a more efficient solution. It became his mantra. And it broke my heart.'

'We should stop him,' said John, glancing behind, as though we might try at once.

'I suppose you're right . . . But I maintain a foolish hope that he might yet be saved and brought back round to reason. I know, I know . . . it's a silly thing, to believe that one so drenched in death might suddenly change.'

Or was it so silly? I wondered, as we walked. After all, hadn't I changed?

14 July 1754

i

By staying at the Green Dragon, we were in the right place to hear of any rumblings against us, and my man Thomas kept his ear to the ground. Not that it was much of a chore for him, of course: listening out for any signs of a plot against us meant supping ale while he eavesdropped on conversations and pressed others for gossip. He was very good at that. He needed to be. We had made enemies: Silas, of course; but, most worryingly, General Edward Braddock.

Last night, I had sat at the desk in my room to write my journal. My hidden blade was on the table beside me, my sword within easy reach in case Braddock launched his inevitable retributive strike straight away, and I knew that this was how it would be from now on: sleeping with one eye open, weapons never far from hand, always looking over our shoulders, every strange face belonging to a potential enemy. Just the thought of it was exhausting, but what other choice was there? According to Slater, Braddock had renounced the Templar order. He was a loose cannon now, and the one thing worse than a loose cannon is a loose cannon with an army at his disposal.

I could at least console myself with knowing that I now had a hand-picked team and, once again, we were assembled in the back room, boosted by the addition of John Pitcairn, a more formidable proposition for either of our two opponents.

As I entered the room, they rose to greet me – even Thomas, who seemed more sober than usual. I cast my eye over them: Benjamin's wounds had healed nicely; John seemed to have cast off the shackles of his commission with Braddock, his preoccupied air replaced by a new lightness of spirit; Charles was still a British Army officer and was worried that Braddock might recall him and, consequently, when not looking down his nose at Thomas wore a concerned look; while William stood at his lectern holding a quill in his hand, still hard at work comparing the markings on the amulet with the book and his own maps and graphs, still perplexed, the telling details still eluding him. I had an idea about that.

I gestured at them to take their seats, and sat among them.

'Gentlemen, I believe I've found the solution to our problem. Or, rather, Odysseus has.'

The mention of the Greek hero's name had a some-what varied effect on my companions and, as William, Charles and Benjamin all nodded sagely, John and

Thomas looked somewhat confused, Thomas being the least self-conscious.

'Odysseus? Is he a new guy?' He belched.

'The Greek hero, you lobcock,' said Charles, disgusted.

'Allow me to explain,' I said. 'We'll enter Silas's fort under the pretence of kinship. Once inside, we spring our trap. Free the captives and kill the slaver.'

I watched as they absorbed my plan. Thomas was the first to speak. 'Dodgy, dodgy,' he grinned. 'I like it.'

'Then let us begin,' I continued. 'First, we need to find ourselves a convoy . . .'

ii

Charles and I were on a rooftop overlooking one of Boston's public squares, both dressed as redcoats.

I looked down at my own uniform. There was still a little of Slater's blood on my brown leather belt and a stain on the white stockings, but otherwise I looked the part; Charles, too, even though he picked at his uniform.

'I'd forgotten how uncomfortable these uniforms are.'

'Necessary, I'm afraid,' I said, 'in order to properly effect our deception.'

I looked at him. He wouldn't have to suffer for long

at least. 'The convoy should be here soon,' I told him. 'We'll attack on my signal.'

'Understood, sir,' replied Charles.

In the square below us an upturned cart blocked the far exit, and two men were huffing and puffing as they tried to turn it the right way up again.

Or *pretending* to huff and puff and turn the cart the right way up, I should say, because the two men were Thomas and Benjamin and the cart had been deliberately tipped over by all four of us a few moments before, strategically placed to block the exit. Not far away from it were John and William, who waited in the shadows of a nearby blacksmith's hut, sitting on upturned buckets with their hats pulled down low over their eyes, a couple of smithies taking a break, lazing the day away, watching the world go by.

The trap was set. I put my spyglass to my eye and looked over the landscape beyond the square, and this time I saw them – the convoy, a squad of nine redcoats making its way towards us. One of them was driving a hay cart and, beside him on the board, was . . .

I adjusted the focus. It was a Mohawk woman – a *beautiful* Mohawk woman, who, despite the fact that she was chained in place wore a proud, defiant expression and sat straight, in marked contrast to the redcoat who sat beside her driving, whose shoulders were hunched and who had a long-stemmed pipe in his mouth. She had a bruise on her face, I realized, and was surprised to feel a surge of anger at the sight of it. I wondered how long ago they'd caught her and how, indeed, they'd managed it. Evidently, she'd put up a fight.

'Sir,' said Charles from by my side, prompting me, 'hadn't you better give the signal?'

I cleared my throat. 'Of course, Charles,' I said, and put my fingers in my mouth and gave a low whistle, watching as my comrades below exchanged 'Ready' signals, and Thomas and Benjamin kept up the pretence of trying to upturn the cart.

We waited – we waited until the redcoats marched into the square and found the cart blocking their way.

'What the hell is this?' said one of the front guards.

'A thousand pardons, sirs – seems we've had ourselves an unhappy little accident,' said Thomas, with open hands and an ingratiating smile.

The lead redcoat took note of Thomas's accent and at once assumed a contemptuous look. He went a shade of purple, not quite angry enough to match the colour of his tunic, but deep enough.

'Get it sorted – and quickly,' he snapped, and Thomas touched a servile hand to his forelock before turning back to help Benjamin with the cart.

''Course, milord, at once,' he said.

Charles and I, now on our bellies, watched. John and William sat with their faces hidden but they, too, watched the scene as the redcoats, rather than simply marching around the cart or even – God forbid – helping Thomas and Benjamin to put the cart straight, stood and looked on as the lead guard became more and more furious, until his temper finally snapped.

'Look – either get your cart right, or we're riding through it.'

'Please, don't.' I saw Thomas's eyes dart up to the rooftop where we lay, then across to where William and John sat ready, their hands now on the hilts of their swords, and he spoke the action phrase, which was 'We're nearly finished.'

In one movement Benjamin had drawn his sword and run through the nearest man, while, before the lead guard had a chance to react, Thomas had done the same, a dagger appearing from within his sleeve which was just as quickly embedded into the lead guard's eye.

At the same time, William and John burst from cover, and three men fell beneath their blades, while Charles and I jumped from above, catching those nearest by surprise: four men died. We didn't even give them the dignity of breathing their last breath with dignity. Worried about getting their clothes stained with blood, we were already stripping the dying men of their uniforms. In moments we had pulled the bodies into some stables, shut and bolted the door and we then stood in the square, six redcoats who had taken the place of nine. A new convoy.

I looked around. The square had not been busy before, but now it was deserted. We had no idea who might have been a witness to the ambush – colonials who hated the British and were glad to see them fall? British Army sympathizers who even now were on their way to Southgate Fort to warn Silas about what had happened? We had no time to lose.

I jumped into the driver's seat, and the Mohawk woman pulled away slightly – as far as her manacles would allow, anyway – and gave me a wary but mutinous look.

'We're here to help you,' I tried to reassure her. 'Along with those held within Southgate Fort.'

'Free me then,' she said.

Regretfully, I told her, 'Not until we're inside. I can't chance an inspection at the gate going wrong,' and was rewarded with a disgusted look, as though to say it was just as she'd expected.

'I'll see you safe,' I insisted, 'you have my word.' I shook the reins and the horses began to move, my men walking either side of me.

'Do you know anything of Silas's operation?' I asked the Mohawk woman. 'How many men we might expect? The nature of their defences?'

But she said nothing. 'You must be pretty important to him if you were given your own escort,' I pressed, and still she ignored me. 'I wish you'd trust us . . . though I suppose it's only natural for you to be wary. So be it.' When she still didn't answer, I realized my words were wasted, and decided to shut up.

When at last we reached the gates, a guard stepped forward. 'Hold,' he said.

I tightened the reins and we drew to a stop, me and my redcoats. Looking past the prisoner, I tipped my hat to the guards: 'Evening, gentlemen.'

The sentry was in no mood for pleasantries, I could tell. 'State your business,' he said flatly, staring at the Mohawk woman with interested, lustful eyes. She returned his stare with a venomous look of her own.

For a moment I mused that when I'd first arrived in Boston I'd wanted to see what changes British rule had wrought on this country, what effect our governance had had on its people. For the native Mohawk, it was clear to see that any effect had not been for the good. We talked piously of saving this land; instead, we were corrupting it.

I indicated the woman now. 'Delivery for Silas,' I said, and the guard nodded, licked his lips then rapped on the door for it to open, for us to trundle slowly forward. Inside, the fort was quiet. We found ourselves near to the battlements, low dark-stone walls where cannons were ranged to look out over Boston, towards the sea, and redcoats with muskets slung over their shoulders patrolled back and forth. The focus of their attention was outside the walls; they feared an attack from the French and, looking down from their battlements, hardly gave us a second glance as we trundled in on our cart and, trying to look as casual as possible, made our way to a secluded section, where the first thing I did was to cut the woman free.

'See? I'm freeing you, just as I said I would. Now, if you'll allow me to explain . . .'

But her answer was no. With a final glare at me she had leapt from the cart and disappeared into the darkness, leaving me to stare after her with the distinct feeling of unfinished business; wanting to explain myself to her; wanting to spend more time with her.

Thomas went to go after her, but I stopped him. 'Let her go,' I said.

'But she'll give us away,' he protested.

I looked at where she had been – already she was a memory, a ghost. 'No, she won't,' I said, and got down, casting a look around to make sure we were alone in the quadrangle then gathering the others to give them their orders: free the captives and avoid detection. They nodded grimly, each of them committed to the task.

'What of Silas?' asked Benjamin.

I thought of the snickering man I had seen at the warehouse, who had left Benjamin to the mercy of Cutter. I remembered Benjamin's pledge to have his head, and looked at my friend now. 'He dies,' I said.

I watched as the men melted away into the night, and decided to keep a close watch on Charles, my pupil. And saw as he approached a group of redcoats and introduced himself. I glanced across the quadrangle to see that Thomas had inveigled himself with another of the patrols. William and John, meanwhile, were walking casually in the direction of a building I thought was probably the stockade, where the prisoners were kept, where a guard was even now shifting and moving to block their way. I looked to check that the other guards were being kept occupied by Charles and Thomas and, when I was satisfied, gave John a surreptitious thumbs-up then saw him exchange a quick word with William as they came to the guard.

'Can I help you?' I heard the guard say, his voice drifting over the quad just as John kneed him in the bollocks. With a low groan like an animal in a trap, he dropped his pikestaff and fell to his knees. Straight away John was feeling at his waist and retrieving a key ring then, with his back to the quad, he opened the door, grabbed a torch from a bracket outside and disappeared inside.

I glanced around. None of the guards had seen what was going on at the stockade. Those on the battlements were diligently staring out to sea; those inside had their attention diverted by Charles and Thomas.

Looking back at the door of the stockade, I saw John reappear then usher out the first of the prisoners.

And suddenly one of the troops on the battlements

saw what was happening. 'Oi, you there, what's your game?' he shouted, already levelling his musket, and the cry went up. Immediately I dashed over to the battlements, where the first redcoat was about to pull the trigger, bounded up the stone steps and was upon him, thrusting my blade under his jaw in one clean move. I dropped into a crouch and let his body fall over me, springing from beneath it to spear the next guard in his heart. A third man had his back to me, drawing a bead on William, but I whipped my blade across the backs of his legs then delivered the *coup de grâce* to the back of his neck when he fell. Not far away, William thanked me with a raised hand then turned to meet another guard. His sword swung as a redcoat fell beneath the blade, and when he turned to meet a second man his face was stained with blood.

In moments, all of the guards were dead, but the door to one of the outbuildings had opened and Silas had appeared, already angry. 'An hour of quiet was all I asked,' he roared. 'Instead I'm awakened not ten minutes later by this cacophonous madness. I expect an explanation – and it had best be good.'

He was stopped in his tracks, his outburst dying on his lips as the colour drained from his face. All around the quad were the bodies of his men, and his head jerked as he looked across to the stockade, where the door hung open, natives pouring out and John urging them to move more quickly.

Silas drew his sword as more men appeared from behind him. 'How?' he shrieked. 'How did this happen? My precious merchandise set free. It's unacceptable. Rest assured, I'll have the heads of those responsible. But first . . . first we clean up this mess.'

His guards were pulling on tunics, strapping swords to their waists, priming muskets. The quadrangle, empty but for corpses a moment ago, was suddenly filled with more troops, eager for retribution. Silas was beside himself, screaming at them, frantically waving at the troops to take up their arms, calming himself as he continued: 'Seal the fort. Kill any who try to escape. I don't care if they be one of us or one of . . . *them*. To approach the gate is to be made a corpse! Am I understood?'

The fighting continued. Charles, Thomas, William, John and Benjamin moved among the men and made the most of their disguises. The men they attacked were reduced to fighting among themselves, not sure which man in an army uniform was friend and which an enemy. The natives, unarmed, sheltered to wait the fighting out, even as a group of Silas's redcoats formed a line at the entrance to the fort. I saw my chance – Silas had positioned himself to one side of his troops and was exhorting them to be ruthless. Silas, it was clear, did not care who died as long as his precious 'merchandise' was not allowed to escape, as long as his pride was not damaged in the process.

I motioned to Benjamin, and we moved up close to Silas, saw that he had spotted us out of the corner of his eye. For a moment I could see the confusion play across his features, until he realized that, firstly, we were two of the interlopers and, secondly, he had no means of escape, as we stood blocking him from reaching the rest of his men. To all intents and purposes we looked like a pair of loyal bodyguards keeping him from harm.

'You don't know me,' I told him, 'but I believe the two of you are well acquainted . . .' I said, and Benjamin Church stepped forward.

'I made a promise to you, Silas,' said Benjamin, 'one I intend to keep . . .'

It was over in seconds. Benjamin was far more merciful with Silas than Cutter had been with him. With their leader dead, the fort's defence broke up, the gates opened and we allowed the rest of the redcoats to pour out. Behind them came the Mohawk prisoners, and I saw the woman from earlier. Rather than escaping, she'd stayed to help her people: She was courageous as well as beautiful and spirited. As she helped members of her tribe away from the accursed fort, our eyes met, and I found myself entranced by her. And then she was gone.

15 November 1754

i

It was freezing, and snow covered the ground all around us as we set off early this morning and rode towards Lexington in pursuit of . . .

Perhaps 'obsession' is too strong a word. 'Preoccupation', then: my 'preoccupation' with the Mohawk woman, from the cart. Specifically, with finding her.

Why?

If Charles had asked me, I'd have told him that I wanted to find her because I knew her English was good and I thought she would be a useful contact within the Mohawk to help locate the precursor site.

That's what I would have said if Charles had asked me why I wanted to find her, and it would have been partly the truth. *Partly*.

Anyway, Charles and I took one of my expeditions, this one out to Lexington, when he said, 'I'm afraid I have some bad news, sir.'

'What is it, Charles?'

'Braddock's insisting I return to service under him. I've tried to beg off, to no avail,' he said sadly.

'No doubt he's still angry about losing John – to say nothing of the shaming we gave him,' I responded thoughtfully, wondering if I could have finished it then, when I had the chance. 'Do as he asks. In the meantime, I'll work on having you released.'

How? I wasn't sure. After all, there was a time when I could have relied on a stiff letter from Reginald to change Braddock's mind, but it had become clear that Braddock no longer had any affinity with our ways.

'I'm sorry to trouble you,' said Charles.

'Not your fault,' I replied.

I was going to miss him. After all, he had already done a lot to locate my mystery woman, who, according to him, was to be found outside Boston in Lexington, where she was apparently stirring up trouble against the British, who were led by Braddock. Who could blame her, after seeing her people imprisoned by Silas? So Lexington was where we were – at a recently vacated hunting camp.

'She's not too far away,' Charles told me. And did I imagine it, or did I feel my pulse quicken a little? It had been a long time since any woman had made me feel this way. My life had been spent either in studying or moving around and, as for women in my bed, there had been nobody serious: the occasional washerwoman during my service with the Coldstreams, waitresses, landlords' daughters – women who had provided solace and comfort, physical and otherwise, but nobody I'd have described as at all special.

This woman, though: I had seen something in her eyes, as if she were something of a kindred spirit – another loner, another warrior, another bruised soul who looked at the world with weary eyes.

I studied the camp. 'The fire's only just been snuffed, the snow recently disturbed.' I looked up. 'She's close.'

I dismounted but, when I saw Charles was about to do the same, I stopped him.

'Best you return to Braddock, Charles, before he grows suspicious. I can handle things from here.'

He nodded, reined his horse round, and I watched as they left then turned my attention to the snow-covered ground around me, wondering about my *real* reason for sending him off. And knowing exactly what it was.

ii

I crept though the trees. It had begun to snow again, and the forest was strangely silent, but for the sound of my own breathing, which billowed in vapours in front of me. I moved fast but stealthily, and it wasn't long before I saw her, or at least the back of her. She was kneeling in the snow, a musket leaning against a tree, as she examined a snare. I came closer, as quietly as I could, only to see her tense.

She'd heard me. God she was good.

And in the next instant she had rolled to her side, snatched up the musket, thrown a look behind her then taken off into the woods.

I ran after her. 'Please stop running,' I called as we flew through the snow-blanketed woodland. 'I only wish to talk. I am not your enemy.'

But she kept on going. I dashed nimbly through the snow, moving fast and easily negotiating the terrain, but she was faster and next she took to the trees, raising herself off the hard-to-negotiate snow and swinging from branch the branch wherever she was able.

In the end, she took me further and further into the forest and would have escaped were it not for a piece of bad fortune. She tripped on a tree root, stumbled, fell, and I was upon her at once, but not to attack, to come to her aid, and I held up a hand, breathing hard as I managed to say, 'Me. Haytham. I. Come. In. Peace.'

She looked at me as though she hadn't understood a word I'd said. I felt the beginnings of a panic. Maybe I'd been wrong about her in the cart. Maybe she couldn't speak English at all.

Until, suddenly, she replied with, 'Are you touched in the head?'

Perfect English.

'Oh . . . sorry . . .'

She gave a disgusted shake of her head.

'What do you want?'

'Well, your name, for one.' My shoulders heaved as I gradually caught my breath, which was steaming in the freezing cold.

And then, after a period of indecision – I could see it playing across her face – she said, 'I am Kaniehtí:io.'

'Just call me Ziio,' she said, when I tried and failed to repeat her name back to her. 'Now tell me why it is you're here.'

I reached around my neck and took off the amulet, to show her. 'Do you know what this is?'

Without warning, she grabbed my arm. 'You have one?' she asked. For a second I was confused, until I realized she was looking not at the amulet, but at my hidden blade. I watched her for a moment, feeling what I can only describe as a strange mixture of emotions: pride, admiration, then trepidation as, accidentally, she ejected the blade. To her credit, though, she didn't flinch, just looked up at me with wide brown eyes, and I felt myself fall a little deeper as she said, 'I've seen your little secret.'

I smiled back, trying to look more confident than I felt, and raised the amulet, starting again.

'This.' I dangled it. 'Do you know what it is?'

Taking it in her hand, she gazed at it. 'Where did you get it?'

'From an old friend,' I said, thinking of Miko and

offering a silent prayer for him. I wondered, should it have been him here instead of me, an Assassin instead of a Templar?

'I've only seen such markings in one other place,' she said, and I felt an instant thrill.

'Where?'

'It . . . it is forbidden for me to speak of it.'

I leaned towards her. I looked into her eyes, hoping to convince with the strength of my conviction. 'I saved your people. Does this mean nothing to you?'

She said nothing.

'Look,' I pressed, 'I am not the enemy.'

And perhaps she thought of the risks we had taken at the fort, how we had freed so many of her people from Silas. And maybe – maybe – she saw something in me she liked.

Either way, she nodded then replied, 'Near here, there is a hill. On top of it grows a mighty tree. Come, we'll see if you speak the truth.'

iii

She led me there, and indicated below us, where there was a town she told me was called Concord.

'The town hosts soldiers who seek to drive my people from these lands. They are led by a man known as the Bulldog,' she said.

The realization dawned. 'Edward Braddock . . .'

She rounded on me. 'You know him?'

'He is no friend of mine,' I assured her, and never had I been more sincere.

'Every day, more of my people are lost to men like him,' she said fiercely.

'And I suggest we put a stop to it. Together.'

She looked hard at me. There was doubt in her eyes, but I could see hope as well. 'What do you propose?'

Suddenly I knew. I knew exactly what had to be done.

'We have to kill Edward Braddock.'

I let the information sink in. Then added, 'But first we have to find him.'

We began to head down the hill towards Concord.

'I don't trust you,' she said flatly.

'I know.'

'Yet you remain.'

'That I might prove you wrong.'

'It will not happen.' Her jaw was set. She believed it. I had a long way to go with this mysterious, captivating woman.

In town, we approached the tavern, where I stopped her. 'Wait here,' I said. 'A Mohawk woman is likely to raise suspicions – if not muskets.'

She shook her head, instead pulling up her hood. 'This is hardly the first time I've been among your people,' she said. 'I can handle myself.'

I hoped so.

We entered to find groups of Braddock's men drinking with a ferocity that would have impressed Thomas Hickey, and we moved among them, eavesdropping on their conversations. What we discovered was that Braddock was on the move. The British planned to enlist the Mohawk to march further north and go against the French. Even the men seemed frightened of Braddock, I realized. All talk was of how merciless he could be, and how even his officers were scared of him. One name I overheard was George Washington. He was the only one brave enough to question the general, according to a pair of gossiping redcoats I eavesdropped upon. When I moved through to the back of the tavern, I found the self-same George Washington sitting with another officer at a secluded table, and loitered close by in order to listen in to their conversation.

'Tell me you've good news?' said one.

'General Braddock refused the offer. There will be no truce,' said the other.

'Dammit.'

'Why, George? What reason did he give?'

The man he called George – whom I took to be George Washington – replied, 'He said a diplomatic solution was no solution at all. That allowing the French to retreat would only delay an inevitable conflict – one in which they now have the upper hand.'

'There's merit in those words, much as I hate to admit it. Still . . . can't you see this is unwise?'

'It doesn't sit well with me either. We're far from home, with forces divided. Worse, I fear private blood-lust makes Braddock careless. It puts the men at risk. I'd rather not be delivering grim news to mothers and widows because the Bulldog wanted to prove a point.'

'Where is the general now?'

'Rallying the troops.'

'And then it's on to Fort Duquesne, I assume?'

'Eventually. The march north will surely take time.'

'At least this will be ended soon . . .'

'I tried, John.'

'I know, my friend. I know . . .'

Braddock has left to rally his troops, I told Ziio outside the tavern. 'And they're marching on Fort Duquesne. It'll be a while yet until they're ready, which gives us time to form a plan.'

'No need,' she said. 'We'll ambush him near the river. Go and gather your allies. I will do the same. I'll send word when it's time to strike.'

8 July 1755

It has been nearly eight months since Ziio told me to wait for her word, but at last it came, and we travelled to the Ohio Country, where the British were about to begin a major campaign against the French forts. Braddock's expedition was aimed at overthrowing Fort Duquesne.

We had all been busy in that time, and none more than Ziio, I discovered, when we did eventually meet and I saw that she had brought with her many troops, many of them natives.

'All these men are from many different tribes – united in their desire to see Braddock sent away,' she said. 'The Abenaki, the Lenape, the Shawnee.'

'And you?' I said to her, when the introductions had been made. 'Who do you stand for?'

A thin smile: 'Myself.'

'What would you have me do?' I said at last.

'You will help the others to prepare . . .'

She wasn't joking. I put my men to work and joined them building blockades, filling a cart with gunpowder in order to make a booby trap, until everything was in place and I found myself grinning, saying to Ziio, 'I can't wait to see the look on Braddock's face when the trap is finally sprung.'

She gave me a distrusting look. 'You take pleasure in this?'

'You're the one who asked me to help you kill a man.'

'It does not please me to do so. He is sacrificed so that the land and the people who live on it might be saved. What motivates you? Some past wrongs? A betrayal? Or is it simply the thrill of the hunt?'

Mollified, I said, 'You misread me.'

She indicated through the trees, towards the Monongahela River.

'Braddock's men will be here soon,' she said. 'We should prepare for their arrival.'

9 July 1755

i

A Mohawk scout on horseback quickly spoke some words I didn't understand but, as he gestured back down the valley towards the Monongahela, I could guess what he was saying: that Braddock's men had crossed the river and would soon be upon us. He left to inform the rest of the ambush, and Ziio, lying by my side, confirmed what I already knew.

'They come,' she said simply.

I'd been enjoying lying next to her in our hiding place, the proximity of her. So it was with a measure of regret that I looked out from beneath a fringe of undergrowth to see the regiment emerge from the tree line at the bottom of the hill. I heard it at the same time: a distant rumble growing louder which heralded the arrival of not a patrol, not a scouting party, but an entire regiment of Braddock's men. First came the officers on horseback, then the drummers and bandsmen, then the troops marching, then porters and camp followers guarding the baggage train. The entire column stretched back almost as far as the eye could see.

And, at the head of the regiment, the general himself, who sat, gently rocking with the rhythm of his horse, his freezing breath clouding the air ahead of him, and George Washington by his side.

Behind the officers the drummers kept up a steady beat, for which we were eternally grateful, because in the trees were French and Indian snipers. On the high ground were scores of men who lay on their bellies, the undergrowth pulled over them, waiting for the sign to attack: a hundred or more men waiting to spring the ambush; a hundred men who held their breath as, suddenly, General Braddock held up his hand, an officer on his other side barked an order, the drums stopped and the regiment came to a halt, horses whinnying and sneezing, pawing at the snowy, frozen ground, the column gradually descending into silence.

An eerie calm settled around the men in the column. In the ambush, we held our breath, and I'm sure every man and woman, like me, wondered if we'd been discovered.

George Washington looked at Braddock then behind, where the rest of the column, officers, soldiers and followers stood waiting expectantly, then back at Braddock.

He cleared his throat.

'Everything all right, sir?' he asked.

Braddock took a deep breath. 'Just savouring the moment,' he replied, then took another deep breath and added: 'No doubt many wonder why it is we've pushed so far west. These are wild lands, as yet untamed and unsettled. But it shall not always be so. In time, our holdings will no longer suffice, and that day is closer than you think. We must ensure that our people have ample room to grow and further prosper. Which means we need more land. The French understand this – and endeavour to prevent such growth. They skirt around our territory – erecting forts and forging alliances – awaiting the day they might strangle us with the noose they've built. This must not come to pass. We must sever the cord and send them back. This is why we ride. To offer them one last chance: the French will leave or they will die.'

By my side, Ziio gave me a look, and I could see that there was nothing she would like better than to prick the man's pomposity straight away.

Sure enough. 'Now is the time to strike,' she hissed.

'Wait,' I said. When I turned my head I found she was looking at me, and our faces were just an inch or so apart. 'To scatter the expedition is not enough. We must ensure Braddock fails. Else he is sure to try again.'

Kill him, I meant, and there would never be a better time to strike. I thought quickly then, pointing at a small scouting convoy that had peeled away from the main regiment, said, 'I'll disguise myself as one of his own and make my way to his side. Your ambush will provide the perfect cover for me to deliver the killing blow.'

I made my way down towards the ground and stole towards the scouts. Silently, I engaged my blade, slid it into the neck of the nearest soldier and was unbuttoning his jacket before he'd even hit the floor.

The regiment, some three hundred yards away now, began to move with a rumble like approaching thunder, the drums began again and the Indians used the sudden noise as cover to begin moving in the trees, adjusting their positions, readying the ambush.

I mounted the scout's horse and spent a moment or so calming the animal, letting her get used to me, before taking her down a small incline towards the column. An officer, also on horseback, spotted me, and ordered me back into position, so I waved an apology then began to trot towards the head of the column, past the baggage train and camp followers, past the marching soldiers, who threw me resentful looks and talked about me behind my back, and past the band, until I came almost level with the front of the column. Close now, but also more vulnerable. Close enough to hear Braddock talking to one of his men – one of his inner circle, his mercenaries.

'The French recognize they are weak in all things,' he was saying, 'and so they have allied themselves with the savages that inhabit these woods. Little more than animals, they sleep in trees, collect scalps and even eat their own dead. Mercy is too kind for them. Spare no one.'

I didn't know whether to chuckle or not. *'Eat their own dead.'* Nobody still believed that, surely?

The officer seemed to be thinking the same thing. 'But sir,' he protested, 'those are just stories. The natives I have known do nothing of the sort.'

In the saddle, Braddock rounded on him. 'Are you calling me a liar?' he roared.

'I misspoke, sir,' said the mercenary, trembling. 'I'm sorry. Truly, I am grateful to serve.'

'Have served, you mean,' snarled Braddock.

'Sir?' said the man, frightened.

'You are grateful to "*have* served",' repeated Braddock, drew his pistol and shot the man. The officer fell back from his horse, a red hole where his face had been, his body thumping to the tinder-dry forest floor. Meanwhile, the report of the gun had scared the birds from the trees and the column suddenly drew to a halt, the men pulling muskets from shoulders, drawing weapons, believing they were under attack.

For a few moments they remained at full alert, until the order came to stand down, and the word filtered back to them, a message delivered in hushed tones: the general had just shot an officer.

I was near enough to the front of the column to see George Washington's shocked reaction, and he alone had the courage to stand up to Braddock.

'General!'

Braddock rounded on him, and perhaps there was a moment in which Washington wondered if he was to receive the same treatment. Until Braddock thundered, 'I will not tolerate doubt among those I command. Nor sympathy for the enemy. I've no time for insubordination.'

Bravely George Washington countered, 'None denied he erred, sir, only . . .'

'He paid for his treachery as all traitors must. If we are to win this war against the French . . . Nay, *when* we win this war . . . It will be because men like you obeyed men like me – and did so without hesitation. We must have order in our ranks, and a clear chain of command. Leaders and followers. Without such structure, there can be no victory. Am I understood?'

Washington nodded but quickly looked away, keeping his true feelings to himself, and then as the column moved off once more, moved away from the front on the pretext of attending to business elsewhere. I saw my chance and manoeuvred my way to behind Braddock, falling into position by his side, just slightly behind so that he wouldn't see me. Not yet.

I waited, biding my time, until suddenly there was a commotion from behind us, and the officer on the other side of Braddock peeled away to investigate, leaving just the two of us up front. Me and General Braddock.

I drew my pistol.

'Edward,' I said, and enjoyed the moment as he swivelled in his saddle and his eyes went from me, to the barrel of my pistol and then to me again. His mouth opened, about to do what, I wasn't sure – call for help probably – but I wasn't going to give him the chance. There was no escape for him now.

'Not so fun on the other end of the barrel, is it?' I said, and squeezed the trigger . . .

At exactly the same time as the regiment came under attack – damn, the trap had been sprung too soon – my horse gave a start and the shot went wide. Braddock's eyes flashed with hope and triumph as, suddenly, there were Frenchmen all around us and arrows began raining down from the trees above us. Braddock pulled on the reins of his horse with a yell and in the next moment was mounting the verge towards the trees, while I sat, my spent pistol in my hand, stunned by the abrupt turn of events.

The hesitation almost cost me my life. I found myself in the path of a Frenchman – blue jacket, red breeches – his sword swinging and heading straight for me. It was too late to engage my blade. Too late to draw my sword.

And then, just as rapidly, the Frenchman was flying from his saddle, as though jerked on a piece of rope, the side of his head exploding into a red spray. In the same moment I heard the gunshot and saw, on a horse behind him, my friend Charles Lee.

I nodded my thanks, but would have to give him more effusive gratitude later, as I saw Braddock disappearing into the trees, his feet kicking at the flank of his steed and casting a quick look behind him, seeing me about to give chase.

ii

Yelling encouragement at my horse, I followed Braddock into the forest, passing Indians and Frenchmen who were rushing down the hill towards the column. Ahead of me, arrows rained down on Braddock, but none found its target. Now, too, the traps we had laid were being sprung. I saw the cart, primed with gunpowder, come trundling out of the trees and scatter a group of riflemen before exploding and sending riderless horses scattering away from the column, while, from above me, native snipers picked off frightened and disorientated soldiers.

Braddock stayed frustratingly ahead of me, until at last the terrain was too much for his horse, which reared up and sent him falling to the ground.

Howling in pain, Braddock rolled in the dirt and briefly fumbled for his pistol before deciding against it, pulled himself to his feet and began to run. For me, it was a simple matter to catch him up, and I spurred my horse on.

'I never took you for a coward, Edward,' I said as I reached him, and levelled my pistol.

He stopped in his tracks, span around and met my gaze. There – there was the arrogance. The scorn I knew so well.

'Come on then,' he sneered.

I trotted closer, my gun held, when, suddenly, there was the sound of a gunshot, my steed fell dead beneath me and I crashed to the forest floor.

'Such arrogance,' I heard Braddock call. 'I always knew it would be the end of you.'

Now at his side was George Washington, who raised his musket to aim at me. Instantly I had a fierce, bittersweet sense of consolation that at least it should be Washington, who clearly had a conscience and was nothing like the general, who was to end my life, and I closed my eyes, ready to accept death. I regretted that I had never seen my father's killers brought to justice, and that I had come tantalizingly close to discovering the secrets of Those Who Came Before but never entered the storehouse; and I wished that I'd been able to see the ideals of my Order spread throughout the world. In the end, I had not been able to change the world, but I had at least changed myself. I had not always been a good man, but I had tried to be a better one.

But the shot never came. And when I opened my eyes it was to see Washington knocked off his horse and Braddock swinging round to see his officer on the deck, tussling with a figure that I recognized immediately as Ziio, who had not only taken Washington by surprise but had disarmed him and had her knife to his throat. Braddock used the opportunity to flee, and I scrambled to my feet, racing across the clearing to where Ziio held Washington firm.

'Hurry,' she snapped at me. 'Before he gets away.'

I hesitated, not wanting to leave her alone with Washington, and more troops on the way no doubt, but she struck him with the hilt of her knife, sending his eyes rolling, dazed, and I knew she could take care of herself. So I took off after Braddock once again, this time both of us on foot. He still had his pistol, and darted behind a huge tree trunk, spinning and raising his gun arm. I stopped and rolled into cover at the same time as he fired, heard the shot thump harmlessly into a tree to my left and without pausing leapt out of my cover to continue the chase. He had already taken to his feet, hoping to outrun me, but I was thirty years younger than him; I hadn't spent the last two decades getting fat in charge of an army, and I hardly broke a sweat as he began to slow. He glanced behind and his hat tumbled off as he mis-stepped and almost fell over the raised roots of a tree.

I slowed, let him regain his balance and continue

running, then chased after him, barely jogging now. Behind us, the sounds of gunshots, of screams, of men and animals in pain, became fainter. The forest seemed to drown out the noise of battle, leaving just the sound of Braddock's ragged breathing and his footfalls on the soft forest floor. Again, he glanced behind and saw me – saw that I was barely even running now, and, finally, he dropped, exhausted, to his knees.

I flicked my finger, engaged the blade and came close to him. Shoulders heaving as he fought for breath, he said, 'Why, Haytham?'

'Your death opens a door; it's nothing personal,' I said.

I plunged the blade into him and watched as blood bubbled up around the steel and his body tautened and jerked with the agony of impalement. 'Well, maybe it's a little bit personal,' I said, as I lowered his dying body to the ground. 'You've been a pain in my ass, after all.'

'But we are brothers in arms,' he said. His eyelids fluttered as death beckoned to him.

'Once, perhaps. No longer. Do you think I've forgotten what you did? All those innocents slaughtered without a second thought. And for what? It does not engender peace to cut your way to resolution.'

His eyes focused, and he looked at me. 'Wrong,' he said, with a surprising and sudden inner strength.

'Were we to apply the sword more liberally and more often, the world would be possessed of far fewer troubles than it is today.'

I thought. 'In this instance, I concur,' I said.

I took his hand and pulled off the ring he wore that bore the Templar crest.

'Farewell, Edward,' I said, and stood waiting for him to die.

At that moment, however, I heard the sound of a group of soldiers approaching and saw I had no time to make my escape. Instead, I dropped to my belly and wormed my way beneath a fallen tree trunk, where I was suddenly at eye level with Braddock. His head turned to me, his eyes gleamed, and I knew he'd give me away if he could. Slowly, his hand stretched out, his crooked finger trying to point in my direction as the men arrived.

Damn. I should have delivered the killing blow.

I saw the boots of the men who came into the clearing, wondered how the battle had gone, and saw George Washington shoulder his way through a small knot of troops to rush forward and kneel by the side of his dying general.

Braddock's eyes fluttered still. His mouth worked as he tried to form words – the words to give me away. I steeled myself, counting the feet: six or seven men at least. Could I take them?

But, I realized, Braddock's attempts to alert his men

to my presence were being ignored. Instead, George Washington had put his head to his chest, listened then exclaimed, 'He lives.'

Beneath the tree trunk I closed my eyes and cursed as the men picked Braddock up and took him away.

Later, I rejoined Ziio. 'It's done,' I told her. She nodded.

'Now I've upheld my part of the bargain, I expect that you will honour yours?' I added.

She nodded again and bade me to follow her, and we began to ride.

10 July 1755

We rode overnight, and at last she stopped and indicated a dirt mound ahead of us. It was almost as if it had appeared from the forest. I wondered if I would even have seen it had I been here by myself. My heart quickened, and I swallowed. Did I imagine it, or was it as though the amulet suddenly woke up around my neck, became heavier, warmer?

I looked at her before walking to the opening then slid inside, where I found myself in a small room that had been lined with simple ceramic. There was a ring of pictographs around the room, leading to a depression on the wall. An amulet-sized depression.

I went to it and took the amulet from around my neck, pleased to see it glow slightly in my palm. Looking at Ziio, who returned my gaze, her own eyes wide with trepidation, I approached the indentation and, as my eyes adjusted to the dark, saw that two figures painted on the wall knelt before it, offering their hands to it as though to make an offering.

The amulet seemed to glow even more brightly now, as though the artefact itself were anticipating being reunited with the fabric of the chamber. How old was it? I wondered. How many millions of years before had the amulet been hewn from this very rock?

I had been holding my breath, I realized, and let it out in a whoosh now, as I reached up and pressed the amulet into the hollow.

Nothing happened.

I looked at Ziio. Then from her to the amulet, where its former glow was beginning to fade, almost as though mirroring my own deflating expectations. My lips moved, trying to find words. 'No . . .'

I removed the amulet then tried it again, but still nothing.

'You seem disappointed,' she said at my side.

'I thought I held the key,' I said, and was dismayed to hear the tone in my own voice, the defeat and disappointment. 'That it would open something here . . .'

She shrugged. 'While this room is all there is.'

'I expected . . .'

What had I expected?

'. . . more.

'These images, what do they mean?' I asked, recovering myself.

Ziio went to the wall to gaze at them. One in particular seemed to catch her eye. It was a god or a goddess wearing an ancient, intricate headdress.

'It tells the story of Iottsitíson,' she said intently, 'who came into our world and shaped it, that life might come. Hers was a hard journey, fraught with loss and great peril. But she believed in the potential of her children and what they might achieve. Though she is long gone from the physical world, her eyes still watch over us. Her ears still hear our words. Her hands still guide us. Her love still gives us strength.'

'You've showed me a great kindness, Ziio. Thank you.'

When she looked back at me, her face was soft.

'I am sorry you did not find what you seek.'

I took her hand. 'I should go,' I said, not wanting to go at all, and in the end she stopped me: she leaned forward and kissed me.

13 July 1755

'Master Kenway, did you find it, then?'

They were the first words Charles Lee said to me when I entered our room at the Green Dragon tavern. My men were all assembled, and they looked at me with expectant eyes, then faces that dropped when I shook my head no.

'It was not the right place,' I confirmed. 'I fear the temple was nothing more than a painted cave. Still, it contained precursor images and script, which means we are close. We must redouble our efforts, expand our Order and establish a permanent base here,' I continued. 'Though the site eludes us, I am confident we will find it.'

'Truth!' said John Pitcairn.

'Hear, hear!' chimed Benjamin Church.

'Furthermore, I believe it is time we welcomed Charles into the fold. He has proven himself a loyal disciple – and served unerringly since the day he came to us. You should be able to share in our knowledge and reap all the benefits such a gift implies, Charles. Are any opposed?'

The men stayed silent, casting approving looks at Charles.

'Very well.' I went on: 'Charles, come, stand.' As he approached me I said, 'Do you swear to uphold the principles of our Order and all of that for which we stand?'

'I do.'

'Never to share secrets nor divulge the true nature of our work?'

'I do.'

'And to do so from now until death – whatever the cost?'

'I do.'

The men stood. 'Then we welcome you into our fold, brother. Together we will usher in the dawn of a new world, one defined by purpose and order. Give me your hand.'

I took the ring I'd removed from Braddock's finger and pushed it on to Charles's.

I looked at him. 'You are a Templar now.'

And at that he grinned. 'May the father of under-standing guide us,' I said, and the men joined me. Our team was complete.

1 August 1755

Do I love her?

That question I find difficult to answer. All I knew was that I enjoyed being with her and came to treasure the time we spent together.

She was . . . different. There was something about her I had never experienced in another woman. That 'spirit' I spoke of before, it seemed to come through in her every word and gesture. I'd find myself looking at her, fascinated by the light that seemed permanently to burn in her eyes and wondering, always wondering, what was going on inside? What was she thinking?

I thought she loved me. I should say, I think she loves me, but she's like me. There's so much of herself she keeps hidden. And, like me, I think she knows that love cannot progress, that we cannot live out our lives together, either in this forest or in England, that there are too many barriers between us and our lives together: her tribe, for a start. She has no desire to leave her life behind. She sees her place as with her people, protecting her land – land they feel is under threat from people like me.

And I, too, have a responsibility to my people. The tenets of my Order, are they in line with the ideals of her tribe? I'm not sure that they are. Asked to choose between Ziio and the ideals I have been brought up to believe, which would I choose?

These are the thoughts that have plagued me over the last few weeks, even as I have luxuriated in these sweet, stolen hours with Ziio. I have wondered what to do.

4 August 1755

My decision has been made for me because, this morning, we had a visitor.

We were at camp, about five miles from Lexington, where we hadn't seen anyone – *not another human being* – for several weeks. I heard him, of course, before I saw him. Or, rather, I should say that I heard the disturbance he caused: a fluttering in the distance as the birds left the trees. No Mohawk would have caused them to behave in such a way, I knew, which meant it was another: a colonial, a patriot, a British soldier; perhaps even a French scout, a long way out of his way.

Ziio had left the camp almost an hour ago to hunt. Still, I knew her well enough to know that she would have seen the disturbed birds; she, too, would be reaching for her musket.

I shimmied quickly up the lookout tree and scanned the area around us. There, in the distance – there he was, a lone rider trotting slowly through the forest. His musket was slung across his shoulder. He wore a tricorne hat and a dark buttoned-up coat; no military uniform. Reining his horse, he stopped and I saw him reach into a knapsack, retrieve a spyglass and put it to his eye. I watched as he angled the spyglass upwards, above the canopy of trees.

Why upwards? Clever boy. He was looking for the tell-tale wisps of smoke, grey against the bright, blue early morning sky. I glanced down at our campfire, saw the smoke that curled its way up to the heavens then looked back at the rider, watching as he moved his spyglass around the skyline, almost as if . . .

Yes. Almost as if he had divided the search area into a grid and was moving methodically across it square by square, exactly the same way that . . .

I did. Or one of my pupils did.

I allowed myself to relax slightly. It was one of my men – probably Charles, judging by his build and clothes. I watched as he saw the wisps of smoke from the fire, replaced his spyglass in his knapsack and began trotting towards the camp. Now he was near, I saw that it was Charles, and I let myself down the tree and into camp, wondering about Ziio.

Back at ground level I looked around, and saw the camp through Charles's eyes: the campfire, the two tin plates, a canvas strung between trees, under which were the skins that Ziio and I covered ourselves with for warmth at night. I flipped the canvas down so that the skins were obscured then knelt by the fire and collected the tin plates. A few moments later, his horse came into the clearing.

'Hello, Charles,' I said, without looking at him.

'You knew it was me?'

'I saw you are using your training: I was very impressed.'

'I was trained by the best,' he said. And I heard the smile in his voice, looked up at last to see him gazing down at me.

'We've missed you, Master Kenway,' he said.

I nodded. 'And I you.'

His eyebrows lifted. 'Really? You know where we are.'

I pushed a stick into the fire and watched the tip of it glow. 'I wanted to know that you are able to operate in my absence.'

He pursed his lips and nodded. 'I think you know we can. What's the real reason for your absence, Haytham?'

I looked up sharply from the fire. 'What *might* it be, Charles?'

'Perhaps you are enjoying life here with your Indian woman, suspended between two worlds, responsible to neither. It must be nice to take such a holiday . . .'

'Careful, Charles,' I warned. Suddenly aware that he looked down on me, I stood to meet his eye, to be on more equal terms. 'Perhaps instead of concerning yourself with my activities, you should concentrate on your own. Tell me, how are matters in Boston?'

'We have been taking care of those matters you would have us attend to. Concerning the land.'

I nodded, thinking of Ziio, wondering if there was another way.

'Anything else?' I asked.

'We continue to look for signs of the precursor site . . .' he said, and raised his chin.

'I see . . .'

'William plans to lead an expedition to the chamber.'

I started. 'Nobody has asked me about this.'

'You haven't been there to ask,' said Charles. 'William thought . . . Well, if we want to find the site, then that's the best place to start.'

'We will enrage the natives if we begin setting up camp in their lands.'

Charles gave me a look as though I had taken leave of my senses. Of course. What did we, the Templars, care about upsetting a few natives?

'I've been thinking about the site,' I said quickly. 'Somehow it seems less important now . . .' I looked off into the distance.

'Something else you plan to neglect?' he asked impertinently.

'I'm warning you . . .' I said, and flexed my fingers.

He cast a look around the camp. 'Where is she anyway? Your Indian . . . lover?'

'Nowhere you need concern yourself with, Charles, and I would thank you to remove that tone from your voice when you speak of her in the future, else I might find myself compelled to remove it forcibly.'

His eyes were cold when he looked at me. 'A letter has arrived,' he said, reached into his knapsack and dropped it so that it landed at my feet. I glanced down to see my name on the front of the envelope, and recognized the handwriting immediately. The letter came from Holden, and my heart quickened just to see it: a link with my old life, my other life in England and my preoccupations there: finding my father's killers.

I did or said nothing to betray my emotions on seeing the letter, adding, 'Is there more?'

'Yes,' said Charles, 'some good news. General Braddock has succumbed to his injuries. He is dead at last.'

'When was this?'

'He died soon after he was injured but the news has only just reached us.'

I nodded. 'Then that bit of business is at an end,' I said.

'Excellent,' said Charles. 'Then I shall return, shall I? Tell the men that you are enjoying life here in the wilds? We can only hope that you grace us with your presence some time in the future.'

I thought of the letter from Holden. 'Perhaps sooner than you think, Charles. I have a feeling I may soon be called away on a business. You have proved yourself more than capable of dealing with matters.' I gave him a thin, mirthless smile. 'Perhaps you will continue to do so.'

Charles pulled on the reins of his horse. 'As you

wish, Master Kenway. I will tell the men to expect you. In the meantime, please give your lady friend our regards.'

And, with that, he was gone. I crouched a little longer by the fire, the forest silent around me, then said, 'You can come out now, Ziio, he's gone,' and she dropped down from a tree, came striding into the clearing, her face like thunder.

I stood to meet her. The necklace she always wore glinted in the morning sun and her eyes flashed angrily.

'He was alive,' she said. 'You lied to me.'

I swallowed. 'But, Ziio, I . . .'

'You told me he was dead,' she said, her voice rising. 'You told me he was dead so that I would show you the temple.'

'Yes,' I admitted. 'I did do that, and for that I'm sorry.'

'And what's this about land?' she interrupted. 'What was that man saying about this land? Are you trying to take it, is that it?'

'No,' I said.

'Liar!' she cried

'Wait. I can explain . . .'

But she had already drawn her sword. 'I should kill you for what you've done.'

'You've every right to your anger, to curse my name and wish me gone. But the truth is not what you believe it to be,' I started.

315

'*Leave!*' she said. 'Leave this place and never return. For, if you do, I will tear out your heart with my own two hands and feed it to the wolves.'

'Only listen to me, I —'

'Swear it,' she shouted.

I hung my head. 'As you wish.'

'Then we are finished,' she said, then turned and left me to pack my things and return to Boston.

17 September 1757

(Two Years Later)

i

As the sun set, painting Damascus a golden-brown colour, I walked with my friend and companion Jim Holden in the shadow of the walls of Qasr al-Azm.

And I thought about the four words that had brought me here.

'*I have found her.*'

They were the only words on the letter, but they told me everything I needed to know and were enough to transport me from America to England, where, before anything else could happen, I'd met with Reginald at White's to fill him in on events in Boston. He knew much of what had happened, of course, from letters, but, even so, I'd expected him to show an interest in the work of the Order, particularly where it concerned his old friend Edward Braddock.

I was wrong. All he cared about was the precursor site, and when I told him I had new details regarding the location of the temple and that they were to be found within the Ottoman empire, he sighed and gave a beatific smile, like a laudanum addict savouring his syrup.

Moments later, he was asking, 'Where is the book?' with a fidgety sound in his voice.

'William Johnson has made a copy,' I said, and reached to my bag in order to return the original, which I slid across the table towards him. It was wrapped in cloth, tied with twine, and he looked at me gratefully before reaching to untie the bow and flip open the covering to gaze upon his beloved tome: the aged brown leather cover, the stamp of the Assassin on its front.

'Are they conducting a thorough search of the chamber?' he asked as he wrapped up the book, re-tied the bow then slipped it away covetously. 'I should very much like to see this chamber for myself.'

'Indeed,' I lied. 'The men are to establish a camp there but face daily attacks from the natives. It would be very hazardous for you, Reginald. You are Grand Master of the British Rite. Your time is best spent here.'

'I see,' he nodded. 'I see.'

I watched him carefully. For him to have insisted on visiting the chamber would have been an admission of neglect of his Grand Master duties, and, obsessed as he was, Reginald wasn't ready to do that yet.

'And the amulet?' he said.

'I have it,' I replied.

We talked some more, but there was little warmth

and, when we parted, I left wondering what lay in his heart and what lay in mine. I had begun to think of myself not so much as a Templar but a man with Assassin roots and Templar beliefs, whose heart had briefly been lost to a Mohawk woman. A man with a unique perspective, in other words.

Accordingly, I had been less preoccupied with finding the temple and using its contents to establish Templar supremacy, and more with bringing together the two disciplines, Assassin and Templar. I'd reflected on how my father's teachings had often dovetailed with those of Reginald, and I'd begun seeing the similarities between the two factions, rather than the differences.

But first – first there was the unfinished business that had occupied my mind for so many years. Was it finding my father's killers or finding Jenny that was more important now? Either way, I wanted freedom from this long, dark shadow that had loomed over me for so long.

ii

And so it was that with those words – 'I have found her' – Holden began another odyssey, one that took us into the heart of the Ottoman empire, where, for the past two years, he and I had tracked Jenny.

She was alive – that was his discovery. Alive and in

the hands of slavers. As the world fought the Seven Years War, we came close to discovering her exact location, but the slavers had moved on before we were able to mobilize. After that we spent several months trying to find her then discovered she'd been passed to the Ottoman court as a concubine at Topkapı Palace and made our way there. Again we were too late; she'd been moved to Damascus, and to the great palace built by the Ottoman governor in charge, As'ad Pasha al-Azm.

And so we came to Damascus, where I wore the outfit of a wealthy tradesman, a kaftan and a turban, as well as voluminous salwar trousers, feeling not a little self-conscious, truth be told, while beside me Holden wore simple robes. As we made our way through the gates of the city and into its narrow, winding streets towards the palace, we noticed more guards than usual, and Holden, having done his homework, filled me in as we ambled slowly in the dust and heat.

'The governor's nervous, sir,' he explained. 'Reckons the Grand Vizier Raghib Pasha in Istanbul has it in for him.'

'I see. And is he right? Does the grand vizier have it in for him?'

'The grand vizier called him the "peasant son of a peasant".'

'Sounds like he has got it in for him then.'

Holden chuckled. 'That's right. So the governor fears being deposed and, as a result, he's increased security all over the city, and especially at the palace. You see all these people?' He indicated a clamour of citizens not far away, hurrying across our path.

'Yes.'

'Off to an execution. A palace spy, apparently. As'ad Pasha al-Azm is seeing them everywhere.'

In a small square thronged with people we watched a man beheaded. He died with dignity, and the crowd roared its approval as his severed head rolled to the blood-blackened boards of the scaffold. Above the square the governor's platform was empty. He was staying at the palace, according to gossip, and didn't dare show his face.

When it was over, Holden and I turned and strolled away, heading towards the palace, where we paced the walls, noting the four sentries at the main gate and the others positioned by arched side gates.

'What's it like inside?' I asked.

'Two main wings: the *haramlik* and the *salamlik*. In the *salamlik* is where you got your halls, reception areas and entertainment courtyards, but the *haramlik*, that's where we'll find Miss Jenny.'

'*If* she's in there.'

'Oh, she's in there, sir.'

'You're sure?'

'As God is my witness.'

'Why was she moved from Topkapı Palace? Do you know?'

He looked at me and pulled an awkward face. 'Well, her age, sir. She would have been highly prized at first, of course, when she was younger; it's against Islamic law to imprison other Muslims, see, so the majority of the concubines are Christians – caught in the Balkans, most of them – and if Miss Jenny was as comely as you say, well, then I'm sure she'd have been quite a catch. Trouble is, it's not like there's a shortage of them, and Miss Kenway – well, she's in her mid-forties, sir. Been a long time since she had concubine duties; she's little more than a servant. I suppose you might say that she's been demoted, sir.'

I thought about that, finding it difficult to believe that the Jenny I'd once known – beautiful, imperious Jenny – had such lowly standing. Somehow I'd imagined her perfectly preserved and cutting a commanding figure at the Ottoman court, perhaps having already risen to the position of Queen Mother. Instead, here she was in Damascus, at the home of an unpopular governor who was himself about to be deposed. What did they do to the servants and concubines of a deposed governor? I wondered. Possibly, they met the same fate as the poor soul we'd seen beheaded earlier.

'What about the guards inside?' I asked. 'I didn't think they allowed men in the harem.'

He shook his head. 'All the guards in the harem are eunuchs. The operation to make them eunuchs – bloody hell, sir, you don't want to know about it.'

'But you're going to tell me anyway?'

'Well, yeah, don't see why I should have to carry that burden all by myself. They hack the poor bleeder's genitals off then bury the bloke in sand up to his neck for ten days. Only 10 per cent of the poor buggers even survive the process, and those guys are the toughest of the tough.'

'Right,' I said.

'One other thing: the *haramlik*, where the concubines live, the baths are in there.'

'The baths are in there?'

'Yes.'

'And why are you telling me that?'

He stopped. He looked from left to right, squinting in the sun. Satisfied the coast was clear, he stooped, grasped an iron ring I hadn't even seen, so well was it covered by the sand below our feet, and yanked it upwards, opening a trapdoor and revealing stone steps descending into the dark.

'Quick, sir' – he grinned – 'before a sentry comes round.'

iii

Once at the bottom of the steps, we took stock of our surroundings. It was dark, almost too dark to see, but from the left of us came the trickle of a stream, while

323

ahead stretched what looked like a walkway used either for deliveries or maintenance of the running-water channels; probably a mixture of both.

We said nothing. Holden delved into a leather knapsack to extract a taper and a tinderbox. He lit the taper then placed it into his mouth and pulled a short torch from the knapsack, which he lit and held above his head, casting a soft orange glow all around us. Sure enough, to our left was an aqueduct, while the uneven path dissolved into blackness.

'It'll take us right under the palace, and underneath the baths,' said Holden in a whisper. 'If I'm right, we'll come up into a room with a freshwater pool, right beneath the main baths.'

Impressed, I said, 'You kept this quiet.'

'I like to have the odd trick up my sleeve, sir.' He beamed. 'I'll lead the way, shall I?'

And with that he moved off, lapsing into silence as we made our way along the pathway. When the torches had burned out, we dropped them and lit two new ones from the taper in Holden's mouth then walked some more. At last the area ahead of us widened out into a shimmering chamber, where the first thing we saw was a pool, its walls lined with marble tiles, the water so clear that it seemed to glow in the meagre light offered by an open trapdoor at the top of some nearby steps.

The second thing we saw was a eunuch, who knelt

with his back to us, filling an earthenware jug from the pool. He wore a tall white *kalpak* on his head, and flowing robes. Holden looked at me with his finger to his lips then began to creep forward, a dagger already in his fist, but I stopped him with a hand on his shoulder. We wanted the eunuch's clothes, and that meant avoiding bloodstains. This was a man who served the concubines at an Ottoman palace, not a common redcoat in Boston, and I had the feeling that blood on his clothing wouldn't be so easily explained away. So I inched past Holden on the walkway, unconsciously flexing my fingers and in my mind locating the carotid artery on the eunuch, coming closer as he finished filling the jug and straightened to leave.

But then my sandal scuffed the pathway. The noise was tiny but nevertheless sounded like a volcano erupting in the enclosed space, and the eunuch flinched.

I froze and inwardly cursed my sandals as his head tilted to look up to the trapdoor, trying to locate the source of the noise. When he saw nothing, he seemed to go very still, as though he'd realized that, if the sound hadn't come from above, then it must have come from . . .

He span round.

There'd been something about his clothes, his bearing, the way he knelt to fill his jug: none of it had prepared me for the speed of his reaction. Nor the skill. For as he swivelled he crouched, and from the corner of my eye I saw the jug in his fist whip up towards me, so fast it would have knocked me down if I hadn't shown a turn of equal speed and ducked.

I had evaded him, but only just. As I scuttled back to avoid another blow from the jug, his eyes flitted over my shoulder and saw Holden. Next, he turned to cast a quick look at the stone steps, his only exit. He was assessing his options: run or stand and fight. And he settled on stand and fight.

Which made him, just as Holden had said, one – *very* – tough eunuch.

He took a few steps back, reached beneath his robes and produced a sword, simultaneously punching the earthenware jug against the wall to give himself a second weapon. Then, sword in one hand, jagged jug in another, he advanced.

The walkway was too narrow. Only one of us could face him at any one time, and I was the nearer. The time to worry about blood on robes was over, and I released my blade, stepping back a little myself and taking a stance ready to meet him. Implacably, he advanced, all the time holding my gaze. There was something fearsome about him, something I couldn't put my finger on at first, but then I realized what it was: he did something no opponent had ever done: as my old nursemaid Edith would have said, he gave me the creeps. It was knowing what he'd been through, the procedure to make him a eunuch. Living through that, nothing held any fear for him, least of all me, a clumsy oaf who couldn't even sneak up on him successfully.

He knew it, too. He knew he gave me the creeps and he used it. It was all there in his eyes, which didn't register an emotion as the sword in his right hand slashed towards me. I was forced to block with the blade and only just twisted to avoid the follow-up which came from his left as he tried and almost succeeded in shoving the broken jug into my face.

He gave me no time to rest, perhaps realizing that the only way to beat both me and Holden was to keep driving us back along the narrow walkway. Again the sword flashed, this time underarm, and again I defended with the blade, grimacing with pain as I used my forearm to stop a secondary strike from the jug then replying with an offensive move of my own, jogging slightly to my right and driving my blade towards his sternum. He used the jug as a shield, and my blade smashed into it, sprinkling earthenware to the stone beneath us, splish-splashing into the pool. My blade was going to need sharpening after this.

If I got out of this.

And damn the man. He was the first eunuch we'd met and already we were struggling. I motioned Holden to stand back and keep from under my feet as I retreated, trying to give myself some space and reorganize myself internally at the same time.

The eunuch was beating me – not just with skill, but because I feared him. And fear is what a warrior fears most.

I crouched low, brought the blades to bear and met his eye. For a moment we stood motionless, engaged in a silent but ferocious battle of will. A battle I won. Somehow his hold over me broke, and all it took was a flicker of his eyes to tell me that he knew it, too; that the psychological victory was no longer his.

I stepped forward, blade flashing, and now it was his turn to edge back, defending well and steadily but no longer with the upper hand. At one point, he even grunted, his lips pulled back from his teeth, and I saw the beginnings of a sweat glow dully on his forehead. My blade moved quickly. And now that I had him retreating, I began to think afresh about keeping his robes free of blood. The battle had turned; it was mine now, and he was swinging wildly with his sword, his attacks becoming more disorganized until I saw my chance, dropped almost to my knees and thrust upwards with the blade, punching up into his jaw.

His body spasmed and his arms outstretched as though crucified. His sword dropped, and when his lips stretched wide in a silent scream I saw the silver of my impaling blade inside his mouth. Then his body dropped.

I'd driven him all the way back to the foot of the steps and the hatch was open. Any moment now, another eunuch would be along to wonder where the jug of water had got to. Sure enough, I heard footsteps from above us and a shadow passed across the hatch. I ducked back, grabbed at the ankles of the dead man and dragged him with me, snatching off his hat and jamming it on my own head.

The next thing I saw was the bare feet of a eunuch as he descended the steps and angled his head to peer down into the pool chamber. The sight of me in the white hat was enough to disorientate him for one precious second, and I lunged, grabbed his robes in my fists and yanked him down the steps towards me, slamming my forehead into the bridge of his nose before he could scream. The bones crunched and broke, and I held his head up to stop blood leaking to his robes as his eyes rolled up and he slouched, dazed, against the wall. In moments he'd recover his senses and shout for help, and I couldn't allow that. So I rammed the flat of my hand hard into his mashed nose, driving splinters of broken bone into his brain and killing him instantly.

Seconds later I'd scampered up the steps and, very carefully, very gently, closed the hatch, giving us at least a few moments of concealment before reinforcements arrived. Somewhere, presumably, a concubine was expecting a jug of water to be delivered.

We said nothing, just slipped into the eunuchs' robes and pulled on our *kalpaks*. How glad I was to get rid of those blasted sandals. And then we looked at one another. Holden had spots of blood on the front of his gown, from where I had smashed the nose of the robe's previous wearer. I scratched at it with a nail but, instead of it flaking off as I'd hoped, it was still wet and smeared a little. In the end, using a complicated series of pained facial expressions and furious nods, we decided by mutual consent to leave the bloodstain and risk it. Next, I carefully opened the hatch and let myself out into the room above, which was empty. It was a dark, cool room, tiled in marble that seemed luminescent, thanks to a pool that covered most of the floor space, its surface smooth, silent yet somehow alive.

With the coast clear I turned and motioned to Holden, who followed me through the hatch into the room. We stood there for a moment or so taking in our surroundings, giving each other cautiously triumphant looks before moving to the door, opening it and letting ourselves out into the courtyard beyond.

iv

Not knowing what lay on the other side, I'd been flexing my fingers, ready to release my blade at a moment's notice, while Holden had no doubt been set to reach for his sword, both of us poised to fight should we be greeted by a squad of snarling eunuchs, a huddle of howling concubines.

Instead what we saw was a scene straight out of heaven, an afterlife filled with peace and serenity and beautiful women. It was a large courtyard paved in black and white stone, with a trickling fountain at its centre and a surround of ornate columned porticos shaded by overhanging vines and trees. A restful place, devoted to beauty, serenity, tranquillity and thought. The trickle and burble of the fountain was the only sound, despite all the people there. Concubines in flowing white silk either sat on stone benches, meditative or doing needlework, or crossed the courtyard, bare feet padding silently on the stone, impossibly proud and erect, nodding courteously to one another as they passed; while among them moved servant girls, dressed similarly but easy to spot because they were younger or older, or not as beautiful as the women they served.

There was an equal number of men, most of whom stood around the edges of the courtyard, watchful and waiting to be called forward to serve: the eunuchs. None looked our way, I was relieved to see; the rules around eye contact were as elaborate as the mosaics. And as two unfamiliar-looking eunuchs trying to negotiate our way around a strange place, that suited us down to the ground.

We stayed by the door of the baths, which was

partly obscured by the columns and vines of the portico, and I unconsciously adopted the same pose as the other guards – back straight, my hands held together in front of me – as my gaze swept the courtyard in search of Jenny.

And there she was. I didn't recognize her at first; my eyes almost went past her. But when I looked again, to where a concubine sat relaxing with her back to the fountain, having her feet massaged by her serving woman, I realized that the serving woman was my sister.

Time had taken its toll on those looks, and though there was still a glimmer of the beauty she'd once been, her dark hair was flecked with grey, her face was drawn and lined and her skin had sagged a little, revealing dark hollows beneath her eyes: tired eyes. What an irony it was that I should recognize the look on the face of the girl she tended to: the vain and disdainful way she gazed down her nose. I'd grown up seeing it on my sister's face. Not that I took any pleasure in the irony, but I couldn't ignore it.

As I stared, Jenny looked across the courtyard at me. For a second her eyebrows furrowed in confusion, and I wondered if, after all these years, she'd recognize me. But no. I was too far away. I was disguised as a eunuch. The jug – it had been meant for her. And maybe she was wondering why two eunuchs had walked into the baths and two different ones had walked out.

Still wearing a confused expression, she stood, genuflected to the concubine she served then began to move over, weaving through silken-clothed concubines as she crossed the courtyard towards us. I slipped behind Holden just as she ducked her head to avoid the vines dangling from the portico and was standing a foot or so away from us.

She said nothing, of course – talking was forbidden – but then again she didn't need to. Lurking behind Holden's right shoulder, I risked a look at her face and watched as her eyes slid from him to the bath-chamber door, her meaning clear to see: *where is my water?* On her face, as she exerted what little authority she had, I could see a reminder of the girl Jenny had been, a ghost of the haughtiness that had once been so familiar to me.

Meanwhile, Holden, reacting to the furious gaze he received from Jenny, bowed his head and was about to turn towards the bath chamber. I prayed he'd had the same flash of inspiration as me, and that he had realized, if he could somehow lure Jenny inside, then we could make our escape with hardly a ruffle caused. Sure enough, he was spreading his hands to indicate there'd been a problem, then gesturing at the door to the bath chamber, as though to say he needed assistance. But

Jenny, far from being prepared to offer it, had instead noticed something about Holden's attire and, rather than accompanying him into the bath house, stopped him with an upraised finger which she first crooked at him and then turned to indicate something on his chest. A bloodstain.

Her eyes widened and again I looked, this time to see her eyes move from the bloodstain on Holden's robes to his face, and what she saw there was the face of an imposter.

Her mouth dropped open. She took a step back then another until she bumped into one of the columns and the impact jogged her out of her sudden, shocked daze and, as she opened her mouth, about to break the sacred rule and call for help, I slipped from behind Holden's shoulder, hissing, 'Jenny, it's me. It's Haytham.'

As I said it I glanced nervously out into the courtyard, where everyone continued as before, oblivious to what was happening beneath the portico, and then I looked back to see Jenny staring at me, her eyes growing wider, already misting up with tears as the years fell away and she recognized me.

'Haytham,' she whispered, 'you've come for me.'

'Yes, Jenny yes,' I replied in a hush, feeling a strange mix of emotions, at least one of which was guilt.

'I knew you'd come,' she said. 'I knew you'd come.'

Her voice was rising, and I began to worry, casting

another panicky look out into the courtyard. Then she reached forward and grasped my two hands in both of hers and brushed past Holden to look imploringly into my eyes. 'Tell me he's dead. Tell me you killed him.'

Torn between wanting her to keep quiet and wanting to know what she meant, I hissed, 'Who? Tell you who's dead?'

'Birch,' she spat, and this time her voice was too loud. Past her shoulder I saw a concubine. Gliding towards us beneath the portico, perhaps on her way to the bath chamber, she'd seemed lost in thought, but at the sound of a voice she looked up, and her expression of calm serenity was replaced by one of panic – and she leaned out into the courtyard and called the one word we had all been fearing.

'*Guards!*'

v

The first guard to come rushing over didn't realize I was armed, and I'd engaged the blade and plunged it into his abdomen before he even knew what was happening. His eyes went wide and he grunted flecks of blood into my face. With a yell of effort, I wrenched my arm round and pulled him with me, ramming his still-writhing corpse into a second man who came rushing towards us, and sent them both tumbling back to the black and white tiles of the courtyard. More arrived, and the fight was on. From the corner of my eye I saw the flash of a blade and turned just in time to avoid it being embedded into my neck. Twisting, I grabbed the assailant's sword arm, broke it and slid my blade up into his skull. I went into a crouch, pivoted and kicked to take away the legs of a fourth man then scrambled to my feet, stamped on his face and heard his skull crunch.

Not far away, Holden had felled three of the eunuchs, but by now the guards had the measure of us and were approaching with more caution, assembling for combat even as we took cover behind the columns and threw worried glances at each other, each wondering if we could make it back to the trapdoor before we were overrun.

Clever boys. Two of them moved forward together. I stood side by side with Holden and we fought back, even as another pair of guards moved in from our right. For a moment it was touch and go, as we stood back to back and battled the guards out of the portico until they withdrew, ready to launch their next attack, inching closer all the time, crowding in.

Behind us, Jenny stood by the door to the bath chamber. 'Haytham!' she called, a note of panic in her voice. 'We've got to go.'

What would they do to her if she was captured now? I wondered What would her punishment be? I dreaded to think.

'You two go, sir,' urged Holden over his shoulder.

'No way,' I called back.

Again came an attack and again we fought. A eunuch fell dying with a groan. Even in death, even with sword steel in their gut, these men didn't scream. Over the shoulders of the ones in front of us I saw more of them pouring into the courtyard. They were like cockroaches. For every one we killed there were two to take his place.

'*Go, sir!*' insisted Holden. 'I'll keep them back then follow you.'

'Don't be a fool, Holden,' I barked, unable to keep the scoffing sound out of my voice. 'There's no holding them back. They'll cut you down.'

'I've been in tighter spots than this one, sir,' grunted Holden, his sword arm working as he exchanged blows. But I could hear the false bravado in his voice.

'Then you won't mind if I stay,' I said, at the same time fending off one of the eunuch's sword strikes and parrying, not with my blade but with a punch to the face that sent him pinwheeling back.

'*Go!*' he shrieked.

'We die. We both die,' I replied.

But Holden had decided that the time for courtesy

was over. 'Listen, mate, either you two make it out of here or none of us do. What's it going to be?'

At the same time, Jenny was pulling on my hand, the door to the bath chamber open, and more men arriving from our left. But still I hesitated. Until, at last, with a shake of his head, Holden whipped round, yelled, 'You'll have to excuse me sir,' and before I could react had shoved me backwards through the door and slammed it shut.

There was a moment of shocked silence in the bath chamber as I sprawled on the floor and tried to absorb what had happened. From the other side of the door I heard the sounds of battle – a strange, quiet, muted battle it was, too – and a thudding at the door. Next there was a shout – a shout that belonged to Holden, and I pulled myself to my feet, about to haul the door open and rush back out, when Jenny grasped hold of my arm.

'You can't help him now, Haytham,' she said softly, just as there came another yell from the courtyard, Holden shouting, 'You bastards, you bloody prickless bastards.'

I cast one last look back at the door then pulled the bar across to lock it as Jenny dragged me over to the hatch in the floor.

'Is that the best you can do, you bastards?' I heard from above us as we took the steps, Holden's voice growing fainter now. 'Come on, you dickless wonders, let's see how you fare against one of His Majesty's men . . .'

The last thing we heard as we ran back along the walkway was the sound of a scream.

21 September 1757

i

I had hoped never to take pleasure in killing, but, for the Coptic priest who stood guard close to the Abou Gerbe monastery on Mount Ghebel Eter, I made an exception. I have to admit I enjoyed killing him.

He crumpled to the dirt at the base of a fence that surrounded a small enclosure, his chest heaving and his last breaths coming in jagged bursts as he died. Overhead, a buzzard cawed, and I glanced to where the arches and spires of the sandstone monastery loomed on the horizon. Saw the warm glow of life at the window.

The dying guard gurgled at my feet, and for a second it occurred to me to finish him quickly – but then again, why show him mercy? However slowly he died and however much pain he felt while it happened, it was nothing – *nothing* – compared to the agony inflicted on those poor souls who had suffered within the enclosure.

And one in particular, who was suffering in there now.

I had learnt in the market in Damascus that Holden had not been killed, as I had thought, but captured and transported to Egypt and to the Coptic monastery at Abou Gerbe, where they turned men into eunuchs. So that is where I came, praying I would not be too late but, in my heart of hearts, knowing I would be. And I was.

Looking at the fence, I could tell it would be sunk deep into the ground to prevent predatory night-time animals digging beneath it. Within the enclosure was the place where they buried the eunuchs up to their necks in sand and kept them there for ten days. They didn't want hyenas gnawing away at the faces of the buried men during that time. Absolutely not. No, if those men died, they were to die of slow exposure to the sun or of the wounds inflicted upon them during the castration procedure.

With the guard dead behind me, I crept into the enclosure. It was dark, just the light of the moon to guide me, but I could see that the sand around was bloodstained. How many men, I wondered, had suffered here, mutilated then buried up to their necks? From not far away came a low groan, and I squinted, seeing an irregular shape on the ground at the centre of the enclosure, and I knew straight away that it belonged to Private James Holden.

'*Holden,*' I whispered, and a second later was crouching to where his head protruded from the sand, gasping at what I saw. The night was cool, but the days were hot, tortuously so, and the sun had burned him so badly it was as though the very flesh had been seared away from his face. His lips and eyelids were crusted and bleeding, his skin red and peeling. I had a leather flask of water at the ready, uncorked it and held it to his lips.

'Holden?' I repeated.

He stirred. His eyes flickered open and focused on me, milky and full of pain but with recognition, and very slowly the ghost of a smile appeared on his cracked and petrified lips.

Then, just as quickly, it was gone and he was convulsing. Whether he was trying to wrench himself out of the sand or struck by a fit I wasn't sure, but his head thrashed from side to side, his mouth yawned open, and I leaned forward, taking his face in both of my hands to stop him hurting himself.

'Holden,' I said, keeping my voice down. 'Holden, stop. Please . . .'

'Get me out of here, sir,' he rasped, and his eyes gleamed wet in the moonlight. 'Get me out.'

'Holden . . .'

'Get me out of here,' he pleaded. 'Get me out of here, sir, please, sir, now, sir . . .'

Again his head began jerking painfully left to right. Again I reached out to steady him, needing to stop him before he became hysterical. How long did I have before they posted a new guard? I offered the flask to his lips and let him sip more water then pulled a shovel

I had brought from my back and began scooping blood-soaked sand from around his head, talking to him at the same time as I exposed his bare shoulders and chest.

'I'm so sorry, Holden, I'm so sorry. I should never have left you.'

'I told you to, sir,' he managed. 'I gave you a push, remember . . .'

As I dug down, the sand was even more black with blood. 'Oh God, what have they done to you?'

But I already knew and, anyway, I had my proof moments later, when I reached his waist to find it swathed in bandages – also thick and black and crusted with blood.

'Be careful down there, sir, please,' he said, very, very quietly, and I could see that he was wincing, biting back the pain. Which in the end was too much for him, and he lost consciousness, a blessing which allowed me to uncover him and take him from that accursed place and to our two horses, which were tethered to trees at the bottom of the hill.

ii

I made Holden comfortable then stood and looked up the hill towards the monastery. I checked the mechanism of my blade, strapped a sword to my waist, primed two pistols and pushed them into my belt, then primed two muskets. Next I lit a taper and torch and, taking the muskets, made my way back up the hill, where I lit a second and third torch. I chased the horses out then tossed the first torch into the stables, the hay going up with a satisfying *whoomph*; the second torch I threw into the vestibule of the chapel, and when both that and the stables were nicely ablaze I jogged across to the dormitory, lighting two more torches on the way, smashing rear windows and tossing the torches inside. And then I returned to the front door, where I'd leant the muskets against a tree. And I waited.

Not for long. In moments, the first priest appeared. I shot him down, tossed the first musket aside, picked up the second and used it on the second priest. More began to pour out, and I emptied the pistols then dashed up to the doorway and began attacking with my blade and sword. Bodies fell around me – ten, eleven or more – as the building burned, until I was slick with priest blood, my hands covered in it, trails of it running from my face. I let the wounded scream in agony as the remaining priests inside cowered – not wanting to burn, too terrified to run out and face death. Some chanced it, of course, and came charging out wielding swords, only to be cut down. Others I heard burning. Maybe some escaped, but I wasn't in the mood to be thorough. I made sure that most of them died; I heard the screams and smelled the burning flesh of those who hid inside, and then I stepped over the bodies of the dead and dying and left, as the monastery burned behind me.

25 September 1757

We were in a cottage, at a table, with the remains of a meal and single candle between us. Not far away, Holden slept, feverish, and every now and then I'd get up to change the rag on his forehead for a cooler one. We'd need to let the fever run its course and only then, when he was better, continue our journey.

'Father was an Assassin,' Jenny said as I sat down. It was the first time we'd spoken about such matters since the rescue. We'd been too preoccupied with looking after Holden, escaping Egypt and finding shelter each night.

'I know,' I said.

'You know?'

'Yes. I found out. I've realized that's what you meant all those years ago. Do you remember? You used to call me "Squirt" . . .'

She pursed her lips and shifted uncomfortably.

'. . . and what you said about me being the male heir. How I'd find out sooner or later what lay in store for me?'

'I remember . . .'

'Well, it turned out to be later rather than sooner that I discovered what lay in store for me.'

'But if you knew, then why does Birch live?'

'Why would he be dead?'

'He's a Templar.'

'As am I.'

She reared back, fury clouding her face. '*You – you're* a Templar! But that goes against everything Father ever . . .'

'Yes,' I said equably. 'Yes, I am a Templar, and no, it doesn't go against everything our father believed. Since learning of his affiliations I've come to see many similarities between the two factions. I've begun to wonder if, given my roots and my current position within the Order, I'm not perfectly placed to somehow unite Assassin and Templar . . .'

I stopped. She was slightly drunk, I realized; there was something sloppy about her features all of a sudden, and she made a disgusted noise. 'And what about *him*? My former fiancé, owner of my heart, the dashing and charming Reginald Birch? What of him, *pray tell*?'

'Reginald is my mentor, my Grand Master. It was he who looked after me in the years after the attack.'

Her face twisted into the nastiest, most bitter sneer I had ever seen. 'Well, weren't *you* the lucky one? While you were being *mentored*, I was being looked after, too – by Turkish slavers.'

I felt as if she could see right through me, as though she could see exactly what my priorities had been all these years, and I dropped my eyes then looked across the cottage to where Holden lay. A room full of my failings.

'I'm sorry,' I said. As if to them both. 'I'm truly sorry.'

'Don't be. I was one of the lucky ones. They kept me pure for selling to the Ottoman court, and after that I was looked after at Topkapı Palace.' She looked away. 'It could have been worse. I was used to it, after all.'

'What?'

'I expect you idolized Father, did you, Haytham? Probably still do. Your sun and moon? "My father my king"? Not me: I hated him. All his talk of freedom – spiritual and intellectual freedom – didn't extend to me, his own daughter. There was no weapons training for me, remember? No "Think differently" for Jenny. There was just "Be a good girl and get married to Reginald Birch." What a great match that would be. I dare say I was treated better by the sultan than I would have been by him. I once told you that our lives were mapped out for us, remember? Well, in one sense I was wrong, of course, because I don't think either of us could have predicted how it would all turn out, but in another sense? In another sense, I couldn't have been more right, Haytham, because you were born to kill, and kill is what you have done, and I was born to serve men, and serve men is what I have done. My days of serving men are over, though. What about you?'

Finished, she hoisted the beaker of wine to her lips and glugged. I wondered what awful memories the drink helped suppress.

'It was your friends the Templars who attacked our home,' she said when her beaker was dry. 'I'm sure of it.'

'You saw no rings, though.'

'No, but so what? What does that mean? They took them off, of course.'

'No. They weren't Templars, Jenny. I've run into them since. They were men for hire. Mercenaries.'

Yes, mercenaries, I thought. *Mercenaries who worked for Edward Braddock, who was close to Reginald . . .*

I leaned forward. 'I was told that Father had something – something that they wanted. Do you know what it was?'

'Oh yes. They had it in the carriage that night.'

'Well?'

'It was a book.'

Again I felt a frozen, numb feeling. 'What sort of book?'

'Brown, leather-bound, bearing the seal of the Assassins.'

I nodded. 'Do you think you'd recognize it if you were to see it again?'

She shrugged. 'Probably,' she said.

I looked across to where Holden lay, sweat glistening on his torso, 'When the fever has broken, we'll leave.'

'To go where?'

'To France.'

8 October 1757

i

Though it was cold, the sun was shining this morning, a day best described as 'sun-dappled', with bright light pouring through the canopy of trees to paint the forest floor a patchwork of gold.

We rode in a column of three, me in the lead. Behind me was Jenny, who had long since discarded her servant-girl clothes and wore a robe that hung down the flank of her steed. A large, dark hood was pulled up over her head, and her face seemed to loom from within it as though she were staring from the inside of a cave: serious, intense and framed by grey-flecked hair that fell across her shoulders.

Behind her came Holden, who, like me, wore a buttoned-up frock coat, scarf and tricorne hat, only he sagged forward a little in his saddle, his complexion pale, sallow and . . . haunted.

He had said little since recovering from his fever. There had been moments – tiny glimpses of the old Holden: a fleeting smile, a flash of his London wisdom – but they were fleeting, and he would soon return to being closed off. During our passage across the Mediterranean he had kept himself to himself, sitting alone, brooding. In France we had donned disguises, bought horses and began the trek to the chateau, and he had ridden in silence. He looked pale and, having seen him walk, I thought he was still in pain. Even in the saddle I'd occasionally see him wincing, especially over uneven ground. I could hardly bear to think of the hurt he was enduring – physical and mental.

An hour away from the chateau, we stopped and I strapped my sword to my waist, primed a pistol and put it into my belt. Holden did the same, and I asked him, 'Are you sure you're all right to fight, Holden?'

He shot me a reproachful look, and I noticed the bags and dark rings beneath his eyes. 'Begging your pardon, sir, but it's my cock and balls they took off me, not my gumption.'

'I'm sorry, Holden, I didn't mean to suggest anything. I've had my answer and that's good enough for me.'

'Do you think there will be fighting, sir?' he said, and again I saw him wince as he reached to bring his sword close at hand.

'I don't know, Holden, I really don't.'

As we came close to the chateau I saw the first of the patrols. The guard stood in front of my horse and regarded me from beneath the wide brim of his hat:

the same man, I realized, who had been here the last time I visited nearly four years ago.

'That you, Master Kenway?' he said.

'Indeed it is, and I have two companions,' I replied.

I watched him very carefully as his stare went from me to Jenny then to Holden and, though he tried to hide it, his eyes told me all I needed to know.

He went to put his fingers to his mouth, but I had leapt from my horse, grabbed his head and ejected my blade through his eye and into his brain and sliced open his throat before he could make another sound.

ii

I knelt with one hand on the sentry's chest as the blood oozed fast and thickly from the wide-open gash at his throat, like a second, grinning mouth, and looked back over my shoulder to where Jenny regarded me with a frown and Holden sat upright in his saddle, his sword drawn.

'Do you mind telling us what *that* was all about?' asked Jenny.

'He was about to whistle,' I replied, scanning the forest around us. 'He didn't whistle last time.'

'So? Perhaps they changed the entry procedure.'

I shook my head. 'No. They know we're coming. They're expecting us. The whistle would have warned

the others. We wouldn't have made it across the lawn before they cut us down.'

'How do you *know*?' she said.

'I don't *know*,' I snapped. Beneath my hand the guard's chest rose and fell one last time. I looked down to see his eyes swivel and his body give one last spasm before he died. 'I suspect,' I continued, wiping my bloody hands on the ground and standing up. 'I've spent years suspecting, ignoring the obvious. The book you saw in the carriage that night – Reginald has it with him. He'll have it in that house if I'm not very much mistaken. It was he who organized the raid on our house. He who is responsible for Father's death.'

'Oh, you know that now, do you?' she sneered.

'I'd refused to believe it before. But now, yes, I know. Things have begun to make sense to me. Like, one afternoon, when I was a child, I met Reginald by the plate room. I'd wager he was looking for the book then. The reason he was close to the family, Jenny – the reason he asked for your hand in marriage – was because he wanted the book.'

'You don't have to tell me,' she said. 'I tried warning you on the night that he was the traitor.'

'I know,' I said, then thought for a moment. 'Did Father know he was a Templar?'

'Not at first, but I found out, and I told Father.'

'That's when they argued,' I said, understanding now. '*Did* they argue?'

'I heard them one day. And, afterwards, Father employed the guards – Assassins, no doubt. Reginald told me he was warning Father . . .'

'More lies, Haytham . . .'

I looked up at her, trembling slightly. Yes. More lies. Everything I knew – my entire childhood, all of it built on a foundation of them.

'He was using Digweed,' I said. 'It was Digweed who told him where the book was stored . . .'

I winced at a sudden memory.

'What is it?' she said.

'The day at the plate room, Reginald was asking me where my sword was kept. I told him a secret hiding place.'

'Was it in the billiards room?'

I nodded.

'They went straight there, didn't they?' she said.

I nodded. 'They knew it wasn't in the plate room, because Digweed told them it had been moved, which is why they went straight to the games room.'

'But they weren't Templars?' she said.

'I beg your pardon.'

'In Syria, you told me the men who attacked us *weren't* Templars,' she said with a mocking tone. 'They *couldn't* be your beloved Templars.'

I shook my head. 'No, they weren't. I told you, I've encountered them since, and they were Braddock's men. Reginald must have planned to school me in the

355

Order . . .' I thought again, and something occurred to me: ' . . . because of the family inheritance, probably. Using Templar men would have been too much of a risk. I might have found out. I might have arrived here sooner. I almost got to Digweed. I almost had them in the Black Forest but then . . .' I remembered back to the cabin in the Black Forest. 'Reginald killed Digweed. That's why they were one step ahead of us – and they still are.' I pointed in the direction of the chateau.

'So what do we do, sir?' asked Holden.

'We do what they did the night they attacked us at Queen Anne's Square. We wait until nightfall. And then we go in there, and we kill people.'

9 October 1757

i

That date above says 9 October, which I scribbled there, rather optimistically, at the end of the previous entry, intending that this should be a contemporaneous account of our attempt to breach the chateau. In fact, I'm writing this several months later and, to detail what happened that night, I have to cast my mind back . . .

ii

How many would there be? Six, on the last occasion I came. Would Reginald have strengthened the force in the meantime, knowing I might come? I thought so. Doubled it.

Make it twelve, then, plus John Harrison, if he was still in residence. And, of course, Reginald. He was fifty-two, and his skills would have faded but, even so: I knew never to underestimate him.

So we waited, and hoped they'd do what they

eventually did, which was to send out a search party for the missing patrol, three of them, who came bearing torches and drawn swords, marching across the dark lawn with torchlight dancing on grim faces.

We watched as they materialized from the gloom and melted away into the trees. At the gates they began calling the guard's name then hurried along the outside of the low perimeter towards where the patrol was supposed to be.

His body was where I'd left it, and in the trees nearby Holden, Jenny and I took up position. Jenny stayed back, armed with a knife but out of the action; Holden and I were further forward, where we both climbed trees – Holden with some difficulty – to watch and wait, steeling ourselves as the search party came across the body.

'He's dead, sir.'

The party leader craned over the body. 'Some hours ago.'

I gave a bird call, a signal to Jenny, who did what we'd agreed. Her scream for help was launched from deep within the forest and pierced the night.

With a nervous nod, the party leader led his men into the trees, and they thundered towards us, to where we perched, waiting for them. I looked through the trees to see the shape of Holden a few yards away and wondered if he was well enough, and I hoped to dear

God he was, because in the next moment the patrol was running into the trees below us and I launched myself from the branch.

I took out the leader first, ejecting my blade so it went through his eye and into his brain, killing him instantly. From my crouching position I sliced up and back and opened the stomach of the second man, who dropped to his knees with his insides glistening through a gaping hole in his tunic then fell face first to the soft forest floor. Looking over, I saw the third man drop off the point of Holden's sword, and Holden look over, even in the dark the triumph written all over his face.

'Good screaming,' I said to Jenny, moments later.

'Pleased to be of assistance.' She frowned. 'But listen, Haytham, I'm not staying in the shadows when we get there.' She raised the knife. 'I want to deal with Birch myself. He took my life away from me. Any mercy he showed by not having me killed I shall repay by leaving him his cock and . . .'

She stopped and looked over at Holden, who knelt nearby and looked away.

'I'm . . .' she began.

'That's all right, Miss,' said Holden. He raised his head and, with a look I'd never seen on his face before, said, 'But you make sure you *do* take his cock and balls before you finish him. You make that bastard *suffer*.'

We made our way around the perimeter back to the gate, where a lone sentry looked agitated, perhaps wondering where the search party had got to; perhaps sensing something was wrong, his soldier's instinct at work.

But whatever instinct he had wasn't enough to keep him alive, and moments later we were ducking through the wicket gate and keeping low to make our way across the lawn. We stopped and knelt by a fountain, holding our breaths at the sound of four more men who came from the front door of the chateau, boots drumming on the paving, calling names. A search party sent to find the first search party. The chateau was on full alert now. So much for a quiet entry. At least we'd reduced their numbers by . . .

Eight. On my signal, Holden and I burst from behind the cover of the fountain base and were upon them, cutting all three down before they even had a chance to draw their swords. We'd been seen. From the chateau there came a shout, and in the next instant was the sharp report of musket fire and balls smacking into the fountain behind us. We ran for it. Towards the front door, where another guard saw us coming and, as I thundered up the short steps towards him, tried to escape through it.

He was too slow. I rammed my blade through the closing door and into the side of his face, using my forward momentum to shove open the door and burst through, rolling into the entrance hall as he fell away with blood sluicing from his shattered jaw. From the landing above came the crack of musket fire, but the gunman had aimed too high and the ball smacked harmlessly into wood. In an instant I was on my feet and charging towards the stairway, bounding up towards the landing, where the sniper abandoned his musket with a yell of frustration, pulled his sword from its sheath and came to meet me.

There was terror in his eyes; my blood was up. I felt more animal than man, working on pure instinct, as though I had levitated from my own body and was watching myself fight. In moments I had opened the gunman and toppled him over the banister to the entrance hall below, where another guard had arrived, just in time to meet Holden as he burst through the front door with Jenny behind him. I leapt from the landing with a shout, landing softly on the body of the man I'd just thrown over and forcing the new arrival to swing about and protect his rear. It was all the opportunity Holden needed to run him through.

With a nod I turned and ran back up the stairs, in time to see a figure appear on the landing, and I ducked at the crack of gunfire as a ball slapped into the stone wall behind me. It was John Harrison and I was upon him before he had a chance to draw his dagger, snatching a fistful of his nightshirt and forcing him to his knees, drawing back my blade arm to strike.

'Did you *know*?' I snarled. 'Did you help take my father and corrupt my *life*?'

He dropped his head in assent and I plunged the blade into the back of his neck, severing the vertebrae, killing him instantly.

I drew my sword. At Reginald's door, I halted, throwing a look up and down the landing, then leaned back and was about to kick it open when I realized it was already ajar. Crouching, I pushed it, and it swung inwards with a creaking sound.

Reginald stood, dressed, at the centre of his chamber. Just like him, always such a stickler for etiquette – he had dressed to meet his killers. Suddenly there was a shadow on the wall, cast by a figure hidden behind the door and, rather than wait for the trap to be sprung, I rammed the sword through the wood, heard a scream of pain from the other side then stepped through and let the door swing closed with the body of the final guard pinned to it, staring at the sword through his chest with wide, disbelieving eyes as his feet scrabbled on the wooden floor.

'Haytham,' said Reginald coolly.

'Was he the last of the guards?' I asked, shoulders heaving as I caught my breath. Behind me, the feet of the dying man still scuffed the wood, and I could hear Jenny and Holden on the other side of the door, struggling to open it with his writhing body in the way. At last, with a final cough, he died, his body dropped from the blade, and Holden and Jenny burst in.

'Yes,' nodded Reginald. 'Just me now.

'Monica and Lucio – are they safe?'

'In their quarters, yes, along the hall.'

'Holden, would you do me a favour?' I asked over my shoulder. 'Would you go and see that Monica and Lucio are unharmed? Their condition may well help determine how much pain we put Mr Birch through.'

Holden pulled the body of the guard away from the door, said, 'Yes, sir,' and left, shutting the door behind him, with a certain finality about the way he did it that wasn't lost on Reginald.

Reginald smiled. A long, slow, sad smile. 'I did what I did for the good of the Order, Haytham. For the good of all humanity.'

'At the expense of my father's life. *You destroyed our family*. Did you think I'd never find out?'

He shook his head sadly. 'My dear boy, as Grand Master, you have to make difficult decisions. Did I not teach you that? I promoted you to Grand Master of the Colonial Rite, knowing that you, too, would have to make similar decisions and having faith in your ability to make them, Haytham. Decisions made in the pursuit of a greater good. In pursuit of an ideal *you* share, remember? You ask, did I think you'd ever find out? And of course the answer is yes. You are resourceful and tenacious. I trained you to be that way. I had to consider the possibility that, one day, you'd learn the truth, but I hoped that when that day arrived you'd take a more philosophical view.' His smile was strained. 'Given the body count, I'm to assume disappointment in that regard, am I?'

I gave a dry laugh. 'Indeed, Reginald. Indeed you are. What you did is a corruption of everything I believe, and do you know why? You did it not with the application of our ideals but with deceit. How can we inspire belief when what we have in our heart is lies?'

He shook his head disgustedly. 'Oh, come on, that's naive rubbish. I'd have expected it of you as a young Adept, but now? During a war, you do what you can to secure victory. It's what you do with that victory that counts.'

'No. We must practise what we preach. Otherwise, our words are hollow.'

'There speaks the Assassin in you,' he said, his eyebrows arched.

I shrugged. 'I'm not ashamed of my roots. I've had

years to reconcile my Assassin blood with my Templar beliefs, and I have done so.'

I could hear Jenny breathing by my side, wet, ragged breaths that even now were quickening.

'Ah, so this is it,' scoffed Reginald. 'You consider yourself a moderate, do you?'

I said nothing.

'And you think you can change things?' he asked with a curled lip.

But the next person to speak was Jenny. 'No, Reginald,' she said. 'Killing you is to take revenge for what you have done to us.'

He turned his attention to her, acknowledging her presence for the first time. 'And how are you, Jenny?' he asked her, raising his chin slightly then adding, disingenuously, 'Time has not withered you, I see.'

She was making a low, growling sound now. From the corner of my eye I saw the hand holding the knife come forward threateningly. So did he.

'And your life as a concubine,' he went on, 'was it a rewarding time for you? I should imagine you got to see so much of the world, so many different people and varied cultures . . .'

He was trying to goad her, and it worked. With a howl of rage born of years of subjugation she lunged at him as though to slash him with the knife.

'*No, Jenny . . .!*' I shouted, but too late, because of course he was ready for her. She was doing exactly what he'd hoped she'd do and, as she came within striking distance, he snatched out his own dagger – it must have been tucked into the back of his belt – and avoided her knife swipe with ease. Then she was howling in pain and indignation as he snatched and twisted her wrist, her knife dropped to the wood and his arm locked around her neck with his blade held to her throat.

Over her shoulder, he looked at me, and his eyes twinkled. I was on the balls of my feet, ready to spring forward, but he pushed the blade to her throat and she whimpered, both of her arms at his forearm trying to dislodge his grip.

'Uh-uh,' he warned, and already he was edging around, keeping the knife to her throat, pulling her back towards the door, the expression on his face changing, though, from triumph to irritation, as she began to struggle.

'Keep still,' he told her through gritted teeth.

'Do as he says, Jenny,' I urged, but she was thrashing in his grip, perspiration-soaked hair plastered to her face, as though she were so revolted by being held by him that she would rather be cut than spend another second in such close proximity. And cut she was, blood flowing down her neck.

'Will you hold still, woman!' he snapped, beginning to lose his composure. 'For the love of God, do you want to die here?'

'Better that and my brother put you to death than allow you to escape,' she hissed, and continued to strain against him. I saw her eyes flick to the floor. Not far away from where they struggled was the body of the guard, and I realized what she was doing a second before it happened: Reginald stumbled against an out-stretched leg of the corpse and lost his footing. Just a little. But enough. Enough so that when Jenny, with a yell of effort, thrust backwards, he tripped over the corpse and lost his balance, thumping heavily against the door – where my sword was still stuck fast through the wood.

His mouth opened in a silent shout of shock and pain. He still held Jenny, but his grip relaxed and she dropped forward, leaving Reginald pinned to the door and looking from me to his chest where the point of the sword protruded from it. When he pulled a pained face there was blood on his teeth. And then, slowly, he slid from the sword and joined the first guard on the floor, his hands at the hole in his chest, blood soaking his clothes and already beginning to pool on the floor.

Turning his head slightly, he was able to look up at me. 'I tried to do what was right, Haytham,' he said. His eyebrows knitted together. 'Surely you can under-stand that?'

I looked down upon him and I grieved, but not for him – for the childhood he'd taken from me.

'No,' I told him, and, as the light faded in his eyes,

I hoped he would take my dispassion with him to the other side.

'*Bastard!*' screamed Jenny from behind me. She had pulled herself to her hands and knees, where she snarled like an animal, 'Count yourself lucky I didn't take your balls,' but I don't think Reginald heard her. Those words would have to remain in the corporeal world. He was dead.

v

From outside there was a noise, and I stepped over the body and pulled the door open, ready to meet more guards if need be. Instead I was greeted by the sight of Monica and Lucio passing by on the landing, both clutching bundles and being ushered towards the stairs by Holden. They had the pale, gaunt faces of the long-incarcerated, and when they looked over the rail to the entrance hall beneath the sight of the bodies made Monica gasp and clutch her hand to her mouth in shock.

'I'm sorry,' I said, not quite sure what I was apologizing for. For surprising them? For the bodies? For the fact that they had been held hostage for four years?

Lucio shot me a look of pure hatred then looked away.

'We don't want your apologies, thank you, sir,' replied

Monica in broken English. 'We thank you for setting us free at last.'

'If you wait for us, we'll be leaving in the morning,' I said. 'If that's all right with you, Holden?'

'Yes, sir.'

'I think we would rather set off as soon as we have gathered together what supplies we need to return home,' replied Monica.

'Please wait,' I said, and could hear the fatigue in my voice. 'Monica. Lucio. Please wait, and we shall all travel together in the morning, to ensure you have safe passage.'

'No, thank you, sir.' They had reached the bottom of the stairs, and Monica turned her face to look up at me. 'I think you have done quite enough. We know where the stables are. If we could help ourselves to supplies from the kitchen and then horses . . .'

'Of course. Of course. Do you have . . . do you have anything to defend yourselves with, should you run into bandits?' I bounded quickly down the stairs and reached to take a sword from one of the dead guards. I handed to Lucio, offering him the handle.

'Lucio, take this,' I said. 'You'll need it to protect your mother as you make your way home.'

He grasped the sword, looked up at me, and I thought I saw a softening in his eyes.

Then he plunged it into me.

27 January 1758

Death. There had been so much of it, and would be more to come.

Years ago, when I had killed the fixer in the Black Forest, it was my mistake to stab him in the kidney and quicken his demise. When Lucio thrust his sword into me in the entrance hall of the chateau, he had quite by chance missed any of my vital organs. His blow was struck with ferocity. As with Jenny, his was an anger born of years of pent-up anger and vengeful dreams. And, as I myself was a man who had spent my entire life seeking revenge, I could hardly blame him for it. But he didn't kill me, obviously, for I'm writing this.

It was enough to cause me serious injury, though, and for the rest of the year I had lain in bed at the chateau. I had stood on a precipice over death's great infinity, drifting in and out of consciousness, wounded, infected and feverish but wearily fighting on, some weak and flickering flame of spirit within me refusing to be doused.

The roles were reversed, and this time it was Holden's turn to tend to me. Whenever I recovered consciousness and awoke from thrashing in sweat-soaked sheets, he would be there, smoothing out the linen, applying fresh cold flannels to my burning brow, soothing me.

'It's all right, sir, it's all right. Just you relax. You're over the worst now.'

Was I? Was I over the worst?

One day – how long into my fever I've no idea – I woke up and, gripping Holden's upper arm, pulled myself into a sitting position, staring intensely into his eyes to ask, 'Lucio. Monica. Where are they?'

I'd had this image – an image of a furious, vengeful Holden cutting them both down.

'Last thing you said before you blacked out was to spare them, sir,' he said, with a look that suggested he wasn't happy about it, 'so spare them's what I did. We sent them on their way with horses and supplies.'

'Good, good . . .' I wheezed and felt the dark rising to claim me again. 'You can't blame . . .'

'Cowardly is what it was,' he was saying ruefully as I lost consciousness again. 'No other word for it, sir. Cowardly. Now just you close your eyes, get your rest . . .'

I saw Jenny, too, and even in my feverish, injured state couldn't help but notice the change in her. It was as though she had achieved an inner peace. Once or twice I was aware of her sitting by the side of my bed, and heard her talking about life at Queen Anne's

Square, how she planned to return and, as she put it, 'take care of business'.

I dreaded to think. Even half-conscious I found it in my heart to pity the poor souls in charge of the Kenways' affairs when my sister Jenny returned to the fold.

On a table by the side of my bed lay Reginald's Templar ring, but I didn't put it on, pick it up, even touch it. For now, at least, I felt neither Templar nor Assassin, and wanted nothing to do with either order.

And then, some three months after Lucio had stabbed me, I climbed out of bed.

Taking a deep breath, with Holden gripping my left forearm in both of his hands, I swept my feet out from underneath the sheets, put them to the cold wooden floor and felt my nightshirt slide down to my knees as I stood upright for the first time in what felt like a lifetime. Straight away, I felt a twinge of pain from the wound at my side and put my hand there.

'It was badly infected, sir,' explained Holden. 'We had to cut away some of the rotted skin.'

I grimaced.

'Where do you want to go, sir?' asked Holden, after we'd walked slowly from the bed to the doorway. It made me feel like an invalid, but I was happy for the moment to be treated like one. My strength would soon return. And then I would be . . .

Back to my old self? I wondered . . .

372

'I think I want to look out of the window, Holden, please,' I said, and he agreed, leading me over to it so that I could gaze out over the grounds where I'd spent so much of my childhood. As I stood there, I realized that, for most of my adult life, when I'd thought of 'home', I'd pictured myself staring out of a window, either over the gardens of Queen Anne's Square or the grounds of the chateau. I'd called both of them home and still did, and now – now that I knew the full truth about Father and Reginald – they'd come to acquire an even greater significance, a duality almost: two halves of my boyhood, two parts of the man I became.

'That's enough, thank you, Holden,' I said, and let him lead me back to the bed. I climbed in, suddenly feeling . . . I hate to admit it, but 'frail', after my long journey all the way to the window and back again.

Even so, my recovery was almost complete and the thought was enough to bring a smile to my face as Holden busied himself collecting a beaker of water and a used flannel, on his face a strange, grim, unreadable expression.

'It's good to see you back on your feet, sir,' he said, when he realized I was looking at him.

'I've got you to thank, Holden,' I said.

'And Miss Jenny, sir,' he reminded me.

'Indeed.'

'We were both worried about you for a while, sir. It was touch and go.'

'Quite something it would have been, to have lived through wars, Assassins and murderous eunuchs, only to die at the hands of a slip of a boy.' I chuckled.

He nodded and laughed drily. 'Quite so, sir,' he agreed. 'A bitter irony indeed.'

'Well, I live to fight another day,' I said, 'and soon, maybe in a week or so, we shall take our leave, travel back to the Americas and there continue my work.'

He looked at me, nodded. 'As you wish, sir,' he said. 'Will that be all for the time being, sir?'

'Yes – yes, of course. Sorry, Holden, to be such a bother these past few months.'

'My only wish has been to see you recover, sir,' he said, and left.

28 January 1758

The first thing I heard this morning was a scream. Jenny's scream. She had walked into the kitchen and found Holden hanging from a clothes dryer.

I knew even before she rushed into my room – I knew what had happened. He'd left a note but he hadn't needed to. He had killed himself because of what the Coptic priests had done to him. It was as simple as that, and no surprise, not really.

I knew from the death of my father that a state of stupefaction is a good index of the grieving to come. The more paralysed, dazed and numb one feels, the longer and more intense the period of mourning.

PART IV

1774, Sixteen Years Later

12 January 1774

i

Writing this at the end of an eventful evening, there is but one question on my mind. Is it possible that . . .

That I have a son?

The answer is I don't know for sure, but there are clues and perhaps most persistently, a *feeling* – a feeling that constantly nags at me, tugging on the hem of my coat like an insistent beggar.

It's not the only weight I carry, of course. There are days I feel bent double with memory, with doubt, regret and grief. Days when it feels as if the ghosts won't leave me alone.

After we buried Holden I departed for the Americas, and Jenny returned to live in England, back at Queen Anne's Square, where she has stayed in glorious spinsterhood ever since. No doubt she's been the subject of endless gossip and speculation about the years she spent away, and no doubt that suits her down to the ground. We correspond, but though I'd like to say our shared experiences had brought us together, the bald fact of the matter is they hadn't. We corresponded because we shared the Kenway name and felt we should stay in touch. Jenny no longer insulted me, so in that sense I suppose our relationship had improved, but our letters were weary and perfunctory. We were two people who had experienced enough suffering and loss to last a dozen lifetimes. What could we possibly discuss in a letter? Nothing. So nothing was what we discussed.

In the meantime – I had been right – I had mourned for Holden. I never knew a greater man than him, and I never will. For him, though, the strength and character he had in abundance just wasn't enough. His manhood had been taken from him. He couldn't live with that, wasn't prepared to, and so he had waited until I was recovered then taken his own life.

I grieved for him and probably always will, and I grieved for Reginald's betrayal, too – for the relationship we once had and for the lies and treachery on which my life was based. And I grieved for the man I had been. The pain in my side had never quite gone away – every now and then it would spasm – and despite the fact that I hadn't given my body permission to grow older, it was determined to do so anyway. Small, wiry hairs had sprouted from my ears and nose. All of a sudden I wasn't as lithe as I once was. Though my standing within the Order was grander than ever, physically I was not the man I once was. On my return to the Americas I'd found a homestead in Virginia on which to grow tobacco and wheat, and I'd ride around the estate, aware of my powers slowly waning as the years passed. Climbing on and off my horse was harder than it had been before. And I don't mean *hard*, just harder, because I was still stronger and faster and more agile than a man half my age and there wasn't a worker on my estate who could best me physically. But even so . . . I wasn't as fast, as strong or as nimble as I had been once. Age had not forgotten to claim me.

In '73, Charles returned to the Americas, too, and became a neighbour, a fellow Virginian estate owner, a mere half-day's ride away, and we had corresponded, agreeing that we needed to meet to talk Templar business and plan to further the interests of the Colonial Rite. Mainly we discussed the developing mood of rebellion, the seeds of revolution floating on the breeze and how best to capitalize on the mood, because our colonials were growing more and more tired of new rules being enforced by the British parliament: the Stamp Act; the Revenue Act; the Indemnity Act; the Commissioners of Customs Act. They were being squeezed for taxes and resented the fact that there was nobody to represent their views, to register their discontent.

A certain George Washington was among the discontents. That young officer who once rode with Braddock had resigned his commission and accepted land bounty for helping the British during the French and Indian War. But his sympathies had shifted in the intervening years. The bright-eyed officer whom I had admired for having a compassionate outlook – more than his commander at least – was now one of the loudest voices in the anti-British movement. No doubt this was because the interests of His Majesty's government conflicted with his own business ambitions; he'd made representations at the Virginia Assembly to try to introduce legislation banning the import of goods from Great Britain. The fact that it was a doomed legislation only added to the growing sense of national discontent.

The Tea Party, when it happened in December '73 – just last month, in fact – was the culmination of years – no, *decades* – of dissatisfaction. By turning the harbour into the world's biggest cup of tea, the colonists were telling Great Britain and the world that they were no longer prepared to live under an unjust system. A full-scale uprising was surely just a matter of months away. So, with the same amount of enthusiasm as I tended my crops, or wrote to Jenny, or climbed out of bed each morning – in other words, very little – I decided it was time for the Order to make preparations for the coming revolution, and I called a meeting.

We assembled, all of us together for the first time in over fifteen years, the men of the Colonial Rite with whom I had shared so many adventures twenty years ago.

We were gathered beneath the low beams of a deserted tavern called the Restless Ghost on the outskirts of Boston. It hadn't been deserted when we'd arrived, but Thomas had seen to it that we soon had the place to ourselves, literally chasing out the few drinkers who were huddled over the wooden tables. Those of us who usually wore a uniform were wearing civilian clothes, with buttoned-up coats and hats pulled down over our eyes, and we sat around a table with tankards close at hand: me, Charles Lee, Benjamin Church, Thomas Hickey, William Johnson and John Pitcairn.

And it was here that I first learnt about the boy.

Benjamin addressed the subject first. He was our man inside Boston's Sons of Liberty, a group of patriots, anti-British colonists who had helped organize the Boston Tea Party, and two years ago, in Martha's Vineyard, he'd had an encounter.

'A native boy,' he said. 'Not someone I'd ever seen before . . .'

'Not someone you *remember* seeing before, Benjamin,' I corrected.

He pulled a face. 'Not someone I *remember* seeing

before, then,' he amended. 'A boy who strode up to me and, bold as brass, demanded to know where Charles was.'

I turned to Charles. 'He's asking for you, then. Do you know who it is?'

'No.' But there was something shifty about the way he said it.

'I'll try again, Charles. Do you have a suspicion who this boy might be?'

He leaned back in his seat and looked away, across the tavern. 'I don't think so,' he said.

'But you're not sure?'

'There was a boy at . . .'

An uncomfortable silence seemed to descend on the table. The men either reached for their tankards or hunched their shoulders or found something to study in the fire nearby. None would meet my eye.

'How about somebody tells me what's going on?' I asked.

These men – not one of them was a tenth of the man Holden had been. I was sick of them, I realized, heartily sick of them. And my feelings were about to intensify.

It was Charles – Charles who was the first to look across the table, hold my gaze and tell me, 'Your Mohawk woman.'

'What about her?'

'I'm sorry, Haytham,' he said. 'Really I am.'

'She's dead?'

'Yes.'

Of course, I thought. So much death. 'When? How?'

'It was during the war. In '60. Fourteen years ago now. Her village was attacked and burned.'

I felt my mouth tighten.

'It was Washington,' he said quickly, glancing at me. 'George Washington and his men. They burned the village and your . . . she died with it.'

'You were there?'

He coloured. 'Yes, we'd hoped to speak to the village elders about the precursor site. There was nothing I could do, though, Haytham, I can assure you. Washington and his men galumphing all over the place. There was a bloodlust on them that day.'

'And there was a boy?' I asked him.

His eyes flicked away. 'Yes, there was a boy – young, about five.'

About five, I thought. I had a vision of Ziio, of the face I'd once loved, when I was capable of doing such a thing, and felt a dull backwash of grief for her and loathing for Washington, who had obviously learnt a thing or two from serving with General Braddock – lessons in brutality and ruthlessness. I thought of the last time she and I had been together, and I pictured her in our small encampment, gazing out into the trees with a faraway look in her eyes and, almost unconsciously, her hands going to her belly.

But no. I cast the idea aside. Too fanciful. Too far-fetched.

'He threatened me, this boy,' Charles was saying.

In different circumstances, I might have smiled at the image of Charles, all six foot of him, being threatened by a five-year-old native boy – if I hadn't been trying to absorb the death of Ziio, that was – and I took a deep but almost imperceptible breath, feeling the air in my chest, and dismissed the image of her.

'I wasn't the only one of us there,' said Charles defensively, and I looked around the table enquiringly.

'Go on, then. Who else?'

William, Thomas and Benjamin all nodded, their eyes fixed on the dark, knotted wood of the tabletop.

'It can't have been him,' said William crossly. 'Can't have been the same kid, surely.'

'Come on, 'Aytham, what are the chances?' chimed Thomas Hickey.

'And you didn't recognize him at Martha's Vineyard?' I asked Benjamin now.

He shook his head, shrugged. 'It was just a kid, an Indian kid. They all look the same, don't they?'

'And what were you doing there, in Martha's Vineyard?'

His voice was testy. 'Having a break.'

Or making plans to line your pockets, I thought, and said, 'Really?'

He pursed his lips. 'If things go as we think, and the rebels organize themselves into an army, then I'm in line to be made chief physician, Master Kenway,' he said, 'one of the most senior positions in the army. I think that, rather than questioning why I was in Martha's Vineyard that day, you might have some words of congratulation for me.'

He cast around the table for support and was greeted with hesitant nods from Thomas and William, both of them giving me a sideways look at the same time.

I conceded. 'And I have completely forgotten my manners, Benjamin. Indeed it will be a great boost for the Order the day you achieve that rank.'

Charles cleared his throat loudly. 'While we also hope that if such an army is formed, our very own Charles will be appointed its commander-in-chief.'

I didn't see exactly, as the light in the tavern was so low, but I could sense Charles redden. 'We do more than merely *hope*,' he protested. 'I am the obvious candidate. My military experience far outstrips that of George Washington.'

'Yes, but you are *English*, Charles,' I sighed.

'*Born* in England,' he spluttered, 'but a colonial in my heart.'

'What's in your heart may not be enough,' I said.

'We shall see,' he returned indignantly.

We would, indeed, I thought wearily, then turned my attention to William, who had been cagey so far, although, as the one who would have been most affected by the events of the Tea Party, it was obvious why.

'And what of your assignment, William? How go the plans to purchase the native land?'

We all knew, of course, but it had to be said, and it had to be said by William, whether he liked it or not. 'The Confederacy has given the deal its blessing . . .' he started.

'But . . . ?'

He took a deep breath. 'You know, of course, Master Kenway, of our plans to raise funds . . .'

'Tea leaves?'

'And you know, of course, all about the Boston Tea Party?'

I held up my hands. 'The repercussions have been felt worldwide. First the Stamp Act, now this. Our colonists are revolting, are they not?'

William shot me a reproachful look. 'I'm glad it's a situation that amuses you, Master Kenway.'

I shrugged. 'The beauty of our approach is that we have all the angles covered. Here around the table we have representatives of the colonials' – I pointed at Benjamin; 'of the British Army' – I indicated John; 'and of course our very own man for hire, Thomas

Hickey. On the outside, your affiliations could not be more different. What you have in your heart are the ideals of the Order. So, you'll have to excuse me, William, if I remain in good humour despite your setback. It's only because I believe that it *is* just a setback, a minor one at that.'

'Well, I hope you're right, Master Kenway, because the fact of the matter is that that avenue of fundraising is now closed to us.'

'Because of the rebels' actions . . .'

'Exactly. And there's another thing . . .'

'What?' I asked, sensing all eyes on me.

'The boy was there. He was one of the ringleaders. He threw crates of tea into the harbour. We all saw him. Me, John, Charles . . .'

'The same boy?'

'Almost certainly,' said William, 'his necklace was exactly as Benjamin described it.'

'Necklace?' I said. 'What sort of necklace?' And I kept my face impassive, tried not to swallow even, as Benjamin went on to describe Ziio's necklace.

It didn't mean anything, I told myself, when they'd finished. Ziio was dead, so of course the necklace would have been passed on – if it was even the same one.

'There's something else, isn't there?' I sighed, looking at their faces.

As one, they nodded, but it was Charles who spoke.

'When Benjamin encountered him at Martha's Vineyard, he was a normal-looking kid. During the Tea Party, he wasn't a normal-looking kid any more. He wore the robes, Haytham,' said Charles.

'The robes?'

'Of an Assassin.'

27 June 1776 (Two Years Later)

i

It was this time last year that I was proved right and Charles wrong, when George Washington was indeed appointed the commander-in-chief of the newly formed Continental Army and Charles made major-general.

And while I was far from pleased to hear the news, Charles was incandescent, and hadn't stopped fuming since. He was fond of saying that George Washington wasn't fit to command a sergeant's guard. Which, of course, as is often the case, was neither true nor an outright falsehood. While on the one hand Washington displayed elements of naivety in his leadership, on the other he had secured some notable victories, most importantly the liberation of Boston in March. He also had the confidence and trust of his people. There was no doubt about it, he had some good qualities.

But he wasn't a Templar, and we wanted the revolution led by one of our own. Not only did we plan to be in control of the winning side, but we thought we had more chance of winning with Charles in charge. And so, we hatched a plot to kill Washington. As simple as that. A plot that would be proceeding nicely but for one thing: this young Assassin. This Assassin – who may or may not be my son – who continued to be a thorn in our side.

ii

First was William. Dead. Killed last year, shortly before the Revolutionary War began. After the Tea Party, William began to broker a deal to buy Indian land. There was much resistance, however, not least among the Iroquois Confederation, who met with William at his home estate. The negotiations had begun well, by all accounts, but, as is the way of things, something was said and things took a turn for the worse.

'Brothers, please,' William had pleaded, 'I am confident we will find a solution.'

But the Iroquois were not listening. The land was theirs, they argued. They closed their ears to the logic offered by William, which was that, if the land passed into Templar hands, then we could keep it from the clutches of whichever force emerged victorious from the forthcoming conflict.

Dissent bubbled through the members of the native confederation. Doubt lurked among them. Some argued that they could never contend with the might of the British or colonial armies themselves; others felt that entering into a deal with William offered no better solution. They had forgotten how the Templars freed their people from Silas's slavery two decades before; instead they remembered the expeditions William had organized into the forest to try to locate the precursor site; the excavations at the chamber we had found. Those outrages were fresh in their minds, impossible to overlook.

'Peace, peace,' argued William. 'Have I not always been an advocate? Have I not always sought to protect you from harm?'

'If you wish to protect us, then give us arms. Muskets and horses that we might defend ourselves,' argued a Confederation member in response.

'War is not the answer,' pressed William.

'We remember you moved the borders. Even today your men dig up the land – showing no regard for those who live upon it. Your words are honeyed, but false. We are not here to negotiate. Nor to sell. We are here to tell you and yours to leave these lands.'

Regrettably, William resorted to force to make his point, and a native was shot, with the threat of more deaths to come unless the Confederation signed the contract.

The men said no, to their credit; they refused to be bowed by William's show of force. What a bitter vindication it must have been as their men began to fall with musket balls in their skulls.

And then the boy appeared. I had William's man describe him to me in detail, and what he said matched exactly what Benjamin had said about the encounter in Martha's Vineyard, and what Charles, William and John had seen at Boston harbour. He wore the same necklace, the same Assassin's robes. It was the same boy.

'This boy, what did he say to William?' I asked the soldier who stood before me.

'He said he planned to ensure an end to Master Johnson's schemes, stop him claiming these lands for the Templars.'

'Did William respond?'

'Indeed he did, sir, he told his killer that the Templars had tried to claim the land in order to protect the Indians. He told the boy that neither King George nor the colonists cared enough to protect the interests of the Iroquois.'

I rolled my eyes. 'Not an especially convincing argument, given that he was in the process of slaughtering the natives when the boy struck.'

The soldier bowed his head. 'Possibly not, sir.'

iii

If I was a little too philosophical when it came to William's death, well, there were extenuating factors. William, though diligent in his work and dedicated, was never the most good-humoured of people and, by meeting a situation that called for diplomacy with force, he'd made a pig's ear of the negotiations. Though it pains me to say it, he had been the architect of his own downfall, and I'm afraid I've never been one for tolerating incompetence: not as a young man, when I suppose it was something I'd inherited from Reginald; and now, having passed my fiftieth birthday, even less so. William had been a bloody fool and paid for it with his life. Equally, the project to secure the native land, while important to us, was no longer our main priority; it hadn't been since the outbreak of war. Our main task now was to assume control of the army and, fair means having failed, we were resorting to foul – by assassinating Washington.

However, that plan was dealt a blow when the Assassin next targeted John, our British army officer, striking at him because of John's work weeding out the rebels. Again, though it was irritating to lose such a valuable man, it might not have affected our plans but for the fact that in John's pocket was a letter – unfortunately, one that detailed plans to kill Washington, naming our Thomas Hickey as the man elected to do the deed. In short order, the youthful Assassin was hotfooting it to New York, with Thomas next on his list.

Thomas was counterfeiting money there, helping to raise funds as well as preparing for the assassination of Washington. Charles was already there with the Continental Army, so I slipped into the city myself and took lodgings. And no sooner had I arrived than I was given the news: the boy had reached Thomas, only for the pair of them to be arrested and both of them tossed in Bridewell Prison.

'There can be no further mistakes, Thomas, am I understood?' I told him when I visited him, shivering in the cold and revolted by the smell, clamour and noise of the jail, when, suddenly, in the cell next door, I saw him: the Assassin.

And knew. He had his mother's eyes, the same jet-black hair, the proud set of his chin. He was the image of her. Without a doubt, he was my son.

iv

'It's him,' said Charles, as we left the prison together. I gave a start, but he didn't notice: New York was freezing, our breath hung in clouds, and he was far too preoccupied with keeping warm.

'It's who?'

'The boy.'

I knew exactly what he meant of course.

'What the hell are you talking about, Charles?' I said crossly, and blew into my hands.

'Do you remember me telling you about a boy I

encountered back in '60, when Washington's men attacked the Indian village?'

'Yes, I remember. And this is our Assassin, is it? The same one as at Boston harbour? The same one who killed William and John? That's the boy who's in there now?'

'It would seem so, Haytham, yes.'

I rounded on him.

'Do you see what this means, Charles? We have *created* that Assassin. In him burns a hatred of all Templars. He saw you the day his village burned, yes?'

'Yes – yes, I've already told you . . .'

'I expect he saw your ring, too. I expect he wore the imprint of your ring on his own skin for some weeks after your encounter. Am I right, Charles?'

'Your concern for the child is touching, Haytham. You always were a great supporter of the natives . . .'

The words froze on his lips because, in the next instant, I'd bunched some of his cape in my fist and thrust him against the stone wall of the prison. I towered over him, and my eyes burned into his.

'My concern is for the Order,' I said. 'My *only* concern is for the Order. And, correct me if I'm wrong, Charles, but the Order does not preach the senseless slaughter of natives, the burning of their villages. That, I seem to recall, was noticeably absent from my teachings. Do you know why? Because it's the kind of behaviour that creates – how would you describe it? – "ill will" among those we might hope to win over to our way of thinking. It sends neutrals scuttling to the side of our enemies. Just as it has here. Men are dead and our plans under threat because of your behaviour sixteen years ago.'

'Not my behaviour – Washington is –'

I let him go, took a step back and clasped my hands behind me. 'Washington will pay for what he has done. We will see to that. He is brutal, that is clear, and not fit to lead.'

'I agree, Haytham, and I've already taken a step to ensure that there are no more interruptions, to kill two birds with one stone, as it were.'

I looked sharply at him. 'Go on.'

'The native boy is to be hanged for plotting to kill George Washington and for the murder of the prison warden. Washington will be there, of course – I plan to make sure of it – and we can use the opportunity to kill him. Thomas, of course, is more than happy to take on the task. It only falls to you, as Grand Master of the Colonial Rite, to give the mission your blessing.'

'It's short notice,' I said, and could hear the doubt in my own voice. But why? Why did I even care any more who lived or died?

Charles spread his hands. 'It is short notice, but sometimes the best plans are.'

'Indeed,' I agreed. 'Indeed.'

'Well?'

I thought. With one word, I would ratify the execution of my own child. What manner of monster could do such a thing?

'Do it,' I said.

'Very well,' he replied, with a sudden, chest-puffed satisfaction. 'Then we won't waste a single moment more. We shall put the word out across New York tonight that tomorrow a traitor to the revolution meets his end.'

v

It is too late for me to feel paternal now. Whatever inside me that might once have been capable of nurturing my child had long since been corrupted or burned away. Years of betrayal and slaughter have seen to that.

28 June 1776

i

This morning I woke up in my lodgings with a start, sitting upright in bed and looking around the unfamiliar room. Outside the window, the streets of New York were stirring. Did I imagine it, or was there a charge in the air, an excited edge to the chatter that rose to my window? And, if there was, did it have anything to do with the fact that today there was an execution in town? Today they would hang . . .

Connor, that's his name. That's the name Ziio gave him. I wondered how different things might have been, had we brought him into this world together.

Would Connor still be his name?

Would he still have chosen the path of the Assassin?

And if the answer to that question was, No, he wouldn't have chosen the path of an Assassin because his father was a Templar, then what did that make me but an abomination, an accident, a mongrel? A man with divided loyalties.

But a man who had decided he could not allow his son to die. Not today.

I dressed, not in my normal clothes but in a dark robe with a hood which I pulled up over my head, then hurried for the stables, found my horse and urged her onwards to the execution square, over muddy streets packed hard, startled city folk scuttling out of my way and shaking their fists at me or staring wide-eyed from beneath the brims of their hats. I thundered on, towards where the crowds became thicker as onlookers congregated for the hanging to come.

And, as I rode, I wondered what I was doing and realized I didn't know. All I knew was how I felt, which was as though I had been asleep but suddenly was awake.

ii

There, on a platform, the gallows awaited its next victim, while a decent-sized crowd was anticipating the day's entertainment. Around the sides of the square were horses and carts, on to which families clambered for a better view: craven-looking men, short women with pinched, worried faces, and grubby children. Sightseers sat in the square while others milled around: women in groups who stood and gossiped, men swigging ale or wine from leather flasks. All of them here to see my son executed.

At one side, a cart flanked by soldiers arrived and

I caught a glimpse of Connor inside, before out jumped a grinning Thomas Hickey, who then yanked him from the cart, too, taunting him at the same time, 'Didn't think I'd miss your going-away party, did you? I hear Washington himself will be in attendance. Hope nothing bad happens to him . . .'

Connor, with his hands bound in front of him, shot a look of hatred at Thomas and, once again, I marvelled at how much of his mother was to be found in those features. But, along with defiance, and bravery, today there was also . . . fear.

'You said there'd be a trial,' he snapped, as Thomas manhandled him.

'Traitors don't get trials, I'm afraid. Lee and Haytham sorted that out. It's straight to the gallows for you.'

I went cold. Connor was about to go to his death thinking I had signed his death warrant.

'I will not die today,' said Connor, proud. 'The same cannot be said for you.' But he was saying it over his shoulder as the guards who had helped escort the cart into the square used pikestaffs to jab him towards the gallows. The noise swelled as the parting crowd reached to try to grab him, punch him, knock him to the ground. I saw a man with hate in his eyes about to throw a punch and was close enough to snatch the punch as it was thrown, twist the man's arm painfully up his back, then throw him to the ground. With blazing eyes he looked up at me, but the sight of me glaring at him from within my hood stopped him, and he picked himself up and in the next moment was swept away by the seething, unruly crowd.

Meanwhile, Connor had been shoved further along the gauntlet of vengeful abuse, and I was too far away to stop another man who suddenly lunged forward and grabbed him – but near enough to see the man's face beneath his hood; near enough to read his lips.

'You are not alone. Only give a cry when you need it . . .'

It was Achilles.

He was here – here to save Connor, who was replying, 'Forget about me – you need to stop Hickey. He's –'

But then he was dragged away, and I finished the sentence in my head: . . . *planning to kill George Washington.*

Talk of the devil. The commander-in-chief had arrived with a small guard. As Connor was pulled on to the platform and an executioner fastened a noose around his neck, the crowd's attention went to the opposite end of the square, where Washington was being led to a raised platform at the back, which, even now, was being frantically cleared of crowds by the guards. Charles, as major-general, was with him, too, and it gave me an opportunity to compare the two: Charles, a good deal taller than Washington, though with a certain aloofness compared to Washington's easy charm. Looking at them together, I saw at once why the Continental Congress had chosen Washington over him. Charles looked so *British*.

Then Charles had left Washington and with a couple of guards made his way across the square, swatting the crowd out of his way as he came, and then was ascending the steps to the gallows, where he addressed the crowd, which pushed forward. I found myself pressed between bodies, smelling ale and sweat, using my elbows to try and find space within the herd.

'Brothers, sisters, fellow patriots,' began Charles, and an impatient hush descended over the crowd. 'Several days ago we learnt of a scheme so vile, so dastardly that even repeating it now disturbs my being. The man before you plotted to murder our much beloved general.'

The crowd gasped.

'Indeed,' roared Charles, warming to his theme. 'What darkness or madness moved him, none can say. And he himself offers no defence. Shows no remorse. And though we have begged and pleaded for him to share what he knows, he maintains a deadly silence.'

At this, the executioner stepped forward and thrust a hessian sack over Connor's head.

'If the man will not explain himself – if he will not confess and atone – what other option is there but this? He sought to send us into the arms of the enemy. Thus we are compelled by justice to send him from this world. May God have mercy on his soul.'

And now he was finished, and I looked around, trying to spot more of Achilles' men. If it was a rescue mission, then now was the time, surely? But where were they? What the hell were they planning?

A bowman. They had to be using a bowman. It wasn't ideal: an arrow wouldn't sever the rope completely, the best the rescuers could hope for was that it would part the fibre enough for Connor's weight to snap it. But it was the most accurate. It could be deployed from . . .

Far away. I swung about to check the buildings behind me. Sure enough, at the spot I would have chosen was a bowman, standing at a tall casement window. As I watched, he drew back the bowstring and squinted along the line of the arrow. Then, just as the trapdoor snapped open and Connor's body dropped, he fired.

The arrow streaked above us, though I was the only one aware of it, and I whipped my gaze over to the platform in time to see it slice the rope and weaken it – of course – but not enough to cut it.

I risked being seen and discovered, but I did what I did anyway, on impulse, on instinct. I snatched my dagger from within my robes, and I threw it, watched as it sailed through the air and thanked God as it sliced into the rope and finished the job.

As Connor's writhing and – thank God – still very much alive body dropped through the trapdoor, a gasp went up around me. For a moment I found myself with about an arm's width of space all around as the crowd recoiled from me in shock. At the same time I caught sight of Achilles ducking down into the gallows pit where Connor's body had fallen. Then I was fighting to escape as the shocked lull was replaced by a vengeful roar, kicks and punches were aimed my way and guards began shouldering their way through the throng towards me. I engaged the blade and cut one or two of the sightseers – enough to draw blood and give other attackers pause for thought. More timid now, they at last made space around me. I dashed out of the square and back to my horse, the catcalls of the angry crowd ringing in my ears.

iii

'He got to Thomas before he could reach Washington,' said Charles despondently later, as we sat in the shadows of the Restless Ghost tavern to talk about the events of the day. He was agitated and constantly looking over his shoulder. He looked like I felt, and I almost envied him the freedom to express his feelings. Me, I had to keep my turmoil hidden. And what turmoil it was: I'd saved the life of my son but effectively sabotaged the work of my own Order – an operation that I myself had decreed. I was a traitor. I had betrayed my people.

'What happened?' I asked.

Connor had reached Thomas and before he killed him was demanding answers. Why had William tried to buy his people's land? Why were we trying to murder Washington?

I nodded. Took a sip of my ale. 'What was Thomas's reply?'

'He said that what Connor sought he'd never find.'

Charles looked at me, his eyes wide and weary.

'What now, Haytham? What now?'

7 January 1778
(Nearly Two Years Later)

i

Charles had begun by resenting Washington, and the fact that our assassination attempt had failed only increased his anger. He took it as a personal affront that Washington had survived – how dare he? – so never quite forgave him for it. Shortly afterwards, New York had fallen to the British, and Washington, who was almost captured, was held to blame, not least by Charles, who was singularly unimpressed by Washington's subsequent foray across the Delaware River, despite the fact that his victory at the Battle of Trenton had renewed confidence in the revolution. For Charles, it was more grist to the mill that Washington went on to lose the Battle of Brandywine and thus Philadelphia. Washington's attack on the British at Germantown had been a catastrophe. And now there was Valley Forge.

After winning the Battle of White Marsh, Washington had taken his troops to what he hoped was a safer location for the new year. Valley Forge, in Pennsylvania, was the high ground he chose: twelve thousand Continentals, so badly equipped and fatigued that the shoeless men left a trail of bloody footprints when they marched to make camp and prepare for the coming winter.

They were a shambles. Food and clothing was in woefully short supply, while horses starved to death or died on their feet. Typhoid, jaundice, dysentery and pneumonia ran unchecked throughout the camp and killed thousands. Morale and discipline were so low as to be virtually non-existent.

Still, though, despite the loss of New York and Philadelphia and the long, slow, freezing death of his army at Valley Forge, Washington had his guardian angel: Connor. And Connor, with the certainty of youth, believed in Washington. No words of mine could possibly persuade him otherwise, that much was for certain; nothing I could have said would convince him that Washington was in fact responsible for the death of his mother. In his mind, it was Templars who were responsible – and who can blame him for coming to that conclusion? After all, he saw Charles there that day. And not just Charles, but William, Thomas and Benjamin.

Ah, Benjamin. My other problem. He had these past years been something of a disgrace to the Order, to put it mildly. After attempting to sell information to the British, he had been hauled before a court of inquiry in '75, headed by who else but George Washington. By now Benjamin was, just as he'd predicted all those years ago, the chief physician and director general of the medical service of the Continental Army. He was convicted of 'communicating with the enemy' and imprisoned, and, to all intents and purposes, he had remained so until earlier this year, when he had been released – and promptly gone missing.

Whether he had recanted the ideals of the Order, just as Braddock had done all those years ago, I didn't know. What I did know was that he was likely to be the one behind the theft of supplies bound for Valley Forge, which of course was making matters worse for the poor souls camped there; that he had forsaken the goals of the Order in favour of personal gain; and that he needed to be stopped – a task I'd taken upon myself, starting in the vicinity of Valley Forge and riding through the freezing, snow-covered Philadelphia wilds until I came to the church where Benjamin had made camp.

ii

A church to find a Church. But abandoned. Not just by its erstwhile congregation but by Benjamin's men. Days ago, they'd been here, but now – nothing. No supplies, no men, just the remains of fires, already cold, and irregular patches of mud and snowless ground where tents had been pitched. I tethered my horse at the back of the church then stepped inside, where it was just as bone-freezing, numbing cold as it was outside. Along the aisle were the remains of more fires and by the door was a pile of wood, which, on closer inspection, I realized was church pews that had been chopped up. Reverence is the first victim of the cold. The remaining pews were in two rows either side of the church, facing an imposing but long-disused pulpit, and dust floated and danced in broad shafts of light projected through grimy windows high up in imposing stone walls. Scattered around a rough stone floor were various upturned crates and the remains of packaging, and for a few moments I paced around, occasionally stooping to overturn a crate in the hope that I might find some clue as to where Benjamin had got to.

Then, a noise – footsteps from the door – and I froze before darting behind the pulpit just as the huge oak doors creaked slowly and ominously open, and a figure entered: a figure who could have been tracing my exact steps, for the way he seemed to pace around the church floor just as I had done, upturning and investigating crates and even cursing under his breath, just as I had.

It was Connor.

I peered from the shadows behind the pulpit. He wore his Assassin's robes and an intense look, and I watched him for a moment. It was as though I were watching myself – a younger version of myself, as an Assassin, the path I should have taken, the path I was being groomed to take, and would have done, had it not been for the treachery of Reginald Birch. Watching him – Connor – what I felt was a fierce mixture of emotions; among them regret, bitterness, even envy.

I moved closer. Let's see how good an Assassin he really is.

Or, to put it another way, let's see if I still had it.

iii

I did.

'Father,' he said, when I had him down and the blade to his throat.

'Connor,' I said sardonically. 'Any last words?'

'Wait.'

'A poor choice.'

He struggled, and his eyes blazed. 'Come to check up on Church, have you? Make sure he's stolen enough for your British brothers?'

'Benjamin Church is no brother of mine.' I tutted. 'No more than the redcoats or their idiot king. I expected naivety. But this . . . The Templars do not fight for the Crown. We seek the same as you, boy. Freedom. Justice. Independence.'

'But . . .'

'But what?' I asked.

'Johnson. Pitcairn. Hickey. They tried to steal land. To sack towns. To murder George Washington.'

I sighed. 'Johnson sought to own the land that we might keep it safe. Pitcairn aimed to encourage diplomacy – which you cocked up thoroughly enough to start a goddamned war. And Hickey? George Washington is a wretched leader. He's lost nearly every battle in which he's taken part. The man's wracked by uncertainty and insecurity. Take one look at Valley Forge and you know my words are true. We'd all be better off without him.'

What I was saying had an effect on him, I could tell. 'Look – much as I'd love to spar with you, Benjamin Church's mouth is as big as his ego. You clearly want the supplies he's stolen; I want him punished. Our interests are aligned.'

'What do you propose?' he said warily.

What *did* I propose? I thought. I saw his eyes go to the amulet at my throat and mine in turn went to the necklace he wore. No doubt his mother told him about the amulet; no doubt he would want to take it from me. On the other hand, the emblems we wore around our necks were both reminders of her.

'A truce,' I said. 'Perhaps – *perhaps* some time together

will do us good. You are my son, after all, and might still be saved from your ignorance.'

There was a pause.

'Or I can kill you now, if you'd prefer?' I laughed.

'Do you know where Church has gone?' he asked.

'Afraid not. I'd hoped to ambush him when he or one of his men returned here. But it seems I was too late. They've come and cleared the place out.'

'I may be able to track him,' he said, with an oddly proud note in his voice.

I stood back and watched as he gave me an ostentatious demonstration of Achilles' training, pointing to marks on the church floor where the crates had been dragged.

'The cargo was heavy,' he said. 'It was probably loaded on to a wagon for transport . . . There were rations inside the crates – medical supplies and clothing as well.'

Outside the church, Connor gestured to some churned-up snow. 'There was a wagon here . . . slowly weighed down as they loaded it with the supplies. Snow's obscured the tracks, but enough remains that we can still follow. Come on . . .'

I collected my horse, joined him and together we rode out, Connor indicating the line of the tracks as I tried to keep my admiration from showing. Not for the first time I found myself struck by the similarities in our knowledge, and noted him doing just as I would have done in the same situation. Some fifteen miles out of the camp he twisted in the saddle and shot me a triumphant look, at the same time as he indicated the trail up ahead. There was a broken-down cart, its driver trying to repair the wheel and muttering as we approached: 'Just my luck . . . Going to freeze to death if I don't get this fixed . . .'

Surprised, he looked up at our arrival, and his eyes widened in fear. Not far away was his musket, but too far to reach. Instantly, I knew – just as Connor haughtily demanded, 'Are you Benjamin Church's man?' – that he was going to make a run for it, and, sure enough, he did. Wild-eyed, he scrambled to his feet and took off into the trees, wading into the snow with a pronounced, trudging run, as ungainly as a wounded elephant.

'Well played,' I smiled, and Connor flashed me an angry look then leapt from his saddle and dived into the tree line to chase the cart driver. I let him go then sighed and climbed down from my horse, checked my blade and listened to the commotion from the forest as Connor caught the man, then I strode into the forest to join them.

'It was not wise to run,' Connor was saying. He'd pinned the driver against a tree.

'W – what do you want?' the wretch managed.

'Where is Benjamin Church?'

'I don't know. We was riding for a camp just north

of here. It's where we normally unload the cargo. Maybe you'll find him th –'

His eyes darted to me, as if looking for support, so I drew my pistol, and shot him.

'Enough of that,' I said. 'Best be on our way then.'

'You did not have to kill him,' said Connor, wiping the man's blood from his face.

'We know where the camp is,' I told him. 'He'd served his purpose.'

As we returned to our horses, I wondered how I appeared to him. What was I trying to teach him? Did I want him as brittle and worn as I was? Was I trying to show him where the path led?

Lost in thought, we rode towards the site of the camp, and as soon as we saw the tell-tale wafting smoke above the tips of the trees, we dismounted, tethered our horses and continued on foot, passing stealthily and silently through the trees. We stayed in the trees, crawling on our bellies and using my spy-glass to squint through trunks and bare branches at distant men who made their way around the camp and clustered around fires trying to keep warm. Connor left, to make his way into the camp, while I made myself comfortable, out of sight.

Or at least I thought so – I thought I was out of sight – until I felt the tickle of a musket at my neck and the words 'Well, well, well, what have we here?'

Cursing, I was dragged to my feet. There were three

of them, all looking pleased with themselves to have caught me – as well they should, because I wasn't easily sneaked up on. Ten years ago, I would have heard them and crept noiselessly away. Ten years before that, I would have heard them coming, hidden then taken them all out.

Two held muskets on me while one of them came forward, licking his lips nervously. Making a noise as if impressed, he unfastened my hidden blade then took my sword, dagger and pistol. And only when I was unarmed did he dare relax, grinning to reveal a tiny skyline of blackened and rotting teeth. I did have one hidden weapon, of course: Connor. But where the hell had he got to?

Rotting Teeth stepped forward. Thank God he was so bad at hiding his intentions that I was able to twist away from the knee he drove into my groin, just enough to avoid serious hurt but make him think otherwise, and I yelped in pretend pain and dropped to the frozen ground, where I stayed for the time being, looking more dazed than I felt and playing for time.

'Must be a Yank spy,' said one of the other men. He leaned on his musket to bend and look at me.

'No. He's something else,' said the first one, and he, too, bent to me, as I pulled myself to my hands and knees. 'Something special. Isn't that right . . . *Haytham?* Church told me *all* about you,' said the foreman.

'Then you should know better than this,' I said.

'You ain't really in any position to be makin' threats,' snarled Rotting Teeth.

'Not yet,' I said, calmly.

'Really?' said Rotting Teeth. 'How 'bout we prove otherwise? You ever had a musket butt in your teeth?'

'No, but it looks like you can tell me how it feels.'

'You what? You tryin' to be funny?'

My eyes travelled up – up to the branches of a tree behind them, where I saw Connor crouched, his hidden blade extended and a finger to his lips. He would be an expert in the trees, of course, taught no doubt by his mother. She'd tutored me in the finer points of climbing, too. Nobody could move through the trees like her.

I looked up at Rotting Teeth, knowing he had mere seconds' life to live. It took the sting out of his boot as it connected with my jaw, and I was lifted and sent flying backwards, landing in a heap in a small thicket.

Perhaps now would be a good time, Connor, I thought. Through eyesight glazed with pain I was rewarded by seeing Connor drop from his perch, his blade hand shoot forward then its blood-flecked silver steel appear from within the mouth of the first luckless guard. The other two were dead by the time I pulled myself to my feet.

'New York,' said Connor.

'What about it?'

'That's where Benjamin is to be found.'

'Then that's where we need to be.'

26 January 1778

i

New York had changed since I last visited, to say the least: it had burned. The great fire of September '76 had started in the Fighting Cocks tavern, destroyed over five hundred homes and left around a quarter of the city burnt out and uninhabitable. The British had put the city under martial law as a result. People's homes had been seized and given to British Army officers; the churches had been converted into prisons, barracks or infirmaries; and it was as though the very spirit of the city had somehow been dimmed. Now it was the Union flag that hung limply from flagpoles at the summit of orange-brick buildings, and where, before, the city had an energy and bustle about it – life beneath its canopies and porticos and behind its windows – now those same canopies were dirty and tattered, the windows blackened with soot. Life went on, but the townsfolk barely raised their eyes from the street. Now, their shoulders were drooped, their movements dispirited.

In such a climate, finding Benjamin's whereabouts

had not been difficult. He was in an abandoned brewery on the waterfront, it turned out.

'We should be done with this by sunrise,' I rather rashly predicted.

'Good,' replied Connor. 'I would like to have those supplies returned as soon as possible.'

'Of course. I wouldn't want to keep you from your lost cause. Come on then, follow me.'

To the roofs we went and, moments later, we were looking out over the New York skyline, momentarily awed by the sight of it, in all its war-torn, tattered glory.

'Tell me something,' Connor said after some moments. 'You could have killed me when we first met – what stayed your hand?'

I could have let you die at the gallows, I thought. I could have had Thomas kill you in Bridewell Prison. What stayed my hand on those two occasions also? What was the answer? Was I getting old? Sentimental? Perhaps I was nostalgic for a life I never really had.

None of this I especially cared to share with Connor, however, and, eventually, after a pause, I dismissed his question with: 'Curiosity. Any other questions?'

'What is it the Templars seek?'

'Order,' I said. 'Purpose. Direction. No more than that. It's your lot that means to confound us with all that nonsense talk of freedom. Once upon a time, the Assassins professed a more sensible goal – that of peace.'

'Freedom *is* peace,' he insisted.

'No. It is an invitation to chaos. Only look at this little revolution your friends have started. I have stood before the Continental Congress. Listened to them stamp and shout. All in the name of liberty. But it's just a noise.'

'And this is why you favour Charles Lee?'

'He understands the needs of this would-be nation far better than the jobbernowls who profess to represent it.'

'It seems to me your tongue has tasted sour grapes,' he said. 'The people made their choice – and it was Washington.'

There it was again. I almost envied him, how he looked at the world in such an unequivocal way. His was a world free of doubt, it seemed. When he eventually learnt the truth about Washington, which, if my plan succeeded, would be soon, his world – and not just his world but his *entire* worldview – would be shattered. If I envied him his certainty now, I didn't envy him that.

'The people chose nothing.' I sighed. 'It was done by a group of privileged cowards seeking only to enrich themselves. They convened in private and made a decision that would benefit them. They may have dressed it up with pretty words, but that doesn't make it true. The only difference, Connor – the only difference between myself and those you aid – is that I do not feign affection.'

He looked at me. Not long ago, I had said to myself that my words would never have any effect on him, yet here I was trying anyway. And maybe I was wrong – maybe what I said was getting through.

ii

At the brewery, it became apparent that we needed a disguise for Connor, his Assassin's robes being a little on the conspicuous side. Procuring one gave him a chance to show off again, and once more I was stingy with my praise. When we were both suitably attired we made our way towards the compound, the red-brick walls towering above us, the dark windows staring implacably upon us. Through the gates I could see the barrels and carts of the brewery business, as well as men walking to and fro. Benjamin had replaced most of the Templar men with mercenaries of his own; it was history repeating itself, I thought, my mind going back to Edward Braddock. I only hoped Benjamin wouldn't be as tough to kill as Braddock. Somehow, I doubted it. I had little faith in the calibre of my enemy these days.

I had little faith in anything these days.

'Hold, strangers!' A guard stepped out of the shadows, disturbing the fog that swirled around our ankles. 'You tread on private property. What business have you here?'

I tipped the brim of my hat to show him my face. 'The Father of Understanding guides us,' I said, and the man seemed to relax, though he looked warily at Connor. 'You, I recognize,' he said, 'but not the savage.'

'He's my son,' I said, and it was . . . odd, hearing the sentiment upon my own lips.

The guard, meanwhile, was studying Connor carefully then, with a sideways glance, said to me, 'Tasted of the forest's fruits, did you?'

I let him live. For now. Just smiled instead.

'Off you go, then,' he said, and we strode through the arched gate and into the main compound of the Smith & Company Brewery. There we quickly ducked into a covered section, with a series of doors leading into warehouses and office space. Straight away I set to picking the lock of the first door we came to as Connor kept watch, talking at the same time.

'It must be strange to you, discovering my existence as you have,' he said.

'I'm actually curious to know what your mother said about me,' I replied, working the lock-pick. 'I often wondered what life might have been like, had she and I stayed together.' Acting on an instinct, I asked him, 'How is she, by the way?'

'Dead,' he said. 'She was murdered.'

By Washington, I thought, but said nothing, except, 'I'm sorry to hear that.'

'Really? It was done by your men.'

By now I'd opened the door but instead of going through I closed it and turned to face Connor. '*What?*'

'I was just a child when they came looking for the elders. I knew they were dangerous even then, so I stayed silent. Charles Lee beat me unconscious for it.'

So I had been right. Charles had indeed left the physical as well as the metaphorical imprint of his Templar ring on Connor.

It was not hard to let the horror show on my face, although I pretended to be shocked as he continued, 'When I woke, I found my village in flames. Your men were gone by then, as well as any hope for my mother's survival.'

Now – now was an opportunity to try to convince him of the truth.

'Impossible,' I said. 'I gave no such order. Spoke of the opposite, in fact – I told them to give up the search for the precursor site. We were to focus on more practical pursuits . . .'

Connor looked dubious but shrugged. 'It doesn't matter. It's long done now.'

Oh, but it did, it did matter.

'But you've grown up all your life believing me – your own father – responsible for this atrocity. I had no hand in it.'

'Maybe you speak true. Maybe not. How am I ever to know?'

Silently, we let ourselves into the warehouse, where stacked barrels seemed to crowd out any light and not far away stood a figure with his back to us, the only sound the soft scratching he made as he wrote in a ledger he held. I recognized him at once, of course, and drew a long breath before calling out to him.

'Benjamin Church,' I announced, 'you stand accused of betraying the Templar Order and abandoning our principles in pursuit of personal gain. In consideration of your crimes, I hereby sentence you to death.'

Benjamin turned. Only it wasn't Benjamin. It was a decoy – who suddenly cried, 'Now, *now*!', at which the room was full of men who rushed from hiding places, holding pistols and swords on us.

'You're too late,' crowed the decoy. 'Church and the cargo are long gone. And I'm afraid you won't be in any condition to follow.'

We stood, the men assembled before us, and thanked God for Achilles and his training, because we were both thinking the same things. We were thinking: when facing superior strength, wrest from them the element of surprise. We were thinking: turn defence into attack.

So that's what we did. We attacked. With a quick glance at one another we both released our blades, both sprung forward, both embedded them into the nearest guard, whose screams echoed around the brick walls of the warehouse. I kicked out and sent one of their gunmen skidding back and smashing his head against a crate, then was upon him, my knees on his chest, driving the blade through his face and into his brain.

I twisted in time to see Connor whirl, keeping low and slicing his blade hand around at the same time, opening the stomachs of two luckless guards, who both dropped, clutching at their gaping stomachs, both dead men who didn't know it yet. A musket went off, and I heard the air sing, knowing the ball had just missed me but making the sniper pay for it with his life. Two men came towards me, swinging wildly, and as I took them both down I thanked our lucky stars that Benjamin had used mercenaries rather than Templar men, who wouldn't have been so swiftly overcome.

As it was, the fight was short and brutal, until just the decoy was left and Connor was looming over him as he trembled like a frightened child on the brickwork floor now slick with blood.

I finished a dying man then strode over to hear Connor demand, 'Where's Church?'

'I'll tell you,' wailed the decoy, 'anything you want. Only promise that you'll let me live.'

Connor looked at me and, whether or not we agreed,

he helped him to his feet. With a nervous glance from one to the other of us, the decoy continued, 'He left yesterday for Martinique. Took passage on a trading sloop called the *Welcome*. Loaded half its hold with the supplies he stole from the patriots. That's all I know. I swear.'

Standing behind him, I thrust my blade into his spinal cord and he stared in blank amazement at the bloodstained tip as it protruded from his chest.

'You promised . . .' he said.

'And *he* kept his word,' I said coldly, and looked at Connor, almost daring him to contradict me. 'Let's go,' I added, just as a trio of riflemen rushed on to the balcony above us with a clatter of boots on wood, tucked their rifle musket butts into their shoulders and opened fire. But not at us, at barrels nearby, which, too late, I realized were full of gunpowder.

I just had time to heave Connor behind some beer barrels as the first of the kegs went up, followed by the ones around it, each exploding with a deafening thunderclap that seemed to bend the air and stop time – a blast so fierce that, when I opened my eyes and took my hands away from my ears, I found I was almost surprised the warehouse was still standing around us. Every man in the place had either hurled himself to the ground or been thrown there by the force of the explosion. But the guards were picking themselves up, reaching for their muskets and, still deafened, shouting at each other as they squinted through the dust for us. Flames were licking up the barrels; crates catching fire. Not far away, a guard came running on to the warehouse floor, his clothes and hair ablaze, screamed as his face melted then sank to his knees and died face down to the stone. The greedy fire found some nearby crate stuffing, which went up in an instant. All around us, an inferno.

Musket balls began zipping around us. We felled two swordsmen on our way to the steps leading up to the gantry then hacked our way through a squad of four riflemen. The fire was rising quickly – even the guards were beginning to escape now – so we ran to the next level, climbing up and up, until at last we'd reached the attic of the brewery warehouse.

Our assailants were behind us, but not the flames. Looking out of a window, we could see water below us, and I cast around for an exit. Connor grabbed me and swung me towards the window, smashing the two of us through the glass so that we dropped to the water before I'd even had a chance to protest.

7 March 1778

i

There was no way I was going to let Benjamin get away. Not having had to put up with life on the *Aquila* for almost a month, trapped with Connor's friend and ship's captain Robert Faulkner, among others, chasing Benjamin's schooner, which had stayed just out of our reach, dodging cannon attacks, catching tantalizing glimpses of him on the deck of his ship, his taunting face . . . No way was I going to let him get away. Especially as we came so near in waters close to the Gulf of Mexico, the *Aquila* at last racing up alongside his schooner.

Which was why I snatched the ship's wheel from Connor, wrenched it hard starboard and with a lurch sent the ship speeding towards the schooner. Nobody had expected that to happen. Not the crew of his ship. Not the men on the *Aquila*, not Connor or Robert – only me; and I'm not sure I knew until I did it, when any crew member who wasn't hanging on to something was thrown violently to the side and the prow of the *Aquila* crunched into the schooner's port side at an angle, breaching and splintering the hull. Perhaps it was rash of me. Perhaps I would owe Connor – and certainly Faulkner – an apology for the damage done to their ship.

But I couldn't let him get away.

ii

For a moment there was a stunned silence, just the sound of ship debris slapping against the ocean around, and the groan and creek of battered, distressed timber. The sails fluttered in a gentle breeze above us, but neither ship moved, as though both were immobilized by the shock of the impact.

And then, just as suddenly, a cry went up as the crew from both ships recovered their senses. I was ahead of Connor and had already dashed to the prow of the *Aquila*, swinging to the deck of Benjamin's schooner, where I hit the wood with extended blade and killed the first crew member who raised a weapon towards me, stabbing him and swinging his writhing body overboard.

Spotting the hatch, I ran to it, hauled out a sailor trying to escape and punched the blade into his chest before taking the steps and, with a final look at the devastation I'd caused, as the two huge ships locked together and began slowly to turn in the ocean, I slammed the hatch closed behind me.

From above came the thunder of feet on deck, the muted screams and gun blasts of battle and the thud of bodies hitting the wood. Below decks, there was a strange, damp, almost eerie silence. But, from further along, I realized, came the slosh and drip that told me the schooner was taking on water. I grabbed a wooden strut as it suddenly listed and, somewhere, the drip of water became a constant flow. How long would it remain afloat? I wondered.

Meantime, I saw what Connor would soon discover: that the supplies we'd spent so long in pursuit of were non-existent – or on this ship anyway.

Just as I was absorbing this, I heard a noise and twisted to see Benjamin Church holding a pistol two-handed on me, squinting along its sights.

'Hello, Haytham,' he snarled, and pulled the trigger.

He was good. I knew that. It was why he pulled the trigger right away, to put me down while he still had the element of surprise; and why he didn't aim directly for me but at a spot slightly to my right, because I'm a right-sided fighter and would naturally dive to my strongest side.

But of course I knew that because I'd trained him. And his shot smacked harmlessly into the hull when I dived, not to the right but to the left, rolled then came to my feet, pounced and was upon him before he could draw his sword. With a fistful of his shirt in my hand I snatched his pistol and tossed it away.

'We had a dream, Benjamin,' I snarled into his face, 'a dream you sought to destroy. And for that, my fallen friend, you will be made to pay.'

I kneed him in the groin. When he doubled over, gasping with pain, I drove my fist into his abdomen then followed it up with a punch to the jaw that was hard enough to send two bloodied teeth skittering along the deck.

I let him drop, and he fell to where the wood was already wet, his face splashing into a wash of incoming seawater. Again the ship lurched but, for the moment, I didn't care. When Benjamin tried to get to his hands and knees I lashed out with my boot, kicking whatever breath he had left out of him. Next I grabbed a length of rope and hauled him to his feet, shoved him against a barrel then wound it around him, securing him fast. His head dropped forward, trails of blood, spit and snot spooling slowly to the wood below. I stood back, took hold of his hair then looked into his eyes, drove a fist into his face and heard the crunch of his breaking nose then stood back, shaking the blood from my knuckles.

'*Enough!*' cried Connor from behind me, and I turned to see him staring at me, and then at Benjamin, with a disgusted look on his face.

'We came here for a reason . . .' he said.

I shook my head. 'Different reasons, it seems.'

But Connor pushed past me and waded through water, now ankle deep, to Benjamin, who regarded him with defiance in his bruised and bloodshot eyes.

'Where are the supplies you stole?' Connor demanded.

Benjamin spat. 'Go to hell.' And then, incredibly, began to sing: 'Rule Britannia'.

I stepped forward. 'Shut your mouth, Church.'

Not that it stopped him. He continued singing.

'Connor,' I said, 'get what you need from him and let's be done with this.'

And at last Connor stepped forward, his blade engaged, and held it to Benjamin's throat.

'I ask again,' said Connor: 'where is your cargo?'

Benjamin looked at him and blinked. For a moment I thought his next move would be to insult or spit at Connor, but instead he began to speak. 'On the island yonder, awaiting pick-up. But you've no right to it. It isn't yours.'

'No, not mine,' said Connor. 'Those supplies are made for men and women who believe in something bigger than themselves, who fight and die that one day they may live free from tyranny such as yours.'

Benjamin smiled sadly. 'Are these the same men and women who fight with muskets forged from British steel? Who bind their wounds with bandages sown by British hands? How convenient for them that we do the work. They reap the rewards.'

'You spin a story to excuse your crimes. As though you're the innocent one and they the thieves,' argued Connor.

'It's all a matter of perspective. There is no single path through life that is right and fair and does no harm. Do you truly think the Crown has no cause? No right to feel betrayed? You should know better than this, dedicated as you are to fighting Templars – who themselves see their work as just. Think on that the next time you insist that your work alone befits the greater good. Your enemy would beg to differ – and would not be without cause.'

'Your words may have been sincere,' whispered Connor, 'but it does not make them true.'

And he finished him.

'You did well,' I said as Benjamin's chin dropped to his chest and his blood splashed to the water that continued to rise. 'His passing is a boon for us both. Come on. I suppose you'll want my help retrieving everything from the island . . .'

16 June 1778

i

It had been months since I'd last seen him, yet I cannot deny I thought of him often. When I did, I thought, What hope is there for us? Me, a Templar – a Templar forged in the crucible of treachery, but a Templar nevertheless – and him an Assassin, created by the butchery of the Templars.

Once upon a time, many years ago, I'd dreamed of one day uniting Assassin and Templar, but I was a younger and more idealistic man then. The world had yet to show me its true face. And its true face was unforgiving, cruel and pitiless, barbaric and brutal. There was no place in it for dreams.

And yet, he came to me again, and though he said nothing – not so far anyway – I wondered if the idealism I'd once had lurked behind those eyes, and it was that which brought him once more to my door in New York, seeking answers perhaps, or wanting an end to some doubt that nagged at him.

Perhaps I was wrong. Perhaps there was an uncertainty that resided within that young soul after all.

New York was still in the grip of the redcoats, squads of them out on the streets. It was years later, and still nobody had been held responsible for the fire that had plunged the city into a grimy, soot-stained depression. Parts of it were still uninhabitable. Martial law continued, the redcoats' rule was harsh and the people more resentful than ever. As an outsider I studied the two groups of people, the downtrodden city folk giving hateful looks to the brutalized, unruly soldiers. I watched them with a jaundiced eye. And, dutifully, I continued. I worked to try to help win this war, end the occupation, find peace.

I was grilling one of my informants, a wretch named Twitch – because of something he did with his nose – when I saw Connor out of the corner of my eye. I held up a hand to stop him while I continued listening to Twitch, and wondered what he wanted. What business did he have with the man he believed had given the order to kill his mother?

'We need to know what the loyalists are planning if we are to put an end to this,' I said to my man. Connor loitered, overhearing – not that it mattered.

'I've tried,' responded Twitch, as his nostrils flared and his eyes darted to Connor, 'but the soldiers themselves are told nothing now: only to await orders from above.'

'Then keep digging. Come and find me when you have something worth sharing.'

Twitch nodded, slunk off, and I took a deep breath to face Connor. For a moment or so we regarded one another, and I looked him up and down, his Assassin's robes somehow at odds with the young Indian boy beneath, his long dark hair, those piercing eyes – Ziio's eyes. What lay behind them? I wondered.

Above us, a flock of birds made itself comfortable on the ledge of a building, cawing loudly. Nearby, a patrol of redcoats lounged by a cart to admire passing laundry women, making lewd suggestions and responding to any disapproving looks and tuts with threatening gestures.

'We're so close to victory,' I told Connor, taking his arm and leading him further down the street, away from the redcoats. 'Just a few more well-placed attacks and we can end the civil war and be rid of the Crown.'

An almost-smile at the edges of his mouth betrayed a certain satisfaction. 'What did you intend?'

'Nothing at the moment – since we're completely in the dark.'

'I thought Templars had eyes and ears everywhere,' he said, with just a hint of dry humour. Just like his mother.

'We did. Until you started cutting them off.'

He smiled. 'Your contact said it was orders from above. It tells us exactly what we need to do: track down other loyalist commanders.'

'The soldiers answer to the Jaegers,' I said. 'The

Jaegers to the commanders, which means . . . we work our way up the chain.'

I looked up. Not far away, the redcoats were still being lewd, letting down their uniform, the flag and King George. The Jaegers were the link between the army high-ups and the troops on the ground and were supposed to keep the redcoats in check, stop them aggravating an already hostile populace, but they rarely showed their faces, only if there was real trouble on the streets. Like if someone, say, killed a redcoat. Or two.

From my robes I drew my pistol and pointed it across the street. I saw Connor's mouth drop open out of the corner of my eye as I took aim at the unruly group of redcoats near the cart, picked one who, even now, was making an off-colour suggestion to a woman, who walked past with swishing skirts and her head bowed, blushing beneath her bonnet. And pulled the trigger.

The report of my gun cracked open the day and the redcoat staggered back, a penny-sized hole between his eyes already beginning to leak dark-red blood as his musket dropped and he fell heavily back into a cart and lay still.

For a moment the other redcoats were too shocked to do anything, their heads swinging this way and that as they tried to locate the source of the gunshot while pulling their rifles from their shoulders.

I began to make my way across the street.

'What you doing?' called Connor after me.

'Kill enough, and the Jaegers will appear,' I told him. 'They'll lead us right back to those in charge' – and as one of the redcoats turned to me and went to jab with his bayonet, I swept the blade across his front, slicing through his white criss-crossed belts, his tunic and his stomach. I laid into the next one straight away, while another, who tried to retreat and find space to raise his weapon and fire, backed straight into Connor and in the next instant was sliding off his blade.

The battle was over, and the street, busy before, was suddenly empty. At the same time I heard bells, and winked. 'The Jaegers are out, just as I said they'd be.'

It was a matter of trapping one, a task I was happy to leave to Connor, and he didn't let me down. In less than an hour we had a letter, and as groups of Jaegers and redcoats ran shouting up and down the streets, angrily searching for the two Assassins – *Assassins, I tell you. They used the blade of the Hashashin'* – who had so mercilessly cut down one of their patrols, we took to the roofs, where we sat and read it.

'The letter's encrypted,' said Connor.

'Not to worry,' I said. 'I know the cipher. After all, it's a Templar invention.'

I read it then explained. 'The British command is in disarray. The Howe brothers have resigned and Cornwallis and Clinton have left the city. The leadership that remains has called a meeting at the ruins of Trinity Church. It's there we should go.'

The Trinity Church was at the intersection of Wall Street and Broadway. Or, I should say, what was left of the Trinity Church was at the intersection of Wall Street and Broadway. It had been badly burned in the great fire of September '76, so badly burned, in fact, that the British hadn't bothered to try to convert it to use as barracks, or to imprison patriots. Instead they'd constructed a fence and used it for occasions such as this – the meeting of commanders that Connor and I fully intended to gatecrash.

Wall Street and Broadway were both dark. The lamplighters didn't come here because there were no lamps to light, none in working order anyway. Like everything else within about a mile's radius of the church, they were blackened and soot-covered, their windows smashed. And what would they illuminate anyway? The greyed-out, broken windows of the surrounding buildings? Empty stone and wooden carcasses fit only for habitation by stray dogs and vermin.

Above it all towered the spire of Trinity, and it was there we headed, scaling one of the remaining walls of the church in order to take up position. As we climbed I realized that what the building reminded me of was an enlarged version of my home at Queen Anne's Square, how it had looked after the fire. And as we crouched in the shadowy alcoves awaiting the arrival of the redcoats, I recalled the day I'd gone back to the house with Reginald and how it had looked. Like the church, its roof had been taken by fire. Like the church, it was a shell, a shadow of its former self. Above us, the stars twinkled in the sky, and I stared at them for a moment through the open roof, until an elbow in my side roused me from my reverie and Connor was indicating down to where officers and redcoats were making their way along the deserted rubble of Wall Street towards the church. As they approached, two men ahead of the squad were pulling a cart and hanging lanterns in the black and brittle branches of the trees, lighting the way. They reached the church and we cast our eyes downwards as they hung more lanterns below. They moved quickly among the truncated columns of the church, where weeds, moss and grass had begun to grow, nature claiming the ruins for herself, and placed lanterns on the font and lectern, then stood to one side as the delegates strode in: three commanders and a squad of soldiers.

Next we were both straining to hear the conversation and having no luck. Instead I counted the guards, twelve of them, but I didn't think it too many.

'They're talking in circles,' I hissed to Connor. 'We'll learn nothing, watching as we are.'

'What do you propose?' he replied. 'That we get down there and demand answers?'

I looked at him. Grinned. 'Well, yes,' I said.

And in the next instant I was climbing down until I was close enough, and jumped down, surprising two of the guards at the rear, who died, their mouths making an O shape.

'Ambush!' went the cry as I piled into two more of the redcoats. From above I heard Connor curse as he leapt from his perch to join me.

I was right. There weren't too many. The redcoats, as ever, were too reliant on muskets and bayonets. Effective on the battlefield, perhaps, but useless at close-quarter combat, which was where Connor and I excelled. We were fighting well together by now, almost a partnership. Before long, the moss-covered figurines of the burnt-out church sparkled with fresh redcoat blood, the twelve guards were dead and just the three terrified commanders remained, cowering, lips moving in prayer as they prepared to die.

I had something else in mind – a trip to Fort George, to be precise.

iii

In southernmost Manhattan was Fort George. Over one hundred and fifty years old, from the sea it presented a vast skyline of spires, watchtowers and long barracks buildings that seemed to run across the entire length of the promontory, while inside the towering battlements were expanses of drill square surrounding the tall dormitories and administrative buildings, all of it heavily defended and fortified. A perfect place for the Templars to make their base. A perfect place for us to take the three loyalist commanders.

'What are the British planning?' I asked the first one, after lashing him to a chair in an interrogation room deep in the bowels of the North End building, where the smell of damp was all-pervasive and where, if you listened carefully, you could just hear the scratching and gnawing of the rats.

'Why should I tell you?' he sneered.

'Because I'll kill you if you don't.'

His arms were bound, but he indicated the interrogation room with his chin. 'You'll kill me if I do.'

I smiled. 'Many years ago I met a man named Cutter, an expert in torture and the administration of pain, who was able to keep his victims alive for days on end, but in considerable pain, with only ...' I flicked the mechanism of the blade and it appeared, glinting cruelly in the flickering torchlight.

He looked at it. 'You promise me a quick death if I tell you.'

'You have my word.'

So he did, and I kept my word. When it was over

I strode out into the passageway outside, where I ignored Connor's inquisitive look and collected the second prisoner. Back in the cell I tied him to the chair and watched as his eyes went to the body of the first man.

'Your friend refused to tell me what I wanted to know,' I explained, 'which is why I slit his throat. Are you prepared to tell me what I want to know?'

Wide-eyed, he gulped, 'Look, whatever it is, I can't tell you – I don't even know. Maybe the commander . . .'

'Oh, you're not the man in charge?' I said breezily, and flicked my blade.

'Wait a minute . . .' he blurted, as I moved to the back of him. 'There is one thing I know . . .'

I stopped. 'Go on . . .'

He told me and, when it was over, I thanked him and drew the blade across his throat. As he died, I realized that what I felt was not the righteous fire of one who performs repellent acts in the name of a greater good but a sense of jaded inevitability. Many years ago, my father had taught me about mercy, about clemency. Now I slaughtered prisoners like livestock. This was how corrupt I had become.

'What's going on in there?' asked Connor suspiciously, when I returned to the passageway where he guarded the final prisoner.

'This one is the commander. Bring him in.'

Moments later, the door to the interrogation room thumped shut behind us, and for a moment the only sound in the room was that of dripping blood. Seeing the bodies discarded in a corner of the cell, the commander struggled, but, with a hand to his shoulder, I shoved him to the chair, now slick with blood, lashed him to it, then stood before him and flicked my finger to engage my hidden blade. It made a soft snicking sound in the cell.

The officer's eyes went to it and then to me. He was trying to put on a brave face, but there was no disguising the tremble of his lower lip.

'What are the British planning?' I asked him.

Connor's eyes were on me. The prisoner's eyes were on me. When he stayed silent I raised the blade slightly so that it reflected the flickering torchlight. Again, his eyes were fixed on it, and then, he broke . . .

'To – to march from Philadelphia. That city is finished. New York is the key. They'll double our numbers – push back the rebels.'

'When do they begin?' I asked.

'Two days from now.'

'June the 18th,' said Connor from beside me. 'I need to warn Washington.'

'See?' I told the commander. 'That wasn't very difficult now, was it?'

'I told you everything. Now let me go,' he said, but

445

I was again in no mood for clemency. I stood behind him and, as Connor watched, opened his throat. At the boy's horrified look, I said, 'And the other two said the same. It must be true.'

When Connor looked at me, it was with disgust. 'You killed him . . . killed all of them. Why?'

'They would have warned the loyalists,' I answered simply.

'You could have held them until the fight was done.'

'Not far away from here is Wallabout Bay,' I said, 'where the prison ship HMS *Jersey* is moored, a rotting ship on which patriot prisoners of war are dying by the thousands, buried in shallow graves on the shores or simply tossed overboard. That was how the British treat *their* prisoners, Connor.'

He acknowledged the point but countered, 'Which is why we must be free of their tyranny.'

'Ah, tyranny. Don't forget that your leader George Washington could save these men on the prison ships, if he was so minded. But he does not want to exchange captured British soldiers for captured American ones, and so the American prisoners of war are sentenced to rot on the prison ships of Wallabout Bay. That's your hero George Washington at work. However this revolution ends, Connor, you can guarantee that it's the men with riches and land who will benefit. The slaves, the poor, the enlisted men – they will still be left to rot.'

'George is different,' he said, but yes, now there was a note of doubt in his voice.

'You will see his true face soon, Connor. It will reveal itself, and when it does you can make your decision. You can judge him.'

17 June 1778

i

Though I'd heard so much about it, I hadn't seen Valley Forge with my own eyes, and there, this morning, was where I found myself.

Things had clearly improved, that much was certain. The snow had gone; the sun was out. As we walked, I saw a squad being put through its paces by a man with a Prussian accent, who, if I wasn't very much mistaken, was the famous Baron Friedrich von Steuben, Washington's chief of staff, who had played his part in whipping his army into shape. And indeed he had. Where before the men had been lacking in morale and discipline, suffering from disease and malnutrition, now the camp was full of healthy, well-fed troops who marched with a lively clatter of weapons and flasks, a hurry and purpose to their step. Weaving among them were camp followers who carried baskets of supplies and laundry, or steaming pots and kettles for the fires. Even the dogs that chased and played at the margins of the camp seemed to do so with a renewed energy and vigour. Here, I realized, was where independence could be born: with spirit, co-operation, and fortitude.

Nevertheless, as Connor and I strode through the camp, what struck me was that it was largely due to the efforts of Assassins and Templars that the camp had improved in spirit. We had secured the supplies and prevented more theft, and I was told that Connor had had a hand in securing the safety of von Steuben. What had their glorious leader Washington done, except for leading them into that mess in the first place?

Still, though, they believed in him.

All the more reason his mendacity should be exposed. All the more reason Connor should see his true face.

'We should be sharing what we know with Lee, not Washington . . .' I said irritably as we walked.

'You seem to think I favour him,' replied Connor. His guard was down and his black hair shone in the sun. Here, away from the city, it was as if his native side had bloomed. 'But my enemy is a notion, not a nation. It is wrong to compel obedience – whether to the British Crown or the Templar cross. And I hope in time that the loyalists will see this too, for they are also victims.'

I shook my head. 'You oppose tyranny. Injustice. But these are symptoms, son. Their true cause is human weakness. Why do you think I keep trying to show you the error of your ways?'

'You have said much, yes. But you have *shown* me nothing.'

No, I thought, because you don't listen to the truth when it comes from my mouth, do you? You need to hear it from the very man you idolize. You need to hear it from Washington.

ii

In a timber cabin we found the leader, who had been attending to correspondence, and, passing through the guard at the entrance, we closed the door on the clamour of the camp, banishing the drill sergeant's orders, the constant clanking of implements from the kitchen, the trundle of carts.

He glanced up, smiling and nodding at Connor, feeling so utterly safe in his presence he was happy for the guards to remain outside, and giving me the benefit of a cooler, appraising stare before holding up a hand to return to his paperwork. He dipped his quill in his inkpot and, as we stood and patiently awaited our audience, signed something with a flourish. He returned the quill to the pot, blotted the document then stood and came out from behind the desk to greet us, Connor more warmly than me.

'What brings you here?' he said, and as the two friends embraced I found myself close to Washington's desk. Keeping my eyes on the two, I edged back a little and cast my eyes to the desktop, looking for something, anything, I could use as evidence in my testimony against him.

'The British have recalled their men in Philadelphia,' Connor was saying. 'They march for New York.'

Washington nodded gravely. Though the British had control of New York, the rebels still controlled sections of the city. New York remained pivotal to the war, and if the British could wrest control of it once and for all, they would gain a significant advantage.

'Very well,' said Washington, whose own foray across the Delaware to retake land in New Jersey had already been one of the major turning points of the war, 'I'll move forces to Monmouth. If we can rout them, we'll have finally turned the tide.' As they were speaking, I was trying to read the document Washington had just signed. I reached to adjust it slightly with my fingertips, so that I could see it clearly. And then, with a silent, triumphant cheer, I picked it up and held it for them both to see.

'And what's this?'

Interrupted, Washington swung around and saw what I had in my hand. 'Private correspondence,' he bristled, and moved to snatch it back before I pulled it away and stepped out from behind the desk.

'I'm sure it is. Would you like to know what it says, Connor?'

Confusion and torn loyalties clouded his features. His mouth worked, but said nothing and his eyes darted from me to Washington as I continued: 'It seems your dear friend here has just ordered an *attack* on your village. Although "attack" might be putting it mildly. Tell him, Commander.'

Indignant, Washington responded, 'We've been receiving reports of Allied natives working with the British. I've asked my men to put a stop to it.'

'By burning their villages and salting the land. By calling for their extermination, according to this order.'

Now I had my chance to tell Connor the truth. 'And this is not the first time either.' I looked at Washington. Tell him what you did fourteen years ago.'

For a moment there was nothing but a tense silence in the cabin. From outside, the cling-clang of the kitchens, the gentle rattle of carts passing in and out of the camp, the stentorian bark of the drill sergeant, the rhythmic crunch of marching boots. While, inside, Washington's cheeks reddened as he looked at Connor and perhaps made some connections in his head, and realized exactly what it was that he had done all of those years ago. His mouth opened and closed as though he were finding it difficult to access the words.

'That was another time,' he blustered at last. Charles always liked to refer to Washington as an indecisive, stuttering fool and, here, for the first time, I knew exactly what he meant. 'The Seven Years War,' said Washington, as though that fact alone should explain everything.

I glanced at Connor, who had frozen, looking for all the world as though he were merely distracted, thinking about something else rather than paying attention to what was going on in the room, then reached for him. 'And so now you see, my son – what becomes of this "great man" under duress. He makes excuses. He displaces blame. He does a great many things, in fact – *except* take responsibility.'

The blood had drained from Washington's face. His eyes dropped, and he stared at the floor, his guilt clear for all to see.

I looked appealingly at Connor, who began to breathe heavily then exploded in anger, '*Enough!* Who did what and why must wait. My people must come first.'

I reached for him.

'*No!*' He recoiled. 'You and I are finished.'

'Son . . .' I started.

But he rounded on me. 'Do you think me so soft that calling me son might change my mind? How long did you sit on this information? Or am I to believe you only discovered it now? My mother's blood may stain another's hands, but Charles Lee is no less a monster, and all he does, he does by your command.' He turned to Washington, who reared back — afraid, all of a sudden, of Connor's rage.

'A warning to you both,' snarled Connor: 'choose to come after me or oppose me, and I will kill you.'

And he was gone.

16 September 1781

(Three Years Later)

i

At the Battle of Monmouth in '78, Charles, despite having been ordered by Washington to attack the retreating British, pulled back.

What had been in his mind to do that, I couldn't say. Perhaps he was outnumbered, which was the reason he gave, or perhaps he hoped that, by retreating, it would reflect badly on Washington and Congress, and he would at last be relieved of his command. For one reason or another, not least of which the fact that it didn't really matter any more, I never asked him.

What I do know is that Washington had ordered him to attack; instead, he had done the opposite and the situation rapidly became a rout. I'm told that Connor had a hand in the ensuing battle, helped the rebels avoid defeat, while Charles, retreating, had run straight into Washington, words had been exchanged, and Charles in particular had used some rather choice language.

I could well imagine. I thought of the young man I'd first encountered all those years ago in Boston harbour, how he'd gazed up at me with such awe, yet looked down on everybody else with disdain. Ever since he had been passed over for commander-in-chief of the Continental army, his resentment towards Washington had, like an open wound, festered, growing worse, not healing. Not only had he talked ill of Washington on any available occasion, denigrating every aspect both of his personality and leadership, but he had embarked on a letter-writing campaign, attempting to win Congress members around to his side. True, his fervour was inspired partly by his loyalty to the Order, but it was also fuelled by his personal anger at having been overlooked. Charles might well have resigned his commission with the British Army and to all intents and purposes become an American citizen, but there was a very British sense of elitism to him and he felt keenly that the commander-in-chief position was rightfully his. I couldn't blame him for bringing his personal feelings into it. Who among those knights who had first assembled at the Green Dragon tavern was innocent of it? Certainly not me. I'd hated Washington for what he'd done at Ziio's village, but his leadership of the revolution, though sometimes ruthlessly clear-eyed, had not been tarred by brutality, so far as I knew. He had chalked up his fair share of success, and now that we were surely in the closing stages of the war, with independence just a declaration away, how could he possibly be thought of as anything but a military hero?

The last time I'd seen Connor was three years ago, when he left Washington and I alone together. Alone. Completely alone. And though older and slower and in near-constant pain from the wound at my side, I'd had the opportunity finally to exact revenge for what he'd done to Ziio; to 'relieve him of command' for good, but I'd spared him, because I was already beginning to wonder then if I was wrong about him. Perhaps it is time to admit that I was. It's a human failing to see the changes in yourself while assuming everybody else remains the same. Perhaps I had been guilty of that with Washington. Perhaps he had changed. I wonder, was Connor right about him?

Charles, meanwhile, was arrested for insubordination following the incident during which he swore at Washington, then court-martialled and finally relieved of duty, and he sought refuge at Fort George, where he has remained ever since.

ii

'The boy is on his way here,' said Charles.

I sat at my desk in my room in the West Tower of Fort George, in front of the window overlooking the ocean. Through my spyglass I'd seen ships on the horizon. Were they on their way here? Was Connor in one of them? Associates of his?

Turning in my seat, I waved Charles to sit down. He seemed swamped by his clothes; his face was gaunt and drawn and his greying hair hung over his face. He was fretful, and if Connor was coming then, in all honesty, he had every right to be.

'He's my son, Charles,' I said.

He nodded and looked away with pursed lips. 'I had wondered,' he said. 'There is a family resemblance. His mother is the Mohawk woman you absconded with, is she?'

'Oh, *absconded* with her, did I?'

He shrugged.

'Don't talk to me about neglecting the Order, Charles. You've done your fair share.'

There was a long silence and, when he looked back at me, his eyes had sparked to life. 'You once accused me of *creating* the Assassin,' he said sourly. 'Does it not strike you as ironic – no, hypocritical – given that he is *your* offspring?'

'Perhaps,' I said. 'I'm really not sure any more.'

He gave a dry laugh. 'You stopped caring years ago, Haytham. I can't remember the last time I saw anything but weakness in your eyes.'

'Not weakness, Charles. Doubt.'

'Doubt, then,' he spat. 'Doubt hardly befits a Templar Grand Master, don't you think?'

'Perhaps,' I agreed. 'Or perhaps I've learnt that only fools and children lack it.'

I turned to look out of the window. Before, the ships had been pinpricks to the naked eye, but now they were closer.

'Poppycock,' said Charles. 'Assassin talk. *Belief* is a lack of doubt. That is all we ask of our leaders at least: belief.'

'I remember a time you needed my sponsorship to join us; now, you would have my position. Would you have made a good Grand Master, do you think?'

'Were you?'

There was a long pause. 'That hurt, Charles.'

He stood. 'I'm leaving. I have no desire to be here when the Assassin – *your son* – launches his attack.' He looked at me. 'And you should accompany me. At least we'll have a head start on him.'

I shook my head. 'I think not, Charles. I think I shall stay and make my final stand. Perhaps you're right – perhaps I have not been the most effective Grand Master. Perhaps now is the time to put that right.'

'You intend to face him? To fight him?'

I nodded.

'What? You think you can talk him round? Bring him to our side?'

'No,' I said sadly. 'I fear there is no turning Connor. Even knowing the truth about Washington has failed to alter his support. You'd like Connor, Charles, he has "belief".'

'So what, then?'

459

'I won't allow him to kill you, Charles,' I said, and reached to my neck to remove the amulet. 'Take this, please. I don't want him having it, should he beat me in battle. We worked hard to take it from the Assassins; I've no desire to return it.'

But he snatched his hand away. 'I won't take it.'

'You need to keep it safe.'

'You're quite capable of doing that yourself.'

'I'm almost an old man, Charles. Let's err on the side of caution, shall we?'

I pressed the amulet into his hands.

'I'm detailing some guards to protect you,' he said.

'As you wish.' I glanced at the window again. 'You might want to hurry, though. I have a feeling the time of reckoning is near.'

He nodded and went to the door, where he turned. 'You have been a good Grand Master, Haytham,' he said, 'and I'm sorry if you ever thought I felt otherwise.'

I smiled. 'And I'm sorry for giving you cause to.'

He opened his mouth to speak, thought better of it, then turned and left.

iii

It struck me, when the bombardment began and I began to pray Charles had made his escape, that this might be my final journal entry; these words, my last.

I hope that Connor, my own son, will read this journal, and perhaps, when he knows a little about my own journey through life, understand me, maybe even forgive me. My own path was paved with lies, my mistrust forged from treachery. But my own father never lied to me and, with this journal, I preserve that custom.

I present the truth, Connor, that you may do with it as you will.

EPILOGUE

16 September 1781

'Father!' I called. The bombardment was deafening, but I had fought my way through it to the West Tower where his quarters were to be found, and there in a passageway leading to the Grand Master's chambers, I found him.

'Connor,' he replied. His eyes were flinty, unreadable. He held out his arm and engaged his hidden blade. I did the same. From outside came the thunder and crash of cannon fire, the rending of stone and the screams of dying men. Slowly, we walked towards one another. We'd fought side by side but never against one another. I wonder if, like me, he was curious.

With one hand behind his back, he presented his blade. I did the same.

'On the next cannon blast,' he said.

When it came, it seemed to shake the walls, but neither of us cared. The battle had begun and the sound of our chiming steel was piercing in the passageway, our grunts of effort clear and present. Everything else – the destruction of the fort around us – was background noise.

'Come now,' he taunted me, 'you cannot hope to

match me, Connor. For all your skill, you are still but a boy – with so much yet to learn.'

He showed me no quarter. No mercy. Whatever was in his heart and in his head, his blade flashed with its usual precision and ferocity. If he was now a warrior in his autumn years, beset by failing powers, then I would have hated to have faced him when he was in his prime. If a test is what he wanted to give me, then that is what I received.

'Give me Lee,' I demanded.

But Lee was long gone. There was just Father now, and he struck, as fast as a cobra, his blade coming within a hair's breadth of opening my cheek. Turn defence into attack, I thought, and replied with a similar turn of speed, spinning around and catching his forearm, piercing it with my blade and destroying the fastening of his.

With a roar of pain he leapt back and I could see the worry cloud his eyes, but I let him recover, and watched as he tore a strip from his robe with which to bandage the wound.

'But we have an opportunity here,' I urged him. 'Together we can break the cycle, and end this ancient war. I know it.'

I saw something in his eyes. Was it some spark of a long-abandoned desire, some unfulfilled dream remembered?

'*I know it*,' I repeated.

With the bloodied bandage between his teeth, he shook his head. Was he really that disillusioned? Had his heart hardened that much?

He finished tying the dressing. 'No. You *want* to know it. You *want* it to be true.' His words were tinged with sadness. 'Part of me once did as well. But it is an impossible dream.'

'We are in blood, you and I,' I urged him. 'Please . . .'

For a moment I thought I might have got through to him.

'No, son. We are enemies. And one of us must die.' From outside there came another volley of cannon fire. The torches quivered in their brackets, the light danced on the stone and dust particles rained from the walls.

So be it.

We fought. A long, hard battle. Not one that was always especially skilful. He came at me, with sword blade, fist and even at times his head. His fighting style was different to mine, something more rough-formed about it. It lacked the finesse of my own, yet was just as effective and, I soon learnt, just as painful.

We broke apart, both breathing hard. He wiped the back of his hand across his mouth then crouched, flexing the fingers of his injured forearm. 'You act as though you have some right to judge,' he said, 'To declare me and mine wrong for the world. And yet everything I've shown you – all I've said and done – should clearly demonstrate otherwise. But we didn't harm your people. We didn't support the Crown. We worked to see this land united and at peace. Under our rule all would be equal. Do the patriots promise the same?'

'They offer freedom,' I said, watching him carefully, remembering something Achilles once taught me: that every word, every gesture, is combat.

'Freedom?' he scoffed. 'I've told you – time and time again – it's dangerous. There will never be a consensus, son, among those you have helped to ascend. They will differ in their views of what it means to be free. The peace you so desperately seek does not exist.'

I shook my head. 'No. Together they will forge something new – better than what came before.'

'These men are united now by a common cause,' he continued, sweeping his bad arm around to indicate . . . *us*, I suppose. The revolution. 'But when this battle is finished they will fall to fighting among themselves about how best to ensure control. In time, it will lead to war. You'll see.'

And then he leapt forward, striking down with the sword, aiming not for my body but my blade arm. I deflected, but he was quick, span and struck me backhanded with his sword hilt above the eye. My vision clouded and I staggered back, defending wildly as he tried to press home his advantage. By sheer dumb luck I hit his injured arm, gaining a howl of agony and a temporary lull as we both recovered.

Another cannon boom. More dust dislodged from the walls, and I felt the floor shake. Blood coursed from the wound above my eye, and I wiped it away with the back of my hand.

'The patriot leaders do not seek to control,' I assured him. 'There will be no monarch here. The people will have the power – as they should.'

He shook his head slowly and sadly, a condescending gesture that, if it was supposed to appease me, had exactly the reverse effect. 'The people never have the power,' he said wearily, 'only the illusion of it. And here's the real secret: they don't want it. The responsibility is too great to bear. It's why they're so quick to fall in line as soon as someone takes charge. They *want* to be told what to do. They *yearn* for it. Little wonder, that, since all mankind was built to serve.'

Again we traded blows. Both of us had drawn blood. Looking at him, did I see an older mirror-image of myself? Having read his journal, I can look back now and know exactly how he saw me: as the man he should have been. How would things have been different if I'd known then what I know now?

I don't know is the answer to that question. I still don't know.

'So because we are inclined by nature to be controlled, who better than the Templars?' I shook my head. 'It is a poor offer.'

'It is truth,' exclaimed Haytham. 'Principle and

469

practice are two very different beasts. I see the world the way it is – not as I wish it would be.'

I attacked and he defended, and for a few moments the passageway rang to the sound of clashing steel. Both of us were tired now; the battle no longer had the urgency it had once had. For a moment I wondered if it might simply peter out; if there was any way that the two of us would simply turn, walk away and go in our separate directions. But no. There had to be an end to this now. I knew it. I could see in his eyes that he knew it too. This had to end here.

'No, Father . . . you have given up – and you would have us all do the same.'

And then there was the thump and shudder of a cannonball strike nearby and stone was cascading from the walls. It was near. So near. It had to be followed by another. And it was. All of a sudden a gaping hole was blown in the passageway.

ii

I was thrown back by the blast and landed in a painful heap, like a drunk sliding slowly down the wall of a tavern, my head and shoulders at a strange angle to the rest of me. The corridor was full of dust and settling debris as the boom of the explosion slowly ebbed away into the rattle and clatter of shifting rubble. I pulled myself painfully to my feet and squinted through clouds of dust to see him lying like I had been, but on the other side of the hole in the wall made by the cannonball, and limped over to him. I paused and glanced through the hole, to be greeted by the disorientating sight of the Grand Master's chamber with its back wall blown out, the jagged stone framing a view of the ocean. There were four ships on the water, all with trails of smoke rising from their cannons on deck and, as I watched, there was a boom as another was fired.

I passed by and stooped to Father, who looked up at me and shifted a little. His hand crept towards his sword, which was just out of his reach, and I kicked it skittering away over the stone. Grimacing with the pain, I leaned towards him.

'Surrender, and I will spare you,' I said.

I felt the breeze on my skin, the passageway suddenly flooded with natural light. He looked so old, his face battered and bruised. Even so, he smiled, 'Brave words from a man about to die.'

'You fare no better,' I replied.

'Ah,' he smiled, showing bloodied teeth, 'but I am not alone . . .' and I turned to see two of the fort's guards come rushing along the corridor, raising their muskets and stopping just short of us. My eyes went from them to my father, who was pulling himself to his feet, holding up a restraining hand to his men, the only thing stopping them from killing me.

Bracing himself against the wall, he coughed and spat then looked up at me. 'Even when your kind appears to triumph ... still we rise again. Do you know why?'

I shook my head.

'It is because the Order is born of a realization. We require no creed. No indoctrination by desperate old men. All we need is that the world be as it is. This is why the Templars can never be destroyed.'

And now, of course, I wonder, would he have done it? Would he have let them kill me?

But I'll never have my answer. For suddenly there was the crackle of gunfire and the men span and dropped, taken out by sniper fire from the other side of the wall. And in the next moment I had rushed forward and, before he could react, knocked Haytham back to the stone and stood over him once again, my blade hand pulled back.

And then, with a great rush of something that might have been futility, and a sound that I realized was my own sob, I stabbed him in his heart.

His body jerked as it accepted my blade, then relaxed, and as I withdrew it he was smiling. 'Don't think I have any intention of caressing your cheek and saying I was wrong,' he said softly as I watched the life ebb out of him. 'I will not weep and wonder what might have been. I'm sure you understand.'

I was kneeling now, and reached to hold him. What

472

I felt was . . . nothing. A numbness. A great weariness that it had all come to this.

'Still,' he said, as his eyelids fluttered and the blood seemed to drain from his face, 'I'm proud of you in a way. You have shown conviction. Strength. Courage. These are noble traits.'

With a sardonic smile he added, 'I should have killed you long ago.'

And then he died.

I looked for the amulet Mother had told me about, but it was gone. I closed Father's eyes, stood and walked away.

2 October 1782

At last, on a freezing night at the frontier, I found him in the Conestoga Inn, where I entered to find him sitting in the shadows, his shoulders hunched forward and a bottle close at hand. Older and unkempt, with wiry, untamed hair and no trace of the army officer he had once been, but definitely him: Charles Lee.

As I approached the table he looked up at me, and at first I was taken aback by the wildness of his red-rimmed eyes. Any madness was either suppressed or hidden, though, and he showed no emotion on seeing me, apart from a look which I suppose was relief. For over a month I had chased him.

Wordlessly, he offered me a drink from the bottle, and I nodded, took a sip and passed the bottle back to him. Then we sat together for a long time, watching the other patrons of the tavern, listening to their chatter, games and laughter which carried on around us.

In the end, he looked at me, and though he said nothing, his eyes did it for him, and so I silently ejected my blade and, when he closed them, slid it into him, under the rib, straight into the heart. He died without a sound and I rested him on the tabletop, as though he had simply passed out from too much drink. Then I reached, took the amulet from his neck and put it around my own.

Looking down at it, it glowed softly for a moment. I pushed it underneath my shirt, stood and left.

15 November 1783

Holding the reins of my horse, I walked through my village with a mounting sense of disbelief. As I'd arrived, I'd seen well-tended fields but the village itself was deserted, the longhouse abandoned, the cook fires cold, and the only soul in sight was a grizzled hunter – a white hunter, not a Mohawk – who sat on an upturned pail in front of a fire, roasting something that smelled good on a spit.

He looked at me carefully as I approached, and his eyes went to his musket, which lay nearby, but I waved to say I meant no harm.

He nodded. 'If you're hungry, I've got extra,' he said genially.

And it did smell good, but I had other things on my mind. 'Do you know what happened here? Where is everyone?'

'Gone west. Been a few weeks since they left. Seems some fella from New York was granted the land by Congress. Guess they decided they didn't need approval from those that lived here to settle.'

'What?' I said.

'Yup. Seein' it happen more and more. Natives pushed out by traders and ranchers lookin' to expand. Government *says* they don't take land that's already owned, but, uh . . . Here you can see otherwise.'

'How could this happen?' I asked, turning around slowly, seeing only emptiness where once I had seen the familiar faces of my people – the people I had grown up with.

'We're on our own now,' he continued. 'No jolly old English parts and labour. Which means we gotta go at it ourselves. Gotta pay for it too. Sellin' land is quick and easy. And not quite so nasty as taxes. And since some say taxes is what started the whole war, ain't no rush to bring 'em back.' He gave a full, throaty laugh. 'Clever men, these new leaders of ours. They know not to push it just yet. Too soon. Too . . . British.' He stared into his fire. 'But it will come. Always does.'

I thanked him and left him, to go to the longhouse, thinking, as I walked: I have failed. My people were gone – chased away by those I thought would protect them.

As I walked, the amulet around my neck glowed, and I took it, held it in my palm and studied it. Perhaps there was one last thing I could do, and that was to save this place from them all, patriots and Templars alike.

In a clearing in the forest I crouched and regarded what I held in my hands: my mother's necklace in one, my father's amulet in the other.

To myself I said, 'Mother. Father. I am sorry. I have failed you both. I made a promise to protect our people, Mother. I thought if I could stop the Templars, if I could keep the revolution free from their influence, then those I supported would do what was right. They did, I suppose, do what was right – what was right for them. As for you, Father, I thought I might unite us, that we would forget the past and forge a better future. In time, I believed you could be made to see the world as I do – to understand. But it was just a dream. This, too, I should have known. Were we not meant to live in peace, then? Is that it? Are we born to argue? To fight? So many voices – each demanding something else.

'It has been hard at times, but never harder than today. To see all I worked for perverted, discarded, forgotten. You would say I have described the whole of history, Father. Are you smiling, then? Hoping I might speak the words you longed to hear? To validate you? To say that all along you were right? I will not. Even now, faced as I am with the truth of your cold words, I refuse. Because I believe things can still change.

'I may never succeed. The Assassins may struggle another thousand years in vain. But we will not stop.'

I began to dig.

'Compromise. That's what everyone has insisted on. And so I have learnt it. But differently than most, I think. I realize now that it will take time, that the road ahead is long and shrouded in darkness. It is a road that will not always take me where I wish to go – and I doubt I will live to see it end. But I will travel down it nonetheless.'

I dug and dug until the hole was deep enough, deeper than that which was needed to bury a body, enough for me to climb into.

'For at my side walks hope. In the face of all that insists I turn back, I carry on: this, this is my compromise.'

I dropped the amulet into the hole and then, as the sun began to go down, I shovelled dirt on top of it until it was hidden and then I turned and left.

Full of hope for the future, I returned to my people, to the Assassins.

It was time for new blood.

List of Characters

As'ad Pasha al-Azm: Ottoman governor of Damascus, unknown–1758

Jeffrey Amherst: British commander, 1717–97

Tom Barrett : boy who lives next door to Haytham in Queen Anne's Square

Reginald Birch, senior property manager for Edward Kenway and a Templar

Edward Braddock, the Bulldog: British General and commander-in-chief of the colonies, 1695–1755

Benjamin Church: doctor; Templar

Connor: Assassin

Cutter: torturer

Betty: servant in the Kenway household

Miss Davy: Mrs Kenway's lady's maid

Mr Geoffrey Digweed: Mr Kenway's gentleman

Edith: Haytham's nursemaid

Emily: chambermaid in the Kenway household

James Fairweather, acquaintance of Haytham's

Old Mr Fayling: Haytham's tutor

John Harrison: Templar

Thomas Hickey: Templar

Jim Holden: private in the British Army

William Johnson: Templar

Kaniehtí:io, Mohawk woman, also known as Ziio; Connor's mother

Edward Kenway: Haytham's father

Haytham E. Kenway

Jenny Kenway: Haytham's half-sister

Tessa Kenway, nee Stephenson-Oakley: Haytham's mother

Catherine Kerr and Cornelius Douglass: owners of the Green Dragon

Charles Lee: Templar

Grand Vizier Raghib Pasha, the most senior minister of the Sultan

John Pitcairn: Templar

Mrs Searle: servant in the Kenway household

Mr Simpkin: on the staff of Edward Kenway

Slater: executioner and Braddock's lieutenant

Tessa Stephenson-Oakley: Haytham's mother

Silas Thatcher: slaver and commander in the King's Troop, in charge of the Southgate Fort

Twitch: informer

Juan Vedomir: traitor to the Templars

George Washington: aide to General Braddock; commander-in-chief of the newly formed Continental Army; Founding Father and future President, 1732–99

Acknowledgements

Special thanks to
Yves Guillemot
Stéphane Blais
Jean Guesdon
Julien Cuny
Corey May
Darby McDevitt

And also
Alain Corre
Laurent Detoc
Sébastien Puel
Geoffroy Sardin
Xavier Guilbert
Tommy François
Cecile Russeil
Joshua Meyer
The Ubisoft Legal department
Chris Marcus
Etienne Allonier
Anouk Bachman
Alex Clarke
Hana Osman
Andrew Holmes
Virginie Sergent
Clémence Deleuze